Always the Last to Know

BOOKS BY KRISTAN HIGGINS

If You Only Knew

On Second Thought

Good Luck with That

Life and Other Inconveniences

Always the Last to Know

Always the Last to Know

Kristan Higgins

BERKLEY
NEW YORK

BERKLEY
An imprint of Penguin Random House LLC
penguinrandomhouse.com

Library of Congress Cataloging-in-Publication Data

Names: Higgins, Kristan, author.
Title: Always the last to know / Kristan Higgins.
Description: First edition. | New York: Berkley, 2020.
Identifiers: LCCN 2019050000 (print) | LCCN 2019050001 (ebook) |
ISBN 9780593199855 (hardcover) | ISBN 9780451489456 (trade paperback) |
ISBN 9780451489463 (ebook)
Subjects: LCSH: Domestic fiction.
Classification: LCC PS3608.I3657 A79 2020 (print) |
LCC PS3608.I3657 (ebook) | DDC 813/.6—dc23
LC record available at https://lccn.loc.gov/2019050000
LC ebook record available at https://lccn.loc.gov/2019050001

Berkley hardcover edition / June 2020
Berkley trade paperback edition / June 2020

Printed in the United States of America
1 3 5 7 9 10 8 6 4 2

Cover image by Cristina Velina Ion / Arcangel
Cover design by Anthony Ramondo and Emily Osborne
Book design by Elke Sigal

This book is dedicated to Huntley Fitzpatrick,
strong and kind, brilliant and fierce.
I am so very, very glad to be your friend.

Acknowledgments

At Berkley, my profound gratitude to my brilliant editor, Claire Zion, for her keen eye and big heart, and to the rest of the brilliant Berkley team: Ivan, Christine, Jeanne-Marie, Craig, Erin, Diana, Bridget, Jin, Angela, Anthony and every single person in art, sales and marketing.

To my agent, Maria Carvainis, who has shaped my career with dedication, enthusiasm and an unwavering eye on the future, thank you, Madame.

Thank you to Mel Jolly, for always remembering what I forget and knowing what I don't, and for being a lovely person in addition to all that. Thanks to my funny, smart, hardworking intern, Madison Terrill, for her innovation and insight these past two summers.

I had no idea what this book was about until I slipped off to Cape Cod in the cold winter and hid for a month, just me, my laptop and my good dog. Thanks to the owner who rented her beautiful house to me; to Luther, the most loyal and sweetest dog, who kept me company and got me outside for walks every day; to Ivan of the Red Sox hat and gold tooth, who helped save a dolphin with me that blustery, cold day, and to the marine wildlife rescuers who actually knew what they were doing, and again to Ivan for driving Luther and me home, even though I was sopping wet and covered in sand.

. . .

Thanks and love to my sister, Hilary Higgins Murray, who listens so well and showed me how to fix all the problems with one word—*amputate*. Who knew? She did!

To Laura Francis, my town's first selectman, for helping me understand just how much there is to do in a small town;

To the folks at Gaylord Specialty Hospital, for the information they provided on stroke and brain injury;

To Stacia Bjarnason, for her time, insight, friendship and laughter;

To Jackie Decker, sister of my heart, for her insider information about painting and art;

To Terence Keenan, the love of my life and my best friend, all in one rather adorable package;

To Flannery and Declan, who are such remarkable, wonderful people and fill my heart with love every single day;

And thank you, readers, for the gift of your time.

Always the Last to Know

CHAPTER ONE

Sadie

"You're engaged? Oh! Uh . . . huzzah!"

Yes. I had just said *huzzah*.

You know what? I couldn't blame myself. *Another* engagement among the teachers of St. Catherine's Catholic Elementary School in the Bronx. The fifth this year, and yes, I was counting.

I couldn't look away from the diamond blinding me from the finger of Bridget Ennis. The stone was the size of a bumblebee, and my hypnotized eyes followed her hand as she waved it in excitement, telling the rest of us teachers—six women, one man—about how *romantic*, how *unexpected*, how *thrilling* it had been.

I had nothing against Bridget. I even liked her. I'd mentored her, because this was her first year teaching. She was twenty-three as of last week; I was ancient at thirty-two (or so it felt in teacher years). It had been raining diamond rings, and despite my having had bubbly hopes on my own last birthday, the fourth finger of my left hand remained buck naked.

Bridget was talking about save-the-date magnets and paper quality and color schemes and flower arrangements and the seventy-nine dresses she was already torn between. Another woman falling victim to wedding insanity. Bridget was the only child of wealthy parents. This did not bode well for me, her sort-of friend. Was it too late to distance myself? *Please don't ask me to be a bridesmaid. Please. Please. I am way too old for this shit.*

"My daddy said whatever I want, and I want it to be perfect, you know?" Bridget looked at me, and I felt the cold trickle of dread. "Sadie, obviously I want you as a bridesmaid." Her pure green eyes filled with happy tears.

Oh, the fuckery of it all.

"Of course!" I said. "Thank you! What an honor!" My cheek began to twitch as I smiled.

"And you, Nina! And you, Vanessa! And of course, Jay's three sisters and my gals from Kappa Kappa Gamma. And my cousin, because she's like a sister to me. Do you like violet? Or cornflower? Off the shoulder, I was thinking, but I think *my* dress might be off the shoulder and . . ." I stopped listening as she began speaking in tongues intelligible only to those addicted to *Say Yes to the Dress*.

This was not my first time around the bridesmaid block. Bridget's would be my sixth stint, and I knew what was coming. Engagement party. Bridal shower. Dress shopping for Bridget. Dress shopping for me and the other eleventeen bridesmaids. A lingerie shower. A household goods shower. Meeting(s) of the families. Bachelorette weekend in some city that caters to large groups of drunken people—New Orleans or Vegas or Savannah, which meant a flight and hotel. Rehearsal dinner. The wedding itself. Brunch the next day. All with or without Alexander Mitchum, my boyfriend, who had not yet proposed, despite his references to a future together, his onetime question about if I'd think about changing my last name from Frost to Mitchum—"hypothetically," he'd added—and the deliberate slowing of my footsteps whenever we passed Cartier on Fifth Avenue.

"You don't have to say yes, idiot," came a low voice next to me. Carter Demming, my best friend at St. Catherine's.

"She's sweet," I murmured back.

"Oh, please. Let her sorority sisters be her bridesmaids. Show some dignity for your age."

"I'm thirty-two."

"Your most fertile years are behind you."

"Thanks, Carter."

"Miss Frost? I need you for a second," Carter said loudly. "Mazel tov, sweetheart," he added as Bridget brushed away more glittering tears.

We left Bridget's cheery classroom and went to the now-empty teachers' lounge, where we teachers discussed which kids we hated most and how to ruin their young lives (not really). Carter posted the occasional *Legalize Marijuana* sticker somewhere, just to torment our principal, the venerable and terrifying Sister Mary.

I was the art teacher here. No, I could not support myself on a teacher's salary at a Catholic school in New York City, but more on that later. I loved teaching, though it hadn't exactly been my dream. Just about every kid loved art. If I didn't have the same stature as the "regular" teachers, I made up for it by being adored.

"So you're thinking about marriage and why you're still single," said Carter, pulling out a chair and straddling it.

"Yep." I sat down, too, the normal way, like a human and not a cowboy.

"So propose already."

"What?"

"Propose marriage to your perfect boyfriend."

"Meh."

"Why should men have to do all the work? Do you know how hard it is to buy the perfect ring, pick the perfect moment and place, say the perfect words and still have it be a fucking surprise? It's very hard."

"You would know." Carter had been married several times, twice to women, once to a man.

"Listen to your uncle Carter."

"You're not my uncle, unfortunately."

"Some men need a shove toward the altar, honey. Shove him. Do you really want to go out into the Tinder world again?"

"Jesus, no."

"Don't become a statistic. Kids are getting married younger and younger these days. Your window is closing. Match and eHarmony worked fifteen years ago, but now they're filled with criminals. As you well know."

"He was a minor felon, and it wasn't exactly listed in his profile. But yes, I see your point."

Alexander (not a felon) and I *had* been dating for a couple of years. Ours had been the classic rom-com meet-cute. I turned around on a wine night with my friends and sloshed my cabernet onto his crisp white shirt. He laughed, asked for my number, and called a few days later. We'd been together ever since.

We had a marriage-worthy relationship by any measure. Maybe it was the distance factor—he was a traveling yacht salesman (someone had to do it)—so we weren't bothered by the slings and arrows of daily life together. He was constant—we saw each other almost every weekend. He brought me presents from his travels—a silk scarf printed with palmetto leaves from the Florida Keys, or honey from Savannah. He'd met my parents, charmed my mother (not an easy task), chatted with my father and wasn't in awe of my older sister, which was definitely a point in his favor. Alex had great stories about his clients, some of them celebrities, others just fabulously wealthy. He was, er . . . tidy, a quality that shouldn't be undersold.

Alexander lived on the Upper East Side, which I tried not to hold against him. His apartment was impressive but soulless. Every time I stayed over, I felt like I was staying in a model home—a place that was interesting and tasteful, but not exactly homey. He'd bought it furnished. Some of his art came from HomeGoods, and since I'd been—correction, *was still*—an artist, that did make me wince.

Sex was great. He was good-looking—his hair a shade I called boarding school blond, which would get nearly white in the summer. His eyes were blue and already had the attractive crow's-feet you'd expect for a guy who sold boats. In a nutshell, he looked like he'd stepped out of a J. Crew catalog, and why he was dating me, I wasn't a hundred percent sure. "You have no idea how hard it is to find a nice girl," he said once, so I guess it was that.

But I wasn't really a girl anymore, not like Bridget. Already past my prime fertility years, according to Uncle Carter, who did tend to know everything.

"Hello?" he said, scratching his wrist. "Sadie. You're in vapor lock. Make a move."

Another fair point. I'd been at St. Cath's for eight years, painting on the side, living in a nine-hundred-square-foot apartment in Times Square, the armpit of Manhattan. "Yeah," I said. "Sure. I could do it. We're seeing each other tonight."

"See? Written in the stars." He winked at me. "Now, I have to go wash the grime from these little motherfuckers off me because I have a date. A sex date, I want you to know."

"I don't want to know."

"Josh Foreman," he said, referring to the security guard who worked at St. Cath's.

"Please stop."

"His hands are so soft. That smile. Plus, he screams like a wildcat in bed."

"And . . . scene." I brought my hands together, indicating *cut*. Carter grinned and left the teachers' lounge.

More evidence of Alexander's plans to marry me someday flashed through my head. Once he'd said, "Margaret's a nice name for a girl, don't you think? I wouldn't mind a daughter named Margaret." Another: "We should look at property on the Maine coast for a summer place. It's so beautiful up there. And Portland has a great art scene."

Maybe it *was* time for me to take action. Juliet, my sister, older by almost twelve years, enjoyed lecturing me on how I floated through life, in contrast to her color-coded, laminated lists for How to Be Perfect and Have Everything. (I jest, but not by much.)

It was just that when I pictured being married, it was never to Alexander.

The vision of a black-haired, dark-eyed boy standing in the gusty breeze came to mind. My own version of Jon Snow, clad in Carhartt instead of wolfskin.

But Noah and I had tried. Tried and failed, more than once, and that was a long time ago.

Carter was right. Why wait? Alexander and I had been together long enough, we had a good thing going, we both wanted kids (sort of, maybe). We weren't getting any younger. I loved him, he loved me, we got along so well it was almost spooky.

Bridget's bumblebee ring flashed in my mind. Call me shallow, but I wanted a big diamond, too. My materialism ended there. (Or not . . . Was it too soon to picture buying a brownstone in the Village? Alexander was loaded, after all. As for a wedding, we could elope. No color schemes or Pinterest boards necessary.)

He was due in around four, depending on traffic. Where was a romantic place in New York in January? It was freakishly mild today—thanks, global warming!—so maybe down on the Hudson as the sun set? The High Line was pretty, and I could go to Chelsea Market and buy some nice cheese and wine. We could watch the sunset and I'd just say it: "I love you. Marry me and make me the happiest woman on earth." And the tourists and hipsters who frequented the High Line would applaud and take pictures and we'd probably go viral.

I imagined calling my dad tonight. He'd be *so* happy. Maybe we wouldn't elope, because I wanted my father to walk me down the aisle. Fine. A small wedding, then. I'd wear a white dress that Carter could help me pick out. Brianna and Sloane could be my flower girls, even if they were a little old for that. I was their only aunt, so may as well. Plus, it would make my prickly mom happy.

Yes. I'd propose tonight, and enter the next phase of my life, where I was sure Alexander and I would be very, very content.

As luck would have it, the temperature took a plunge, as weather in the Northeast is cruel and fickle. What had been sixty-two was the low forties by the time Alexander met me in front of the Standard, an odd-looking hotel that straddled the High Line. "God, it's freezing," he said as the wind blew through us. "I found a parking spot on Tenth, but I didn't know it would be this cold."

"Oh, it's not so bad!" I said. I had a plan, and I was sticking to it. "Just brisk! The sunset will be gorgeous." Or it wouldn't. There was only one other couple who seemed to be sightseeing, everyone else hunched against the weather and hurrying to wherever New Yorkers hurry.

"Christ. I didn't dress for this." Alexander wore a brown leather jacket over a blue oxford shirt and bulky sweater, khakis and expensive leather shoes. I'd dressed to be beautiful—pretty black knit dress, hair in a ponytail (now being undone by the wind), the necklace he'd given me for Christmas and a cute red leather jacket that did nothing to keep me warm. Should've worn pants. And a parka.

"Well, come on," I said. "We don't have to stay too long. It'll be fun."

He followed me down the sidewalk, past clumps of grass and dead flower bushes. Come spring, this most elegant of New York's parks would be filled with color and life, but as it was, it was a little, uh, barren.

Shit. Well, I'd make it quick. "Sunset's in ten minutes," I said.

"I'll be dead by then."

"I'll revive your cold, hard corpse. Or at least give it a really strong attempt, then go into the Standard and drown my sorrows at the bar."

He laughed, and my heart swelled a bit. He really was a good, kind person. Great husband material. Never too demanding, always cheerful . . . the opposite of Noah, which was probably no coincidence, and I shouldn't be thinking of Noah, I reminded myself. I glanced at the other couple. Would they film us when I got down on one knee? Also, *should* I get down on one knee? These were my only black tights.

"I cannot *believe* you're saying this!" Ah. They were fighting. Not a great sign.

I really wanted the light of the sunset to spill onto us, which it would in about six minutes. Being a painter who had once loved skyscapes, I was an expert on natural light. "How was your day, hon?" I asked, trying to kill time.

"Oh, fine," he said, putting his arm around me. "Pretty sure I nailed down a sale to a hedge fund guy. He wants it made from scratch, of course." He detailed the many requirements this guy had for his boat—private master deck, helipad, indoor garden, sauna, steam room and gym.

"So just a little wooden boat to paddle around in, then," I said.

He smiled. "It's a living. Are we about done, babe? I'm starving."

"I bought cheese." I pulled the block out of my bag. Shit. We'd have to bite right into it, since I didn't have a knife.

"Hon. It's forty degrees out here. Maybe thirty-five. It's supposed to snow tonight."

"It's not so bad. See? That other couple's brave. Plus, we're Yankees. This is practically summer."

He glanced at the other couple. "They have winter coats on."

They did, both dressed in those down coats with patches that announced them as explorers of Antarctica. The woman crossed her puffy arms. "Are you shitting me, Dallas?" she practically yelled.

"Oh," murmured Alexander. "Maybe this *will* be fun after all."

"I never said I wanted to be exclusive! That was all in your head!" the unfortunately named Dallas answered.

"How many women have you been seeing, you cheating bastard? Belinda? Are you seeing that whore again?"

"She's not a whore!"

"So that's a yes! Jesus! We're done, asshole. If I have an STD, I will slit your throat and burn your apartment to the ground."

She stomped past us, cutting us a look. "Hi," I said.

"Fuck you," she snapped.

Alexander laughed. The cheater skulked past us, arms folded, head down against the wind.

"Okay, so that was fun," Alexander said. "They do have the right idea about leaving, though. This cheese is almost frozen, and I don't really see eating it here. What do you say, babe? Shall we go? Grab a drink somewhere with heat?"

Do or die. "Right. Okay." Shit. We were sitting. I scrambled to my feet. "Um, can you stand up for a second?"

"About time. Do you want to go out for dinner?" The cold wind whipped his blond hair, and his ears were bright red.

"Just one thing first." I looked into his eyes, which were watering a little from the wind. Just then, the sun slipped behind a bank of clouds that had come out of nowhere. So much for fiery skies burnishing the moment.

It didn't matter. I loved him. He was rock solid, this guy, and we . . . we had such a good thing going. Before I changed my mind, I knelt down. Felt my tights catch on the rough surface of the walkway.

"You all right?" he asked.

"Alexander Mitchum, will you marry me and make me the happiest man—shit, I mean *woman*—alive?" The wind gusted again, blowing my hair into my face.

"Uh . . . what are you doing, Sadie?" His face was incredulous.

"I . . . I'm proposing." My heart felt like the sun, abruptly swallowed in clouds. *Do not make me go back on those dating websites, Alexander Mitchum.*

"I'm the one who's supposed to propose."

"Okay! Sure. Go for it." Thank *God.*

He laughed a little. "Well, babe . . . I'm not ready. There are things I need to have in place. A ring, for one."

"We can get one later. Cartier is open till seven. Probably. Not that I checked."

He laughed. "Well, I'd like to surprise you. When the time comes."

"I'm down on one knee here, Alexander."

"Get up, then! This is crazy." He pulled me to my feet. I felt my tights tear. "You nut. It's the man's job to propose."

Sexist, really. "It seemed like a good idea. I mean, we've been together two years. We're the right age." I forced a smile.

"What is the right age, really? Is there an age that's wrong?" he asked, but he kissed my forehead. "I'll do it when the time is right. Okay?"

Well, didn't I feel stupid. "Okay."

"I want the moment to be when we're not freezing our asses off in the dark. Don't worry. It'll be perfect."

My heart felt weird. Happy weird, or disappointed weird? "I mean, now that we're talking about it . . . you could just . . . ask."

"No. I want it to be really romantic. Not on a night so cold my balls are retracting."

"Got it."

In case there was any doubt that my plan sucked, those dark gray clouds opened and a cold rain started to fall.

"I'm gonna pass out if I don't eat soon. Want to grab something, then go back to my place and fool around so we can salvage this night?"

"Sure."

Feeling like a dolt, I followed him to the stairs that led to street level.

Alexander's phone chimed. He studied it, then looked up. "Shit, babe," he said. "I have to go up to Boston. That idiot Patriots player is pitching a fit over a painting of himself that was supposed to be hung on the ceiling over his bed, and the designer put it on the wall instead. What time is it? Damn. I'll have to drive up tonight." He looked at me. "Want to come? We could grab some fast food on the road and stay overnight. A suite at the Mandarin with some spa time tomorrow, maybe?"

That was the thing about Alexander. He was so thoughtful. But my feeling of ineptitude lingered.

"I think I'll just go home. I have a painting due Sunday."

"Gotcha." We stood there awkwardly. "Want me to drive you home?

"Subway's faster," I said.

"Okay."

"Well. Drive safely."

"I will. Talk to you, babe." He kissed me quickly and strode off.

It really was cold. I started walking toward Eighth Avenue to catch the subway. Soon, I'd be home. Maybe I'd take a shower to warm up. Order Thai food and work on that blue-and-white "like Van Gogh except not as swirly" painting I'd been commissioned to do. Bitter sigh, followed by the reminder to be grateful that I had these gigs at all and wasn't living in a paper bag.

Just then, my phone rang. Juliet, who almost never called me. "Hi!" I said. "How are you?"

"Listen, Sadie," she said, her voice strange, and instinctively, I stopped walking, my free hand covering my ear so I could hear her better. "Dad had a stroke. He's in surgery at UConn, and it's pretty bad. Get here as soon as you can."

CHAPTER TWO

Barb

I was in a meeting with the head of the town crew, discussing his zealous use of salt so far this winter and the complaints about undercarriage rust I'd been fielding, when I got the call.

Yes, being first selectman of a small town in Connecticut was a nonstop thrill fest. I smiled at the thought. Truth was, I loved my job. Even moments like this.

It was my last appointment of the day, and I didn't have any committee meetings tonight. Maybe I'd head over to Caro's if John was already parked in front of whatever war documentary he was watching these days. If she didn't have plans, that was.

"Yeah, well, people always bitch and moan if they skid half an inch, so I can't win for losing here, Barb," Lou said.

"We're halfway through the salt budget, and we've only had two inches of snow so far. You know we'll have at least four or five more storms this year."

"Like I said, I'm the one who gets blamed!"

Lindsey, my secretary, opened the door.

"Barb?" she said, her voice almost a whisper. "I'm so sorry, but you need to take this call. Right away. Lou, out you go."

I picked up the phone. "This is Barb Frost, how can I help you?" I said in my warm, mayoral voice. Most people who called my office wanted to complain about something, and I found that being polite always shocked them a little. I grew up in Minnesota, where manners were drilled into us. This was New England.

"Mrs. Frost, it's George Macon." George was a paramedic in town, but I didn't think we had any issues with the first responders. I hoped he wasn't going to ask for new equipment. They just got a new ambulance last year.

"How can I help you, George?" I said.

"I'm really sorry to have to tell you this, Mrs. Frost. Your husband is on his way to the ER, and he's unresponsive and not breathing on his own. Seems like he took a bad fall off his bike. Can someone drive you to the hospital? Right now?"

Gosh. *Right now* sounded real ominous, all right. My mouth moved for a moment before the words came out. "Of course. Thank you." I hung up.

Mind you, I'd always been good in emergencies. My mind could prioritize needs and get things taken care of in near-perfect order. When Juliet was eight and sliced open her hand so deeply the blood was pulsing out of it with every beat of her heart, I wrapped it tightly, told her to keep it over her head, and put her in the car rather than calling 911, mentally doing the math on how long it would take the ambulance crew to get there versus how quickly I could take her to the hospital myself. At the same time, I was wondering if I should tourniquet her arm, but I was thinking that might cut off her blood supply. I remembered my purse so I'd have our insurance card and grabbed her Pooh bear for comfort. Got a blanket to tuck around her in the car in case she was going into shock. We were at the hospital in under ten minutes, and I only went ten miles an hour over the speed limit, because I didn't want to drive like a crazy person and cause an accident. That wouldn't have helped anyone, for Pete's sake.

When Sadie was bitten by the neighbors' dog, same thing. Ice for her face, call to the police to secure the dog and get proof of rabies vaccination, call to Caro to ask her to pick up Juliet from school, call to the hospital to tell them we'd be needing the plastic surgeon, not some resident who wanted to practice stitching, thank you very much. Six months later, you could barely see the scar.

But now . . . with John in the ambulance already . . . I felt kind of . . . well . . . frozen.

Because tomorrow, I was planning to tell my husband that I'd be filing for divorce.

And even with that, and though I'd often pictured myself a happy widow . . .

I did not ever see this moment actually happening.

Unresponsive. Not breathing.

"Barb?"

I looked up. I was still at my desk. Lindsey, the dear girl, had her coat on. "Why don't I drive you?" she said. Guess she knew, then.

"That's—that's a good idea, Linds. Thank you, hon."

My hands were shaking as I grabbed my purse. Things seemed to be moving in slow motion. I should've been well on my way to the hospital right now, but instead, I wasn't quite sure what to do next.

"Don't forget your coat," she said, because I had.

Then time sped up, and we were on 95, and I had Juliet on the phone, and she would be on her way as soon as her sitter got there. I don't know what I said to her, to be honest.

"Do you want to call your other daughter?" Lindsey asked, and no, I didn't, because it didn't seem fair to Sadie, not if ten minutes from now I'd be telling her her dad was . . . was dead.

My throat was tight. I kept swallowing, but it didn't help.

The doctor was waiting for me in the hallway of Lawrence and

Memorial, which I knew wasn't a good sign. I wondered if Westerly would've been a better choice. But maybe not. Maybe this place was better for unresponsive, not-breathing patients.

"Mrs. Frost, I'm Dr. Warren," she said. "We're going to have to chopper your husband to UConn, okay? He's getting a CAT scan now, but I'm pretty sure he's got a ruptured aneurysm with massive bleeding. His condition is grave, I'm sorry to say, and he'll need surgery as soon as possible to relieve the pressure. We need you to sign these forms."

Grave? Massive? Did she have to say *massive*? My breathing was loud enough that I could hear it.

"Just sign here, and here, and initial here."

Forms. Yes, God forbid we just treated him. God forbid I got to stand by my husband and hold his hand and reassure him.

An old man was wheeled in on a gurney into a stall. Because the ER *was* like a barn. There were barns nicer than this, frankly, with all this beeping and noise and chaos and people in different-colored scrubs. Barns were beautiful, peaceful places. Sadie had taken horseback riding lessons, and the barn had been so gosh-darn pretty, but she lost interest after—

"You can see him now," the doctor said.

Oh. The old man . . . the patient they'd just parked . . . that was John. I could barely see him amid all the people in there, the equipment. He was in a neck brace. Intubated, too. His face was bloody, his eyes shut. There were electrodes and wires and an IV, and he looked so unlike himself that I nearly told the doctor there'd been a mistake.

But those were his hands. Old man hands, but wearing the ring I'd put on it fifty years ago. He'd aged well, but his hands looked old now. Then again, they may have looked old for some time. I couldn't remember the last time I'd noticed. We weren't the hand-holding type.

People were talking, but I didn't listen to what they said. They weren't talking to me, anyway.

"He's very healthy," I said. "He's been taking real good care of himself. Swimming, running, riding his bike. He wants to do a triathlon in the spring. I told him, 'John, don't be crazy, you're seventy-five years old.'"

No one was listening. I didn't blame them. He was *massively bleeding*. They had important things to do.

I suddenly remembered one sunny Sunday morning in the winter, just weeks after our wedding. The sunlight had streamed into the bedroom, turning it buttery and warm, and his hair—he'd had such thick, glorious hair back then, light brown and all crazy if he didn't comb it down. I'd thought those freckles on his shoulders so endearing. We made love . . . maybe the first time when it wasn't awkward, because that's how inexperienced we'd both been. Both of us virgins on our wedding night, hardly typical for the crazy seventies. But I'd been brought up with old-fashioned values, and John had been, too.

Anyway, we were pretty happy with ourselves that morning, since we'd finally figured out this sex thing, and we spent the whole day in bed, eating toast and then leftover spaghetti, reading the Sunday *Times* until it got dark. Then we showered and dressed and went to the movies. Can't remember what we saw.

"Go ahead, Mrs. Frost, talk to him," someone said, putting a hand on my arm. A nurse. Gosh, she seemed so young. Beautiful skin. Her eyes were kind.

"John?" I said, looking down at him. I wanted to call him honey, or darling, but it had been so long since either of us used a term of endearment for the other. "John, don't worry. I'm here. You're being taken care of. Darling." I put my hand over his.

Please don't die.

The thought came as a shock, a lightning strike right to the heart. We could do better, couldn't we? It wasn't too late?

"Here are his things," someone said, thrusting a plastic bag at me.

"Mom! Oh, my God, Daddy!" Juliet was there, and started to hug her father, but he was too confined. She hugged me instead, her body shaking.

"I know, honey, I know," I said. "He's going to UConn, and they'll do everything they can for him. World-class medicine, don't you know."

"Mrs. Frost." It was the doctor again, with some papers in her hand. "He's ready to go. The CAT scan did show a significant bleed, but no head or neck fractures. The chopper is here. Are you okay to drive to Farmington?"

"We're fine," Juliet said, then looked at me. "Riley London's watching the girls and Oliver's on his way home. I'll drive. Do you have your car? Can someone drive it home?"

The details of emergencies. Who drove which car? Did Lindsey have my coat? Did I thank her for driving me? Would she cancel all my appointments for tomorrow? Oh, wait, it was Friday. Should we take Route 9 or Route 2? What was the traffic like? Did I need the ladies' room before we left? I did.

It's strange how your body keeps going when your life is falling apart. I needed to go to the bathroom—I was seventy years old, of course I did. I washed my hands, aware that I was in a hospital with a lot of sick people. It was flu season. It wouldn't help anyone if I got sick.

My husband might be dead right now.

Juliet had pulled her BMW to the entrance. I got in and buckled up. "I didn't text Sadie," she said. "I wasn't sure if you told her anything yet. I thought it might be better if we knew something first. When he's stable. Or . . . if he doesn't make it. I hope someone can drive her. She's gonna take this hard."

Exactly my thoughts. "Are *you* all right to drive, sweetheart?"

"I'm a rock, Mom." Her voice shook a little, but she was. She really was. She drove efficiently and safely, always using her turn signal.

We didn't talk much. But she reached over and took my hand and squeezed it. "Whatever happens," she said, "we'll get through it."

By the time we got to Farmington, John was already in surgery. He was still alive, the nurse told us, but it was a critical situation, given his age and the location of the aneurysm.

According to the paramedic report, John had been riding his bike. In January, down Canterbury Hill Road, and honestly, why? I mean, sure, he had to have his hobbies, and when he started that whole silly running/biking/swimming thing last year, I was relieved that he'd found something to keep him occupied. But riding a bike in January? That's just foolish, even if today had been real nice.

"Based on his injuries, the doctor thinks he had the stroke first and then fell smack onto the pavement, which is why his face is banged up," the nurse said. "He didn't raise his hands to protect himself." She demonstrated how someone would instinctively cover their face. "He has a concussion on top of the stroke, and his nose is broken, but the bleeding is the big problem right now."

"Will he live?" Juliet asked. My strong girl, asking the hard questions.

"These things are hard to predict," she said. "Try to keep good thoughts. We'll tell you more as soon as we know." She put a hand on my arm. "I'm sorry. I know this is incredibly hard. I wish we had more information."

"Thank you. You're very kind."

"I'll call Sadie," Juliet said.

"Oh. Yes. Do you want me to?" I asked. "Maybe I should, don'tcha think?"

"No, Mommy. You sit down, okay? I'll be back in a few. I'll bring you a coffee and a snack. There's a Starbucks here. I'll be right back. Text me if there's any news." She smiled suddenly. "I can hear your Minnesota."

"Oh, can you, now?" I asked, exaggerating the accent as a joke, and we managed a little laugh. It was true; stress brought out the accent.

Off she went, and as ever, I was so grateful that she was mine, and here.

The family waiting room on this floor looked like an airport lounge, sleek and cheerful. I found a chair and sat down, still in my winter coat. The chair was meant to look like a Morris chair, sturdy and reassuring. A good choice for this place.

When we first moved to Stoningham, I'd loved tag and estate sales and combed half the state looking for antiques that needed a little sanding, some repairs. John still worked in family law then, and we had to be smart about money, what with all the house costs we had—new kitchen, bathrooms, a leak in the roof, a new boiler. But we also had to furnish the place.

One day, I'd come across a beautiful wooden chair with leather cushions and clean lines. It cost ten dollars. I brought it home, cleaned and oiled the leather, polished the wood, and presented it to John when he came home that night. He'd been so pleased. So pleased. It was a vintage Morris chair, we learned, and John sat in it every night until he moved it to his study.

It was the best gift I'd ever given him.

I wondered when he moved it from the living room into the study.

The bag I'd forgotten I was holding gave a strange buzz. Right. John's things were in there, those slippery, strange clothes that were thin as paper but somehow kept you warm. Honest to Pete. He was too old to be an athlete. I'd tell him that if he lived. He could take up fly-fishing or something. My fingers closed on his phone and pulled it out.

It was his work. John still did some consulting here and there. Shoot. I should tell them, shouldn't I? He loved some of those folks. I typed in his code (0110, our anniversary), but it didn't work. He must've changed it after being hacked or something, not that he said anything to me. I typed in his birthday. That didn't work, either. Sadie's birthday. There.

His screen was lit up with texts. I put on my reading glasses.

After a second, I took off my reading glasses and put the phone down. Held down the little button so it would turn off. My face felt hot, my hands like ice. My heart felt sick and slow, flopping like a dying bird.

I glanced around. Could anyone tell? Were they looking at me? Did they know?

No. Everyone else was worried about their own people. I should worry about John. His brain was bleeding. Juliet would be back in a minute.

Shame. That's what I felt. Shame and humiliation, and fear that everyone would see on my face what I had just learned.

CHAPTER THREE

Juliet

On the day her father had his stroke, Juliet Elizabeth Frost was considering leaving her perfect life and becoming a smoke jumper in Montana—husband, children and job be damned.

The thing was, her life really *was* perfect. Excellent health, fabulous education, a career as an architect that earned her a ridiculous salary. She had a husband who loved her *and* was from London with a dead-sexy accent to boot. They had two healthy daughters and lived in a beautiful home overlooking Long Island Sound. Juliet drove a safe, fancy but not too pretentious German car. They brought their daughters on vacations to places like New Zealand and Provence. She spoke French and Italian. Her boobs had survived nursing two babies, and while they might not be perky anymore, they weren't saggy, either.

She knew a lot of successful, intelligent women, though her mother was her true best friend. She tolerated her younger sister and was sometimes even fond of her. Her father, who had always been distracted where she was concerned, had recently morphed into a raging asshole . . . and Juliet was going to have to tell her mother about it. Soon.

None of this explained why she was currently sitting in her closet, having a panic attack, hoping she'd faint.

The girls were at school, thank God, and Oliver was at work, designing jet engines. It was lucky that Juliet was working from home today, because last week, when she had a panic attack at work, and the idea of her coworkers, her boss, and *Arwen* seeing her hyperventilating and crying and possibly fainting . . . no. She'd had to get down eight floors and rush into the Starbucks on Chapel Street, and thankfully, the restroom was free. The first time it hadn't been, and she'd slid to the floor and had to pretend she was having a sugar crash in order to keep the barista from calling the ambulance.

Today, the panic attack had just sneaked up on her right during the conference call with her team at DJK Architects, one of the best firms in the U.S. Seemingly out of nowhere, it came . . . that creeping, prickling terror that started in her feet and slithered up her legs, making her knees ache, her heart rate accelerate. *Keep your shit together*, she ordered herself. Her boss, Dave, was drawing out the goodbyes with his usual jargon . . . "So I think we all have our action points" and "we've really drilled down on the issue," all those stupid clichés. Would it kill him to just end the damn meeting?

Her heart was beating so hard, and she was trying not to blink too fast, but the sweat was breaking out on her body, chest first, then armpits and crotch, back of the legs, forehead. In another ten seconds, she'd start to hyperventilate.

"Arwen, e-mail me those numbers, okay?" she said. Her voice sounded strained and thin.

"Already done."

Of course it was. "Great! Talk soon, everyone!" Her voice was a croak. She clicked the End button, closed the computer just in case the feed was still live, and bolted for the closet.

Sometimes, the hyperventilation caused her to pass out, which was actually a lot easier than talking herself down, that forced slow breathing, the mantra of *you're fine, you're fine, you're fine, slow down, slow down, slow down.* Fainting was lovely. If she fainted, everything grayed out gently, giant spots eating up her vision, and it felt as if she were falling so slowly.

Then she'd wake up, normal breathing restored, on the carpeted floor of her expansive closet—because so far, four of the six panic attacks had been in the closet, conveniently—safe among her shoes and sweaters. Like a nap. Like anesthesia. Juliet loved anesthesia; last year, she'd had to have a uterine biopsy, and the IV sedation was the best feeling she'd had in ages. She wished she could've stayed in that state, that lovely, floating, almost unconscious state, for a long time. Totally understandable why people got hooked on those drugs.

The attack was passing. No pleasant fainting this time, apparently. She'd have to shower again, since she was damp with sweat, and change, and get her current outfit to the dry cleaner's. If Oliver noticed their dry-cleaning bill had seen a significant bump, he hadn't said anything. Then again, that was her job: pick up dry cleaning on the way home from the office.

None of these was the reason she was sitting hunched in her closet.

The problem was Arwen.

No. No, she wasn't the problem. Juliet hated women who blamed other women for their issues . . . or maybe their own lack of success.

But the problem was maybe Arwen. Arwen Alexander, Wunderkind.

Yes. Fuck it, Juliet's heart started racing again. *Come on, fainting! You can do it!* A laugh/sob popped out of her lips.

The panic grew. Fast. Like a mushroom. Like cancer. How had she been reduced to sitting in a fucking closet with the full-on shakes when she had a perfect life?

In the past few months, everything Juliet took for a fact seemed fluid. She'd always wanted to be an architect, but did she anymore? Somehow, inexplicably, it felt like she was living the wrong life. How could that be? Every detail had been planned, mapped out, worked for and achieved. Harvard, check. Yale, check. Oliver, check. Two healthy daughters, check and check and thank God. This house that she'd designed in the town she loved. Check. Parents who loved her and had a solid (ha!) marriage.

But suddenly it all felt wrong. Never before had Juliet questioned that she was on the right path . . . until now.

Was she a good mother? A good wife? She loved her girls, of course she did. She'd *die* for them. Kill anyone who threatened them with a song in her heart and a smile on her lips. She did everything she could for them, and from the outside, it probably looked like she was a good mother.

She just didn't *feel* like it these days. Brianna had grown sullen and withdrawn—she was twelve, so it wasn't the world's biggest surprise. But the thing was, Juliet hadn't done that with her mother. She *adored* her mother, every day, every year. Sloane was right behind Brianna at ten . . . Would she stop talking to her, too? Oliver had been a little . . . distant, maybe. And if there was one thing Juliet couldn't stand, it was distant. Her father had been that way (except with Sadie). And Dad had been *especially* distant with Mom.

Of course things stopped being hot and heavy after fifteen years of marriage. You couldn't keep that shit up, no matter how hard you tried, how many thongs you bought. Things became expected and comfortable, and that was *good*, wasn't it? Even if she tried really hard to be spontaneous and exciting, she and Ollie knew each other inside and out. Would she find herself walking her parents' path, barely speaking, being invisible to the other?

This seeping dread, this flight response . . . why did it feel so real? Was she a fake somehow, in both work and life? Why was Arwen so terrifying when she was perfectly . . . fine?

Shit, shit, shit. This was what happened. One little crack, and the whole building comes down.

Juliet stood. Her legs felt shaky, and her hair looked greasy. There were circles under her eyes.

That faint would've been welcome. A little nap.

Instead, she went to her computer and Googled "how to become a smoke jumper in Montana." Very conveniently, the U.S. Forest Service was hiring. So she would need a little experience fighting wildland fires. She'd get it. Juliet was in great shape. She liked heights and fires (though more of the bonfire/fireplace type). She was brave—always the first to jump in the water, or try waterskiing or leap off the platform while zip-lining. She was an adrenaline junkie who had just emerged from hiding in her closet.

The idea of being far, far away doing heroic things had such pull, such promise. Her sister Sadie would probably do it. Move to Montana, be handed a job, meet a cowboy who happened to also be a billionaire and spend the rest of her life traveling and getting massages on various beaches, because that's how life unfolded for Sadie. Juliet worked and planned for everything; Sadie skipped off to New York City, doing things in the most irresponsible, unplanned, carefree way possible. *No money? No problem. I can waitress! I can work in a tattoo parlor! I'm an artist, you see. Things are different for us, since we're pure and superior. No career? No worries! Something will come along. In the meantime, look at this hovel I'm living in after Mom and Dad remortgaged the house to put me through college!*

In typical Sadie fashion, she got a cute little job at a cute little school and somehow started earning money on paintings that allowed her to buy a cute little apartment and then found a cute wealthy boyfriend. Sadie never had to work for a thing. Juliet worked every fucking day, every fucking minute. Did people think Oliver just saw her and fell in love? Oh, no. She had to *work* for him. The guy was absolutely wonderful—handsome and charming and smart and kind and funny—and *everyone* had wanted him. Juliet had taken one look at him and thought, *Game on.* She'd had to *earn* him, which she had.

All work, all the time, every part of her life. Me time? Please. Juliet brought work with her on every weekend away, every vacation. She took a bubble bath for effect, only when Oliver had come home from a trip, and she'd run the bath and sprinkle flower petals in and light candles the way no one ever did in real life, and it was all for seduction, to say, "Sure, we've been married for fifteen years, but I'm still a voracious sex beast, you betcha!" Long walks on the weekends or after school were to incorporate health and outdoor time into the girls' lives, even if Juliet's brain was fogged with all the work she had to do to earn that fat salary, how late she'd have to work to make up the time spent walking, how to help Sloane catch up on reading and make gluten-free, peanut-free, dairy-free cupcakes for Sloane's class and later have sex with Oliver so he wouldn't forget he loved her, or take Mom out to dinner because she deserved it, or plant flowers in the front yard because Oliver's British mother loved gardens and had once said a house without a garden is a house without a soul, and then what about the mentorship thing she'd promised to do for Yale, and the workshop (not keynote) she was giving at the annual American Institute of Architects conference on risk management (not the sexy one Arwen was doing on "breaking boundaries") and right, their cleaning lady had moved and Juliet hadn't found another one yet so she had to clean the house because she liked things tidy and couldn't relax if things were messy.

"Shit," she said aloud. "Next time, faint, you idiot."

She left her closet, intending to take a shower, but there was her phone, buzzing on the desk of her study.

Mom. She always took calls from Mom.

"Sweetheart," her mother began, "I'm real sorry to have to tell you this, but your dad's been in an accident, and he's hurt. Real bad. I'm on my way to Lawrence and Memorial."

Her heart thudded hard, rolling in a sickening wave—once, twice, three times.

"I'm on my way," Juliet said, her voice firm. "Hang in there, Mom, I'll be there in twenty minutes."

Smoke jumper. She would make a great smoke jumper.

CHAPTER FOUR

Sadie

In the blur of terror that followed Juliet's call, I rented a car and drove through the snarl of traffic between Manhattan and Connecticut, doing eighty miles an hour when I could, slamming on the brakes when I saw taillights. Even though I'd tried calling Alexander as soon as I hung up with Jules, he wasn't answering. He had a habit of keeping the phone off while he drove, which was not at all convenient at this moment. After leaving six messages, I called Carter and told him instead, hiccuping with sobs.

"Oh, sweetheart," he said. "Good luck. I'm here for anything you need. If you want me to call Sister Mary or anything, if you need me to water your plants, let me know."

The whole way there, tears streaked down my cheeks and I had to fight not to break down. My dad had been my idol growing up—always encouraging, upbeat and fun . . . not to mention the parent who actually liked me. He taught me to play poker and swim and never said art school was a bad idea. He told me I was pretty and never criticized my clothes, even in my goth stage. He came to visit me once a month in the city, and still held my hand when we were crossing the street. He couldn't be dying. Not without me there.

All my life, there'd been a clear division in the family. Juliet "Perfection from Conception" was Mom's; I, the lesser child in just about every measurable aspect except artistic ability, was Dad's. He never seemed to think he got the short end of the stick.

"Please don't die, please don't die," I chanted under my breath. Who else would root for me the way he did? Who else would be so . . . so delighted at every turn of my life? It seemed that all my childhood, Mom had lectured on everything from posture to how to clean the bathroom to grades, and Dad had been right behind her, sweeping away the criticism with a grin or a wink and maybe a trip to the ice cream parlor. Everything he did let me know I was loved, whereas everything Mom did let me know I was wrong.

There was a reason I rarely came back to Stoningham, and when I did, it was only for a day. And there was a reason my father came to visit me in the city, sleeping on the pullout couch, thinking it was the best fun ever. Those were always like old times, when I was little and afraid of thunderstorms, and Dad would tell me stories about girl warriors who rode monsters they'd tamed into battle.

My chest felt like it was being crushed. Where the hell was Alexander? Why wasn't he calling me?

Finally, after an eternity, I pulled into the UConn Health Center's giant parking lot, threw my shitty little rental in park and ran to get inside, slipping and sliding, since the rain had frozen when the temperature dropped, and it was a good ten degrees colder up here.

An orderly directed me to the family waiting area, and I ran there, too.

Mom, Jules and Oliver were in the waiting room, Jules looking worried, Mom a thousand miles away.

"Is he—" I began, but my voice choked off.

"Unconscious but alive," Oliver said, getting up to hug me. "He made it through surgery. We're waiting for the doctor to tell us what we can expect."

My sister got up and we hugged awkwardly, too. She stepped on my foot, and my hair got tangled in her earring for a second.

"Hi, Mom," I said.

"Hello, Sadie." Her voice was expressionless. Shock, I guessed. She was clutching a plastic bag to her chest. I kissed her cheek, and she still didn't look at me. "Hello, Sadie," she repeated, and I felt a twinge of sympathy.

"Hi, Mom. You doing okay?" She was younger than Dad, and I'd heard that seventy was the new forty, but still.

"I'm fine," she said. My hands were shaking, but she seemed utterly calm.

"Can I see him?"

"He's resting."

"I'd like to see him."

"Sure, sure," said Jules. "Come on. We're only allowed a few minutes an hour, but come say . . . well." Her voice choked off, and she took a shaky breath.

We walked down a long, brightly lit hallway and went into a room.

Oh, God. Oh, Daddy.

He was on a ventilator, his face swollen, a cut on his nose, a black eye. His head was shaved and bandaged. "Jesus," I whispered.

"They had to drill into his head to relieve the bleeding," Jules said.

He didn't look like himself, but it was him, all right. Those were his outrageous eyebrows. That was his wedding ring on his left hand, his class ring from Boston College on his right. The scar on his arm from when he had a bad break in college.

"It's a wait-and-see situation," Jules said, and her voice was uncharacteristically soft.

I didn't know where to touch my father; he looked so small in the hospital bed.

"Daddy?" I whispered, putting my hand on his chest, over his heart. "It's Sadie. I'm here. I love you so much, Daddy."

That was all I was allowed. A nurse told us he needed quiet, and Jules led me back to the waiting room.

"What happened?" I asked, and Oliver, the diplomat in the family, filled me in.

It was such a Dad move, deciding to go for a bike ride on a nice day, winter be damned. Apparently he had a stroke and fell, then lay there for an unknown amount of time before someone saw him and called 911. They missed the golden hour, that window after a stroke when intervention can make a huge difference. "A pity, really," Oliver said. The vast understatement of that word made me want to smack him.

My tears kept falling. My mother stared into space. Juliet checked in with the babysitter and sat next to Mom. They murmured to each other. Oliver smiled every time I looked at him. I kept checking my phone to see if Alexander had turned on his—Boston wasn't that far, and I'd texted, too. But he was one of those people who would forget his phone was off until hours later.

A few friends from St. Catherine's had texted; I guess Carter had put the word out. Even Sister Mary sent me a message, saying she'd pray for my family.

An hour ticked past. A couple of times, I had to get up and go to the window so I wouldn't sob in front of my family, in case Mom said something like, "There's no point in crying, Sadie. Save that for when he dies." Not that she would. But I kept imagining that kind of thing—Juliet sighing and rolling her eyes at me, or my annoyingly chipper brother-in-law saying something British, like, "Stiff upper lip, Sadie! No need to get all collywobbles!"

Where was Alexander? Where was the doctor? (He probably had a good excuse, like saving someone's life, but I was still irked.)

It started to snow, first just a few drifting flakes, then a near white-out. The TV on the wall showed meteorologists peeing themselves with glee, standing at intersections where cars slid by to report that, yes, it was snowing. If one of those sliding cars hit them, it would be natural selection.

My father's condition had rendered me vicious, it seemed.

Finally, as I stared out the window at the "polar vortex" (because calling it *snow* was so yesterday), Alexander's name flashed on my phone. I told him the grim news.

"Babe, I'm so sorry. I'll be there as soon as I can," he said. "You know me and driving with the phone off. But I'll keep it on, and I'm getting right back in the car."

"Is it snowing there?" I asked.

He hesitated. "Yeah. Pretty hard."

"Here too. Why don't you call in the morning? Stay in Boston tonight. The forecast is eight to twelve inches."

"That's what she said."

My jaw clenched. "Not now, Alexander."

"Sorry. Just trying to make you laugh."

"I know." I paused. "I miss you."

"I miss you, too. I'm so sorry about this, babe. I know how much you love your dad."

The tears started again, stinging the now-raw skin under my eyes. "Thanks, honey," I said, my voice husky.

"Love you, Sadie."

"Love you, too."

I went back to rejoin the family. No one looked up.

"No word from the doctor?" I asked.

"Alas, no," said Oliver.

Alas? I tried not to be annoyed, but Oliver . . . he was perfectly nice. If he lacked substance in my opinion, I guess it didn't matter. He was a good father, a good husband, and a brilliant son-in-law, at least according to Mom.

I Googled "stroke with cerebral hemorrhage" on my phone, then decided it would only lead to terror. May as well hear from the doctor first. I sighed. Studied my family. I'd seen them at Christmas, just a few weeks ago, but that seemed like millennia now.

Jules looked frazzled, which was rare, but who could blame her? Her hair was perfectly straight, smooth and dark blond, shoulder length, but now it was tangled, as if she'd been sleeping. Her clothes were wrinkled, too. Usually, she was so put together—her personal style could be called understated hip. Always quality stuff, always a little boring unless you looked closely and saw that her shirt was asymmetrical or she was wearing a wicked cool silver ring. As ever, she was Mom's guard dog, sitting by her side, reminding her to drink some water, offering her a Life Saver.

She didn't offer me a Life Saver.

And then there was Oliver, terribly handsome as always, brown hair, green eyes, his teeth blindingly white and straight (he'd gotten braces when he and Juliet were engaged, succumbing to the pressures of American orthodontic standards). He was scrolling through his phone, and I wanted to rip it out of his hands and hit him on the head with it. Every time he caught me looking, he gave that knee-jerk smile. *Oliver,* I wanted to say, *my father might be dying and I realize I'm probably the only one who would really miss him, but could you stop flashing your perfect teeth at me?* He'd always been nice to me . . . and also had never made an effort to do more than exchange pleasantries. Then there was the way Juliet showed him off, like he was a prize cow at the state fair. "This is my *husband*, Oliver Smitherington." It was that last name, probably. How could you have sex with someone with such a silly last name?

And Mom. Right now, she was a frickin' statue, her blunt white bob perfectly in place, mascara unsmudged by tears. Why *would* she cry? She practically hated my father. Tolerated him at best, and while it didn't feel great to think of my mother as a user, she had sure used Dad. His name, his hard-earned money. She hadn't had her own job till last year.

That being said, she looked pale and alone right now. I'd expected Auntie Caro, Mom's closest friend, to be here, since they'd been besties since before I was born. But no. Mom just stared into the distance, probably planning a tag sale to get rid of Dad's things.

"How are you doing, Mom?" I said.

"Fine."

"This must be very hard for you."

She blinked. "What's that, Sadie?"

"This must be hard for you," I repeated more loudly, getting an evil look from Jules. "Having your husband of fifty years in a life-threatening situation. Brain bleed. Surgery."

"I don't need a summary, Sadie. Of course it's hard."

"Don't be a jerk," Juliet told me.

"Well, it's a little odd, all of you stone-faced here. Except you, Oliver." He smiled again. Jesus.

"Want some sackcloth and ashes?" she asked. "Sorry if we're keeping it together. You keep doing you, though."

Finally, the doctor appeared, a tall, handsome African American man wearing scrubs and a white doctor jacket with his name stitched over the pocket. *Daniel Evans, MD. Neurosurgery.*

God. Brain surgery. *Please make it, Daddy. Please don't die.*

"I'm so sorry," he said. "We had another emergency right after your . . . uh, Mr., uh . . ."

"Frost," Juliet and I said in unison.

"Yes, of course. So." He sat down. "Your father—and husband, Mrs. Frost—had a significant bleed, as we suspected. Right now, he's resting, as you know. We're keeping him on the ventilator to help his breathing, more as a precaution than anything else, since he had started breathing on his own again in the ambulance on the way here."

My insides started to quiver. It sounded so dire.

"I wish I could tell you what to expect. There *is* damage to the part of the brain that controls speech, we're sure of that. There's also bruising from the fall, which has caused some swelling. But he survived the surgery. It's going to be one step at a time. Now, I'm sure you have questions."

"Will he wake up?" I asked.

He tilted his head. "We don't know yet. Brain injuries are hard to predict. Every one is different. All I can say now is he's stable but critical. The next couple of days will tell us more. Where do you folks live?"

"Stoningham," Juliet answered. Mom still hadn't said a word.

He nodded. "Why don't you go home and get some rest? We'll call if his status changes."

"That's a good idea," Oliver said.

"No, it's not," I said. "He'll want us close by."

"We've been here for hours," Juliet said. "And we can't camp out in his room, Sadie. It's critical care."

"Well, I'm not going," I said. "If something . . . happens, I want to be here."

"We have the girls," Oliver said.

"I'm aware of that, Oliver. You guys go. The girls need you. I know that."

"Thanks, Dr. Evans," Jules said. "We appreciate your kindness."

He shook our hands, his face somber, and left.

"Too bad you're dating a yacht salesman," Juliet said.

I ignored that. "I can sleep right here if I have to, but I want to be close by."

"That's fine," Mom said. "But I'll go home with Juliet, I think. It's been quite a shock."

The obligatory hugs were doled out, and they left.

My mom might be a widow soon. For all her flaws as a wife, that had to be scary. They'd been married fifty years. God. Fifty years tomorrow.

I went to the nurses' station and asked to see my father again. He was in the same position, but then again, he'd been heavily sedated, I guessed.

He looked awful. It was hard to imagine he could survive—the bandage on his head, the tube coming out of his mouth, some stitches on his eyebrow, the bruising.

"I'm here, Daddy," I said. "I'm right here. You and me, just like always." I told the nurses where I'd be, and they were so nice, telling me to get some food. One of them gave me a blanket.

If my father died in the middle of the night, he wouldn't be alone. There'd be someone who loved him to hold his hand and thank him, and I was glad it was me, because honestly, I couldn't imagine Juliet or my mother doing it.

CHAPTER FIVE

Barb

I tried to remember when my marriage went from real good to fine to not bad to downright nonexistent, and could not pinpoint a time. No, I couldn't.

Once, John and I loved each other. I didn't have any doubt about that, no sir. It could be said that we didn't know each other real well in those early days, but we were happy.

It was the infertility that started the downward slide. John didn't try real hard to understand my pain, and being a second-generation Norwegian and daughter of a Minnesotan farmer, maybe I didn't know how to share the full heft of it. We Minnesotans don't like to complain.

But it didn't take a genius to understand that I *was* suffering. Looking back, I think John wanted to pretend I *didn't* suffer, because that would get him off the hook for a problem he couldn't fix.

Then, when we *were* blessed, of course my focus was Juliet. Unfortunately, having a baby didn't bring us a heck of a lot closer, which was partly my fault. I can see that now.

But isn't that what good mothers do? I was a stay-at-home mom in an age (and a town) where most of us *did* stay home, or only worked part-time. I'd wanted more than anything to be a mother. I wasn't about to put my little baby in someone else's care. Absolutely not! She was my whole purpose in life, don't you know. I wouldn't have had it any other way.

But John didn't get it. He didn't see all that I did. It used to make me downright crazy when he would comment on her progress or abilities. "We had a lot of fun this afternoon," he said one Sunday in August when he'd taken her to the beach, practically giving himself the father of the year award. "Do you know what a great swimmer she is?"

"Who do you think taught her?" I snapped. "And did you forget the sunscreen? She looks mighty pink to me."

The same with reading. "Our four-year-old is reading chapter books!" he exclaimed, as if he was telling me something I didn't know. Me, who spent every day with her, who read to her for hours, who gave her her love of books. I wanted him to see that, to credit me, to honor those hours, those *years*, when everything I did was for the good of our daughter. I was a wonderful mother. I told Juliet I loved her all the time, and that was something I never heard growing up, no sir. I was generous and thoughtful and affectionate. I set boundaries so she got enough sleep, ate nutritious meals, respected others and herself, was brave but not foolish. She was my life's work.

And while John would give me a card on Mother's Day and make me a breakfast that used every pot and pan in the kitchen, and tell me to "take the day off from housework" (so I could do twice as much on Monday), he just didn't see it. Or he pretended not to. When he "babysat" Juliet so I could do exciting things like grocery shopping all by my lonesome, I'd come home to find him reading with her parked in front of the TV, watching something other than the shows I allowed (half an hour a day on weekends, nothing on school days). He didn't notice that the house was sparkling clean, even when she was a tiny baby, because the house had *always* been sparkling clean, and let me tell you, it wasn't because he knew his way around a scrub brush.

He thought Juliet had just come out a certain way, as if she raised herself.

Sometimes, I had to grit my teeth when people told us what a great kid she was, and John would glow with pride. He'd say things like, "Well, my mom loves poetry, too," forgetting that I read poetry to our daughter (and no one had ever read poetry to me, you can be sure about that). *He* sure didn't read poetry—and he was related to Robert Frost, maybe! He rarely made it home in time to read anything at all to Juliet.

The truth was, John didn't do a lot with our daughter except provide. And he *was* a good provider. I valued that. Of course I did, and I still tried to be a good wife, asking him how his day went, arranging our social life because he certainly didn't. I'd invite the partners of his firm over for dinner and make sure everything was delicious and beautiful, and he'd say, "That was nice, hon," and then try to put the moves on me, and ignore the fact that I had just made a dinner for twelve people and was darn tired. But I'd have sex with him, and when he was sound asleep, I'd go downstairs and clean up the mess from dinner.

His personal habits began to scrape my nerve endings raw. When we were new to Stoningham and I had nothing but the house and volunteering to occupy my time, it was absolutely fine if he left a towel on the bathroom floor or didn't rinse out the sink after he shaved. I was a housewife, so I didn't mind cleaning up after him, though it reminded me that when we both worked full-time, I still did ninety-five percent of the housework.

But now, raising our beautiful, wonderful daughter, that towel and sink told me he didn't think anything had changed. That he was too important to put his own dang towel on the rack or in the laundry basket, that three seconds of sink rinsing was beneath him because he was a lawyer and I was *just* a mother.

Again, in hindsight, I probably should've said something about this.

His own mother appreciated me, because she'd *been* me. When his parents came to visit, John and his father would play golf, while Eleanor and I admired Juliet, because really, isn't that what grandmothers do? She cooed and praised and held her granddaughter close. Once, when it was just the two of us, Juliet asleep in her arms, she said, "No one knows how much of your soul you give to your baby. They think it's just luck or chance that your baby sleeps through the night, or doesn't pitch a tantrum when you're leaving a store, or knows to say thank you. They think you were tapped by a fairy wand, and they ignore all the hours you put in, shaping them."

Gosh, it felt so good to be truly seen that way! Sad to say, Eleanor died when Sadie was three months old. I wondered if things would've been different if she'd lived. I bet she would've helped, and maybe recognized that I had postpartum depression, because she was a smart one, that Eleanor. She was always kind and wise. Much more so than my own mother, may she rest in peace.

But as it was, both John and I lost our mothers in the span of six months, and right smack in between those deaths, we had a newborn. Seemed like God was laughing at all those years of trying to have Juliet, and then, when Juliet was almost twelve, surprise!

John felt very heroic, taking care of Sadie, changing diapers and getting up in the middle of the night . . . something he'd almost never done with Juliet. He loved to tell me how much he did, as my breasts felt like they were being sliced by knives and turning hard as rocks. When my incision needed to be restitched because I'd had a coughing fit (don't the doctors just love to tell you how you were responsible for everything that goes wrong?), John told me how he'd brilliantly arranged for Caro to pick up Juliet for Girl Scouts. Not only that, he'd taken a casserole I'd made the month before out of the freezer, so dinner was all set. I'd been saving that casserole for when he went back to work and was traveling, when I'd be alone with our baby and adolescent, when all household and child-related responsibilities would be on me and me alone. "It's good, isn't it?" he said at dinner that night. "Who made this?"

He was just so . . . obtuse sometimes. Most times, to be honest.

Just as Juliet and I had our own little world, he had one with Sadie.

Juliet loved her little sister, but their time together was limited; she had homework and projects, activities and friends. The sides were pretty clear—Sadie and John, Juliet and me. I couldn't help resenting his adoration of Sadie, because Juliet had gotten none of that. Sometimes I'd see her face as she watched her father giving horsey rides to Sadie, or drawing with her for an hour after supper, and I knew she was hurt.

When Juliet left for college, things got worse in our marriage. He was critical of how I interacted with Sadie, telling me I was too strict, that Sadie was a free spirit, that I had to be more flexible. If I said, "No more cookies, Sadie," he'd inevitably sneak her one more. If I said it was bedtime, he'd give her fifteen minutes longer. He came home every night at six thirty and it seemed like all he did was pick at me regarding Sadie. Why was she in her room? So what if she'd told her teacher math was stupid and she wouldn't do her assignments? Everyone hated math. Were we having pork chops again? Didn't we just have them?

And he said these things in an amiable way, so if I were to say, "No, John, that was in April. I make a meal plan so we never have the same dinner twice in any month, and I've done that since the day we were married. Haven't you noticed?" he'd say, "Okay, okay, I'm sorry. My mistake. I didn't mean to offend you." Then he'd wink at Sadie, or sigh if she wasn't in the room, letting me know I was the bad guy here.

He always, always took her side. "She's not Juliet. She's her own person, Barb."

"I know that! But she needs more boundaries and focus, John! I spend all day with her, and you breeze in for two hours of fun after all the hard things are done."

"What's so hard about your life, Barb?" Again, said in a condescending way.

You can see there was no winning these arguments.

By the time Sadie finally left for school, I was fifty-eight years old, tired and awfully relieved. And this time, John was the one who cried on the trip home. I've got to admit, it felt a little bit like justice.

I did hope that once we were alone, things would improve between us . . . hoped that my constant irritation with him would fade and we could become close again. But there was always a disconnect. If I put my hand on his leg in bed, he'd say, "Oh. I'm sorry, hon. I'm exhausted." The next night, he'd be completely up for it if you get my meaning, and *I'd* be fighting to stay awake. If we did have sex, it was rare that we recaptured that old sunshiny feeling. Instead, it was just a box to be checked. Sex with husband. Done, thank heavens.

Men didn't understand how hard it was to get in the mood. I hated movies when one kiss was enough for the woman and three seconds later they were doing it. Men thought that was normal. They took it personally if you weren't like that, and please. I wasn't twenty-five anymore. Men didn't realize that we women had to talk ourselves into the mood a lot of the time, had to go through the motions until they were sincere, had to deal with the consequences of an aging reproductive system. Dryness. Hot flashes. Urinary tract infections. Less sensitivity. Cysts. All men had were penises that were or were not erect.

We started sleeping in different bedrooms during Sadie's sophomore year of college, when his snoring took a turn for the louder and my bladder got me up two times a night. When we watched TV together, he'd sit in the recliner, and I'd sit on the couch, and ten minutes later, he'd be asleep.

John worked. I volunteered. Though he was Sadie's favorite parent, I was the one who knew her college schedule. I was the one who made her retake her math requirement at the community college so she could graduate. I asked Genevieve London, who lived here in Stoningham and was quite a force in fashion, if Sadie could have an internship in the design department, hoping her art degree could somehow support her. (Sadie turned that internship down, FYI.)

And yet, I was always the mean parent, always the odd man out. I wondered what it was like to be loved by Sadie, to be respected, to have her come up and put her arm around my waist. Must've been real nice, I thought. If I put my hand on her hair or tried to give her a hug, she'd act all surprised and give me a look that said, *What are you* doing?

It was just so . . . draining.

To fill myself up, I turned to the place where I felt most like myself: Juliet. And her family, of course. But Juliet especially. There, with them, I was the best, truest version of myself. Happy, funny, helpful, listening intently as Juliet told me something about work or her friends, offering advice when asked. "That's a great idea, Mom," she'd say, or "I knew you'd have the perfect words."

I volunteered, as I always had in Stoningham. I was on the school board, the historical society, the garden club, the Friends of the Library. There were hardly any year-rounders I didn't know by name. Shopkeepers greeted me gladly; teachers would come to me with problems; newcomers to town were steered to me for guidance on how to fit into our tight-knit little community. I knew the pastor, the priest and the rabbi. I recommended volunteer groups—trash pickup, the food pantry, adopt-a-grandparent, the after-school program.

John knew I did these things, but they didn't interest him. He played golf; he was on the fishing derby committee, which meant I wrote a check for $500 for the Scouts each spring, and John went and talked to the other dads.

And still I tried. It's the woman's job to steer the relationship, Caro told me (which didn't prevent her divorce, mind you). So over dinner, I'd ask John about his day and get the customary answer . . . "Nothing exciting. Just the usual." If I offered up what I did, his eyes would glaze over, and he'd say, "Hm?" in response. We took to reading instead of talking as we ate.

Holidays were generally wonderful, because of Juliet and the girls. I'd bake and decorate and play special music—all the things my childhood lacked out there in cold Minnesota. Juliet and her girls would help or admire, and Sadie would come home and sometimes even say something nice, like, "The house looks pretty, Mom" or "It smells so good in here."

Times like these, I'd look at my husband and smile, thinking, *Aren't we so lucky? Two healthy children. Two healthy grandchildren. A lovely son-in-law. A beautiful home.* Sometimes, I'd even say it. "Sure are," he'd answer, and that would be it.

It was hard, feeling nothing but irritation toward him. Harder and harder with every passing year. When he retired at sixty-eight, my heart sank, because after all those years, he would be here, every day, day after day, getting in the way, pretending to try to be helpful but gumming it up enough so I'd shoo him away. He'd clean up the kitchen, which to him meant putting the dishes in the dishwasher and running tepid water into the pans. He wouldn't wipe off the counters or empty the drain catch . . . The bits of food would just sit there until I took care of it. Inevitably, I couldn't take the mess, so I'd start cleaning the pots and pans, and John would say, "Oh, I meant to do that! I'll do it now."

But of course, he didn't. If he'd meant to do it, he *would've* done it. If he really and truly wanted to be helpful with the laundry, say, he wouldn't have poured bleach right into the washing machine—on darks, no less—three times in a row.

"For a smart man, you sure can be dumb," I said, trying to keep things light.

"It's not a big deal," he said. "There's a learning curve."

"And there's three hundred dollars' worth of clothes ruined because you didn't read the instructions or listen to me." The thrifty Norwegian in me was furious.

"I didn't like that shirt, anyway."

"Well, I liked mine a lot."

"Barb. It's not a big deal. Buy another one. You don't have to get so upset all the time."

"I'm not upset. I'm stating a fact."

"I'm *sorry*," he said in that condescending way that really meant, *I'm sorry you're being so petty, and I'm sorry I have to deal with this, and I'm sorry you don't realize I'm the most wonderful thing in the known world.*

I'm not sure when I started picturing widowhood as my happy alternative. John was healthy, but he was a man. He played golf. Weren't there lightning strikes on golf courses? He drove down to the city to see Sadie, and you know how those New York drivers are.

It wasn't that I wanted him to die. I just didn't want to be married anymore.

"I think there's something called divorce," Caro said one blissful night when John had decided to stay over in the city (on the pullout couch in Sadie's apartment, pretending to be twenty again, it seemed. We could afford a hotel room, after all).

I sighed. "We've been married for fifty years almost, don't you know. Do people get divorced after that long?"

"Yes, but between now and your death—let's say twenty-five more years—how do you want your life to be?" she said, taking a sip of her margarita. She had a point.

I thought for a moment. "Exactly the same, minus him."

I'd already done some research. We were comfortable because of John's work, but he never made partner. Too unambitious, too friendly to move up in the world. If we got a divorce, both of us would take a hit financially, which I told Caro. "I love this house and everything in it. I don't want to have to move in with Juliet or live in some three-family house in New London and worry about paying my bills." Caro had divorced long ago. But she had family money, and she'd gone back to school and become a public relations consultant and made a real good income. Real good.

She nodded slowly. "So . . . I guess we have to murder him." She flashed her beautiful smile. "Or . . . or what? Is there any chance you can make things better? It's not like he's a horrible man."

"No, he's not horrible."

"Trying to get along again would probably be better than murder or divorce."

"Probably." I smiled, but the thought made my shoulders sag. Another task for me to do. You could bet John's friends weren't telling him to be a more loving husband.

"As I tell my clients, fake it till you make it. You never know. If you pretend to be in love, maybe you'll fall back in love again. So much of happiness is the habit of positivity." Another sunny smile.

"I'm very glad to have you as my best friend, Caro," I said, my voice a little husky.

"Oh, Barb! I'm glad to have you, too! I love you! And I love this margarita! Please tell me there's more."

We spent the rest of the night chatting, and she drank a bit too much and stayed over in the guest room, which she could do without a single phone call explaining her actions. She had two boys a little older than Juliet; one lived in Vermont, and the other in New York City, so just like that, we were having a sleepover. I couldn't remember the last time I'd had so much fun with anyone except Juliet. Next to my daughter, Caro was my best friend. She lived around the corner and had brought over a cake the very first day we moved in. We clicked right away.

I took her advice, even though my heart wasn't in it. I tried. I made a point of lining up things to do with John, or for the two of us and with other couples, like our newlywed days. Caro had a steady beau named Ted (she refused to use the word *boyfriend*), and the four of us took ballroom dancing lessons, though John was clumsy as an ox on the dance floor. Karen, the dance instructor, would laugh till she cried sometimes, making us laugh, too. When Caro ruptured her Achilles tendon on a hike, we dropped out. There was a bowling league we tried, but I had some arthritis in my wrist, and it was painful. We went on a wine-tasting tour of Connecticut. Booked a trip to Italy with a group, which John summarized as "on the bus, off the bus; on the bus, off the bus" for the girls. Sadie lectured us about how shallow those bus tours were, and how we should've asked her for recommendations instead, since she was an expert on all things Europe (in her own mind, at least).

I'd thought our trip was quite nice. I liked the ease of the coach, not having to wonder where we'd stay each night, knowing a fairly decent hotel was part of the package. No, we didn't explore and wander on our own, but we saw some beautiful churches and countryside. Why did John have to poke fun at it?

It was the same as always, somehow. If we had a good time, John always credited someone else. "That Caro is a spitfire" or "Ted has the funniest stories, doesn't he?" or "Boy, that museum had some amazing pieces!" There was never a "thanks for looking that up and buying the tickets and getting me out of my chair when I was whiny about going in the first place." He never called *me* a spitfire or complimented me on telling a good story, even though Caro and Ted laughed and laughed when I told them about my childhood war with that giant goat we'd had.

No, John just gave me a look. *Her one fun story from childhood. Here we go again.*

And in the entire time I was faking it, hoping to make it, John never reciprocated. He didn't bring me flowers. He didn't suggest we do something, go somewhere. He just showed up, sometimes after I had to pitch it to him, to win him over to the idea of seeing a darn movie.

Exhausting.

Sex, which had become rote during the infertility years, became something I just didn't want to bother with anymore. I knew I was supposed to care, but a person got tired of asking, don't you know. A person can feel real bad for having to ask. John didn't seem to notice. I stopped trying to do couple things. He didn't seem to care. We stopped talking almost completely. It was better than forcing a meaningless conversation.

So when I got the call that he was probably dying, the grief came as a real shock. Not as big a shock as the adultery, but that came an hour or so later.

CHAPTER SIX

Barb

WORK: Babe, I miss U so much! Last week seems like a thousand years ago. I can't stop thinking about how U make me feel. I have NEVER come that hard before. I swear I thought I was dying. U ARE EVERYTHING TO ME!

JOHN: SAME!!! You're amazing. I've never felt this way. All I think of is you, you, you. Us together. God! I feel like a new man!

WORK: That thing U did with your tongue has me on FIRE just thinking about it.

JOHN: You deserve to be worshipped. Your body is incredible. God, I wish I had more "golf" weekends!!! LOL!

WORK: You can put your iron in my hole anytime.

OMG, I can't believe I said that!

JOHN: Keep talking, sex kitten. You make me roar like a tiger!!!!

WORK: I want U. All the time, any time, every time. When can we meet again??? I'm dying for U.

JOHN: Soon. But never soon enough, my love!!!

WORK: The things I could do to U for an entire weekend . . . week . . . month . . . lifetime! My ♥ swells just thinking about it!!! Will we ever be that lucky?

JOHN: My heart is swelling too and not just my heart!!! LOL!!! We will make it happen!! I want to spend the rest of my life with you. You make me HAPPY.

WORK: I am so hot for U right now. If I saw U, I'd be all over you in SECONDS. I am so PROUD of U for taking your happiness into your own hands and not feeling guilty. LIFE IS TOO SHORT!

JOHN: IKR? I didn't know what happiness WAS before this. I get hard just thinking about you! Have to go now. I want to do some cycling for our TRIATHLON together! I can't even believe I'll be doing this. I am a new man because of you!!! Miss you miss you miss you!!!

A series of emojis followed John's last text. A red heart. A smiley face with heart eyes. A smiley face blowing a kiss. A purple heart. A smiley face with a tongue hanging out. Another red heart.

Then there was the abundance of exclamation points. The words in capital letters. The acronyms (I had had to look up IKR, which stood for "I know, right?"). The poor comma usage and use of the letter *U* instead of the onerous three-letter word. I might not have set the academic world on fire, but for Pete's sake.

Clearly, John had been going through a second puberty.

"My God," Caro said, handing the phone back. "I—I don't know what to say, except let's kill the bastard." Her cheeks got red the way they always did when she was mad.

"Well," I said. "The wife is always the last to know. Isn't that what they say?"

It was two days after John's accident. Caro stopped by after getting the message that John was in the hospital, and (unfortunately) still alive. The girls were at the hospital . . . Well, Sadie was. Hopefully Juliet was home right now, getting a little TLC from Oliver and the girls.

"Fuck him," Caro said, throwing up her hands. "How dare he have a mistress! Fuck him, Barb!"

"Apparently, 'WORK'"—I used air quotes—"is fucking him plenty." It felt strange to curse. Kind of good, too. I'd read an article that said people who cursed were more honest. All those years of saying *heck* and *gosh darn* . . . they were over now.

"Are you okay?" Caro asked. "You seem so . . . calm."

"Well, you know, he's most likely dying."

"I hope he does." Caro covered her mouth with her hand. "Sorry."

"I hope so, too."

We were quiet a minute.

Thank *God* for Caro, a friend for so long, privy to just about all the issues and troubles and joys I had ever had. She was the only one who knew how hard it had been for me to get pregnant with Juliet. She was the one I called in shock when I found out about my pregnancy with Sadie. The one who'd consoled me when I dropped Juliet off at Harvard, so proud and devastated at the same time. Caro had been my campaign manager for my run for first selectman—*Barb Frost for Stoningham: The Name You Trust.*

Caro was also the only one who knew I had been planning to file for divorce.

"So let's text her back," Caro said, taking a sip of the bourbon she'd brought over, good friend that she was.

"You think so?"

"Yeah. Why not?"

The last few texts were, obviously, from WORK, since John had been too busy having a hole drilled in his head. There was some joke in there, but I wasn't in the mood.

WORK: Babe, haven't heard from U. U OK? Love U and miss U!

Thinking of U and us and the way we are together. Miss U!

Starting to worry. Is it HER? Pls call me. ♥ ♥ ♥ x 10000000!!!

"'Is it her?'" I read. "That would be me, I'm guessing."

"Answer her. Just to buy time for when you can think of what you want to say."

"And say what? 'Hey there. This is John's wife. You can have him. By the way, he's brain damaged.'"

Caro snorted. "Sounds good to me."

I sighed and let my head rest against the back of the couch. "This would really hurt the girls. Sadie especially. She thinks her dad walks on water."

"So tell her. Take no prisoners."

"Would you tell the boys?"

"In a heartbeat." That was probably a lie. Caro and Rich, her ex, had divorced with grace and humor, and I still didn't understand how they'd pulled it off. Those two still had dinner together once a month. Caro went to his wedding, for heaven's sake!

That's what I'd been hoping for, if not expecting. An amicable divorce where we still saw each other on the holidays. If he wanted someone else, I wouldn't have cared, not once the divorce was final.

It was the deceit that had my panties in a twist, as the young people said. He'd cheated on me. Had there been other women? Was WORK the first time he'd had an affair?

I'd probably never know, would I?

I closed my eyes. The bourbon made a nice warm spot in my chest, and after two nights without sleep, I could use some relaxing. When I left the hospital earlier today, Sadie gave me the stink eye for saying I needed to go home. Juliet told me to take a long bath and make sure I ate a real dinner. Such was the difference between my two children. I'd only just walked in the door when Caro came in like an angel with bourbon, and a long, comforting hug to boot.

John had a mistress. He was young again. He had discovered what happiness was, did things with his tongue and was now in a medically induced coma.

"I want to find out who she is," I said suddenly. "I mean, Caro, who the hell would want that old windbag? She sounds like she's twenty-three. He's seventy-five years old, don't you know! And he's got that horrible nose! Thank God the girls took after me. That there's a blessing, you know what I'm saying?"

Caro laughed. "I love when you talk Minnesotan to me."

"It's because I'm a little drunk. I think I had a breakfast bar in the car this morning, so this is my dinner." I held up the glass. Caro always had the good stuff. Woodford. John was cheap when it came to liquor. He'd never bought a bottle of wine that cost more than ten dollars.

Caro squeezed my hand. "By the way, yes. Thank God they both look like you. But some women will do anything for a man. Especially a married man." She stood up. "I'm gonna call for a pizza. I'd offer to cook you something, but I just don't love you that much."

I started laughing, the exhausted, wrung-out kind of laughter that was hard to stop.

A mistress! Who'da thunk it?

From the kitchen, I heard Caro calling Wood Fire. "It's a rush job, okay? A pizza emergency for the first selectman." Caro's voice was soothing and warm, and people just loved her. I sure did.

People loved me, too. They should. I loved being useful, loved helping out and being friendly. The only two people who didn't love me were my husband and Sadie. Well, Sadie probably loved me. She just didn't like me all that much.

"So why would someone want a married man?" I asked when Caro came back from the other room. "Especially an old married man?"

"Money, honey. For one, he's close to death. Whoops. Sorry. I meant figuratively. I bet she's some young slut who figures he'll leave you, marry her, and then she'll get all his money."

"You know, we're not exactly rolling in it. We did fine. We have enough for retirement. No one's going to inherit much other than this house."

"Which our trashy whore probably doesn't know," Caro said. "For two, he's already proven he's a keeper for someone. 'Married fifty years? Oh, he's a family man!' She never thinks, 'If he cheated *with* me, he'll cheat *on* me.' Because that could *never* happen. Her vagina is so special, it has unicorns in it."

I snorted again.

Caro took a sip of bourbon. "And for three, she gets a rush off the competition."

"How are you an expert on this?"

"I read articles on the Internet."

I smiled, but it died a quick death. "The thing is, Caro, I didn't know we were competing. I thought John was just . . . done. You know. In the bedroom. He never . . . you know. Made a move. Not that I minded. We were barely talking these past ten years."

"Fuck him. I'm going with smothering. It's the best way for everyone."

"I'm trying to feel angry here. I didn't want to stay married, and neither did he, apparently, but I'm not the one who snuck around. And now look! If she'd take him off my hands, I'd be grateful."

"Of course you would!" Caro said staunchly. "You were all set to ditch him. He didn't deserve you, Barb."

"I know." Another sip of bourbon.

And yet . . . and yet there was the embarrassment.

My husband was cheating on me. It was so ridiculous and cliché. WORK made him feel young again. Wow. Breaking news, people. Screwing around behind your wife's back is exciting. Dating a younger woman makes you feel like a stud.

It was *pathetic*. There was no other word for it. He was acting like every idiot man who'd ever cheated on his wife. And like teenagers discovering sex, he thought he invented all those feelings.

I had been planning to take the high road. Divorce him. Bury the corpse that was our marriage.

Cheating had never occurred to *me*. I took those vows seriously, you bet I did.

I'd worked so hard to make our home a lovely place, and even harder raising our girls. If Sadie and I rubbed each other the wrong way sometimes, it didn't matter too much. They were fine girls. Good people. Juliet designed those amazing buildings, and Sadie taught little children to appreciate art. There was so much to be proud of.

But it had always been *me* who did the work. John was the provider, and I made it so he didn't have to lift a finger around the house. He liked it that way. Who wouldn't?

But when it came to the marriage, the nuts and bolts of it, the conversing, the staying close, the intimacy and the social life, I felt it should've been more mutual. He had done nothing. Those dance lessons, going to the annual scholarship auction, the bird-watching club, the bowling league . . . none of those things had been his idea. Women were responsible for what the couple did. It wasn't fair, but it was true. John agreed to do this and that, but he never suggested a damn thing.

Then, being turned down for a little love, some affection, well, that stung. Before I'd thrown up my hands regarding sex, his absentminded professor bit had hurt when he failed to notice a filmy nightgown or the fact that I'd sprayed the pillowcases with perfume, moisturized my skin like it was religion. I'd been a nice-looking woman. Still was. John, he had to be reminded to take a shower, for Pete's sake! He'd go for days without shaving, looking like a bum. That potbelly, his drooping man-breasts. He didn't care if I found him attractive. But WORK . . . oh, she inspired him to do a triathlon!

I had wondered about his sudden interest in the gym last fall. About those new clothes he'd bought with Sadie on one of his visits to the city—shirts with floral prints, like something a girl would wear, and pants that stopped an inch above his anklebone. He'd even taken to wearing a little porkpie hat, and I had to stop myself from rolling my eyes, he looked so dang ridiculous. He wasn't fooling anyone. He wasn't from Brooklyn, and he wasn't thirty years old.

But apparently, WORK found him just amazing.

A flash of hatred hit me like lightning. For him and WORK both.

"Okay, here goes," I said, sitting up abruptly. I took the phone and started texting. "'My darling, so so SO'—all caps—'sorry to not be able to answer you,' exclamation point, exclamation point, exclamation point. 'Family crisis going on here. Miss you and love you too. Will be in touch very soon. Longing to see you,' exclamation point, exclamation point, exclamation point." I looked at Caro. "How do you get those little happy faces and hearts?"

"Pass it over," Caro said. She tapped a few keys, and handed the phone back. "Are you going to send it?"

"Watch me." I hit the blue arrow, and a second later, we heard the swish of the text going out into the wide world.

"Cheers," Caro said, toasting me with a smile. "And the pizza's here, too. A good omen."

In between going back and forth to the hospital and taking care of the work that couldn't wait, I found that I was having an odd bit of . . . well, not *fun*. Satisfaction, that was it.

I'd texted WORK twice more, soothing her (his?) concerns about when they'd get together. Imitating my husband's idiot language was simple, and WORK suspected nothing. Just sent more drivel about sex and passion and fires and what they could do to each other at the earliest possible convenience.

If John was gay, that would make things a lot better. Living in a straight marriage, yearning for a man . . . everyone could understand that. I'd be kind to his boyfriend, welcome him, even. Maybe we'd all be friends. Brianna and Sloane could have two grandfathers, since Oliver's dad had died when Oliver was twelve. John would finally admit that it was never me that was the problem; it was his fear of coming out, but now that he had, he would thank me for the most wonderful daughters in the world. We'd be a happy, loving, modern family, laughing and cooking elaborate dinners, and this new man (Evan, I thought, Evan was a nice name) . . . Evan would help me decorate at Christmas and bring the most delicious pies to Thanksgiving and compliment me on a turkey that was absolutely delicious, because I did do a great turkey.

On the third text exchange, however, WORK had referenced her breasts and how she loved when John worshipped them, so that was the end of the happy gay fantasy, which was a real shame, because I had been getting awfully fond of Evan there.

I wasn't crushed. I wasn't heartbroken.

I was *furious.*

John had made my life into a cliché. *My wife of fifty years doesn't understand me. Finally, I can talk to someone! Life had become so routine, so gray. I wasn't living . . . I was just existing. You, my beloved WORK, have changed all that.*

And meanwhile, John just wouldn't die. No sir. He kept on keeping on, leaving his daughters in misery, leaving me to stare at him as he slept in the hospital bed. For fifty years, I'd accepted his flaws. I knew I wasn't perfect. I knew I had to work at life, not one of those people like Sadie, who seemed to have people falling into her lap. Yes, I wanted to divorce him. I *deserved* a divorce.

John, on the other hand, had been sneaking around, becoming an athlete at seventy-five, having sex with another woman for God knew how long, all the while wearing me down with his neglect until I felt like a ghost in my own marriage.

How dare he find happiness with another woman? How dare he leave me in charge of him now, this brain-damaged old man with a catheter?

Honest to Pete, Caro was right. If I thought I could get away with it, I'd put a pillow over his face and smother the old fool.

CHAPTER SEVEN

John

Something is wrong with his wife's face. It's too soft. Saggy. Her eyes aren't gentle anymore.

He thinks she might be . . . not sick, that's not right, but something like that.

The years have rushed by in a river. There's an old man living in his room. John isn't sure who he is. His wife doesn't notice. It's not his grandfather, but he looks familiar. He'd ask his wife, but he can't make words come out.

She smells nice. Not the way she used to, but the smell makes him feel safe, and safe is the best feeling, even if she doesn't stay near him very long. Those ungentle eyes. Shark eyes, flat and cold when they should be . . . different. He wishes she would sit against him and put her head on his shoulder. He wishes she would let him hold her hand longer, but if he does manage to grab it, she gives it a firm pat and pulls away. If he had words, he would tell her he loves her, but words are gone now, and hearing comes and goes.

There is another woman who is here quite a lot. She talks and sits with him and sometimes gives him food. Her eyes are the same color as his wife's but not flat. He knows her, but he can't remember her. Some children come and go, but John doesn't know them. They make a lot of noise and fling themselves around, and they're scary . . . so fast and strong. Their mother is another someone he used to know. She talks to him in a brisk, kind way. Maybe she's someone he works with at the . . . the . . . the place you go in the day to make money.

There is a big man here, too. John doesn't know him, but the big man helps him and talks to him. John has been hurt somehow. He thinks it was a car accident. His legs must be broken, because walking is so hard, and his knees hurt.

John knows he's been . . . changed. He's not sure how.

Trying to figure these things out is too hard. If he thinks or listens too much, his head hurts, and he falls asleep. He just wants to be outside, working in the garden, but when he looks out the window, summer is gone. John doesn't know what month it is or what he's supposed to do today. The people who make him do things—the women, the big man, his wife—come and go. Maybe they tell him what to do, but he's not sure.

Other people come and go. A man with strange words that John can't understand, but who hugs him and smiles. Another person he should know. A woman with long hair twisted into ropes. She is not here for him, he knows, but she comes anyway because she is . . . she is that way of being when a person is kind for no reason. Her voice makes him happy and sleepy. Like warm rain.

There is the man who was a boy but isn't a boy anymore who comes, first to the place for sick people, then to the other place where his warm-rain friend was, and now to his grandfather's house. Sometimes, he brings a baby. He is a father, this boy who is grown up now. They have dark hair, father and son, and the young man lets John hold the baby, who laughs.

Images flash through his head too fast to make sense—a girl with blond hair and freckles with that dark-haired boy, and colors, and John once held her hand as they crossed a street in a place with many lights. Once she cried because of that dark-haired boy who's now a man.

Then, there's nothing. Nothing but emptiness and gray and the horrible feeling of loss. Time passes, swirling past him, knocking him down, pulling him out into the sea of puzzling memories, and there's nothing he can hold on to, so he falls asleep, and sleep is what he likes best.

His wife comes in. Her name is sure in his mind. Barbara. His Barb. He's not sure why they're not in the little red house anymore. She says words, and he looks at her, smelling her good smell, loving her, wishing she wasn't always leaving. But she is. She does.

Then it's later, or another day, and John can't remember where he is. But the boy is here again with his little one, and a toolbox—*toolbox* jumps right into his head, and he knows it's the right word. John reaches out and the man puts the baby into his arms and sits there a minute, his hand on the baby's head, making sure John knows how to hold him.

He does.

The baby looks up at him with dark eyes, then smiles. John feels his mouth move, and he looks at . . .

. . . the name is coming . . .

. . . *Ned. Neil. Nick* . . .

Noah!

And Noah smiles, then opens the toolbox and starts doing things. John is not sure what or why.

The baby makes noises, but John knows they are not words, and it's such a relief, letting the sounds just be sounds, and nice sounds at that. Happy sounds. Then the baby puts his head against John's shoulder, and John's eyes get wet, because he remembers this feeling. He had a baby once, too. Maybe more than one. He knows how to hold this baby, yes he does. One arm under the baby's bottom, one hand resting on his back, feeling the breath going up and down, up and down.

Then those thoughts are gone, and there's just the baby, and the smell of his head, and the feeling of his dark silky hair, and the soft, sweet warmth of his weight as the baby breathes. Up and down. Up and down.

CHAPTER EIGHT

Sadie

Moving back to Stoningham was not something I'd ever wanted to do.

But move back I did. Who else would take care of my father? Jules was too important and busy and had Brianna and Sloane and Oliver. Mom was first selectman, and the truth was, I think she stopped loving my father decades before. Maybe before I was born, aside from one obvious coupling.

I couldn't leave him alone. He stayed in the critical care unit at UConn for ten days, then was transferred to Gaylord, a specialized rehab center, where his healing would really begin.

It became apparent that Dad wasn't going to die, despite being seventy-five years old and all that had gone wrong. In addition to the stroke, he'd had a bad concussion. It was complicated, the handsome neurosurgeon told us. Only time would tell, which, you know, I'm glad Stanford and Johns Hopkins had taught him. Only time would tell, huh? Great. Try not to overwhelm us with complicated medical terms, Doc.

I mean, I understood. Of course I did. Words like *apraxia*, *aphasia*, *neuroplasticity*, *executive functioning* and *hemiparesis* became part of my daily vocabulary. Dad had all kinds of therapy at Gaylord—physical, speech, aqua, occupational, community reentry, where they'd take patients to the grocery store or a restaurant. There was a robotic suit of some kind that helped him relearn to walk. He was given an iPad, which he didn't understand, even when the therapists guided his fingers.

What I wouldn't give for an e-mail or message from him saying, "Don't worry, sugarplum. I'm in here. Just give me a little time. Love, Dad." Instead, he stared blankly, then turned his head to the window.

I came every day, driving back and forth from the city every night, practically living in my rental car, which was full of fast-food wrappers and half-drunk coffees from Dunkin'. Sometimes Alexander came with me, but it was generally easier if he didn't. He was one of those guys who didn't know what to do around a sick person. He was a peach, though, always ready to take me out to dinner or sending me flowers, checking in during his travels.

Dad started walking again, first with one of those belts and a walker, then with crutches, then on his own, though he tended to list to one side. He could almost dress himself. He could hold a fork, but not always on command—apraxia, the PA told me, where the messages between his brain and muscles got scrambled. He tried to talk a few times, but only managed strangled, labored noises, which broke my heart.

It was wrenching. There was no other word for it. My father had always been so smart, so playful in his dry way, open for anything. All the times he'd come down to the city to see me over the years, doing anything I suggested, from going to a performance where the woman drenched herself in what she said was menstrual blood and Dad and I had to sneak out the back because we were laughing so hard, to taking the Staten Island Ferry back and forth for the view. We'd ridden bikes along the Hudson River Greenway, eaten street meat with gusto and gone to a scotch tasting that left us both tipsy and giggly. He'd even taken me for a carriage ride in Central Park. "You're my princess, after all," he'd said, and we snuggled under the blanket to the sounds of the horse's hooves.

He was my hero.

"He would hate this," Juliet said on a day when we happened to be visiting Gaylord at the same time. We were waiting for Dad to come back from the pool with one of his therapists, both of us itchy and tired. "Sometimes I think it would've been better if he—"

"Jules! That's our father! No, it wouldn't have been better if he'd died! He's getting better every day."

She sighed, sounding exactly like Mom. Speaking of Mom, she was down the hall making a phone call. Whenever she was here, she spent as little time near Dad as possible.

"Here he is, and he did great!" said Sheryl, wheeling Dad back into the room.

"How was the pool, Dad?" I asked. "The pool? Did you like it?" *Keep it simple* was one of the things we'd learned.

He didn't answer.

"Hey there," said a woman. Janet, the sister of another patient. "How's it going, John? Did you eat that chicken for lunch? It was pretty good, wasn't it? I liked the spinach. Nice touch. How you girls doing? You doing okay?"

I liked Janet. Her brother had had a traumatic brain injury and was a patient down the hall. She was devoted to him, visiting every day. But she also wandered up and down the hall when he was sleeping or in therapy. Janet dressed in overalls most of the time, granny glasses and big, clunky clogs. She chatted to my father like he was an old friend.

It was strange, the unwilling little community of family members, all of us here for shitty reasons. My mother spent most of her time talking with them, and Jules was fairly helpless. But I didn't mind the nitty-gritty of helping my father. While it broke my heart that he was struggling, I knew he'd get better. It would take time and work, but he was on his way. I had to believe that. A life without my dad—the old dad—was not something I was prepared to imagine.

"He seems to have plateaued."

"Well, shit," Jules said.

We were at a meeting with the team, the therapists and doctors and nurses, Mom, Jules and Oliver, me.

"So at this point," Dr. McIntyre continued, "because he's doing well with the tasks of daily living, we usually send the patient home. Often, that improves their mental capacity, being around familiar things and people."

"He can't come home," Mom said.

"Of course he can," I said. "Where else would he go?"

"Rose Hill has an adult wing now."

"No. He's not going into a home, Mom. You have to give him a chance."

"Rose Hill *is* an excellent facility," the team leader murmured.

"But he should be home! He deserves to be home. His odds of recovering are better there, just like you said."

"We can't predict anything, sadly," said the doctor. "I'm sorry, I realize it's incredibly frustrating, but it's best to focus on the amazing progress he's already made and set small goals for the future."

"Like what?" Jules asked.

"Maybe some intelligible words. Of course you want him to be the man you knew before, but right now, just saying 'hungry' or 'tired' would be a breakthrough. We have to manage expectations."

"Won't he need a caregiver?" Mom asked.

"Yes. He won't be able to be left alone until his cognition is significantly better."

Mom, Jules and I exchanged looks. "None of us has medical training," Mom said, and I felt a guilty flash of relief.

"No, of course not. We'll arrange for therapists and some nursing help. You're not alone in this."

"Thank God," Mom said.

"But there should be a point person, someone who lives with him or very close by. Mrs. Frost, since you—"

"No. It won't be me. I have a more-than-full-time job, and I'm seventy years old."

Wow. I mean, yes, her age was a factor, but boy, she couldn't get those words out fast enough.

"I also have a full-time job, plus two kids," Juliet said. She glanced at Oliver, who nodded and smiled, the asshole.

"I live in New York City," I said. They looked at me. "But yeah, I'll do it." I closed my eyes. "Of course I will. I'll . . . move home. It'll take me a week or two, but yeah." Shit. But of course I would.

"Good girl, Sadie," my mother said.

I shrugged. It wasn't like I wanted to, but who else would take care of Dad?

In the week that followed, I listed my apartment with Airbnb so it would earn me some money while Dad was recovering. Carter helped me touch it up with a new comforter and throw pillows and the like. I put my personal stuff in crates and brought them with me. Jules let me put some things in her basement.

Sister Mary gave me a leave from St. Catherine's, and all my friends there took me out the night before I left. I tried not to cry as Alexander drove me east to my hometown.

The first couple of weeks, I barely left the house, too busy learning things from the nurses, therapists and equipment people and trying not to kill my mother.

Old Barb seemed devoid of any midwestern capability where Dad was concerned. Instead, she did everything she could to distance herself from my father, becoming conveniently invisible when my dad needed a bath, or physical therapy, or just some damn company. Jules came by and sat next to his bed, but she checked her phone constantly.

"Do you have to do that?" I snapped.

"I'm working, okay? Insurance doesn't cover all of this, and I don't want Mom and Dad to drain their retirement. So I'm making up the difference, if it's all right with you."

I sat back, chastened. "Sorry," I muttered, ever the little sister.

"It's okay," she said. "We all do our part." Gaylord had provided the names of a few occupational and physical therapists, and (I guess with Juliet's help) we hired a physical therapist named LeVon Murphy to stay with Dad from eight until four five days a week to keep working on his improvement. LeVon was amazing, calm and funny, and all three of us Frost women loved him. He was also big and strong, so he could do things like lift Dad if necessary.

My part was the nitty-gritty, apparently. The sponge baths. The occasional change of linens when he wet the bed. "Look," I told him the first time, LeVon looking on to supervise. "We're both uncomfortable with this. But I love you, Dad, and you washed me when I was little, so now I'll take care of you. And when you're better, we can both get hypnotism to forget this." I thought he might have smiled. Well. His mouth moved, either in horror or humor or reflex. It was hard to say.

When he looked at me, I sensed he was striving to say something. "It's me, Dad. Sadie. Can you say my name?" He didn't. If he grew restless, I'd hold his hand and stay positive. "You're getting better every day. The brain is incredible. You just have to relearn things."

It was like a bad dream. Dad, unable to talk; me in my old room, which had been redone about half an hour after I left for college; Mom and me trying not to bicker over dinner. At least Caro would pop in, alleviating the tension. My nieces would come over, Brianna a little freaked out by seeing Grampy this way, Sloane oblivious and happy.

New York seemed far, far away.

After three weeks of living at home, I told my mother I needed to get out of the house.

"Well, I can't stay here alone with him, Sadie!" she said. "That's your job."

"LeVon isn't here today, and Dad is still your husband!" I snapped.

"He just needs company. Is that so hard? Can you just sit with him for half a damn hour so I can get some fresh air?"

"Fine. Go," she said. "Be back before lunch, please." She hated watching him eat, which I admit wasn't the prettiest sight.

Shit. I so wished it had been her. In her case, a nursing home would've been more than enough.

I left the house. It was March now—eight weeks since Dad's stroke, and mud season for New England, but the air had the promise of spring. The sky was pale blue, the breeze brisk, blowing the fug off me and bathing me in the smell of salt air.

I walked away from town, toward the tidal river. When I came to the wooden footbridge that spanned it, I took a seat the way I had when I was a kid, my legs dangling, the river gurgling past below me, the long reeds along the bank golden in the sunlight. My dad and I used to play Poohsticks, dropping twigs in on one side, then looking over the other to see whose came out from under the bridge first.

In the distance, the Sound was empty; all the boats were still in dry dock.

I lay down, the boards warm and strong under my back, soothing the ache I didn't realize I had till now. I'd been doing a lot of heavy work, packing up my apartment, helping Dad get in and out of bed, moving furniture around their house to make it more accessible. Right now he was using a walker, and they had a lot of furniture that got in the way. My mother loved antiques, and it seemed like they all weighed three times what modern stuff did.

I hadn't been back in Stoningham for more than two days in a row in eons. The sound of the river, the distant slapping of the waves against the shore, the shrill cries of the gulls were comforting—sounds I hadn't realized I'd missed till now—and the sun was warm, even if the air was cool.

A few tears slipped out of my eyes and into my hair. I thought I'd cried myself out over my father's stroke, but apparently, I hadn't.

He'd get better. I had to believe that.

"Sadie?"

I jolted into a sitting position, my heart jackrabbiting.

Of course I'd known I'd run into him. Somehow, I just hadn't prepared myself for it.

"Noah." I blinked, then shielded my eyes from the sun. It took a minute to see him clearly.

He had a baby in one of those front-pack carriers.

A *baby*.

The fabric of the carrier blocked all but the baby's black hair on top, and tiny feet clad in little blue socks on the bottom.

A baby. A baby who, I imagined, looked a lot like the man carrying him. My speeding heart dropped to my stomach.

"I was really sorry to hear about your dad," Noah said.

"Yeah. Thanks." I tried to smile. "Thank you. Thanks for the card." He'd sent one when Dad was still at UConn.

"How's he doing?"

"Um . . . he's doing okay. Slow going." The little blue feet kicked, and I remembered to blink.

"Heard you're back to help out."

"Yeah." I paused. "Is that . . . your baby?"

I wanted him to laugh and say, "God, no, it's my sister's," but of course he didn't have a sister. He could've been babysitting for a friend, and—

"Yes. This is my son. Marcus." He looked down at the little black head and smoothed the unruly hair with undeniable tenderness. "Sixteen weeks old."

Jesus God in heaven.

Now I was blinking too fast. *Do not cry, Sadie. Don't you dare cry.* "Um, wow! A son! Wow! Congratulations. I didn't . . . no one told me . . . Congratulations! Are you, uh, married?"

He leaned against the railing of the footbridge, his face losing expression. "No. Michaela Watkins is the mom. We're coparents."

"*Mickey* Watkins?"

"Yeah."

I swallowed. Okay. Mickey Watkins had been our classmate from third or fourth grade on. And she was gay.

"We both wanted to be parents, and nothing else seemed to be working out," he said.

I realized a response was required. "Wow. Um . . . congratulations."

"Yeah. Thanks." He stood stiffly, the wind ruffling his hair, and looked to the left of me. On the other hand, I couldn't stop staring at him. The unshaven face that never could grow a proper beard. His long lashes and slight scowl. His big hands, one on the baby's back, the other on his hip. He should've looked ridiculous—brooding hot dad with baby in carrier meets ex-lover.

He didn't look ridiculous at all.

I became aware of the fact that I should speak. And maybe close my mouth. "Mickey. How is she? That's . . . this is a big surprise."

"I'm sorry," he said, an edge in his voice. "Should I have consulted you? Asked if it was okay?"

"No!" I scrambled to my feet. "I just . . . I mean, I knew you'd been engaged, but I, uh . . . I didn't . . ."

"That didn't work out. Also, I thought you were never coming back to this godforsaken town, as you called it, and now I have a four-month-old and all of a sudden, you're living here again. If I'd known you were coming back, maybe I wouldn't have impregnated a lesbian."

"I'm here to take care of my father, Noah. Not have your babies."

"Oh, I know. Believe me, I know. Nothing else could've gotten you back here to this hellhole."

I was quite sure I'd never called Stoningham a hellhole. "Still bitter, are we?"

"Yes."

His hair, which had been short a couple of years ago (thank you, Facebook), had grown longer and wild again, and I was glad.

"Can I take a peek at your baby?" I said.

He scowled properly, then undid two clips and lifted out his son. I went over to them.

The baby was asleep, but I could tell he was Noah all over, tiny black eyebrows, the full cheeks, the perfect mouth. "Hey, little one," I whispered, and touched his cheek. It was as soft and perfect as a puppy's ear.

"Okay, that's enough," Noah said, repacking him. "Look. You're here. I'm really sorry about your dad and I hope he gets better. But you left a mark, Sadie. We're not gonna be friends. I can't do that. I'm not your backup plan."

Oh, the *ego*. "Was I humping your leg just now, Noah? Or begging you to marry me? Because I must've missed that part."

"I'm just being clear. You'll ruin me all over again, and I have a son to raise now. So if we run into each other, it's not old home week. Okay?"

I pursed my lips. "Got it. But before you go, I have to point out that you were as stubborn as I was, Noah. We could've been together if you'd been open to anything but your own life plan. So you ruined me, too."

"Yeah, right. Heard about your rich boyfriend."

"And I heard about your event planner. So neither of us has been sitting around nursing a broken heart. Good for us."

"You did exactly what you wanted to, Sadie."

"And so did you, Noah!" I dropped my voice, remembering the baby. Noah glared at me, somehow still looking as hot as Jon Snow, even with a baby carrier on. Maybe *because* of the baby carrier.

"Hey! Sadie! How the hell are you, woman!"

It was Mickey Watkins, dressed in running gear.

"Hey," I said, recalibrating fast. "I just met your son! Wow! Congratulations!"

"Right? He's the cutest baby in the entire world, isn't he? Hi, Marcus! It's Mommy! Who shouldn't be running with two breasts full of milk!" She put her hands over her boobs, ever without a filter, just like

I remembered, and I grinned. "God, this hurts! The second I see him, I'm leaking like a bad radiator. Look at this." She moved her hands, and yep, there were two big wet spots. She went to Noah and kissed her son's little head, and Noah smiled.

"You two okay?" Mickey asked.

"We were just yelling at each other," I said.

"We're fine," Noah said at the same time.

"Sorry about your dad," Mickey said.

"Thanks. He's doing okay."

"Glad to hear it. Hey, you should come by sometime. I'll let you sniff Marcus's head. It's good for the soul."

"Mickey," Noah muttered.

"What? Am I supposed to hate her because you loved her once? Get over yourself, straight boy." She looked at me and winked. "Well, I can't run with these milk jug boobs. Noah, where's your car? I have to nurse this little guy or I'll explode. Sadie, great seeing you. I mean it about coming over. Noah and I share custody. Three nights with him, three with me. Have you ever seen a breast pump? Clearly invented by a man. It's a fucking torture device. Anyway, take care, hon! See you soon!"

Off they went, leaving me in a state of shock. After a minute or two, I started back toward home.

Noah had a child. With Mickey Watkins, one of the best people in our year, a funny, boisterous girl—woman now—who was always full of life and laughter. Good. Her genes would balance out the Prince of Gloom's over there.

Noah was a *father*.

It was a lot to take in.

"Hey," I said when I got to the house. Jules was there, eating lunch at the table with Mom. "Thanks for telling me Noah and Mickey Watkins had a baby together."

"So? You two have been done for ages," Mom said.

"Completely slipped my mind," Jules said.

I sighed. Reminded myself that I had a nice boyfriend and didn't care what Noah did. "Where's Dad?"

"Asleep," said Mom, taking a hostile bite of her sandwich.

I went to check on him; we'd turned the dining room into his room until he could handle the stairs. I fixed his blanket and sat in the chair. He wasn't sleeping, just staring ahead.

"Remember my boyfriend, Dad? Noah? He's a father," I told him. "He made a baby with Mickey Watkins from our class. It's a boy. Also, he's still mad at me."

Dad said nothing. *He could've had you*, I imagined Dad saying. *Inflexible, that one. Not a good quality in a spouse. I should know.*

For some reason, I had a lump in my throat. Even if I shouldn't. The heart wants what the heart wants, and the heart can be a real idiot.

CHAPTER NINE

Sadie

Ever since I could remember, I'd wanted to leave Stoningham, because even though I loved it, I hated it. It was so smug. So content. So adorable. So assured of itself. In a way, it was like my sister, never questioning its value. *Welcome to Stoningham. You're lucky we let you in,* the town seemed to say. *If you play your cards right, we might let you stay.*

The fact that my mother viewed Stoningham as an achievement, rather than a place, definitely colored my views as a teenager, when I felt it was my duty to think the opposite of everything she did. When I was little, it was paradise, of course—a rocky shore with a couple of sand beaches, huge stretches of marsh, land reserves, the gentle Sound always murmuring, that one part of the shore where the Atlantic roared in, unfettered by Long Island. There was Birch Lake, still so pristine and quiet, surrounded by old-growth forest with gentle paths for walking. We had the most beautiful skies, and they were my first paintings. Skyscapes in pastels or watercolors, those endless shades of blue, violently beautiful sunsets in the winter, summer skies smeared with colors.

But it was a small town. A tiny town, and so stuffy it was hard to breathe sometimes, especially if you were Juliet's not-as-smart-or-athletic sister, or the daughter of Barb Frost, Queen of Committees and Volunteerism, daughter of John Frost the lawyer, and yes, related to *that* Robert Frost.

Being average was difficult.

I had one talent, though, and I would use it to get away, distance myself from the smugness, the familiar, the "aren't you Barb's daughter?" of Stoningham.

Looking back, it's hard not to be a little embarrassed. Girl from tiny town in Connecticut goes to New York to become artist. Wears black and pierces nose. Fails to set the art world on fire. Becomes waitress, then teacher, then sells out. Eventually goes home to help ailing parent.

The thing was, I'd been sincere. At eighteen, my heart was pure, my determination boundless. I was talented . . . I'd won first prize in the annual Stoningham art show since I was fourteen and even sold three paintings at Coastal Beauty Art Gallery in Mystic. I'd placed third in the Young Artists of Connecticut Competition, Acrylics.

I couldn't remember a time when I didn't draw or paint. I loved it so much—the smells, the textures, the way a single flicker of a brush could take you on a journey, how the slightest color variation could make all the difference. I loved mixing paints, the sweet perfection of a new brush, like the smallest baby animal, so soft and innocent and full of potential. I loved seeing something come from nothing. And not just something, but an experience. Not just a picture, but *emotions*, an entire story in a frame. There was nothing else I wanted to do.

Of course I was going to New York to study art! What other city in America was there for art? (Aside from Austin, Denver, San Francisco, Chicago, etc., but I was young and ill-informed.) New York it would be.

Dad was encouraging—"Of course! Follow your dream, sugarplum!" Mom was baffled.

"An *art* major?" she cried, as if I'd said *assassin for drug cartel.*

"What are you going to do with an art major? Your sister is an *architect*!" Just in case I'd forgotten what Perfection from Conception did for a living.

Speaking of Juliet, who was also sitting in judgment, she laughed. "You're adorable. Do you like living in cardboard boxes?"

"Have you ever been to a museum?" I asked in my oh-so-sophisticated way.

"I've *designed* museums, Sadie."

"Then you should remember that they're just places to hold art. Have you ever bought a painting? Seen a movie?" I raised an eyebrow at my mother in response to her snort of disapproval. "People who think art is a waste of time should have to live in a world without color."

"Have you ever been poor?" Jules asked. "Ever eaten at a soup kitchen?"

"This might come as a shock to you, Jules, but money and luxury aren't everything." She'd just built her house on the water, tearing down an old gray-shingled cottage to construct what was admittedly a fabulous home with views from every angle. "You're all very narrow-minded," I said. "Except you, Daddy."

"Well," he said. "If you can't follow your dreams now, baby, when can you?"

"See?" I said, hugging him.

"Oh, super, John," Mom said. "She needs to have something to fall back on. Something practical."

"What if she's the next Jackson Pollock?" Dad said.

"Then she'll kill herself in a car crash while drunk-driving," said my sister.

"Keith Haring, then," Dad said.

"AIDS."

"Vincent van—ah, shit. Georgia O'Keeffe, then."

"She lived to be ninety-eight," I said. "Guess art isn't *always* fatal. But I do appreciate the support."

My mother would not be convinced. She wore my dad down until he agreed that I should double major in studio art and art education. I had nothing against teaching. I pictured myself in a Tribeca studio, allowing worshipful artists in every Saturday for a master class. At least one of them would be named Lorenzo and be madly in love with me. So off to Pace University I went. (Columbia and the School of Visual Arts had rejected me, thanks to mediocre grades, I told myself.) But hey. It was still New York, and I was going.

In doing so, I broke Noah Pelletier's heart, and he broke mine.

High school sweethearts. The only boyfriend I'd ever had. Wise beyond his years, stoic, hardworking, a fifth-generation townie and my first love. He was wrenchingly beautiful—eyes so dark they were nearly black, full lips that made him look a little grumpy unless he smiled, and wild, curly unkempt black hair that framed his face.

We'd been friends since before I could remember. When we were small, we'd go over to each other's houses to play once in a while, and as we grew older and play-dates stopped being a thing, he remained one of the nicer boys in school—quiet, good at sports, a mediocre student, like me. We sat next to each other in band during fourth and fifth grades, me on flute, him on clarinet, neither of us very good, though he practiced more. He always picked me to be on his team in gym class. Smiled at me during recess. Once, he got hit in the head with a baseball, and I walked him into the nurse's office, holding his arm to make sure he didn't fall. In junior high, we didn't see each other much, since he was busy being a guy and playing soccer, and an art teacher had told me I had "a real gift."

Then high school started. Something had happened to Noah over the summer. His voice dropped an octave and his hands were suddenly big and strong. He'd grown a few inches, and when he smiled at me, it felt . . . profound. I could practically feel my heart changing—a lifetime of good-natured affection suddenly turning into a pounding, beautiful ache.

In the front yard of my parents' house was a beautiful Japanese maple tree, and in the fall, it grew so red it glowed. That was the color of my heart when Noah looked at me, and all freshman year, my paintings were filled with red and black, the black of his hair and eyes, the pure Noah-red of my love. Noah Sebastian Pelletier, he of French Canadian descent, a boy who looked as if he would've been at home in the Canadian Rockies on his own, sitting by a fire, watching the stars, the wolves surrounding him in recognition of his wild beauty and soul.

Hey. I was a teenage girl. It was my job to think this way. I dared not draw him, afraid my mother would find the pictures and lecture me about sex. Or worse, tell me I could do better than a blue-collar boy—Mom was such a snob, and couldn't resist telling people that my sister had married a man who was somehow related to British nobility. My mother might call his mother and tell her we were too young to be in love, and that would be worst of all . . . because Noah was not in love with me.

Unfortunately. His gentle, "Hey, Sadie," in the halls of Stoningham High, the occasional scraps of conversation about assignments or, once in a while, an amused smile when he caught my eye when our peers were goofing around . . . same as he was with everyone. There was nothing special between us, and it made my heart hurt in the most pleasurable way, pulsing with that pure, glorious crimson. Once, we sat together at the mandatory holiday pageant, watching Gina Deluca, who was two years ahead of us, do an interpretive dance of Mary giving birth to Jesus, and we laughed silently till tears ran down our faces, Noah's hand covering his face as his shoulders shook, peeking at me through his fingers, both of us laughing harder in that wonderful, uncontrollable way. Oh, I relived that moment thousands of times. Thousands.

The summer between sophomore and junior years, I was fifteen, being on the younger side of my class, since Mom had kicked me into kindergarten when I was four. One sunny, perfect afternoon when the gulls drifted on air currents and red-winged blackbirds called to each other, I took my sketchbook down to the tidal river. The school fields were nearby, and I'd heard some sportsball type of yelling, but I was on another plane. When I was drawing or painting, I was adrift in the moment . . . It irritated my mom that she'd have to say my name over and over before I'd lift my head, but to me, it was the best, most beautiful way to be, alone in a world of my own making. I'd go for hours without eating or drinking. I could sit in the cafeteria at lunchtime and not hear a word . . . unless it was said by Noah.

This day, I was sketching with a new set of graphite pencils, a gift from my father, focused on the sway of the reeds and the curve of the piping plover's head as it darted along the muddy edge of the river. The sun was hot on my hair, the gentle gurgle of the tidal river was music, and the quick steps of the little bird were so cunning and sweet. All of it flowed from my pencil onto the paper, and I was in a state of utter bliss.

Then a black-and-white ball bounced down the hill, and instinctively, I stopped it with my foot before it hit the river and was carried out to sea. It took me a second to put the pieces together: soccer ball. Intruder. Sports. Boys.

Noah.

He stood there, hands on his hips, his legs already a man's legs, tan and muscled, appropriately hairy, which I suddenly found *extremely* attractive. Sweat dampened his T-shirt, and his cheeks were ruddy, his hair tangled and unruly and glorious.

"Hey, Sadie," he said with a half grin, and my stomach contracted with a strong, hot squeeze.

"Hi," I managed.

"Thanks for saving the ball."

"Sure."

He glanced at my sketchbook. "Wow. That's incredible."

The heat of pride (and lust) crept up from my chest, tickling my neck. "Thanks."

He sat down next to me, taking the ball under his arm, the smell of his sweat and grass from the soccer field enveloping me. "You having a good summer?"

"Mm-hm." My cheeks were hot, and I kept my eyes on the drawing to avoid melting into a puddle of lust. "Are you?"

"Sure."

I sneaked another look at him. Long lashes on top of that wild beauty. His face had taken on more definition in the past year, and I had to swallow. I wanted to draw that face. Heathcliff. He was Heathcliff of the moors, if I ignored the Ramones T-shirt and gym shorts.

"I should get back," he said.

"Oh, right. Sure." My conversation game was red-hot.

"All right if I kiss you?"

I may have twitched. "I . . . What did you say?"

He grinned and half shrugged, so I leaned toward this wild boy, and our lips met, a soft, gentle kiss. The deep scarlet in my heart flared with such heat and beauty, I already loved him.

When the kiss ended, he rested his forehead against mine, his eyes still closed. "Wanna be my girlfriend?" he whispered.

"Okay."

"You sure?"

"Yes."

And that was that.

My parents didn't mind too much; I was that age when kids started dating, and everyone knew the Pelletiers as a good, solid family. Besides, Juliet was pregnant, and our mother was obsessed with throwing her a ridiculous shower (as she'd been obsessed with the wedding two years before). Me having a boyfriend barely registered.

Noah's parents didn't mind, either. He was an only child; they loved him and welcomed me, seeing me as a nice girl for their boy, though his mom's forehead did pucker when I mentioned traveling and applying to schools in San Francisco and Barcelona.

Noah had a job on the weekends; his father was a general contractor, and a lot of his work was expanding houses for the summer people that populated Connecticut's long, gentle shoreline. He'd worked on Juliet's house, in fact. Noah would put in long hours most Saturdays and Sundays, not returning till late, when he would come to my house or, if it was super late, to my window, tossing pebbles against the screen until I came out. In these cases, *I* was Juliet. Juliet Capulet. Or Montague. I always forgot who had which last name.

"Hey, Special," he'd say softly, and that glowing red would pulse in every molecule of my being. You bet I'd sneak out to be with him . . . to the town green down the block, where we could lie on a blanket and kiss, or, in the off-season, to the dock of one of the summer "cottages," the waves lapping and lifting us as we fitted together, wrapped so tightly around each other it almost hurt.

In school, his black eyes would rest on me like I was the only person in the world. My friends were jealous; not only was I dating the cutest, nicest boy, but he *loved* me, and made no secret about it. He *loved* me. When we were together, everyone else fell to the wayside, and every spare minute was given to each other. It made my friends irritable, but I couldn't help it. I was smitten. Utterly, completely in love.

For our first Valentine's Day together, I gave him my first big canvas oil painting—a periwinkle-blue sky just before sunrise, golden clouds tipped with the same color of glowing, lush vermillion that lit up my heart. He hung it in his bedroom and took down all his movie posters and memorabilia so my painting was the only thing on that wall.

Oh, the kissing, the sweaty tangle of young limbs and heated murmurs that painting saw . . .

In our junior and senior years, Noah went to a vocational school part-time, taking a bus to New London on Thursdays and Fridays to learn carpentry, since he loved woodworking as much as I loved painting. I thought we were perfect for each other, both of us artists, though he'd laugh when I said that and say making door frames or coffee tables wasn't exactly art. Though I'd never thought of myself as unhappy before, being with Noah—so seen, so important . . . it taught me what happiness was.

He had one flaw: he wanted to stay put. He wanted life to be exactly like his parents' and grandparents'. He wanted to marry me in a few years and raise a bunch of kids, preferably five. (How many teenage boys say they want five kids?) I loved that he saw us together, because I did, too. Just . . . not here. I pictured us traveling, hiking on the moors or walking through the streets of Rome, on the Great Wall, in the spice markets of Mumbai. How we would fund this was unclear, but we were young. We could, er, backpack or however it was that people without rich parents traveled.

But as graduation drew closer, things got a little prickly. Noah had no problem with my plans for the next four years, but there was always a hint of condescension somewhere in there. Like once I'd gotten this "see the world/live in the city" bug out of my system, I'd understand that Stoningham was the only place to be.

But there was no way on earth I wanted to live in the town I'd grown up in. A thousand year-round residents, thick with pretension because of the brushes with celebrity or true wealth—Genevieve London of the handbag empire; an Oscar-winning actress who spent all of two weeks a year in her six-thousand-square-foot house. I didn't want to run into the same people on the same streets in the same places I'd already been every day of my life. Staying here was an admission of fear of something greater . . . or a total lack of ambition. Only people like Juliet, with her Ivy League degrees and brilliant success, could come back to Stoningham without seeming like a loser. Or so it seemed to me.

I didn't want to be Barb and John's daughter and Juliet's not-as-amazing sister. I didn't even want to be called "Noah's girlfriend." I wanted to be myself . . . with Noah, still my parents' daughter, but I wanted to be Sadie Frost, yes, *that* Sadie Frost, the artist.

Change. The word was a siren call that filled me with an energy and thrill I couldn't describe. When you grow up in Connecticut, you're defined by the absence of things. We had hills but not mountains. A shoreline, but not really the ocean. Farms, but not exactly farmland. Cities, but either scarred by urban blight or too small to hold their own with Boston and New York just a train ride away.

New York. Oh, New York. All the songs were true. I wanted to be in the hard, glittering city, with its harsh reflections and sharp-toothed skyline, its roar and breath, to meet new people, to *not* have my family history ambling beside me, to be the only one who defined me. I was eighteen. I ached for it the same way I ached for Noah, with the same molten red longing.

The fact that he had none of this desire baffled me. I thought we were *supposed* to want these things. Noah did not. He was utterly happy with the idea of waiting me out.

I didn't hate Stoningham, but God, it was relentless in its familiarity. Every street, every inch of shoreline, every type of weather was something I'd lived over and over and over. The sameness was squeezing the life out of me.

We didn't make any promises about the future . . . Each of us figured the other would see the light. Their light. I went off to New York, and the first thing I put up in my dorm room was a picture of Noah and me, our arms around each other on the town dock, both of us smiling. His curly hair whipped in the breeze, and my eyes looked more blue because of the sky and water behind us. Breaking up was not in my plans. Ever. We were meant to be. We could find a way where we were both happy and fulfilled. We were different from other high school couples. Our love, I was certain, would last forever.

I was wrong.

CHAPTER TEN

Barb

I never liked my name. I should've changed it when I was sixteen.

Barb. Barb Frost. Barbara Marie Johnson Frost. The most boring, unremarkable, midwestern name on every level. Oh, Frost was a fine last name, especially given that John was somehow related to Robert Frost. I'd been so excited by that when we first met. How thrilling, being related to the great poet! To have that gentle, insightful, famous blood running through your veins! Gosh!

"Well, I don't know about that," John had said, and maybe I should've taken more notice, because it was true. Turned out, there was nothing poetic about him.

At our wedding, his mother told me no one was quite sure how Robert Frost was connected to them . . . It was more of a rumor than anything that could be fact-checked at the time. Not that it mattered, but it seemed like John had been keeping that from me. *Maybe* related to Robert Frost is different from *being* related to Robert Frost. As for the name John, well, it was the most common name in the English-speaking world, wasn't it? At least no one called him Jack. Jack Frost. Jeez Louise, that would've been horrible.

When I finally had a baby, I gave her the most poetic name in the world. Juliet Elizabeth Frost. A beautiful name for a beautiful girl. I only wanted one baby, I'd already decided; I had three sisters and three brothers, and it wasn't the way they show it in books. I remember reading *Cheaper by the Dozen* and feeling so cheated. We Johnson kids were no happy gang of seven romping and singing and helping each other, heck no. My oldest brother, fifteen years my senior, barely knew I was alive, and Elaine, older by sixteen months, picked on me endlessly. I was the fifth child, lost in the middle blur. My father never got my name right on the first try, and my mother was exhausted and exasperated all the time. I shared a room with my sisters, and all our clothes were hand-me-downs from our wealthier cousins, first to Nancy, then Elaine, then to me, then to Tina, who at least had the honor of being the baby of the family.

Seven children in nineteen years. Russell, Nancy, Henry, Elaine, me, Arthur and Tina. We weren't poor, but we weren't comfortable, either. We didn't go hungry, but that was because we had a small farm, and Dad could always slaughter a pig. No vacations except for one time when we piled into the gigantic station wagon and drove for ten hours to an aunt's rented house on a lake, where there was one bathroom for thirteen people. We kids slept on the floors of various rooms and porches, trying to make friends with cousins we had never met. The mosquitoes were relentless, and the lake water was murky and brown. Tina was still wetting the bed at night, which became my responsibility somehow. Every other summer was unbroken, just a stream of long days and hard work, endless laundry and cooking, loading hay, feeding the pigs, weeding our vast garden, crushing grubs between our fingers with no relief from the prairie sun. I hated it.

I was a not-bad student, not that anyone noticed. Solid Bs, the occasional A. I blamed my name. Barbara Marie Johnson. She doesn't sound much like a valedictorian, does she? Not someone who'd get a scholarship to St. Olaf or Columbia. My oldest brother went into the Army; Nancy went to secretarial school; Henry became a mechanic; Elaine got pregnant and married the summer after she graduated.

All I wanted was to get away. I took a few courses and became a legal secretary, then I applied for jobs up and down the East Coast. No way was I going to stay in Minnesota, no sir. When I got a job offer in Providence, Rhode Island, I took it sight unseen. I had just turned eighteen, since I'd skipped fourth grade, much to Elaine's annoyance. Without much fanfare, I moved to Rhode Island, so small and charming and eclectic compared to Minnesota!

I loved Providence. It was busy and cultured, with the colleges and the restaurants and such. I told people my name was Barb, which sounded a little more energetic than Barbara. Barbie was out. I couldn't go by my initials—B. M. or B. J. (A girlfriend told me what BJ stood for, and gosh, I was shocked.) Bobbi was too popular at the time. I tried BeBe, but it didn't take. Barb was the best I could do.

The law firm that had hired me was large and paid well. I shared a cute apartment with two other girls, and buckled down at being a grown-up, learning to drink a gin and tonic (my family was dry in every sense), painting old furniture I got at garage sales. I learned to accessorize and shop at thrift stores for good-quality clothes and tried to look professional and a little sassy at work. Sometimes people teased me about my accent, which I didn't even know I had, and I tried to tone it down.

I worked hard at my job, one of dozens of legal secretaries at the firm. I needed to stand out, so I was first in the department every day, last to leave. I learned my boss's preferences and rhythms, handing him the paper and a coffee just the way he liked it ("You don't have to do that, Barb!" he'd say every day, pleased that I did). In addition to making sure my work was absolutely immaculate, I put his wedding anniversary and kids' birthdays on my calendar to remind him. I offered to order flowers for his wife or call restaurants for reservations. I was friendly and respectful and didn't miss a day.

It worked. He recommended that I get promoted to paralegal, because this was back in the day when you didn't need to have a degree for that. You just had to be sharp. And I was.

Soon it felt natural, being perky and cheerful and making the most out of my ordinary looks with makeup and flattering hairstyles. Elaine was "the pretty one" in our family, Tina "the feisty one," Nancy "the smart one." I didn't have a title—once, my father called me "the angry one," and I burst into tears, scaring him. I'm not sure I ever forgave him for that. It should've been "the hardworking one."

I had to work just as hard socially. I didn't come from a close-knit, adoring family like Becky, one of my roommates. I wasn't beautiful, like Christine, one of the other secretaries, who made men fall silent and forget what they were saying. I was just Barb Johnson, cheerful, hardworking, helpful. So when it came to parties or dating, I studied the other girls and learned how to flirt, talk, walk with my hips swaying just enough. I was making the best of what I had. That was something I *had* learned from my parents.

I met John at a company cocktail party. I worked in Real Estate; he worked in Family (one of the lower-earning divisions). But he was nice-looking and had a gentle voice, and he seemed to like me quite a bit, laughing at my jokes, smiling as I spoke. We dated for six months before he proposed, saying he loved me. I loved him, too. I thought I did, anyway. He was a perfectly nice young man with good prospects. I liked kissing him. I liked his hands on me, but I kept things chaste, because who marries the cow if you get the milk for free, even if this was the wild seventies?

That makes me sound cold, doesn't it? Well, you have to know, there was no romance in my upbringing. My parents married each other because they were both immigrants, both Norwegian, both Lutheran, and my father had land.

John would be a good husband. There was nothing to dislike, no skeletons, no weird fetishes or unkindness. We wanted the same things—stability, family, comfort.

When my parents finally agreed to come to Rhode Island to meet him and his parents, my father opened by saying a big wedding wasn't in the budget and there was nothing wrong with city hall. John's parents exchanged a glance. His mother said, "Oh, please, let us throw the kids a wedding. John's our only child, and we love Barb like a daughter already!"

I felt so pathetically grateful. My own parents didn't care, but Eleanor Frost did. Our wedding was small but tasteful—forty guests, a fancy lunch at the Hotel Adelade. I invited my siblings, but none of them came. Tina was in a snit because I didn't want her to be a bridesmaid, Nancy was pregnant and the rest of them didn't have the money or time or interest to come, frankly. Nancy sent a card and a casserole dish, which, given that she already had four kids, was truly thoughtful.

I stayed at the law firm, relishing both my job and our domesticity. John and I weren't setting the world on fire, but I read a few books about making a happy marriage, and we *were* happy, back then. We bought a real cute house on a lovely street in Cranston. On Friday nights, we had cocktails and a nice dinner, just us two, sometimes going out, sometimes me making a fuss and trying something from *Mastering the Art of French Cooking*, because the books said to make an effort and show your appreciation. On Saturday nights, we went out with friends—bowling or the movies, Mexican food. We had sex on Tuesdays and Fridays, and sometimes on Sunday mornings, too.

I loved being married. The rhythm of it, the safety. When I woke up in the middle of the night, I'd snuggle against John's back, so grateful to belong.

I loved being a wife. Loved doing little things to make him feel special—cranberry orange muffins on the weekends, or a note tucked into his briefcase.

Maybe more than him, I loved *us*. The unity of us. He'd roll his eyes in sympathy when I endured my mother's phone call each month, knowing that she peppered me with a litany of complaints and dissatisfactions. When *he* called his mother (every other day), I'd run my hand through his hair or give him a kiss on the cheek, glad he was a good son, a good man, then take the phone and update Eleanor on the girlier things in our life—how I'd planted tulips, could I have her recipe for those delicious potatoes with the rosemary and such.

When I was twenty-three, I decided it was time for a baby. Keep in mind I was a midwesterner, and twenty-three in Minnesota was a full-on grown-up, and we'd already been married for more than two years. John agreed. He'd be a wonderful dad, so solid and reliable, so unwavering, especially if our baby was a boy.

As I said, I only wanted one child. Growing up in a sloppy litter of children, I never wanted my child to feel unloved or pushed aside. Though John said he'd been a bit lonely without siblings, he'd also felt completely loved by both parents. He had no idea how lucky he was in that respect.

So it was settled. We had enough in the bank, we had this marriage thing down, and it was time. I repainted the empty bedroom pale yellow and started shopping at antiques stores on the weekends, buying a nice old mantel clock and some porcelain Winnie-the-Pooh figurines that would look so sweet on a bookcase. Threw myself into baking, dreamily imagined my little one running in from the school bus to eat a chocolate chip cookie warm from the oven, chattering about his or her day.

I got pregnant right away. Oh, gosh, we were so happy. We wanted to wait to tell folks, just in case something went wrong, but we celebrated, just the two of us. I think that's when I loved John the most, and he loved me the most, too. He worshipped my body, in awe, even if I wasn't showing. My tender breasts, the veins that were suddenly so visible through my pale skin. He'd bring me an Awful Awful from Newport Creamery—a milkshake that got its name from being awful big, awful good.

A miscarriage never crossed my mind, not until I felt the warm rush of blood, and helpless terror flooded through me.

By the time we got to the hospital, it was over. Ten weeks. Not uncommon, especially with first pregnancies. Nature's way of sensing a problem with the fetus.

I'd never thought of it as a fetus. That had been our baby. Our son. Though the doctor didn't say, I knew it was a boy.

I was *so* glad we hadn't told anyone, because I felt an awful sense of shame. I couldn't put it into words. On the one hand, I believed the doctor when he said it wasn't my fault. On the other, I hated my stupid, stupid body. My mother had seven children! My sister Nancy was on her sixth! Elaine had three!

John was kind. And sad. But you know, it felt like it was my fault, no matter what anyone said. I missed that baby. Gosh, I missed him.

All I wanted was to get pregnant again, and fast. As soon as I recovered, we started trying again. Figured since I got pregnant right away the first time, it'd be no problem the second.

We were wrong.

The weeks turned into months. That was fine, I told myself. I loved John, loved working as a paralegal, loved keeping our house perfectly tidy and appealing. If I lay awake in bed at night, tears slipping into my hair, well, of course I was taking it hard. Now that I'd had a taste of that kind of love, I needed another baby to heal my heart. I wanted to be a mother so much, I ached with it.

The second year I didn't get pregnant, we saw a doctor. Nothing was wrong with either of us, and I was still young. "You're not infertile," the doctor said, "because you *did* get pregnant. Keep trying." I cried in the parking lot, and John tried to console me.

I found myself growing brittle. It was harder to keep smiling, to stay perky. My mind drifted at work, and I made mistakes, too busy wondering if *this* month would be when nature deigned to let me have—and keep—what everyone else seemed to get so easily. John was sympathetic enough, but it was hard to put into words just how empty

I felt. Like all the work and time I'd put into getting to this point in life meant nothing, not without a baby. What good was I if I couldn't be a mother? Oh, I knew it was harder for some women, of course I did. But when Tina called with the news that she was having twins, I hung up, then called back later, saying a storm had knocked out our phone lines.

Babies were everywhere but in my womb.

I went on Clomid, but had to go off it because of the blinding headaches it caused. "There's nothing medically wrong with either of you," the doctor said, and I quit his practice and found someone else.

The second year of trying turned into a third year.

It wasn't *fair.* Going out with other couples was harder now; once we'd all been in the same boat; now Ellen was having her second and was tired, and the Parsons couldn't get a babysitter, and Abby and Paul had exciting news, and I didn't want to see them anymore. Friday night dinners, which had been such fun and felt so grown-up, were now morose. Why us? When would it happen? What if something was really wrong? Should we be trying to adopt now? Could we afford a trip to Korea? Colombia? Russia? We were on three agencies' lists, and not once did we make it to the interview stage.

Then John's grandfather died, and much to his surprise, John inherited the old man's home in Stoningham, Connecticut. When we pulled up to the house, I sat there, stunned silent. Grandpa Theo had been living with his sister in Maine for years and years. I'd never even been to Stoningham. Didn't know this house existed.

It was absolutely beautiful. A Greek Revival that needed some work, but was elegant and large and so . . . so classy. As I wandered through, taking in the huge windows, the columns, the pilasters, friezes and cornices and other words whose meaning I didn't even know, I fell in love. A front hall with a curving, graceful staircase. Fireplaces. A front parlor, a study, a family room, a dining room, a sunny if dated kitchen. Five bedrooms upstairs. Five!

A far cry from our run-down farmhouse in Nowhere, Minnesota. Our house in Cranston was cute but humble, not a place where we could have more than two couples over because the rooms were so small. But *this* house . . . this was heaven! The town, the house, the small enclosed yard, the nearby library, the smell of salt in the air, the cheerfully painted businesses on Water Street . . . honest to Pete, I was in heaven.

Stoningham was what a person thought of when they heard the word Connecticut—a little village of Colonials and Victorians, old cemeteries, posh boutiques, several restaurants, the historical society, the garden society, Long Island Sound sparkling, dotted with the white sails of boats.

Suddenly, marriage seemed wonderful again, new lifeblood injected into our lives. We needed this, John and I. The change. The freshness. We moved, John commuting half an hour or so to Providence. I decided to quit my job and devote myself to the house, which hadn't been lived in for nearly a decade. *This* was where I was meant to be. This would be where my child would be born. We would belong here in a way I'd never belonged anywhere. I'd been the girl who lived on that cow farm outside of town, one of the many Johnson kids. I'd been Barb from Minnesota in Providence, and since I worked the whole time we lived in Cranston, we still hadn't met some of our neighbors.

But in Stoningham, I could be someone. I *wanted* to be someone here, to fit into Stoningham's effortless grace, to be known by name, to have our house on the tour of homes at Christmas, to be recognized by the society ladies, because this was a town that had society ladies. Being a Frost was suddenly relevant; while we may or may not have been related to the poet, the name Frost was carved in granite on three war memorials here—Silas, Obadiah and Nathaniel.

I wasn't a paralegal anymore; I was the wife of an attorney. He'd gone to Boston College and Northeastern, and suddenly, that mattered more. He had a pedigree (maybe), and I would reflect that in everything I did, starting with our home. And once that was done, maybe God would grace me with a pregnancy, because this was where my child should be raised.

I threw myself into the town and was received graciously. Welcomed, even. I met Caro from around the corner. She was married, had one infant son and was desperate for an adult to talk to. I joined the Friends of the Library and asked for advice about the restoration of our columns from the head of the historical society, who was pleased that I took the house's history so seriously. John bought a little sailboat and we joined the yacht club.

I still didn't get pregnant, though. Years passed. *Years* of trying, that one brief pregnancy. Four different ob-gyns. No diagnosis.

It was devastating. Everywhere I went, I felt judged. I *wasn't* childless by choice. I was broken somehow. Everywhere I looked, there were pregnant women, children, babies. In the summertime, when the population doubled, there were so many beautiful children everywhere that I would cry. "Don't worry, honey," John said one night. "It'll happen, and if it doesn't, well, we're happy just the way we are."

I wanted to punch him. Hard. I was *not* happy, not on the inside! Couldn't he see that? I almost hated him, living the same life as always, staid and unruffled, driving back and forth to Providence, reasonably successful but ever complacent. How dare he be happy when I wanted to drop to my knees and sob?

When a woman can't get pregnant, the world judges her. The husband, gosh, he's just a great guy, releasing millions of sperm for his wife's selfish, snobby egg to reject. He's so patient, so understanding, so good-natured, so supportive (of *her* problem). *That John*, I imagined people thinking. *He sure is a saint*.

I was *barren*. That hateful word. I wanted to be lush, fertile, inviting, warm, nurturing . . . and instead, my uterus was an empty white room with sharp angles and immaculate floors.

One of my former coworkers was Japanese, and she told me once that women who couldn't have children were called stone women. I felt like stone, all right. I went through the motions, sex becoming only about procreation. I snapped at John. My smile felt hard as I volunteered on committees and worked in the garden. When Genevieve

London, the most influential and beloved of all Stoningham's residents, told me I'd done a "truly stellar" job on the fund-raiser for a new wing in the library, I almost broke down. *I don't care about that!* I imagined sobbing on her shoulder. *I just want to be a mother.*

I spoke with adoption agencies, longing for the Victorian days when you could just go to an orphanage and pick out a child. "This one's adorable! We'll take her!"

Caro was the only one I told. She'd just had her second boy, and I'd gone over with a hot dish. She let me hold him, and I must've looked sad, because she said, "Are you okay, honey?"

"Oh, sure," I said. "It's just . . . we've been having some trouble on the baby front." A few tears dropped onto her son's tiny, perfect head. "He's awfully precious, Caro."

She got me a tissue and gave me a hug. "If you ever want to talk about it, or borrow the boys, I'm here." And she let me hold that baby a long, long time.

And then, finally, when John had stopped asking if I was late, when I was speaking to adoption agencies in nine states and three countries, it happened. John and I had gone through the motions the night before, and when I woke up in the morning, I knew. I just knew.

Those first three months, I was so careful, holding myself together with all I had. I told God I was grateful and waited, waited for every day to pass, to bring me closer to my child. When I went to the doctor at fifteen weeks and she pronounced everything normal and healthy, I burst into tears. Only when I started to show did I confirm that yes, I was pregnant.

That beautiful, rich, sacred word. *Pregnant.* I called my family, and they answered in typical Minnesotan fashion. "Oh, that's nice, Barbara. Didja hear Tina's pregnant again, too?" I hadn't shared my difficulties with them, but their nonchalance infuriated me.

Caro was wonderful. She threw her arms around me and cried with happiness. Took me shopping for maternity clothes and understood that I was too superstitious to want a baby shower.

What a completely terrifying time those nine months were! "Enjoy," people would say, and I'd look at them like they were crazy. Enjoy? When I could hold my baby, I would enjoy. For now, I was wrapped in fear, walking a razor's edge, taking such good care of myself and yet held hostage every minute.

John figured we were "out of the woods" once I hit the fourth month, unaware that I prayed ferociously and almost constantly, begging and bribing and cajoling and threatening God to give me a healthy child, to spare me another miscarriage. I would be the best mother. I would love my baby so much. I already did. I would make God so proud of me. Please. Please. Please. With every roll and push of the baby, I was struck by wonder . . . and fear. Oh, I loved this baby so much. So much.

When I went into labor, I was the most ready person in the world. None of this "please, it hurts too much, I can't do it," not for me. Gosh no. And it didn't hurt—well, of course it did, but not nearly as much as they tell you it will.

I was ready, and my baby was ready, too—two hours after John and I got to the hospital, she was here.

A daughter. Oh, the joy that filled my heart when they told me! I'm sure I would've felt the same way if it had been a boy, but upon hearing, "It's a girl, Mrs. Frost!" my heart overflowed with gratitude and joy and sheer, utter bliss.

Juliet Elizabeth Frost. My precious, wonderful miracle. I knew, in that moment, I would never love anyone as much.

Not even my second daughter. I'm not proud of it, but there it is just the same.

CHAPTER ELEVEN

Juliet

One Wednesday in late October, months before her father's stroke, when the sky was deep, pure blue and the last of the spectacular foliage was still lighting up the Yale campus, Juliet sat at the Union League Cafe, waiting for Arwen to arrive for their mentorship lunch. She'd been warmly greeted by the maître d' and put at a lovely table by the window, where she watched Yalies nearly get killed as they attempted the difficult task of crossing the street. They might be among the smartest in the world, but they lacked life skills, which Juliet could say, since she was a graduate.

She looked at her watch. Ten after one.

When she'd started the mentorship program at DJK Architects, Juliet thought a monthly lunch would be a relaxed, informal way to discuss issues, goals, the company structure, projects . . . whatever the youngling needed. All her other protégés had loved these lunches, and not to brag or anything, but Juliet had a damn good reputation for supporting and nurturing young talent, at Yale, in the Association for

Women in Architecture and Design (AWA+D had given her an award for that just last year, thank you) and especially at DJK. Not a single new hire there hadn't benefited from Juliet's guidance or support, especially the women.

And not a single one of her mentees had ever been late to a mentorship lunch. It would be highly disrespectful.

Arwen was late.

Juliet wanted to bring it up somehow—the fact that while Arwen was talented and hardworking, there was a pecking order to be acknowledged. A ladder to be climbed, even if Juliet herself had given Arwen the chance to skip a few rungs. That, at thirty-one, Arwen still had a lot to learn, and Juliet would very much love to teach her, so she should be a little bit more respectful and drop the attitude. And . . . and yet . . .

Maybe the attitude was just confidence. Would a man be told to check in with his mentor more often if he was doing perfectly fine work? Would a boss tell a man to be less confident in his abilities? Did women do things differently because they were women? Was this more about Juliet's ego than Arwen's? Did Juliet just wish she'd been that confident, that—

Holy shit.

There was her father. Her father and a . . . woman. A . . . girlfriend.

Until that moment, she didn't know he had a girlfriend.

She knew the woman was his girlfriend because he was kissing her.

Really kissing her. Right there on Chapel Street, making out like they were teenagers who'd just discovered tongues. People had to go around them, they were so locked in.

That couldn't be her dad. Sure, he looked exactly like him, but maybe . . . nope. It was her father. They broke apart, gazed at each other, smiling, laughing.

Gross. Grotesque, that's what it was.

The woman was tall, with dyed black hair and sharp, strong features. For a second, Juliet thought it might be a man and almost wished it was—Gay Dad would be so much better than Cheating Dad—but no, it was indeed a woman.

Dad had his hand on her ass now. God! Get a room, people! No, don't, she quickly amended. Shit! This couldn't be happening. Her father? Her mild father, whose exciting life consisted of reading John Grisham novels and doing the crossword puzzle, maybe taking a walk in the afternoon, followed by a nap? This couldn't be happening.

They kissed again, deeply—Juliet shuddered—and then, finally, kept going, down Chapel toward the green.

It was as if the scene had been staged for her benefit. What were the odds that her father would decide to make out with a woman on Chapel Street? Three blocks from where she worked? *Was* it staged? Was it a prank? Who would think this was funny? Did he do this so Juliet would tell Mom?

What the actual fuck?

She realized she was half standing, watching them.

"Can I help you, ma'am?" said the server.

"Uh . . . uh . . . I'll have a martini," she said. Her heart was pounding. "Dry, three olives. Chopin, please."

Her father was having an affair.

She sank back into her seat and pulled out her phone, thinking she'd call her mom right away. No. No, not Mom. Oliver. He was calm. He'd know what to do.

"All right, darling?" he said, which was his customary greeting.

"I . . . I just saw my father kissing another woman."

There was a moment of silence. "You must be mistaken, love. John Frost, with a bit on the side? I rather doubt it."

"Oliver. I just saw him outside the restaurant where I'm having lunch."

There was a pause. "Was it a joke?"

"No!" she said, though she'd been thinking the same thing. "His tongue was down her throat! His hand was on her ass!" She glanced around apologetically, lowering her voice.

"That's . . . astonishing," he said.

"I know!"

"Deep breaths, my love," he said. "Christ, if this is true, I'm gobsmacked."

Arwen walked in the door, wearing a white dress that fit her perfectly, black stilettos, and a huge wonking single pearl on a gold strand. Bright red purse. Heads turned, as they always did for Arwen. "I have to go," she said to Oliver.

"Love you, darling. Ring me later."

"Juliet. So sorry I'm late." Arwen bent down and kissed Juliet on either cheek. Weird, since they'd seen each other in the office two hours ago. Probably some body language domination trick.

"No worries. It's fine. It's fine."

Arwen tipped her head. "You sure? You look upset."

There was that tremor of fear. "I'm great," Juliet said, adjusting her posture.

"Your martini, madam." The server set it down. "And for you, miss?"

"Perrier, please. Unless you feel uncomfortable drinking alone, Juliet. Alcohol makes me sleepy, so I never drink at lunch."

Fuck. Alcohol made Juliet sleepy, too. She'd already lost this pissing match. "No. I'm fine. I . . . " *I just saw my father snogging another woman*. "I'm good. It's nice to see you, especially since we had to miss last month's lunch."

"How long do they go on, these mentorship meetings?" Arwen asked. The implication was clear. She no longer needed or desired them.

"We never set a formal policy, but generally, three years," Juliet said, making it up on the spot. The truth was, all her previous hires *loved* going out with her, viewing it as special time with the likely next partner of DJK. "How are you? How are things?"

"Excellent." She took her nonalcoholic drink from the server and nodded thanks, looking both elegant and warm at the same time. Juliet could feel the sweat breaking out under her arms. Her face was still flushed. Arwen took a sip of water and tilted her head. "Pardon me for asking a personal question, Juliet, but are you having a hot flash?"

Fuck you. "No," Juliet said, trying to laugh. "I'm forty-three. A little young for that."

"My mom started when she was your age." A sympathetic smile.

"Well, *my* mom had a baby at my age."

"Really? Are you planning to have another?"

You'd love that, wouldn't you? Me on maternity leave. "No, no. Two is just fine. Wonderful. The best."

Her father was having an affair. Would her parents get a divorce? A sudden lump rose in her throat. She took a drink of the vodka, its burn welcome. "Tell me about the stadium project. Ian said there was some confusion on ADA compliance."

"No. He was mistaken." She smiled. "It's going beautifully, and even a little bit ahead of schedule. Now. What shall we order?"

When Juliet got home that night, she was exhausted and wired at the same time. Oliver had fed the girls already, and Sloane was in bed, Brianna doing homework (i.e., messaging her friends).

"I've got a lovely big martini ready when you are," he said. "Salmon, couscous and brussels sprouts, with a fat slab of chocolate cake I picked up at Sweetie Pies just for you."

"You're amazing," Juliet said. "I'll go say good night to the girls and be right back."

Sloane was already sleepy, her Patronus being an elderly cat who slept and liked to be petted. "How's my girl?" Juliet asked, sitting on the edge of her bed, stroking Sloane's silky hair.

"I'm good, Mommy. How are you?"

"I'm fine." There was that lump again. What would the girls say if their grandparents divorced? Oliver's mother lived in London, and while she was fabulous and descended with gifts once or twice a year, it wasn't the same. Oliver's dad had died when he was twelve.

Sloane and Brianna saw their Frost grandparents at least three times a week.

Shit.

"Do you want me to sing your good-night song?" she asked.

"No, Daddy already did. He makes up funny rhymes." She smiled sweetly. Yes. Oliver did everything better than she did.

"Okay. Sleep tight, little one," she said, kissing Sloane on the forehead, nose and lips. Soon, if she were like her sister, Sloane wouldn't want kisses anymore and would say things like, "Did you brush your teeth today?" and slice away at Juliet's heart, one translucent layer at a time.

But maternal love was required to be unconditional, so Jules went into Brianna's room, knocking once.

"What?" her oldest said.

"Hi, sweetheart," she said.

"Why did you work so long today?"

"It's Thursday. I always work till seven on Thursdays. You know that. That way I get to be home when you're done with school on Monday, Tuesday and—"

"*Okay*. Fine. I remember. Sorry." She widened her eyes as if Juliet had been screaming at her.

"How was school?"

"Fine."

"Any quizzes or tests or fun things?"

"No. It was boring. Um, I'm kind of busy, if you don't mind. Ackerly and I are doing math homework."

Ackerly was the most poisonous of Brianna's friends, and one of these days, she would take Brianna down. Juliet could see the handwriting on the wall. "What about Lena? She's good in math, too." Lena hadn't been over lately, and Brianna had stopped talking about her as much as she used to. The two had been friends since preschool.

"Mom. Ackerly is also good in math. If it's okay with you."

Juliet opened her mouth to say, *I don't trust her* or *Watch yourself with that one* or *Lose the attitude, Bri, or you're grounded.* "Watch your tone," she said, the best she could manage.

"Okay. Sorry. Good night."

"Good night. Love you, baby. Lights out in half an hour."

There was no response. Juliet closed the door and went down the stairs, pausing in front of a beautiful black-and-white photo of Brianna as a baby. Back when she loved her mother. God, those dimples! Her father's huge, smiling eyes, and Juliet's square chin, and those dimples.

When was the last time Brianna had smiled at her?

Juliet knew this was normal. Teenage girls were hormonal and beginning that process of pulling away from their mothers especially. Because how could you bear to leave if you didn't hate your mother a little bit? Except Juliet never had. She'd cried and cried when Mom had dropped her off at Harvard, and had to pretend to love it for six weeks before it became true. It was only because Barb was so diligent in checking in, coming to visit, sending care packages, that Juliet made it through her freshman year. She was her mother's favorite, she knew.

And Sloane was hers. Mothers shouldn't have favorites. She loved both girls the same. But she *liked* Sloane a lot more these days. If Brianna could give her something to work with, it would be easier.

Please, God, she thought, *don't let Sloane ever get to this point.*

Oliver was waiting, shaker in hand. He loved making cocktails to a fault, trying the Tom Cruise moves from that terrible movie.

"All right, darling? Must've been a terrible shock, seeing your dad today."

"Yep."

"Sloanie-Pop still awake?"

"Just barely."

"And Brianna?"

"Doing homework." She sat down on the stool. Remembered she

hadn't kissed him that day, and since she'd vowed never to be one of those wives who took her man for granted, got up and kissed him, then sat back down. "So."

"Right. I've been thinking about the situation," Oliver said, the ice clacking around in the shaker. "Thanksgiving is in three weeks. Perhaps wait till after to address all this muck? Your mum does love that holiday." He rattled the shaker dramatically over one shoulder, then poured her drink. "And her turkey *is* the stuff of legend."

Her second martini of the day. She'd had to drink hers at lunch, since Arwen had thrown down the gauntlet, and fought the afternoon sleepiness that it caused out of sheer will.

But if ever a day called for two martinis, it was today.

"Do you think she'll leave him?" Juliet said, her voice low.

"I would leave *you*, darling. And you'd have me murdered and thrown in the ocean in tiny bits and pieces."

"They've been married almost fifty years, Ollie." Her throat was tight. "How can you cheat on someone after fifty years?"

"Oh, my darling, there, there." He came around the counter and put his arms around her, and she clutched his shirt. "I've no idea. Your father's a twat."

"What do I do? Tell him I saw? Tell her? Order him to tell her or I will? Ignore it? I mean, it's not like they have the best marriage in the world. God. Maybe they have an open relationship."

"Well, darling, Barb has been incredibly busy this year, and—"

She jerked back. "And what? That gives my father permission to cheat on her?"

"No! Not at all. It's just that perhaps things on the home front have . . . I'm going to stop talking now. This is awkward, isn't it? Go on, love. What were you going to say?"

"Nothing. I have to let this sit a little while."

"Good plan. Maybe talk to a friend? Saanvi?"

Saanvi was one of their summertime neighbors. She worked in

New Haven, too, at the hospital, and sometimes she and Juliet had lunch or, more rarely, a glass of wine after work. She couldn't see bringing up her parents' marriage, though. Too personal.

The truth was, Barb was Juliet's best friend. In any other circumstance, Barb was the one she'd go to.

Juliet wiped her eyes and let Oliver kiss her on the cheek. They ate dinner, and since it was late, went to bed, where they made love, tenderly and quietly, since Brianna had ears like a bat. "I love you, sweetheart," he whispered just before he fell asleep.

"I love you, too," she said, but the words almost made her cry.

Her father loved her mother, once. Now look.

Ten minutes later, Oliver sound asleep, Jules got out of bed, put on her bathrobe and went to her study. Googled "why do married men cheat?"

All the clichés were true. Boredom. Trying to reclaim lost youth. Not getting enough at home. The thrill of the chase. Lack of communication.

The hard fact was, if someone wanted to cheat, they could. If someone wanted a divorce, he or she could just end things. *I don't want to be married anymore. Well, not to you.* And just like that, your carefully built life would crumble.

Juliet's mother had built a life *so* carefully. She had always put the family first, and Dad had reaped those benefits. The beautiful home, the respect of the community, Juliet and Sadie themselves, and now, by extension, Oliver, Brianna and Sloane. She saw how hard her mother tried—she'd always seen it. Cooking lovely meals, the house always a haven, trying to make conversation with topics such as "tell me the happiest thing that happened to you today" at dinnertime. She remembered her parents taking ballroom dancing classes, going to Scotland, learning about wine.

So if Barb couldn't pull it off, who could?

Oliver was perpetually happy, and not tremendously empathetic to people who weren't, always a little confused as to why they didn't just shrug off what they couldn't control and focus on the positive.

Which made it hard to talk to him about difficult, complicated matters like her parents. Or Arwen, since he said things like, "Sounds like you picked a winner in that one!" or "That's bloody fabulous for her!" missing the point entirely.

It was hard to talk about the fact that Brianna made her feel sad and tired these days, and not liking her own child made her feel small and mean. She couldn't say out loud that she liked Sloane better, and she couldn't discuss the fear that Brianna would be able to tell, the same way Sadie knew Juliet was the favorite, and this was karma getting Juliet back for being their mom's favorite.

And now, it would be hard to talk about the creeping terror that if her father could somehow justify cheating on her mother, Oliver would see his point.

CHAPTER TWELVE

Barb

I hadn't wanted another child. I was too old. My husband and I were *both* too old to have another child. It was absurd. We had one, and she was—forgive me—perfect.

Juliet had been that way since birth. Since conception, to be honest, because I hadn't had one day of nausea or swelling or heartburn. And my body was miraculous. I could do everything she needed—nurse her, soothe her, intuitively know when she was about to wake up at night, or when she was coming down with a cold.

She was a happy, healthy, beautiful baby, speaking in full sentences by her first birthday, smiling, a good sleeper. She began reading at three. She was a friend to all her classmates, especially those who seemed to need a little more—the boy who wet his pants every day in kindergarten, or the girl who had a speech impediment. Teacher after teacher told me she was exceptional.

She was Mommy's girl. John loved her, of course—who wouldn't?—but he worked more during her childhood. He switched from family law to regulatory compliance, which required him to travel out of state once or twice a week. Sometimes, he'd stay overnight or come home very late, and I loved those mother-daughter nights.

Juliet was the purpose that had been missing in my life, because marriage wasn't enough, and work had been a placeholder for me. Our house and my role in town were just to prepare the way for Juliet. I was born to be her mother, and we lived in a beautiful world built by the two of us. I made sure she got enough fresh air, taking her for walks every day, first in the pram, then holding her hand. We took our big canvas tote to the library and filled it with books, even when she was tiny, and I read to her for hours. I made nutritious meals and snacks, way ahead of the curve regarding organic, locally sourced food. I chose my words carefully, always explaining to her why she shouldn't touch something rather than just "because I said so." Even my voice changed, and my flat upper-midwestern accent morphed into the blander, more cultured Connecticut non-accent.

Every day was bliss. It truly was.

John faded into the background. I never hired a babysitter. Every few years, John's mother would visit from Seattle, where they'd retired, and spend a week with us. Eleanor would urge John and me to go out, and we would, but I was anxious, never able to relax the way I sensed I was supposed to. I only wanted to be home with my precious, wonderful daughter. The very word was magical. My mother-in-law deserved a little time alone with her, though, so I did it.

Home, our gracious, warm, inviting home, was made more perfect because of Juliet. Her artwork hung on the fridge, and I couldn't seem to take enough photos of her. Her room was a delightful chaos of books and stuffed animals and projects. I turned one of the extra bedrooms into her own library, filling it with books she had loved, did love, would love. Oh, the happy hours we spent there, reading together!

My parents visited only once (we bought them tickets, but even so, you'd think they were being sent to a work camp in Outer Mongolia). They'd never seen the house before, and all my mother had to say was, "Aren't you the fancy-pants now?" My father commented that I "fawned over" Juliet, and maybe I could send some money Elaine's way, since I liked to flash it around so much. Who needed a house with five bedrooms when you had one single kid?

We didn't invite them back. Still, I sent them a Christmas photo of Juliet each year; though they had more than twenty grandchildren by then, I felt they should see her utter perfection.

By the time she was nine, Juliet was doing algebra and reading at a twelfth-grade level. She took ballet and was wonderful, even dancing the part of little Clara in *The Nutcracker*. She was helpful and thoughtful and funny, doing her chores without being asked, taking on extra-credit projects or tutoring other kids just because she liked to.

In the evenings, when her homework was done, she'd snuggle up next to me on the couch and say, "What are you doing, Mommy?" The fact that she, this bright star, was interested in me . . . it touched my heart in a way I couldn't explain. Even though she was clearly smarter than I was, she never made me feel unneeded. She asked me to teach her needlework—her room was filled with pillows and sachets I'd embroidered, and her closet full of gorgeous sweaters knit by my own hand. She wanted to learn to knit, too, so we could do it together. I loved to bake, and she loved to help. We picked flowers and arranged them, and the house shimmered with our love.

Then, when Juliet was eleven, that magical age when she was starting to ask questions about the world, as we started to be able to really talk about life, and our relationship began to bloom with that added gift of friendship, my mother was diagnosed with stomach cancer. It had already spread to her intestines and liver, and she didn't have long to live.

It surprised me—that panicky sensation, the primal yearning for my mother, no matter how mediocre she'd been. I found myself crying uncharacteristically, and eating at all hours, something I'd never done. My mother was dying in slow agony, and when she was gone, I'd lose the chance to ever win her approval.

By the time I visited in March, the cancer had spread to her brain and bones, and she was thrashing around on the bed like a trapped animal. Oh, I cried and cried when I saw her—that poor skinny body, her skin bruised, face sallow. The hospice nurses said it could happen anytime, but that tough old bird just wouldn't die, as much as she wanted to. She lasted and lasted, in constant, grueling pain, and it was torture. There was just no other word for it.

I ate my emotions. My period was light, then stopped for a month or so, which I attributed to stress. It had happened to Caro when her husband was deployed. Then Mom finally did die, and I went back for the funeral with John and Juliet.

So I didn't suspect pregnancy, not after all the trouble I'd had. I was old enough to start flirting with menopause. Nancy had hit it at thirty-nine, Elaine at forty-three. Besides, John and I had only had two very mediocre . . . couplings . . . this entire year.

Well, I *was* pregnant, turns out. No signs this time. No flash of knowing. I had no idea until I saw a chiropractor for back spasms.

"How many weeks are you?" she asked, and I actually laughed.

"I'm not pregnant," I said. "My mom died recently, and I stress-ate. I . . . oh."

Oh, no. The crying. The hunger. I hadn't been eating my emotions; I'd been eating for two. I went from the chiropractor to my regular doctor, and yep. I was pregnant. Almost halfway along.

Juliet was in sixth grade, high school and teenage years just around the corner, not a time I wanted to be distracted by an infant. My god, an infant! Middle-of-the-night feedings, spit-up, dragging around a diaper bag for two years, ever in need of a shower. What had been a privilege with Juliet now seemed like a terrible burden.

Surprisingly, John was thrilled. Even more so than when I was pregnant with Juliet. "It'll be a second chance," he said, and I snapped back with, "A second chance at what?"

"At family life," he answered, and I may have hissed at him.

Juliet, true to form, was happy, though she admitted that my pregnancy was "kind of gross and embarrassing." I couldn't disagree. To know your parents were having sex when you're in junior high school (even if it had been practically an immaculate conception) *was* gross and embarrassing.

I hoped the baby would be a boy, because then I wouldn't have to compare him to Juliet. His name would be Nathaniel, I thought, after one of his ancestors who'd fought for the Union and died in the Civil War. A fine New England name. Nathaniel Robert Frost. Though the pregnancy was a shock, I loved the baby as it wriggled and writhed in me. It was the unknown that had me worried.

And God, I was tired. I wasn't quite forty, but I felt eighty. I'd nod off as I tried to read the paper, yawned constantly. My back hurt as if someone had hit me with a baseball bat, and my ankles were swollen. I had pregnancy-induced hypertension, and my cheeks were flushed and hot all the time. I couldn't sleep, and I had heartburn so horrible I had to keep a huge vat of antacids with me at all times. Even at night.

I went into labor early on a Tuesday morning. It was brutal. Maybe because I was older, but I felt like I actually might die. Hours and hours of contractions, fiery knives of pain shooting down my legs, my back clenching and spasming. I vomited and had diarrhea, and my throat burned with bile. How could I survive this? All through that day into the night, into the next morning, I suffered and labored and endured. With every contraction, I felt desperate, trying to claw my way away from the wrenching, twisting pain. Was this how my own mother had felt with cancer? How could she have endured it?

After fifty-four hours of labor and no progress, only five centimeters dilated, they finally decided to take the baby via C-section because "mother failed to progress."

As always, my fault.

"The worst of both worlds," the nurse chuckled. I was too exhausted to answer. They took me to the operating room and stabbed my back with a needle that felt as big as a chopstick and then, when the epidural had taken effect, sliced me open.

It hurt. They say you'll feel nothing, and they lie. As the doctors yanked and pulled, elbows-deep in my body, tears slipped into my hair.

Those were my insides they were jerking around! How would the baby be healthy after such a battle? How could I love the little thing when all I felt was failure and exhaustion, literally torn apart by the savagery of childbirth?

"It's a girl!" Dr. Haines said, holding her up for a glimpse. I saw a huge, whitish baby with dark hair before they whisked her off.

"Is she all right?" I asked.

"Looks perfect to me!" said the jolly nurse.

John was crying with joy. "Another girl!" he said. "Oh, honey, I'm so happy."

"Nine pounds, nine ounces! She's a bruiser! Apgars are all nines, too. Guess we know what your lucky number is, guys!"

Another daughter. I'd been so sure it was a boy. I closed my eyes, so wrung out that I started to fall asleep.

"Barb, look! Our little girl! Isn't she beautiful?"

I forced my eyes open.

She wasn't very pretty, her head tubular from all that time stuck in the birth canal. She seemed giant compared to how I remembered Juliet, who'd been seven pounds even. The baby's eyelids were bruised and her face looked swollen. Her little rosebud mouth moved, and she opened her eyes.

I loved her. Oh, thank God, I loved her.

"Hello, little one," I whispered. John kissed her forehead, and put her face against mine, and the softness of her cheek was so beautiful. "Hello, sweetheart."

Then she started to cry. She started to *scream*. I had to turn my head away, because she was right against my ear.

"Sounds perfect!" said the irritatingly cheerful nurse.

It was startling that a newborn could make that much noise. "There, there, little one," John said, holding her close, and just like that, the baby stopped crying.

"Aw. She loves her daddy," said Dr. Haines. "Barb, I'm stitching you up, but you can snuggle her in a few minutes, okay?"

John was crooning to the baby, telling her she was beautiful, Daddy's little angel, and I fell into a deep, black sleep, unable to wake up for her first two feedings.

Having a C-section is much worse than giving birth the other way. With every move, it felt as if my insides were going to spill out onto the floor. Flashes of white-hot pain seared through my abdomen. When they made me get out of bed, I fainted. They made me pedal my feet to avoid blood clots, but I got one anyway, which they said was because I didn't get out of bed soon enough (ignoring the fact that unconscious people do have trouble on that front). My leg throbbed and burned. I couldn't hold the baby by myself for the first two days, because I was too weak. All I wanted to do was sleep, but they kept waking me up to feed her. I had to have a pillow over my stomach to protect my incision.

She didn't want to nurse. She screamed and screamed, her body shaking with rage as I tried to offer my breast again and again. They brought in a special nurse who was an expert, and she wrestled the baby close to me. When she latched on, I gasped in pain. My entire body was drenched in sweat as my sutured uterus contracted.

Juliet came to the hospital to meet her new sister. That was the bright spot of my six days there. I got mastitis, the cure for which was nursing more. My incision got more sore, not less, but I couldn't take any effective pain medications because I was nursing. My nipples started to bleed. That was the last straw. She could be bottle-fed. It was fine.

John picked her name. Sadie. Like a factory worker in World War II. He suggested Barbara as a middle name, to which I said, "Don't curse her with that." I know it was meant to be a compliment. But honestly. Sadie Barbara Frost? How would that look on a diploma?

And so her middle name was Ruth, after his grandmother. It was fine. It would grow on me, hopefully. I didn't have any other suggestions.

Looking back, I realize I had postpartum depression. In those first few months, however, I just thought I was a failure.

When she was asleep, I loved her. When she was awake, it soon became clear that she didn't prefer me. She wanted John, and he took a partial leave so he could work from home to help. When Juliet was born, he'd taken all of two days off.

But for Sadie, he was here, and it *was* helpful. He'd make me lunch and feed the baby, walk the floor with her, take her for a ride or put her in the carriage and tell me to rest and bounce back.

I didn't bounce back.

I was exhausted but couldn't sleep. The surgery and its complications took a lot out of me, and I just didn't bond with the baby the way I wanted to. The way I had with Juliet. I had a coughing spell a few days after I came home and tore my stitches, so that fun event had to be repeated.

I started to resent Sadie, the way she wouldn't be comforted by me, the exhaustion from the moment I woke up, dreading the long day ahead. When John went back to work full-time, I held Sadie as she cried and fussed—colic, teething, always something—and I'd look at the clock and count the minutes until Juliet would get off the school bus. Then I'd feel that love. I'd find enough energy to make dinner and pretend I was fine, because when my older daughter was around, I did feel so much better, gosh, yes.

I waited for my second-born to love me the way Juliet had. She didn't. She didn't hate me, of course not, but we just didn't have that special connection. Sometimes I'd see her looking at me, and I swore she knew. What was it about me that she sensed? That I was a fake? That I hadn't wanted her as much as I'd wanted Juliet? Was I a terrible mother?

During this same time, Juliet and I became closer than ever. Whether she knew it or not, I think she saved me. The sweet girl would bring me a cup of tea without asking if I wanted one, or she'd pick me flowers from the garden, knowing I was too tired to do it myself. That Mother's Day, she gave me a card that said, "After intensive research and based on my own experiences, this fact cannot be denied: you are the best mother in the history of the world." That was also the day

Sadie cried and cried; she was teething, so I rubbed her gums, and she bit down hard, slicing my finger with her razor blade of a new tooth. My finger bled a shocking amount, and it throbbed for the rest of the day.

That about summed things up. I kept trying to get my second-born to love me, and everything I did was wrong, whereas my first daughter continued to adore and *like* me. I tried. I really did. You can't compare your children, all the authorities said, and I tried not to. I wanted to make room for Sadie. I tried to. But John was her favorite, and my poor body was ravaged by the pregnancy and birth. While I had bounced back in weeks after Juliet, it took nearly a year before my incision stopped hurting, before I could pee normally again.

Decades later, when postpartum depression came into the social conversation, I recognized that I'd had it with Sadie. It didn't solve anything, but it was good to know. But once again, something in me had been wrong. Always, always my fault.

As Sadie grew, our relationship didn't change much. If she woke from a nightmare, she called out for Daddy, not Mommy. She wanted him to push her on the swing, him to take her to the library on Saturdays, him to make her macaroni and cheese. (They both thought Kraft was better than my homemade version, which I found ridiculous. If there's one thing a Minnesotan knows, it's how to make a baked dish with noodles in it, thank you.)

Juliet started high school when Sadie was two, and the dreaded countdown began for the time she would leave me. Every minute of those four years with her was precious, every drive, every morning when I made her breakfast, every weekend, every little moment we had together. Sadie would go to bed at seven or seven thirty—the earlier the better, as far as I was concerned. I let John read to her at night, telling myself it was only fair, since he'd missed out on those times with Juliet. It also gave me more time with Juliet, who told me about her classmates, her papers, which teachers were better, who was going to the spring dance.

When she was at school, I'd try to play with Sadie, but neither of our hearts were in it. If I made her a fort, she'd want to be in it alone. She told me hide-and-seek was only fun with Daddy and "Jules." She didn't like to bake or knit or pick flowers. If I drew with her, she was lost in her own little world. I'd ask her what she thought of my picture, and she'd say, "It's nice. Will you make lunch now?"

But Juliet never let me down, was never sullen, didn't have sex as a teenager, managed to have a nice group of friends without too much drama. She went to Harvard, and I sobbed all the way back from Cambridge. After that, I visited her once a month, trying not to let on that I needed those visits, that they sustained me. At college, she'd introduce me all around, and she was *proud* of me. Of me. "This is my awesome mother," she'd say, putting her arm around me and resting her head on my shoulder. "My best friend." We'd go shopping and have lunch and stroll around campus, hand in hand. Yes. We still held hands. Sadie only let me hold hers if we were crossing a street, and only because I insisted.

Juliet was so . . . kind. So *generous*. I was more grateful than I could put into words. Meanwhile, Sadie didn't seem to notice me, didn't take my advice. I loved my second child, but she was her father's girl, lost in her head, dreamy, unaware of her surroundings, sloppy, heedless of my requests to put her dirty laundry in the basket or bring her plate to the counter. I tried to engage, to feel as close, but she wasn't interested. When I asked if she wanted me to read her a story, she'd say no, she could read herself, though she let John read *The Lord of the Rings* to her out loud, a story that so bored me, I couldn't stay in the room.

I told myself not to mind. I had Juliet, after all. Juliet who, after graduating with honors from Harvard, chose Yale to get her degree in architecture. She asked if I'd come down for lunch every Wednesday. She met Oliver, who was the loveliest young man in the world. A month after they graduated—Oliver from the School of Engineering, Juliet once again with honors—Oliver drove up from New York City to Stoningham and asked me if he could have my blessing to marry my girl. Me. Not John. Of course I said yes, and he asked me what kind of ring I thought Juliet would like. I pointed him in the right direction, and when she called me the next week, we cried with joy together. (And she *loved* the ring.)

Oliver started calling me Mum in a way that made me feel flushed and proud. His mother was wonderful, and when she visited to talk about the wedding, we got along so well! Oliver was an only child, and Helen adored Juliet (as she should have), and asked to pay for half the wedding so it could be as extravagant as possible.

"I adore them together, don't you?" she asked, and we bonded over our love of our offspring.

Juliet and I spent the most wonderful year talking about colors and flowers, church readings and dresses, without a single cross word or bridezilla moment. We went to New York to pick out her dress, just the two of us, because that was how she wanted it, and oh, yes, I cried when she came out, smiling . . . beaming, really. It seemed that just yesterday, we'd been playing in her room, or I was wrapping her up in a big towel after her bath, breathing in the smell of her clean skin, making her laugh.

My beautiful little girl.

Sadie was eleven when Juliet and Oliver got married, a tomboy with a sketchbook who said she didn't want to be a junior bridesmaid, "whatever that was." It was fine. It was better, really, without a sullen tween sighing dramatically and reading Sylvia Plath as the other bridesmaids laughed and chatted.

The wedding was every mother-of-the-bride's dream. Every detail was gorgeous, from the cream and apricot flower arrangements to the delicious hazelnut cake. At the reception, Juliet thanked me for being a perfect mother in front of 250 guests, and said she could only hope to be half as good a mom as I was.

When she and Oliver moved into their Chelsea apartment, she asked for my help decorating it, "since you have such great taste, Mom." There was a second bedroom painted in pale blue, my favorite color, and the bed had feather pillows on it, because Juliet knew I preferred them. My favorite tea was always in their cupboard, and Oliver was always wonderful when I visited for the occasional weekend, making us dinner the first night, then sending us out for some "lovely mum and daughter time." The theater, or shopping, or best of all, just a long, drawn-out dinner at a quiet restaurant with my favorite person in the world.

Meanwhile, Sadie embraced every cliché of a teenage girl. The weariness, the cynicism, the all-black clothing. She became obsessed with painting, giving minimal effort in her other classes, lecturing me on the importance of art over all else.

"Really?" I said. "Over medicine? Do you think art is more important than, gosh, I don't know, saving lives?"

"Life isn't worth living without art," she said airily. Spoken like someone who'd never been sick.

Honest to Pete. Did she think art would count for more than actual learning? We argued over her mediocre grades, but John always took her side. "As long as you're doing your best, sweetheart, we don't care about your marks." Which was a total lie. Juliet had had the highest GPA of any child from Stoningham in a generation! She got into all eight Ivy League schools! Sadie never even made the honor roll, and it wasn't because she wasn't smart. She just didn't try.

Then, that boyfriend. Did she think I was blind, the way she looked at Noah Pelletier? He was a nice enough young man, but I knew about teenage boys and what they were after. She only rolled her eyes when I talked about unwanted pregnancy, as if she already knew so much more than I did.

That was her attitude about anything. Whatever I said, she treated it as if she was vastly more intelligent than I was. If Juliet thought I was the best mother in the world, how dare Sadie dismiss and avoid me, or worst of all, simply *tolerate* me? Endure me, as if I was such a burden, such an embarrassment?

Art school. Honestly. It would've been one thing if she'd gotten into . . . wherever one goes if one is good enough. Rhode Island School of Design, or Savannah College of Art and Design, with a plan toward historic restoration or something like that. Instead, she went to Pace, a school I'd never heard of, so she could become an artist. Oh, she had talent, not that it meant anything in the cold, hard world.

Then Juliet got pregnant. Again, I was included in every detail. She brought me to a few appointments so I could hear my grandchild's heartbeat. I came down four days before her due date and pampered her, and when she went into labor, I went to the hospital with them, right into the labor room, so welcomed and included, so needed. I held her hand and told her she was strong and amazing and I loved her so much, and when the baby finally came out, Juliet clutched my hand, crying tears of joy.

A girl.

They named her Brianna. "After you," Juliet said. "I know you never loved your name, so we took letters from Barbara Marie Johnson and made Brianna. So she's your namesake in a special way, Mommy."

Was there ever a more perfect daughter?

And so, as Sadie drifted like a butterfly, living her New York dream of art, poverty and waitressing, my older daughter continued to be my pearl. When Brianna was one, they moved back to Stoningham. Juliet called me several times a day just to talk and invited John and me for dinner a few times each month, and came to our house most Sunday afternoons.

If Sadie had given me anything more than scraps from her heart, I could've done better, but the truth is, I got tired of trying. Sadie had her father; I had my Juliet, and Oliver, and Brianna, and a few years later, another beautiful granddaughter, Sloane.

John was a bit disappointing as a grandfather, frankly. He was fine when a child was deposited on his lap, but he wasn't all that enthusiastic. He still worked a few days a week and played golf (the most unimaginative hobby in the world). Twice a year, he went away for a golf weekend with his friends, and I loved being in the house without him.

Sometimes he'd go to the city to see Sadie and take her out to dinner and spend the night in a hotel down there, or at her place, once she got an apartment of her own.

"You never did that when I lived there," Juliet said, a rare rebuke from our gentle girl.

"Didn't I?" was his response, and I felt the venom well up in my throat, like one of those dinosaurs that could spit acid. Still, I held my tongue.

I continued to be a contributing member of Stoningham, working on committees and serving on boards. I watched my granddaughters when asked—unlike me, Juliet and Oliver liked to go out, and it was a joy to be the one to care for the girls. I'd read to them, or bake cookies with them, or do crafts and let them take an extra-long bath, and when they were asleep, I'd fold some laundry or pick flowers. Juliet's house was beautiful, and she had a cleaning lady, but I still liked to fuss and tidy.

It was so nice to be wanted.

I thought about divorcing John. It had been so long since we'd done anything meaningful together, connected in any way. But there was that affordability thing. The thought of losing my house.

Then Bill Pritchard said he wouldn't run again for first selectman.

"You should run, Mom," Juliet said over dinner at her house when John was on a golfing weekend. The girls were in bed, and we were enjoying a glass of wine on the deck on the top of their house, which overlooked the Sound.

"Oh, absolutely," Oliver concurred. "Can you imagine how shipshape this town would be if you were in charge, Mum?"

"That community center project would be in the bag, that's for sure," Juliet said. She put her hand over mine. "You should do it. You'd be amazing."

"Honey, I'm almost seventy."

"And? You have more energy than I do. And organizational skills. And smarts. And everyone adores you."

The idea took root. I *was* good at organizing. I'd been on every committee there was. Being Juliet's mother still carried cachet in this town; everyone loved her (and Sadie, too, just not as much . . . she'd left Stoningham years before, after all, impatient to shake the small-town dust from her shoes).

I won in a landslide. John had the nerve to be surprised on election night. "Well, holy crap, Barb. Who could've called that?" he said right there in the school gym, loud enough to be overheard. I saw a few people give him a strange look. An angry flush crept up my chest. Where had he *been* all these years we'd lived in Stoningham? Didn't he know how hard I worked, how many people respected me, how much I'd given to this community? How dare he be surprised by my success?

Then he took to calling me Queen Bee at home. "Please stop," I said. "It's really not funny, and it's sexist besides."

"Oh, it's a little funny," he said. "And it's not sexist in the least. The queen bee is the most important—"

I stopped listening. He loved those nature documentaries that never ended, some British man extolling the virtues of ant colonies or monkey dexterity.

Divorce. I'd give it a year, and then we'd move on. Shouldn't your husband be the one who truly believed in you? We'd be fine financially, now that I was working, and I'd save every penny of my salary this year. I could probably get the house, and even if I didn't, well. I'd cross that bridge.

A year. I threw myself into the town. Applied for grants. Talked to almost every single year-round resident about their concerns. I *did* get the old school approved for a community center, and I didn't even have to raise taxes to do it, thanks to a hefty state grant and what Juliet called my velvet glove approach with the summer people, asking them to donate in a way they couldn't refuse.

Not only that, we bought Sheerwater, that magnificent old house on Bleak Point, after Genevieve London died, got it listed on the National Register of Historic Places and got the land approved as a park, the house available for weddings and reunions and other functions. I was on a roll. I worked with the chamber of commerce to increase our tourism outreach, catching some of the casino crowd on their way *to* the casinos, rather than on the way back, when they were broke. We got rid of the stoplight that wasn't needed and drove everyone crazy and wooed a salmon fishery to open on the old paper mill site. Clean energy, ecologically responsible and employing seventeen full-time people.

It was a brilliant year. Juliet was so proud of me, and I knew this because she told me. Often. When that first year was up, I decided to wait till after the holidays to tell John I wanted a divorce. Why punish the grandkids over Christmas? Because of course they'd be upset. Our fiftieth anniversary was January 10; I'd do it then, since the fact that we barely acknowledged the date would provide a perfect lead-in. I was tired of dragging the corpse of our marriage behind me. It was over.

On January 9, he had the stroke.

Four hours after I got the call from the paramedics, I found out my husband had a mistress.

CHAPTER THIRTEEN

Juliet

"We're just so sorry to hear about your father," said Dave Kingston, one of the partners at DJK Architects, the *K* in the DJK. "If there's anything you need—extra time off, more flexibility to work from home—you just let us know."

"Thank you, Dave. I really appreciate it. And the flowers were beautiful. My mom really appreciated them." The fact that part of Juliet would rather see her father die than deal with his adultery . . . well, best not to go there right now. A wave of love for that same father washed over her, and she had to swallow the tears in her throat. *Not now. Not now.* It was becoming her mantra.

Juliet sat in the conference room of DJK with Dave; Dave's personal assistant, the ever-silent and slightly terrifying Laurie, who took notes at every meeting Dave ever had; and Arwen Alexander. That Arwen was here was . . . disturbing.

Dave had been Juliet's boss since he hired her out of Yale. He wasn't a bad boss, not by a long shot, but he had a way of letting her know how grateful she should be to work there. She hadn't missed the *extra* time off, the *more* flexibility.

She'd taken all of three days off, thank you. The firm's HR policy gave her three *weeks* of sick time, which included family illness. The last time Juliet had taken a sick day was four years ago, because, like their mother, the girls almost never got sick, having the immune systems of Greek deities. And when Juliet worked from home, she worked longer hours than if she were at the office, and she had the time sheets and productivity to prove it. But at the age of forty-three, she felt her worth to the company was something she shouldn't *have* to prove. She'd been here almost seventeen years and worked on many billion-dollar buildings, delighting clients, leading teams, dealing with crises and labor issues, managing projects on time and sometimes even under budget, which, in the world of large-scale construction, was akin to calling Lazarus forth from his tomb.

Her work spoke for itself. Or it used to. In the past six months, there'd been a tremor in the Force. Lots of tremors, actually.

"So," Dave said. He cleared his throat. "I think we'll use this as an opportunity to give Arwen a little more responsibility. I'm putting her on the lead for the Hermanos headquarters."

The tremor became a quake. The new home of a Fortune 500 company under Arwen's lead? Why? Juliet was completely capable of doing her job.

"Absolutely. Anything I can do to help," Arwen murmured.

"I appreciate that," Juliet said, keeping her voice low and pleasant. "But I'm really fine. Totally in the game. Thanks just the same, Dave."

"Let's see how it goes. Great. Good meeting. I feel reassured. Again, anything you need. Anything at all. Thanks, Arwen, that'll be all."

Arwen put her hand over Juliet's and gave it a quick squeeze. "I really am so sorry about your dad." She left, leaving a hint of jasmine in the air. Even her perfume was gorgeous.

When the door closed, Juliet fixed Dave with a firm look. "I do not need Arwen taking over my responsibilities, Dave. I'm the project manager. She has her plate full already."

"You know what? I think you're right, but we'll try this out just the same. It'll be good for you. Good talk. I like that we're thinking outside the box. Let's circle back and see if we can move the needle on this project. Great! Good! We're all on the same page. Give your mother my best." He stood up, and Silent Laurie closed her laptop and trailed after him, but not before she gave Juliet a look that seemed to say, "Watch your back, sister."

Juliet sat alone in the big room, Dave's cliché business-speak ringing in her ears and the too-familiar waves of dread lapping at her feet.

Two years ago, Juliet had recruited Arwen to join DJK Architects. It had seemed so innocuous at the time.

Recruitment was part of Juliet's job, unofficially . . . to keep an eye out for young talent, especially female talent. Not that anyone made extra time for her to do this—the partners had never said, "Juliet, take two days a month and dedicate them to finding young female architects so we don't look so middle-aged white male around here, okay?"

It was just a given, since she was the highest-ranking woman at DJK, the only firm she'd ever worked for. The message was she was lucky to work here (and she was), so this would be paying it forward. Sure. She was happy to do it, frankly. There *weren't* enough women in architecture, and she could help solve that in her corner of the industry. The firm was international, with branches in seven states and sixteen countries. Bringing in new perspectives was only going to help everyone, from the partners to the clients to the world, who'd get to see beautiful buildings designed by people from all backgrounds.

Arwen came to her attention because of her work at another firm. She'd been Architect II—basically responsible for daily design—on a hospital wing in Denver, and it was gorgeous *and* ahead of schedule. Her name was mentioned in a small article about the building, and Juliet did a little poking. UCLA undergrad, master's at SCI-Arc, the

Southern California Institute of Architecture. She had five years of experience on big projects.

Juliet did her thing: flew to San Diego, where the other firm was based, and took Arwen out to dinner while Oliver and the girls frolicked on the beaches and went to the botanical gardens. Arwen was sharp, good-natured and a little in awe of Juliet.

"I can't believe Juliet Frost is taking me out for dinner," she said the first night as they sat at Juniper & Ivy. "You've designed some of my favorite buildings ever. That hotel in Dubai? And the hospital in Cincinnati? Next level."

But Arwen was happy at RennBore, she said. The weather in San Diego would be hard to beat. Why would she want to move to New Haven?

Game on. Juliet pitched her hard, extolling the loveliness of New Haven, the Yale School of Architecture, the proximity to New York and Boston, the beauty of the state with its many small towns and cities, the vibrant cultural scene (a bit of a stretch, but hey). Then it was onto salary and benefits packages, international opportunities, which would take Arwen years more at a huge firm like RennBore. Arwen considered it, and Juliet took her out again the next night to field any questions.

She finally won Arwen over by offering her a position as Architect III, a jump that usually took a few more years for someone so young, and a step right below Juliet herself as Senior Architect/VP Design. It would be fine. Juliet would work with her closely, and Arwen was talented, smart and hardworking.

She joined DJK within a month. A press release had been sent out and picked up by every major architecture magazine. *Arwen Alexander Leaves RennBore for DJK/Connecticut as AIII.* A few interviews came Arwen's way, in which she mentioned her heroes in architecture, including Juliet and Dave Kingston (smart girl, mentioning a partner, even if Dave spent most of his time golfing and drinking scotch). Arwen worked hard. Designed well, took critiques, adjusted her designs when needed, credited other team members. There was nothing—absolutely nothing—wrong with her work.

But here's the thing about architects. Every generation, there are two or three innovative, change-the-field-forever people. I. M. Pei, Frank Lloyd Wright, Mies van der Rohe, Zaha Hadid . . . architects who invented entire schools of design. They were the geniuses who created buildings the likes of which the world had never seen before. Sometimes that was a good thing (Frank Lloyd Wright's Fallingwater), and sometimes not (Frank Lloyd Wright's Guggenheim . . . can't win 'em all). But they were the geniuses, the innovators, the type who changed the landscape, literally and figuratively.

And then there's every other architect. Ninety-five percent of the best architects in the world designed buildings and interiors that were dazzling and beautiful, but built on the shoulders of those greats. Juliet felt she was in that category—creative, energetic, sometimes even brilliant—but not someone who was going to invent a new way of thinking.

Arwen, too, was a solid designer with a lovely portfolio. A little derivative, in that she clearly borrowed from her idols, but that was the way of the world, in everything from literature to fashion. Not everyone was Lin-Manuel Miranda, but that didn't make them a bad songwriter. Not everyone was Gianni Versace, but that didn't mean they didn't make beautiful clothing.

Juliet thought Arwen had some flair. With experience, Juliet thought, Arwen could rise to Juliet's own level, and sure, maybe surpass her . . . in a decade or so, after she'd learned more about the craft and worked with more senior architects. Hopefully, Arwen would become bolder and more confident, develop her own style and voice.

And then, six months into her employment at DJK, abruptly and without explanation, Arwen became the It Girl of Architecture.

Suddenly, articles about feminism and sexism in the industry appeared, with Arwen giving quotes . . . something Juliet didn't know until the piece ran in the *Times*. It was nothing new, nothing that hadn't been said by dozens of female architects before, but it got buzz. Then

Architectural Digest asked Arwen to comment on the booming architecture in China and its impact on the future of cities, even though she'd never been to China or designed a building there.

Juliet had. She'd been lead on a massive retail and office center in Hangzhou, and an apartment building in Chengdu.

The CEO of a Fortune 100 company that DJK had just landed said, "We'd like Arwen Alexander on the team." Dave and Juliet exchanged quick glances.

"Absolutely!" Dave boomed. "You got it! She's a keeper, that one!"

All fine. Juliet had been planning to put Arwen on this project anyway. But . . . why had he asked for her by name? Why all this attention? Had Arwen hired a really good PR firm? Was she connected in ways Juliet was unaware of? It wasn't that the girl—woman—was without talent. But she was a long way from superstar. Maybe someday, but those other greats, like Zaha Hadid, had been dazzling from day one. And Arwen, as solid and reliable as she was, was not dazzling.

That was a minority opinion, apparently.

Arwen was listed as the number one Forty Under Forty in *Architectural Review*, a "bolt of lightning with her stunning designs and razor-sharp outlook."

Juliet had turned forty just three months before that article ran. Not being included . . . it stung.

Arwen was quite attractive, which didn't hurt, but nonetheless, it was a shock for Juliet to see her photo on the front page of the style section in the *Los Angeles Times*. She was asked to give workshops and even a TED talk.

Apparently, her work was setting the world on fire . . . and Juliet, her boss, was scratching her head. It was great for the firm, this sudden outpouring of adoration, but Juliet was a little . . . baffled. Glad for her success and its echoes on DJK, and yet . . . why Arwen? Juliet had been an architect for more than a decade and a half. She knew brilliance when she saw it, and Arwen was good. She could be great. She was a far cry from brilliant.

Juliet was not the only one to think so.

"I just don't get it," muttered Kathy Walker, an interior architect who'd been Juliet's first female friend at DJK. "Do you?" She lowered her voice to a whisper. "We've had better. You're *way* more talented than she is."

"We work in a subjective field," Juliet said. Kathy was a friend, but also a gossip, and if Juliet said anything that showed the slightest flicker of faith in Arwen, word would spread. Juliet would die before she seemed jealous. Women in architecture had it hard enough without other women backstabbing or gossiping about them.

"Maybe all this adoration is because she's"—Kathy looked around—"young."

Oh, that word. That terrifying word. "Don't be catty. She's doing great stuff."

But of course it had crossed her mind. Juliet was only eleven years older than Arwen. But apparently, those were akin to dog years, and it sent a quiver of fear through her, a shameful fear she couldn't admit to anyone. She'd always been a solid presence in the architecture world, often asked for quotes or sound bytes, speeches, articles.

Then, just like that, she was yesterday's news.

After Arwen had been working at DJK for a year, Juliet went out for drinks with some of her closest architect friends, all of them women. They were in Chicago for a one-day design showcase, a PR kind of thing. Arwen was in Maui, checking the site of a hotel expansion, and Juliet suspected she'd been DJK's second choice as spokesperson for the Chicago gig.

Whatever. The drinks arrived, and within seconds, the issue Juliet knew was coming arrived. "Tell us about your whiz kid," said Yvette.

"She's doing very well," Juliet said. She couldn't be anything but positive, and she suspected the group knew it.

Silence dropped over the table. "What's said in Chi-Town stays in Chi-Town?" suggested Lynn. Everyone nodded, except Juliet.

"I'm sorry, Juliet," Yvette said, "but what's the big deal with her?

She's not exactly special. Forgive me for saying so, but there it is. All of a sudden, it's like there's only one female architect in the world, while the rest of us have been slogging it out for decades."

"Maybe it's timing," Juliet said. "You know how it is. Sometimes you just get attention."

The other women murmured. A few looks were exchanged—disappointment, maybe, that Juliet wasn't going to throw her protégé under the bus.

"Do you ladies know I love opera?" Susan said. She was the oldest of the group at sixty-five and, at one time or another, had been a mentor to every other woman at the table. "I even studied it in college, believe it or not. Music performance minor."

"You're so cool," Juliet said with a smile.

Susan smiled back, her face kind. "One time, my husband and I went to hear Pavarotti sing. And from the first note out of his mouth, my body just broke out in goose bumps. Everyone in that building *knew* we were hearing the greatest tenor in three generations." She took a sip of her martini. "Then, a few years later, we heard Andrea Bocelli. You know, the handsome one?"

"He's blind, you know," said Linda.

"Yes, dear, everyone knows that," said Susan. "So we went to the concert, and Bocelli was good. Very good. It was very entertaining. The crowd was in love." She paused. "But he's no Pavarotti. He's not even a great opera singer. He's a pop star who sings opera, Elvis Presley and Christmas carols. Which is not to take away from his talent, his spark. But if you love opera, if you *know* opera, he's a mediocre singer who gives a great performance."

"By which you're saying . . ." said Lynn.

"This young woman we're discussing is no Pavarotti."

Juliet was so relieved, she closed her eyes. It wasn't just her.

The week following the conference, Santiago Calatrava, one of the actual living legends of architecture, was quoted saying Arwen Alexander was the most exciting new voice out there.

Susan sent Juliet an e-mail. Guess I was wrong about Andrea Bocelli. What do I know?

A week later, Arwen was nominated for the AIA Young Architects Award and the Moira Gemmill Prize for Emerging Architecture.

No one at DJK had ever been so recognized. Juliet's friends, those women at the table in Chicago, went silent. Arwen was on the rise, and you didn't cast aspersions on a woman on the rise no matter what she did or did not bring to your field.

It was the elephant in the room. If there were any men who shared the opinion that Arwen was a Bocelli, not a Pavarotti, they didn't dare say it, especially after Santiago had praised her.

Arwen was no dummy. Without saying a word, the dynamic in the office changed. She stopped popping into Juliet's office to chat, or asking if she wanted to grab a glass of wine before heading home. Her clothes got better—she'd always had style, but now it was Armani and Christian Louboutin, Tom Ford and Prada. She bought a Tesla. She moved from a rental in downtown New Haven to an incredibly hip and spacious loft in a former manufacturing building and had a party for the entire staff plus spouses, and did all the cooking herself. Apparently, she'd developed a passion for Northern Indian cuisine when she spent a summer there during college. Oliver, who had lived in New Delhi for a few years as a teenager, said Arwen's samosas were the best he'd ever had. Traitor.

Architects were paid well. But not that well. Family money? A rich lover? Arwen never mentioned anyone, and she lived in the loft alone. As far as Juliet knew, she was single.

Juliet still offered input and guidance on Arwen's projects, because that was her job . . . but there was that tremor. Arwen seemed to tolerate her advice now, not seek it. Dave and the rarely seen Edward Decker, the *D* in DJK and the other living partner, stopped by Arwen's office to chat when Edward graced the New Haven office with his presence. Once, it had been Juliet he stopped by to see.

It was chilling. It was as if architecture were a river, and Juliet had been a white-water rafter for all these years. Suddenly she'd been turned into a rock, the water flowing around her, the raft way, way ahead.

Well. She was a rock sitting in a conference room who had better get to work while she still had a job. Her phone chimed, reminding her the girls had a half day. Oliver had taken off three days on Christmas break, so this was definitely her turn.

Leaving the office early had never felt like a liability before.

Snap out of it, she told herself. *You have a lovely marriage.* (Which reminded her, she should have sex with Oliver tonight, because it had been almost a week and he got grumpy if he went too long. He'd been so wonderful about Dad and deserved some attention.) *You have two healthy children. (Who haven't had a full week of school since mid-September; honest to God, who sets these school calendars?) You love your job. (Even if your star is sinking, you feel helpless and you're having panic attacks in your closet.) You were raised by parents who love you. (Take the girls to see Dad, and try to get Brianna not to sob when she sees him, and also check in with Mom and see how she is, because there's something she's not telling you.)*

That smoke-jumping job looked awfully great right about now. The mountains. A cabin. A good dog. Lots of books and a woodstove, and no one around who needed anything.

Juliet felt like crying. Like crying and eating an entire box full of Dunkin' Donuts Boston Kremes.

If she'd known how hard it was to have it all, she would've asked for less.

CHAPTER FOURTEEN

Barb

John had come home, and I wasn't feeling real thrilled.

Oh, go on, now. He'd been cheating on me for God knows how long with some floozy, and now he needed a full-time caregiver, and guess who won that prize?

The six weeks without him had been hard, of course—I visited him almost every day while still handling the myriad duties of first selectman, from going to the Winter Concert at the elementary school to commissioning a summer traffic study to getting more money for the library budget, because what was a town without a decent library?

But on those nights when I got home from Gaylord, which took a solid hour and fifteen minutes, or on those even better nights when I just couldn't find the energy to go, I'd pour myself a glass of wine and make a sandwich. Watch *Broadchurch* on Netflix—gosh, what a show!—or see if Caro wanted to come over and visit. In the mornings, I got up at seven; John liked to get up at five so he could go to the gym (and now I knew why), so the extra sleep was bliss. I'd make my coffee

(I liked it stronger than John did, and always had to dump out his weak brew and wash the pot out, because God forbid he did that himself). I made oatmeal, one of the rare dishes from my childhood I had loved. John hated oatmeal. Said it gave him the dry heaves just looking at it.

I hadn't realized how much room he took up. How much space he demanded.

There was less laundry. Less noise, because John loved those punishing Russian composers. He often walked around in those silly clip shoes he wore to ride his bike. The house was immaculate again without his workout gear littering the place—the pants with the padded behind, his aerodynamic helmet, gloves, Day-Glo shirts, water bottles, running shoes. (I'd called them sneakers and been schooled in what may have been our last conversation.)

I had never lived alone. I'd gone from my parents' house to an apartment with roommates to marriage.

Living alone, I was finding, was rather wonderful. I just didn't want it *this* way, a husband trapped in a brain that no longer worked the way it used to. Almost every night, I'd wake up and think about him, not being able to speak, confused, needing help with everything from going to the bathroom to getting out of bed. Was he scared? Was he in pain? What was he thinking? Did he miss home? Did he miss WORK and all her texts and wonder why she hadn't visited him? Did he even know his children? Did he remember me?

Then the tears would slip out of my eyes, down my temples and into my hair. He was a liar and a cheater and hadn't been a good husband even without that. But no one deserved what he was going through. And I was going to have to suck up my hurt and stay with him and do my best to take care of him. And I would, because I'd meant those marriage vows, even if he'd forgotten his.

Sometimes, being an honorable person was quite the dang burden. Here I was, trapped in the in-between space of being a devoted wife and a wronged woman, a wife who'd wanted to leave my husband and was stuck with him forever now. And not even him. A husk of his former self.

He came home, requiring my dining room to be turned into his bedroom, the beautiful walnut table put in storage along with the chairs and the highboy that had been John's grandfather's. I packed it all up with Caro and Sadie one Sunday; Juliet had been in Chicago on a business trip. We made room for a hospital bed and a bureau, made sure he had ample space so he wouldn't trip and a cleared path to the downstairs bathroom, which luckily had a shower. He was brought home, and the next phase started, and I was so tired already.

Yes, I had help—LeVon Murphy was just wonderful, a cheerful, strong and handsome man who came at eight and left at four. He handled John's physical and occupational therapy, took him for walks, tried to engage him with puzzles and problem solving. Sometimes he stayed for dinner, and it was so nice, having a man who complimented me on my cooking and helped wash up. In addition to LeVon, a speech and language therapist came three times a week.

And Sadie was here, sleeping in her old room. I had to give her credit. She stepped up. She did the grocery shopping, the housework, took John to his doctors' appointments and kept a log of who said what and when. Filled his prescriptions and sat with him, talking, bringing her paints over, sometimes even bringing Brianna and Sloane to do art therapy, saying it was good for John to have the kids around. She wiped her father's face at dinner with a tenderness that made me almost jealous. Would she have done that for me? I doubted it.

Sadie and I picked at each other. I didn't mean to, and some of my comments were harmless enough—*Do you think you'll get a job?*—but Sadie always found a way to take offense. That calm sense of being alone faded with her there, tromping up and down the stairs, reading aloud to her dad, asking me question after question about his care.

Not that John seemed to notice she was here. He looked at everyone like a curious chickadee, head tilted. Or he'd fall asleep in the middle of a conversation.

Even in his current state, he could make me feel irrelevant. It wasn't a fair thought, but it came nevertheless.

One night, Sadie plunked herself down in the sitting room, where I was knitting a rainbow sweater for Sloane. John was in the dining room, and the TV we'd moved from his study was on. "Mom," she said, "I think I'm going to move out."

"Is that so?"

"Yes." There it was, the edge to her voice.

"Okay, then." Sometimes there was nothing to do but agree with my younger daughter. Truth be told, it was no picnic having her here.

"I'll come over every day after LeVon leaves and help out till Dad's bedtime."

I sighed. "I'm finding a home health aide to keep an eye on him when I'm not here."

"I just *said* I'll do it."

"And I just said no." My voice was sharp. "It's not your job to take care of your father. He'd hate that, and you know it. You've been real great, Sadie, and of course you can visit and spend as much time here as you like. But you should be living your own life. So go ahead. Move out. There's a real cute fixer-upper that just came on the market if you're looking to buy. Then again, I don't know how much you make with those paintings of yours, or if you've managed to save anything on a teacher's salary, or if that rich boyfriend of yours is ever going to propose, but let me know if I can help."

Sadie's jaw was like iron, because of course I said the wrong thing. I always did to her way of thinking. "I'll come over every day, Mom."

"Good. That'd be real nice for your father."

"Great." She stood up and left the room.

Always the two of us rubbing each other the wrong way, scraping and chafing like corduroy pants that were too tight.

John's phone chimed. I kept it with me at all times for obvious reasons.

Ah, WORK. She was a faithful correspondent, that was for sure.

Baby, me so horny! LOL!!! But totally true, too! R U back from Cali? Hope U R not too sad!!!

Broken heart, red heart, smiley face blowing kisses, a cat with heart eyes, a lipstick imprint, a smiling devil, fire and, inexplicably, a chicken. Best not to know why that poor chicken was included.

So this was love? This was what John had wanted? A semiliterate lover who communicated through tiny cartoons?

I had been texting WORK for weeks now. John's mother, may she rest in peace having died before Sadie was born, had once again gone on to her great reward . . . at least, that's what I told WORK. Guess John and his lover had never gotten around to talking about family, too busy being new and happy and horny again.

The estate, I had told the other woman, was complicated with many valuable pieces of art and furniture to be dealt with. Not to mention the house on the water in Santa Barbara. The response had been immediate:

OMG! I love SB! Babe, do U need company??? I can come help and we could spend some time together doing all sorts of dirty things! LOL!

An emoji of an eggplant had followed. Caro hooted over that one. "You are too much, Barb! Hey. If WORK is a moneygrubbing whore, she deserves what's coming."

I set my knitting aside and considered what to write. It was probably time for John to come home from his poor mother's second funeral. I put on my reading glasses, glanced to make sure Sadie wasn't hovering, and typed.

Baby, me so horny, too!!!! Not too sad, bc Mom was 105. I didn't know she was such an art collector! The Sotheby's guy went cray-cray.

John's IQ had dropped well before his accident, so I felt no compunction about making him sound like an idiot.

WORK: Really??? Can't wait to hear!!!

"I bet you can't," I muttered.

> JOHN: So many wonderful surprises! Much to discuss. When can we meet??? I miss U!!!

WORK: ANYTIME! Love you so much, tiger!!!

I sighed.

> JOHN: Will be in touch soon! Love you too, my sweet honey angel kitten!!!

Nothing appeared to be too nauseating with these two.

I then took a screenshot of the exchange and texted it to Caro.

> I'm going to meet the other woman. You in?

The answer was immediate.

Holy crap, yes.

Caro was worth her weight in diamonds.

After that, I read for a while. When it was time for me to go to bed, I got up first to check on John. Sadie was in there, just getting up from the chair next to his bed.

"I was reading to him, and he fell asleep," she said, her voice husky. "Just like he used to do for me."

"That's real nice of you, honey. I'm sure he appreciates it."

For once, there was no hostility or subtext. "Well. Good night, Mom," Sadie said. She went upstairs, the sixth stair creaking reliably, just like it had when she used to sneak out to meet Noah Pelletier.

I sat down next to John. "You used her birthday so you could text your mistress in secret," I whispered. "How do you think she'd feel about that, her perfect dad having an affair? I was in labor with her for two and a half days, John Frost. How dare you use her birthday?"

He didn't answer, as he was asleep. "You know, if you'd asked me for a divorce, I'd have burst into song, mister. I would've said yes so fast, it would've given you whiplash. But no. It was more fun to sneak around, I guess. Maybe you were never going to divorce me. After all, I'm a darn good housekeeper, aren't I?"

God! I couldn't bear it. I hated him, this man I once loved. Once, I'd felt so lucky that he'd married me. I'd taken such pride in the life we'd made. The old love, dusty from neglect, was still there, and yet, the knowledge of his affair was a corrosive acid, eating away at it.

"I'm going to meet your lover," I said. "I'll report back. Tiger."

I got up and then sat back down, fast and furious. "I tried, John. I made room for you right until you had the nerve to be surprised that I won that election. Not once did you say, 'Good job, Barb,' or 'I'm proud of you.' Not once in this entire year! Instead, you found an idiotic woman who can't even spell, because why, exactly? I wasn't good enough? Because I had the nerve to get older? Maybe this stroke is exactly what you deserved."

Tears spurted out of my eyes. Oh, the *fury*. Sometimes it felt exactly like grief.

CHAPTER FIFTEEN

Sadie

My mom, who thought she knew everything, was irritatingly correct about the little house for sale.

It had a leaking roof, one tiny bathroom on the first floor with a rusting iron tub and no shower, two bedrooms, one of which was too small to fit a twin bed (so they called it a bedroom because . . . ?) and floors that sloped so much, a marble would roll from one end of the house to the other. The kitchen was outfitted with harvest-gold appliances and Ikea's cheapest cabinets. One cupboard gaped open like a loose tooth. The kitchen was big enough for maybe four people, and the living room had stained beige carpeting and drafty windows. There was no garage, and the basement was made from stone and had a dirt floor and evidence of a recent squirrel rager, based on the litter and tiny little footprints in the dust on the workbench.

We went outside and walked around the . . . well, the structure. It wasn't quite a house just yet. Juliet closed her eyes and shook her head.

"I'll take it," I told Ellen, the real estate agent.

"Seriously?" she said. "I mean, great! It's a . . . unique property."

It was.

"You're an idiot," Juliet said, tilting her head to squint at the house. It did look straighter that way. "Looks like it'll collapse in a strong wind."

"Ah, what do you know? You're just an *architect*. By the way, do you do any pro bono work?"

She smiled a little, which was nice to see. Jules hadn't smiled much since Dad's stroke. She did have a point about the building in front of us. But I was one of the few people in Connecticut who viewed an eleven-hundred-square-foot house as spacious, and if there was another house I could afford in Stoningham before I won Powerball, it was invisible, like Wonder Woman's plane.

"I'll draw up the papers," said Ellen, getting into her car before my sanity was restored.

"You can live with me, you know," Juliet said.

"We'd kill each other. It might scar the girls, seeing their mother and aunt lying in pools of blood."

"True. Well, you have a nice view, I'll give you that."

"That's why I bought it," I said, turning around to look out to sea, like the wife of a sea captain from long ago. Or like a regular person who enjoyed pleasant views. Because the view was *incredible*. The house, teetering though it may have been, was on what had become a nature preserve, which meant it couldn't be expanded or torn down for a rebuild (which is what would've happened in a heartbeat otherwise, and a grotesque "cottage" would sit here now). Ten years ago, a monster storm had devastated this area, and none but this house had survived. The owner died in the fall, and the market for tiny, decrepit houses was soft, so I was in luck.

"You haven't signed anything yet," Juliet said. "It's my professional opinion that you shouldn't. I happen to know a few things about buildings, Sadie. This is a money pit."

"I enjoyed us getting along for ten minutes," I said.

"Seriously. You'll regret this. I can loan you some money for a rental if you need it. A rental with a flushing toilet and everything."

"I'm only staying in Stoningham till Dad gets better, and I'm not working. I'll spruce this place up, slap on some paint and sell it at a profit."

"Stop watching HGTV. It's all make-believe." She sighed and looked at me critically, as our mother taught her. "Hard to believe you have enough money for anything more than a paper bag."

"Please. I can afford an entire refrigerator box."

"You're a teacher at a Catholic school."

"It's my art, Jules. Some people actually like what I do."

She got that constipated look I loved so well.

As an architect of super-fabulous buildings, my sister could have recommended me to some of her clients, or commissioned me to make lobby art for, say, that corporate headquarters she designed in San Fran a couple of years ago.

She did not. She wasn't in charge of artwork, she said, and besides, DJK usually went with . . . *other* artists.

By which she meant *important* artists. And hey. I got it. Plus, I didn't want to make it because my sister used nepotism and threw me a bone. Still, it would've been nice to be able to turn her down (and have her competitors start a bidding war for me, but so far, nada).

I put my hands on my hips. "Well, I have my work cut out for me. Want to drive me to Home Depot?"

"Will you let me make you a list, at least?"

"No thanks! I got this." I smiled.

Her jaw hardened. Oh, it would drive her crazy to have me buy laminate flooring, some fake plants and a couple of throw pillows to sex the place up, but that was exactly my plan. There was nothing wrong with Ikea chic. I should know. I'd been living with it since college. My apartment was currently drawing $175 a night on Airbnb, thanks in large part to my new throw pillows.

I'd make this house adorable, too, thank you. And, as my mother pointed out, I did have a rich boyfriend. If he wanted to help me out, that would be quite lovely, especially as I was ninety-five percent sure he was going to propose, now that Dad's crisis had stabilized and he was on the mend.

"Instead of having me chauffeur you around, why don't you borrow the Volvo while you're home? That little shitbox you're renting is a death trap. You get hit in that, you're dead."

Death trap, money pit, shitbox. So judgy. "Can I have your Porsche instead?"

"No."

"I had to try. Sure, I'll take the Volvo. Thank you so much, Jules." It *was* awfully nice of her.

She nodded. Pushed her hair back and sighed again, looking at my house.

"Everything okay, Jules?" I asked. "Aside from Dad?"

"Sure. Listen. About Dad. I think you better . . . prepare yourself. He might be like this for the rest of his life. Which could be really short."

"Jesus. Why don't you dig his grave while you're talking?"

"Just facing facts."

"The facts are, the brain is very elastic. People have come back from far worse. Clara, that nurse at Gaylord? She said they've had people in comas who—"

"I know," she snapped. "I was there, remember?"

"Well, don't you *want* him to get better?"

"Of course I do!"

"Then stop being so pessimistic! A caregiver's attitude can really affect—"

"Get in the car, okay? I have to help Brianna with a history project."

Two days later, it was official. I was a property owner.

My house—such nice words, *my house*!—did need a bit more work than perhaps I acknowledged, now that I was here. Alexander, who was in Sausalito at the moment, the poor bastard, had very sweetly covered the cost of moving my furniture from Juliet's to here, and the movers had just left after cursing and sweating and wrestling my bed up the narrow stairs, for which they received a generous tip. Otherwise, I had a couch, a table for two, a chair and some pots and pans and kitchen stuff. A couple of lamps. My books and pictures were still at Juliet's, but I wanted to sleep here tonight and get the feel of the place.

I also wanted to put some distance between my mother and me. Her disapproval of whatever I did, had done and would do seeped into every interaction we had. Even my care of Dad seemed to irk her, and her own lack of tenderness irked me right back. I had paintings to do, and she hated the smell. Even though their house was huge, there never seemed to be enough room for the two of us.

Hence, my purchase.

Perhaps not the best decision.

Did I mention I had no neighbors? Fifteen years in New York City had made me used to that safety in numbers thing. In the entire time I'd lived there, I'd never once been scared.

But I was kind of scared now. What if Connecticut had a serial killer? What if those giant coyotes that ate cats marked me as a slow runner?

I should get a dog. I *would* get a dog. I glanced at my watch. Shit. Six o'clock and already dark. Allegedly, my heat was on, but it was cold in here. I did have a fireplace, but Jules told me I'd burn to death if I tried to make a fire.

Maybe I'd go to my parents' house to sleep. Get the dog tomorrow, preferably a large, vicious, loyal-to-only-me type, and see if Alexander would be back from California and wanted to spend the weekend in scenic Connecticut doing a little house renovation. We'd be a team, like that irritating couple on the house-flipping show that I did indeed watch. Except that we'd be adorable. In fact, maybe we'd get our own show. I knew art and had great taste, and Alexander was rich and photogenic. What else did you need?

The knock on the door made me scream.

"Jesus!" yelled the person. I peeked out the window.

It was Noah.

No baby this time. Just him, looking irritable and beautiful.

"Hi," I said, opening the door.

He didn't answer.

"Hello, Noah," I said, enunciating.

"Your mother sent me."

I sucked in a breath of cold air. "Why? Is my dad okay?"

"He's fine. She wanted me to check your house." I closed my eyes in relief. "But I can go if you want. Which would be my preference."

"You're so very sweet, Noah. Come on in. What little heat I have is racing out of here."

He came in, brushing past me.

Damn. He smelled so good—wood and polyurethane and laundry detergent. "How's your baby?" I asked.

He deigned to allow half his mouth to twitch in a smile. "He's great."

I nodded. "Good. Well. What do you think?"

"Money pit."

"That's what Jules said. I'm glad you let your hair grow again, by the way." *No, Sadie. Nope. Don't say that. Too late. You did.* "I saw your picture on Facebook. That's all. Nothing big. I wasn't stalking you." *Please stop.* "It was when you were engaged, that's all. All our classmates were talking about it." *Sigh.*

He just looked at me with those dark, dark eyes. As opposed to looking at me with his teeth, for example. God. I needed a drink.

You have a boyfriend, some distant part of my brain sang happily. *He's very nice to you! You almost always have an org—*

"I don't like the sound of that furnace," Noah said. "Okay if I go downstairs?"

"Sure! Yeah! It's super dark, though, because there's no light down there. Which is what happens in the absence of light. Darkness."

"Are you drunk?" he asked.

"I wish. I'm just feeding off all that brooding masculinity of yours." I snorted and regretted it deeply.

Noah sighed, took a flashlight out of his toolbox, which I hadn't noticed before, and found the cellar door, which was easy, because it was right in front of him.

I took a few cleansing breaths. Texted Alexander that I missed him.

It would just take some getting used to, seeing Noah again. He was my first love. Of course I still had a soft spot for him. There would always be a place in my heart for—

"Sadie! Can you come down here and hold the flashlight, please?"

"Coming!" I groped my way down the stairs. Lightbulbs. I definitely needed to buy some lightbulbs. Shouldn't have dismissed Jules and her list quite so fast. Noah was at the hulking black thing (furnace, I assumed), doing something with his hands. Something manly and hard and dirty.

He handed me the flashlight, which I pointed in his eyes. "Sorry," I said, shining the light at his feet.

"Your filter is filthy."

"So are my . . . never mind. Filthy filter. Got it. Should I call someone? Or buy something?"

"You have someone." Oh, my heart! "I'll be right back."

"Are you—" Nope. He was already up the stairs. I heard my front door bang closed.

I had to get a grip. Yes, he was gorgeous. What did I expect? That he'd become Nick Nolte in my absence? And yes, that brooding Jon Snow act was doing things to my lady parts.

But he had a child, and I had a serious, long-term, almost engagement going on, and Noah didn't even want to be friends. I could respect that.

Except it seemed to trigger dirty thoughts that had the added benefit of irritating him, which, I had to admit, was kind of fun. Maybe I was just overtired. Maybe I needed something to distract me from Dad's condition, which made me cry if I thought about anything other than a full recovery. Every time I thought about him, lost in his own brain, panic slithered around my heart.

Whatever the case, I shouldn't mess with Noah.

But once, we'd been so happy together.

Noah came thumping down the stairs. "This is a furnace filter. You need to change it once a month on your model. Watch me so you can do it yourself next time."

I watched. It didn't seem difficult, not in those capable hands. That frickin' beautiful hair. His soft voice. I bet he was a great dad.

"All done."

"Okay. Thank you." Finally, a normal sentence. "Are you seeing anyone these days?"

"Not your business."

"Sorry."

We went upstairs—him in front, which gave me a perfect view of his ass, and I'm sorry, how could I miss it? The radiators were clicking with what I assumed was heat.

"I appreciate this, Noah."

"Don't do any construction on this house without checking with me, all right? I might not like you anymore, but I don't want you dying. Your mother would be crushed."

"Or relieved. But yes, I see your point."

He finally looked me in the eye, and his expression softened a little. "I really am sorry about your dad."

"He's getting better. You know, when it first happened, I was scared, but he's . . . he's good. He's improving."

"I brought Marcus over to see him the other day. You were at the grocery store, LeVon said. I hope that's all right. We, uh . . . we visited him at Gaylord, too. Figured it would be okay."

The image of my first love, bringing his beautiful baby to my father, punched me in the heart. "Thank you, Noah," I whispered. My eyes were suddenly wet. "It's really kind of you."

He nodded once. "Well. Enjoy your new place."

"Thanks. Have a nice night."

"Don't tell me what to do."

And there it was, that tug of a smile on his beautiful face. Then he was gone, and my house was warmer because of him. The quiet settled around me, bringing with it all the memories of how Noah and I had failed each other.

CHAPTER SIXTEEN

Sadie

I thought when Noah came to visit the city I was obsessed with, he'd understand. He'd never been to New York before, aside from the obligatory eighth-grade field trip. I wanted him to drink in the architecture, the life and pulse of the city. I thought he'd appreciate the glittering skyscrapers and gracious brownstones, the cobbled, uneven streets of SoHo, the thrum and rush of noise, the smells of street food and the variety, my God, the *newness* of every single block.

He came to visit for the first time on Columbus Day weekend of my freshman year. He didn't love a thing. In fact, he hated it. "How can you live here?" he asked the second night, rubbing his forehead. "You can't hear yourself think. How do you paint?"

My mouth dropped open. "I'm getting really good!"

"You were good already."

I made a disgusted noise. "Anyone can do a pretty landscape, Noah," I said patiently. Landscapes had been my forte in high school, and they won me those prizes at our town's art contest (which meant nothing, I had quickly learned). "I'm really growing as an artist. It's mind-blowing, what I don't know yet, and how good I could get."

I stopped in front of a gallery; we were in SoHo, and you couldn't swing a cat in this neighborhood without hitting a posh space staffed by black-clad beautiful people who spoke three languages. "*This* is art," I said, pointing to the sole oil painting in the window. "It's so much more than a pretty picture. This says something."

"Looks like blobs of black tar to me," he said.

"It's a statement on materialism and abstraction," I said. "There's a tension here, a grittiness and impact. It's a dissonant whole worldview about what's real and what we want to be real."

"It's black blobs, hon," he said. "That painting you did of the blood moon rising? Now *that's* beautiful."

I sighed. "Yeah, well, I'd kill to have been the one to come up with this. You know how much it goes for?" I knew, because my class had had a field trip here just last week (hence my knowledge of dissonance and such). "Three hundred *thousand* dollars, Noah."

His eyebrows jumped. "Jesus. But then you'd have to look at the goddamn thing. Whereas if someone bought one of your paintings, they could actually feel happy."

"Noah . . . knock it off." But I smiled, even if I felt somehow slighted by his compliment. Happiness because of a painting? How *plebeian*. Why not just frame a picture of your dog? (I mean, yes, I did have a picture of my dog, the late, great Pokey, who died when I was eleven.) But art was supposed to do more.

I went home for Christmas break, but only for ten days, because I was going to Venice for the remainder. And oh, that beautiful city was everything I'd imagined. It spoke right to my heart, the crumbling buildings, the canals, the decrepit, genteel beauty, the patterns of bricks, the beauty imbued in everything, even the rainspouts. I loved the garbagemen who chatted animatedly with each other, smoking, but who paused to give me an appreciative glance with "*ciao, bellissima*." The riotous glory of stained glass in every church, the beautiful window boxes and brightly painted shutters. I took the water taxi to Murano and watched handsome men blowing glass, their arms brown and scarred. The beauty of the city, the foreignness of it, filled up parts of my soul I didn't even know I had.

When I got back to school, I signed up for a summer session in Barcelona and found a waitressing job so I could pay for it.

A quick trip home, travel on break, back to New York. It became my pattern. My painting changed; the gentle landscapes that had gotten me into Pace were cast aside. Now I did mixed-media and monochromatic paintings. I tried sculpting. I started wearing only black (I know, I know). I got my nose pierced.

Noah visited when he could, which wasn't often. He was apprenticing as a carpenter, working six days a week. When we were together, in bed, skin against skin, his light scruff gently scraping my cheek, our fingers intertwined, the red glow returned. But he kept asking about the next break, when I'd come home. When I did go back to Stoningham, I felt itchy—my mother, still the same but only on more committees; Juliet, securing her status as favorite by giving birth to a girl she and her perfect husband named after my mother.

And Noah. His love was so big and fierce it was like a dragon, waiting for me.

I could feel the resentment growing in him.

My return visits consisted of Noah and me sleeping together whenever and wherever possible, and seeing the two friends I'd kept in touch with from high school. My dad was the only one who asked me the questions I wanted to answer, who listened with real interest as I described the wonder of the Duomo di Milano's rooftop, the hundreds of different shades of green in Ireland, that moment when I stood at the very tip of South Africa, one foot in the Indian Ocean, one in the Atlantic, and compared the shades of blue. He was the only one who didn't ask when I was going to come home, the only one who believed I could succeed out in the world.

New York had its hooks in me, and I believed with all my heart that I would make it.

When you're a student in that city, all you see around you is what you could become. It is a city of wanting—wanting to live in that neighborhood, have that view, stride through that lobby every day. Wanting to show at this gallery, eat at this restaurant, be a regular at that bar. Wanting to shop at that boutique, wear those clothes, be invited to that person's parties. Wanting to know all the city's secrets.

I started bicycling all over the city, and the overriding emotion I felt was a combination of wonder and hunger. When I saw a woman who seemed to have it all, I wanted to be her—the confidence, the look, the way she belonged, the casual grace and comfort she exuded just walking down the street or sitting in a restaurant. Me, I'd almost killed myself gawking at a particularly beautiful building on the Upper East Side, and a cop yelled at me when I attempted to zip through the intersection on a yellow light, which apparently wasn't done in the Big Apple. Everywhere I went, I wondered, *Who* are *these people? How do they pull it off? How do they make it?*

I wanted to weave myself into the fiber of this city. I wanted to paint it, eat it, breathe it, own it. I wanted to be right without even wondering what right was. I wanted to live in a building with character and flair. I wanted to walk into an art exhibition and have people murmur—"Oh, my God, Sadie Frost is here." I would be that strangest anomaly—a warm, welcoming, super-successful New Yorker who knew everything and shared everything. The parties I would throw! The students I would mentor! The love and admiration of my peers and teachers! I would be celebrated, and I would give back.

Except I wasn't, and I didn't.

The thing about going to art school is that you're surrounded by talent. I might've been the best artist in my graduating high school class, but as I hit the end of my sophomore year of college, I started to see that I was . . . average. Skilled. We'd *all* started off as talented kids. All of us had different strengths. But while I'd been great at the technical aspects of art, now was the time where my professors were using words like *fragility*, *vision*, *articulation* . . . and they weren't using them on my pieces.

That was okay. I'd learn. I'd change. I could refine my voice and clarify my point of view. My travels had deepened and educated me—didn't I backpack through Europe with ten bucks in my pocket? Didn't I sleep under a tree in the Parc Municipal in Luxembourg? I bought breakfast for the old woman who begged for food outside Temple Expiatori del Sagrat Cor in Barcelona and talked to the heroin addicts of Manchester. Surely all those things made me a *real* artist. I would take it all and express it, beauty and darkness both, hope and despair, rage, loneliness, love . . .

"Sadie," my professor sighed during my senior year conference, "you have to stop trying to be what you're not." She pointed to the angry scribbles of charcoal. "This is what you *think* art should be."

I tried not to let my confusion show. Wasn't that the point?

She tilted her head. "Do you even know what you want to say with your art?"

"Of course I do," I said. "It's the melding of rage and darkness with the, um, the scope of architectural beauty and . . . uh, poverty. But hope, too. That things will change. For the better."

She grimaced.

"How is this worse than Zach's work?" I asked, because yes, my classmate had also done a series of black charcoal abstracts and gotten a show at Woodward Gallery in fucking SoHo.

My teacher folded her hands. "Zach's work shows a modernist fusion and battle of urban life and nature. It's a poem to the fragility and strength of humanity. The minimal quality of movement, the strength of message . . . if you don't see the difference, Sadie, I'm concerned."

I cried on the phone that night to Noah. "She's wrong," he said. "You're fantastic, Sadie. You are. You just have to . . . I don't know. Find your audience."

"You mean, paint pictures of sunsets and sell them to the summer people?"

"Well, yeah. What's wrong with that, Special?"

It was the wrong time to use that nickname, beloved though it had always been. I had just been told I was anything but special. "I want more, Noah! I don't want to be stuck in that stupid town, painting stupid pictures of stupid clouds!"

He answered with silence.

Right. I'd given him that painting of clouds, and he'd just hung it in the little apartment he'd rented over the hardware store. He'd sent me a picture of it there.

"I'm sorry," I said belatedly.

A few weeks later was the senior art show. Our school sent out invitations to art buyers and critics, gallery owners and collectors. Some students got a big break this way, and I was hopeful, anxious . . . and a little desperate.

Noah came, as well as my parents. "Your stuff is the best here," he said, ignoring the fact that everyone seemed clustered around Zach the charcoal boy and Aneni, a woman who painted strange animals with miraculous detail.

My work *wasn't* the best. I knew it, and so did everyone except Noah. Dad told me he was so proud of me and couldn't wait to see what was next . . . which, in my funk, I interpreted as "keep trying and maybe you'll get better someday." My mother bought one of Zach's paintings. "Imagine what this will be worth in ten years," she said, and I wanted to bite her.

I latched on to one woman who owned a gallery in Greenpoint, my voice high and fast as I tried to describe the references to Warhol and my love of Venice in my sculpture, only to find that her gallery had closed last month and she was going back to school to become a physician's assistant. The art critic from the *Village Voice* glanced at my display as she moved across the space and didn't even slow. My heart cracked.

I didn't sell a single piece, except to my dad.

My parents were staying at a hotel; Noah came back to my dorm room. My mind buzzed and fretted as I swallowed the sharp tears in my throat.

I hadn't been discovered. All those trips, the thousands of photos I'd taken, the open heart and mind I'd kept for four years had resulted in the *Village Voice* reviewer walking right past and my father pity-buying the Zach knockoff.

I'd have to keep working. Be more daring. Be different. It would be hard, but wasn't it better this way? Who cared if you were discovered at a school show, especially at Pace (which had been good enough until this moment but had now completely failed me as an institution).

No. A much better story would be of Sadie Frost who, believe it or not, was told she was unoriginal by her own art professor! I'd be in the same league as J. K. Rowling, who was rejected a zillion times, or Gisele Who Married Tom Brady, once told her nose was too big for modeling. Bill Gates. Oprah. I'd be in great company, goddamnit.

Then Noah got down on one knee.

"I know we're young," he said. "But I've loved you since I was fifteen years old, Special. Marry me. Come home. I promise we'll be happy."

The timing . . . it really sucked.

"Are you kidding me?" I asked, my voice squeaking with disbelief.

His dark eyes lost their light. "No."

"Noah. Honey. Come on. I haven't accomplished one thing I want to. I can't marry you! I can't quit before I even get started!"

He stood up. "I'm not *asking* you to quit. I just want us to be together. I love you. You love me. Why are we wasting time?"

"Because I have to be here!" I said. "Noah, I've never wanted to live in Stoningham. That's your dream. Mine is something different. You move *here*, and we'll see how it goes."

He wasn't going to move here. It was loud. Dirty. Crowded. The air smelled bad.

"I have to stay here," I said. "And you know what? I love it here. This is where I have to be right now. If I leave, I'll never prove I'm good enough." My voice broke.

"Sadie. You're more than good enough."

"You're the only one who thinks so, and Noah, I'm sorry, you just don't know that much about art."

"I do know about you, though."

Tears slid down my cheeks. "Then you know I have to stay."

"I've saved money so we can travel, and I'll build us a house where you can have a studio with the right light—"

"You're not listening to me. We're twenty-two, Noah. I'm not getting married this young. And I don't want to move back to Connecticut. Maybe ever."

He closed his eyes.

"So let's just keep going this way," I said, reaching for his hand. "Long-distance. We'll figure something out. Weekend lovers. It's not perfect, but it's enough."

"No. It's not."

The weight of those words seemed to squeeze all the air from the room. "Are you going to dump me because I have ambition, Noah?" I asked. My throat felt like I'd swallowed a razor blade.

"I'm just saying you can have ambition and work from anywhere in the world. I'm asking you to make a life with me. I thought it's what we both wanted. You can't raise a family if one parent doesn't live in the same state."

"Okay, it's way too early to be thinking about raising a family," I said. "You can work from anywhere, too, Noah. You could get a job here in a heartbeat. There's a housing boom, in case you didn't notice."

"I don't want to live here. I hate this city."

"Well, I hate Stoningham."

"No, you don't! You just think you have to because it's small and quiet. It's not part of the story you made up about how New York would fall over itself when you came to town."

Oh. His words sliced me right through the heart. They were so big and painful—and true—that I was frozen where I stood.

And then I said, "So you won't move for me, and I won't move for you. I guess we're at an impasse." I couldn't bring myself to say, *I guess we're breaking up.* Not to the wild boy who loved me. Whose pet name for me was Special. Who lit up my heart in such glorious, vibrant, pulsating color.

"All right, then." His eyes were shiny. I'd never seen him cry before, and I couldn't now. I looked away. "I'll wait for you, Sadie," he said, his voice rough. "But not forever."

"Same." The lump in my throat was strangling me. I still couldn't meet his eyes, and while I was staring out the window, he left.

At dinner that night, my mother asked, "Why isn't Noah here?"

"We're taking a break," I answered, the words wooden and hard in my mouth. I drained my martini, even though I hated martinis, but it was what Zach had ordered the last time we'd all gone out, and . . . and God, I was so fucking unoriginal.

My dad squeezed my hand. "These things happen," he said kindly. "Don't worry, sugarplum."

"Marriage is an outdated institution," Mom said. Dad sighed and let go of my hand.

I cried so much that for the next month, there were salt deposits in my eyelashes. It felt like Noah had slammed the door on my pulsing heart. Why did *I* have to move? Why wouldn't he even *try* living here? Why was there no compromise? What was this sexist bullshit?

And then I'd flip. *Should* I move home? What would happen to me if I did? Would I hate him for cutting my dreams short? How long was I going to try to be an artist in this vicious, competitive city? Was he right? Did I want five black-haired babies? The truth was, I wasn't sure. I didn't hate babies, but I didn't stare at them or fawn over them like some of my friends.

He would wait, he'd said. Apparently in silence, because we didn't talk to each other for a month.

Not many high school couples stay together, I rationalized. Not many twenty-two-year-old men really know what they want. Sure, I could marry Noah, and within a decade, we'd be stale and old and bitter, scratching to make ends meet in a town that catered to the wealthy. Our kids would grow up in the weighted gloom the way I had, tiptoeing around their parents' disappointment in each other. We'd inevitably divorce, and those five kids and I would resent him. Or worse, they'd love him better. Who wouldn't?

I'd picture his face, his wild beauty and curly hair, the rare smile with the power of the sun, and I'd cry again.

But I had to try. I'd always only wanted to be a painter, and I knew I had to give it my best shot. I had just graduated. It was too early to call myself a failure.

With a little help from my dad, I was able to rent a shared apartment in Hell's Kitchen, the only part of Manhattan that had resisted gentrification. It was a grubby, stuffy place with two roommates, not counting the cockroaches. Mala never left the apartment and barely spoke, just sat with her face practically touching her phone, thumbs twitching away. (I had no idea how she paid her bills, if she worked, if she had friends or family . . . She never offered anything.) Sarah was a violinist and only came home with her friends to cook giant vegan meals and leave all their dirty dishes in the tiny kitchen for days at a time.

Two months after my graduation, there was a knock on the door. I opened it to see Noah standing there with a duffel bag. I burst into tears and wrapped myself around him, sobbing with relief and love.

"I'll try it. Okay? I'll try." His eyes were shiny again, and we fell into bed without another word.

He got a job in construction—not finish construction, which was what he did back home—trim work and custom cabinets and, occasionally, a piece of furniture. Here, he worked with a company that built skyscrapers—Juliet had connections and got him the job. So every day, he went to work with metal and cement, thirty or more stories above the ground.

Noah was afraid of heights. I remembered the summer I got him to jump off a rock into the Sound, and how he'd been shaking, how it took half an hour of my talking him into it, and when he did and we surfaced in the briny water, he'd kissed me, and I pushed his wet curls off his face and loved him so, so much. I knew he was doing this for me, just as he had jumped for me, too.

I worked, too, waitressing at a sleek restaurant in Tribeca (hoping my proximity to the heart of the art world would grant me a lucky break). I made a website featuring my artwork, dropping in the fact that I was (probably) a distant relative of Robert Frost . . . anything that would help. It didn't. During the days, I painted in the tiny living room, my easel on the couch because there wasn't enough floor space for me, the canvas, my paints and brushes, and Mala, staring at her phone, cackling occasionally.

Noah and I didn't have a lot of leisure time together, but at least we were here. When we could, we'd take walks, because that's the best thing to do in New York. We'd poke around St. Mark's Place, or get some street meat near Central Park. I told him about the city, the history, the art, the famous people who'd thrived here and loved it here.

He was trying. I could see that. And he was failing. To him, the city was too loud, too hard, too full of chaos. He didn't sleep well, and dark circles appeared under his eyes. He didn't smile as much as he used to. He had always been the quiet one in our relationship, but now, he was rivaling crazy Mala in silence.

As Heathcliff needed the moors, so my wild boy needed to go home. Stoningham was as lovely a town as there was, but I knew it wasn't the pretty streets and green that Noah loved. It was the birdsong, the tide, the sound of the wind in the marsh grass, the way a storm would roll up the coast and light up the horizon with lightning. The deep woods with their three-hundred-year-old oaks and maples, the farmland and stone walls that wandered through forest and field, marking out the history of the land. He missed working with wood;

his job was now pouring cement. He missed his parents and knowing everyone he ran into.

One night, I woke up and looked at him. He was asleep, his lashes like a fanned sable brush on his cheeks, the scruffy beard that never seemed to fill out. He'd lost a little weight, and he didn't have it to lose. With his arm over his head, his ribs seemed too sharp.

My city was hurting him.

In the morning, I made him breakfast as Mala stood near the window with her goddamn phone. "Mala, could you give us a minute?" I asked. She shot me a dark look and stomped to her room.

"I've been thinking," I said to Noah, setting his eggs and toast down in front of him. "I think you should move back, honey. I know you hate it here."

He took a deep breath, the relief clear on his face. "Will you come, too?"

"No. I have to stay, and you have to leave."

"Are you breaking up with me?"

"No. I just can't stand seeing you so unhappy." My eyes filled. "I love you, after all."

He looked at his plate. "I love you, too. I want a life with you, with kids and everything, but I can't wait forever."

"Fair enough." Was it, though? Was it fair to ask someone to give up trying to get what they'd always, *always* wanted?

It was a wretched goodbye. I cried. A lot. My tiny bed seemed huge without him. And yet . . . and yet it was easier, too, without him looking like a beaten dog, without him silently judging my paintings, knowing he thought I should be drawing puffy clouds or dogs romping on the beach, rather than trying to stretch and grow. I missed him. I was glad he was gone. I loved being here, doing what I was. I hated being without him.

I tried to get an agent and absorbed their feedback—*nice color palette but the content is a bit too familiar . . . once you've honed your eye . . . not taking new clients at this time . . . have you considered taking an art class?* I had taken four *years* of art classes, for crying out loud! I could teach art classes! I had a double degree, thank you very much.

That was okay, though. Content too familiar . . . I could use that. Every failure, I told myself, was a step closer to success, even if it didn't feel that way.

I lugged my portfolio to the galleries who would see me, and sent countless e-mails to those who wouldn't. I was suckered into paying hundreds of dollars to be featured in a show for a week . . . the "gallery" a former garage that still stank of diesel, the promised opening consisting of cheap wine in plastic cups, with not even a dozen people attending. I entered contests, paying the fees with my hard-earned waitressing money, never once placing. But I tried to learn and absorb from every experience. New York was a harsh teacher, but the best teacher, too.

Months passed. A year. Noah came to visit twice, and I went home to Stoningham to see my parents and nieces from time to time. We were still together. We talked on the phone almost every day. Then less. Then a little less.

My art school friends started leaving the city . . . It was so expensive, so competitive. Only Aneni stayed—even Zach, my professor's favorite student, left for Cincinnati and a job at an advertising company. *So much for your wunderkind*, I wanted to say.

Aneni, she of the amazing and bizarre animal drawings, was our school's pride and joy. She was showing at all the hot places and guest lectured at the Art Students League. Every time she had an opening, I was invited, and she hugged me and introduced me around to her friends, gallery owners, critics. Once in a while, someone would say, "Send me your info" or "Stay in touch," but it never leveraged into anything.

Aneni . . . she had a true gift. You could see it a mile away, because her paintings were like nothing I'd ever seen before. I was so happy for her, because she was incredibly nice, but I couldn't lie. I was also jealous. Really, really jealous. How had she done it? Her viewpoint was so clear, her drawings incredibly precise, beautiful and odd. Was it because she was from Zimbabwe that she had such a different point of view? Why did I have to grow up in Connecticut, a state no one (except Noah—and my mother) took seriously?

Of course, I tried to figure out what my art was missing. I knew I could be better, clearer, more. As the months passed, I stayed resolutely openhearted. I took classes when I could afford them, listened to my teachers and tried, so hard, to be better. I pored over the great works at MoMA, the Guggenheim, the Met, the Frick, the Whitney. I went to galleries and studied the paint strokes, the textures, the voices.

I still loved painting with all my heart. It was more like painting didn't love me. Or the art world didn't. I'd stare into gallery windows and think, *Is that piece really so special, or did someone just anoint it?* And if it was anointed, how could I get some of that holy oil, hm?

Then one of my professors sent me a link to a teaching job at St. Catherine's, a small Catholic elementary school in the Bronx. I applied, and the rather terrifying nun, Sister Mary, seemed to like me. I was good with kids for the same reason I didn't seem to burn for them—to me, they were entertaining little aliens. Wanting kids never felt as real to me as painting did. I knew what I wanted there. Kids? They were . . . nice. Fun. Kinda cute.

At any rate, I took the job. I had a solid education, appreciated health care and didn't mind the tiny paycheck, since waitressing was pretty lucrative.

Carter, who taught third grade, took me under his wing, and suddenly, I had new friends, not in the art world. Normal people, many of whom had been at St. Cath's for decades and had children older than I was. There was a handful of us in our twenties and thirties.

The job was nice. The art room was bright and cheery, and I got hugged a lot.

Noah was furious. If I could teach in the Bronx, why not Stoningham? He saw it as a betrayal, and we stopped speaking for a while. Fine. The way he seemed to be watching and waiting for me to give up made me want to kick him, anyway. Then he sent me a card with a bluebird on the front. Inside, he'd written, "I still love you." Nothing else.

I made him a pastel, one of those easy skyscapes that virtually anyone could draw, and wrote on the back, "I still love you, too."

So we weren't quite apart, even if we weren't together.

When we saw each other the next time I went to Stoningham, we were practically strangers.

"How's teaching?" he asked as we sat in his mother's kitchen.

"It's really nice." It was so strange to feel awkward around him, of all people on earth. We seemed to be having trouble making eye contact.

"Painting going okay?" he asked.

"Yep." I didn't tell him about the galleries and rejections and meh feedback, not wanting to give him ammo in his argument for me to come back home. "How's carpentry going?"

"Good."

"Great."

We'd never been like this before. He drove me to New London to get the train, and when I got my ticket, he kissed me, hard and fierce and beautiful, and if we'd kissed like that when we first saw each other, maybe things would've been different.

I still waitressed downtown. I grew to hate Mala, who never even tried to be nice. I cleaned up after Sarah, who was a pig but pleasant. I painted and critiqued my own work and painted more, still not able to pinpoint what I was trying to accomplish with my work, other than make somebody see its value.

But something started to happen. Two years out of college, no longer shielded by my student status, I *was* becoming a New Yorker. I knew which subways to take, which street would be clogged with tourists, how to avoid the Yankees fans swarming to the stadium for a day game. I didn't worry about what to wear and knew which boutiques were cool and cheap. I painted all summer, and my work was getting better. I even sold a few pieces at those studio open houses where you paid to play.

Then one of the moms at St. Catherine's approached me. She was an interior decorator and wondered if I'd do pieces on commission to match the rooms she was doing. It was too hard, she said, to find art that matched exactly right. Maybe she could give me some paint colors and fabric swatches, and I could make something that would fit on the wall she had in mind?

I didn't hesitate in saying yes. Why the hell not? Would Aneni? Never.

My first piece for Janice, the decorator mom, was a ten-by-five-foot painting for over a couch. "Here's the couch fabric, and the throw pillows," she said, handing me swatches of fabric. "Make it with some texture in it, swirly, you know? Like that one with the stars in it by the dude who cut off his ear? Super! Oh, and sign it. My client will love having an original piece."

So I made it—an oil painting in sage, apricot and lavender with swirly brushstrokes (like Van Gogh, you betcha). Was it a complete sellout? Yes, it was. Did I earn five hundred bucks? Yes, I did.

Janice was thrilled. She came back to me again, and then again, and then it became part of her selling point: original artwork made *just for your house*. It gave me an idea, and I contacted half a dozen more decorators. Selling out, with the emphasis on sell. I was loyal to Janice and kept my prices low, but I asked for triple that with the other folks, and they didn't blink. Apparently, some artists were quite fussy about being told what to do and how to do it. Not me.

Later that year, I quit my waitressing job (which never did produce any contacts) and ditched the horrible little apartment in Hell's Kitchen, Mad Mala and Sloppy Sarah. Juliet alerted me to a "motivated seller" with a place in Times Square (the worst neighborhood in all five boroughs to any true New Yorker). But the apartment was affordable, and nicer than I could've gotten in any other neighborhood. Juliet loaned me the money for a down payment (we artists had no pride), and just like that, I had a one-bedroom place of my own, lit up at night by the garish lights of enormous, flashing advertisements.

I still tried to paint more than just the couch paintings, as I took to calling them. I still took the occasional class, still entered contests with influential judges, still sent e-mails to those galleries that could make a career. I was still young. But however mundane, I was also selling art . . . made, alas, to match comforters or bathroom tile. Between that and teaching the little darlings at St. Catherine's, I was making a living. At painting. Not a lot of people could say that. Not even Zach of Cincinnati.

Besides, it would make another great story, I told myself. Philip Glass had once been a cabdriver. Kurt Vonnegut had sold cars. David Sedaris had been an elf at Macy's. Oprah Winfrey had worked at a grocery store.

"This is an early Sadie Frost!" someone might brag someday of my couch paintings. That purple-and-blue horror I'd done to cover a sixty-inch flat-screen TV? It might sell for millions.

Noah still came to visit, but I could sense his heart hardening toward me. It almost felt like he wanted me to fail. He viewed my apartment as proof I didn't want to get married, but for crying out loud, we were twenty-four years old. I *didn't* want to get married! Not now! I was getting tired of his broody bullshit. He was an artist, too, though he hated when I said it. Only in bed did we recapture that beautiful, fierce glow and remember why we were together.

I settled into this new phase of my adulthood, one in which I could pay my bills and go out for dinner once in a while, get cable, if not HBO. Carter lived on the Upper West Side (family money) and he and I hung out a lot. One of Janice's clients asked to take me to coffee to thank me for her "stunning" watercolor, and we started going to yoga classes together. Alexa, the sixth-grade math teacher, and I both loved to wander through the New York Botanical Garden, which wasn't far from St. Catherine's.

I made good use of the city, believe me . . . I went to author readings at the 92nd Street Y and student recitals at Juilliard. My father came to visit, the only other person in our family who loved New York—not even Juliet, the architect, enjoyed being here. But Dad loved it. He thought my apartment was perfect, and loved walking as much as I did. We went out for dinner to my favorite little Italian place in the Village, and then meandered through Washington Square Park, where some kid from NYU was doing ballet while her friend played the violin. Sometimes, Dad would even stay over, insisting on sleeping on the pullout couch rather than taking my bed. "It's fun, sugarplum," he said, and we talked and talked.

He understood my ambition. "I wanted to be a writer," he told me once. "Law school was supposed to be temporary. But then, you know . . . we moved to Stoningham, and your mom loved it so much, and then Juliet came along. It never seemed like the right time to quit my job and try to write a novel."

"You could still do it, Dad!" I said. "There's no age limit. You're retired now! You should start tomorrow!"

"Well . . . I don't know about that. I think the urge is gone now. Besides, your mother thinks I'm enough of an annoyance without me talking about a crime novel."

"She'd probably love for you to have a hobby." And get out of her space, I thought. But she wasn't exactly the encouraging type (unless your name was Juliet Elizabeth Frost).

"Well. I'm very proud of you, Sadie. Not everyone is brave enough to go for it, and here you are. My fierce little girl, making it in the Big Apple."

No one else felt that way. No one had said they were proud of me in a long, long time. Noah used to, but not anymore, not if it meant me staying here. Our love for each other was becoming a clenched fist of frustration and uncertainty.

Love is not all you need. Don't believe that lie.

On my twenty-fifth birthday, Noah called. "I need to see you," he said, and it didn't sound promising. We weren't a couple, not really, not in his eyes, and yet we weren't not a couple. I gathered we were about to come to a conclusion.

When I saw him in Grand Central Station, my old love for him hit me like a wave, tumbling me in its force. I still loved him. I'd always love him. And when he saw me, his face softened just a little, an almost smile there on his lips. He never could grow a proper beard, but he looked sixteen if he shaved, and it was so . . . so endearing. My heart glowed that scarlet color that only Noah could bring.

"Hey, stranger," I said, and gave him a big hug. We hadn't seen each other in months, and he seemed bigger—broader shoulders, more muscle, and there was a sudden lump in my throat at the idea that my wild boy was now a man.

He wanted to go to a nearby restaurant and "get this out of the way."

"Sure thing," I said, nervousness and irritability fluttering in my stomach. I took him to a tourist-trap Irish pub just across the street, and we ordered beers and burgers. He could barely look at me.

So there was someone else, I guessed, and for a minute, I had to bend my head so I wouldn't cry.

"How've you been?" I asked, my voice a little rough.

"I want you to marry me," he said.

My head jerked back up. Not what I expected.

He was scowling.

"I want you to marry me and come home. I love you. I've never loved anyone but you, Sadie. But I'm not waiting anymore."

"This sounds vaguely like a threat, not a proposal," I said.

He didn't answer. The waitress brought us our beers and wisely slipped away.

"Sadie . . ." He looked away. "Do you still want to get married?"

I sat back in the red booth, choosing my words carefully. "I don't want to be with anyone but you, Noah. I love you. But I'm not sure I want the same life you do. You always had our future mapped out, and there doesn't seem to be any room for compromise."

"I did compromise! I lived here for four months."

"And you hated it, just like you promised you would."

"I can't help that. You're the one who sent me away." He glowered.

"I didn't send you away, Noah. I put you out of your misery."

The waitress brought us our burgers. "Enjoy," she said. We ignored her.

"Stoningham sucks the life out of some people," I said. "I know you're not one of them, but I am."

"That's ridiculous."

"Thank you for being so understanding."

He scowled.

I rolled my eyes.

"Are you happy, Sadie?" he asked.

"Yes. Mostly." Content, maybe. Climbing my way to happiness.

"Because from here, it looks like you're killing time. Being a teacher, doing those paintings you hate, listening to sirens and car horns all day, taking your life into your hands every time you cross the street. You gave it a shot. It didn't work. Come home and be with me."

My jaw clenched. "Wow. So now that I've failed—at least the way you define it—I should come home and marry you and get pregnant."

He leaned forward. "I *love* you. Doesn't that matter at all? Because to me, that's everything."

"It doesn't sound like everything. It sounds like everything *you* want, with no room for me. Why can't we be together, me in the city, you in Stoningham? Lots of people have long-distance relationships."

"You can't raise a family that way!"

"So that's it? Your way, or nothing?"

"What would I tell our kids? Mommy doesn't love you enough to live with you?"

"I don't see me having kids anytime soon, Noah. And certainly not because you bullied me into it."

We glared at each other over our cooling burgers.

"So you're saying no, is that it?" he asked. "Because I'd like an answer. The waiting period is over, and I'm not gonna chase after you all my life."

"This is a very hostile marriage proposal."

"Don't make jokes, Sadie. Give me an answer. Will you marry me?"

There was no right answer I could give.

"I'm so sorry, Noah," I whispered. "I love you with all my heart, but I don't want that life right now."

His face didn't change. He just looked at me with those dark, dark eyes, then glanced away and swallowed. Twice. He pulled out his wallet and put two twenties on the table. Then he left me at the table with our untouched burgers and unfinished beers.

Sitting there in that pub, I think I knew. A love like that didn't come along every day. No other man was going to light my heart up in shades of red so beautiful it hurt. I loved Noah, loved his gentleness and kind heart, how hard he worked. I loved his smile, his mouth, the way he looked on the water with the wind blowing in his tangled hair. I knew that being with someone who thought you were the most wonderful, precious thing in the world didn't happen very often, and maybe would never happen again.

But I wasn't going to marry a man who'd proposed via ultimatum.

Three years after I'd turned Noah down in that stupid Irish pub, he got engaged.

My sister told me about it. We were having a perfectly nice, perfectly bland chat about her perfect life when she said, "Hey, by the way, Noah's getting married. Gillian something. You guys were pretty hot and heavy, weren't you?"

I didn't answer.

Noah was getting married. To someone who was not me. *Married.* As in living together. Sleeping together, waking up together, eating together, and probably having kids together.

My sister's words sat in my stomach like stones. "That's nice," I said belatedly, but Jules was already talking about the perfect vacation she'd be taking.

I'd managed to avoid imagining Noah with someone else. It was much more romantic to think of him staring out at the horizon, wind whipping his hair, arms crossed, his heart still mine. Occasionally, he showed up in my dreams, at times happy, sometimes angry and, worst of all, sad.

You can try to talk yourself out of loving someone. You can pitch it all the right ways, ways that make sense. *We wanted different things. It was beautiful while it lasted. Not every relationship is meant to be forever. I'll always have a soft spot for him. You never forget your first love.* And all that makes sense . . . in your head, if not your heart. I still loved Noah, and sometimes I'd find myself walking down a street and letting out a growl of frustration. Why couldn't he have at least tried to love my city, to open his heart to it? Why did he view Stoningham, that beautiful, pretentious, infuriating, lovely little town, as the be-all and end-all for our lives?

And who the hell was this Gillian person he was marrying?

A quick Facebook search brought me to her page. Gillian Epstein, the future Mrs. Noah Pelletier. She was an event planner—Epstein Events, not a very creative name.

Neither was she subtle about their engagement; her profile picture was her hand on a man's chest. Noah's chest. On her finger was a very pretty solitaire. Other photos showed the two of them at McMillan Orchards, in what was obviously their engagement photo shoot. I knew this because her page wasn't private, and there were thirty-seven pictures captioned *Engagement Photo Shoot!!!* A lot of Stoningham people had weighed in on how beautiful they were, how happy they looked, couldn't wait for the wedding, a year and a half away, for the love of God. If you were going to do it, just do it.

I didn't like the look of her. She was pretty, but very done. Those too-perfect eyebrows. Eyelash extensions (or very blessed). She looked . . . smug. Oh, she was nice-looking, of course. Quite pretty.

But it was Noah's face I really studied. His hair was cut short. Why on earth would he cut that beautiful, curly black hair? He looked—he was—older. I blew up the picture to see if he was really smiling, if his dark eyes crinkled and sparkled in that special way I remembered, and shit, yes, he did look happy.

My wild boy.

Tears spilled out of my eyes, surprising me. Obviously, I could've been his wife. I'd said no for all good reasons. He was uncompromising, and that wasn't a good sign for a marriage. We didn't want the same things, no matter how much we loved each other. So of course he was moving on. He deserved happiness, and I felt a hot, fast burn of shame that I hadn't been able to give it to him. No. I'd broken his heart instead.

Then again, he'd broken mine, too. It was a mutual devastation.

So I would be glad for him. I took my unjustified sense of betrayal and stuffed it down deep. Before I could talk myself out of it, I took out my pastels and drew him a little card with a heart-shaped cloud on it and wrote, *Congratulations on your engagement. I'm happy for you, Noah.* I didn't sign it. I didn't have to.

He didn't answer, nor did I expect him to. I just wanted him to know I wasn't resentful or furious or sobbing on my desk . . . even if I'd sobbed a little.

In a way, his engagement freed me. I didn't have to justify or prove myself, because Noah wasn't out there, watching and waiting and judging anymore. I relaxed, not knowing my heart had been clenched with tension until it loosened. Something softened in me. Now when I saw that New York confidence, when I read about Aneni's latest show, I felt the familiar sense of wonder, but it was no longer infected by envy. Maybe I'd never be them, those brilliant, sharp-edged, confident New Yorkers, but it was okay. I was doing just fine.

I got a couple of raises at St. Catherine's—Sister Mary seemed to like me. Teaching was more fun than I'd expected, introducing the kids to Picasso and Seurat, Jackson Pollock and Georgia O'Keeffe. I was told I was loved multiple times throughout the day, and was the beneficiary of many hugs. At least once a month, a kindergartener or first grader would propose. It was good for the ego, all those bright eyes and happy faces, and it was nice to leave them, too, and return to my lovely apartment in the armpit of the city.

Though I was embarrassed by their utter vapidity, the couch paintings were profitable. I could bang out one of those in a couple of hours, depending on the medium and size. If it looked like something you'd buy at Target, so be it. I still got to sign my name and deposit a sizable check. I took down my website, since nothing I was doing needed to be immortalized in cyberspace.

I saw friends often and enjoyed the nights when I was alone, despite the urge to machete my way through Times Square on the way home every night. (Tourists taking pictures of neon signs should be thrown in jail. There. I *was* a true New Yorker.) I even dated a little. A slurry of first dates, one regrettable hookup, then a nice person named Sam. We dated for a few months—he was a funny guy who did something with the waste water of New York City. I liked him very much. We never had a bad time together. One night, when we'd been together long enough that we didn't wonder if we were going to spend the weekend together, he said (in bed, no less), "I think I'm falling in love with you, Sadie."

I replied with, "Oh, wow, that's so . . . flattering."

Thus ended Sam and me. I was grateful he broke it off before we got more entangled in each other's lives. Breaking another heart was not something I could handle. And besides . . . *I think I'm falling in love with you*? Kind of tepid. I'd never had to ponder that with Noah. It was, to quote the great Stevie Wonder, signed, sealed, delivered. Done.

Once in a while, I'd check Gillian's Facebook page. She was the kind of bride who gave me a rash—obsessed with the *me*-ness of the upcoming day. "Which bouquet do you like best?" she'd ask. Sure, sure, she was an event planner, but come on. She had Pinterest boards of dresses, bouquets, centerpieces, bridesmaid dresses. She had a bachelorette weekend with her twelve closest friends in Miami (those poor women . . . I imagined it cost them *thousands*), and every photo showed Gillian's blinding white teeth in a near-feral smile. She wore a tiara that said *BRIDE*, in case we were unclear.

In short, she was milking every drop of attention she could possibly get, and while I tried not to hate her, I failed. She had a countdown to the wedding on all her pages. Every frickin' day, she mentioned something wedding related, even posting a picture of the white corsety thing she'd be wearing under her gown. For Pete's sake, as my mother would say.

Then, four months before the "Big Day," there came a cyber-silence (not that I was stalking her or anything). Five days later, she posted that she appreciated all the concern and kindness, but she and Noah were going their separate ways. No one was to blame, and they'd stay friends. He was wonderful, and she wished him only the best.

I clicked off immediately, shoving aside the shameful rush of satisfaction. Their breakup was too personal for me to read about, even if she'd posted it for all to see. Noah didn't have a Facebook page, except for his business: Noah Pelletier Fine Carpentry, on which he posted pictures of kitchen cabinets and decks and, in one case, a rather magical tree house made for one of the summer people.

I didn't send a card this time. Somehow, some way, even though we hadn't spoken for years now, I felt responsible for his heartache.

CHAPTER SEVENTEEN

John

Here are the things he knows.

The old man in the house . . . it's him. He finally understands how the mirror works, and that old man is *him*. He's gotten much older. He looks like his father.

The big man who helps him is named LeVon. He is a friend, but not really, because he works for John. But John thinks of him as his friend and would like to talk to him, but talking isn't happening.

He has had something called a stroke and a BLT. Or not a BLT, but something like that. A BLT is a sandwich with bacon, and John likes bacon. But the thing he has means his brain has been hurt. His little daughter tells him not to worry about this because he'll be better soon. His big daughter says less. She is less happy than his little daughter, even though she has very pretty little girls herself. This means she is a mother now. John doesn't remember that, or the little pretty girls, and that makes his eyes wet and sloppy.

When the little pretty girls are here, he likes it. Their voices are like birds, chirping and fast. He can't understand most of the words they say, but sometimes it clicks. *Grampy. Nana. Upstairs. Cookies.* These he knows. They run to him and kiss him and are gone, like the . . . the . . . the flower-bugs that float and drift. Flutter-bugs. Flutter-byes. Something like that. He knows he is close with the word, and also wrong with the word.

John also knows his wife doesn't love him anymore. She is important in some way, and she doesn't like him very much, but she isn't unkind. John tries to remember why she doesn't love him, but he can't remember or understand why that would be.

Barb. Barb. He wants to talk to his Barb. When he tries to make his mouth say her name, he only hears a wheezy old man—his now-self—making horrible sounds, so he stops trying. A bossy lady comes to see him and tries to get him to talk, but those sounds are too awful. Sometimes, if he moves his mouth too much, he drools, and this makes him feel small and stupid.

Barb.

Barb.

She looked so pretty on their wedding day, back in the long-ago.

They lived in a little red house in the long-ago. Not this house. Things were better there, but then there was something very sad, and she was different. Closed and locked. Case closed.

Case closed. Those words mean something to him, but he's not sure why.

Barb lives here now. In his grandfather's house. It's her house now, not his. Not theirs.

Barb wanted something very much in the long-ago. Was it this house? No. But something to do with this house. A boat? No, but almost a boat, with the same starting sound, that's what the bossy lady says when she tries to make him talk. The starting sound. Boat. Bank. Baby.

Baby. She wanted a baby. So did he. Lots of them. He wanted four, because four was a nice number, many but not too many. But they couldn't find the baby. No, not *find*. Get the baby. No, not that, either. They couldn't buy the baby?

Have the baby. They couldn't have a baby, and Barb was pretending to be happy, but she wasn't. She would have people over and make meals and light candles and pretend-smile, and he hated it. The . . . *untruth* of it. She would do those things and then he'd hear her crying in the bathroom, but she wouldn't talk to him. *Fine. Fine.* That was a word he knew was a lie when Barb said it.

She had . . . pretended, pretended happiness, and did things with people John barely knew, and filled their days with people and work and . . . and . . . and there were always *things* in the way, *her* things, her projects and papers, and he just wanted it to be the two of them, like the time in the little red house, when home was home, not a place to do so much. Always, there were the new people who thought Barb was fine, fine.

One night in the long-ago, he heard that noise, that horrible again-noise of Barb crying in the bathroom, the slight echo, how hard she tried to be quiet, how she'd run the water so he wouldn't know. He wanted to go in and tell her not to cry, that he would . . . find . . . no, not find, but do *something* to help. But she didn't want him to know she was crying, which was why she had the water turned on.

He almost went in. He put his hand on the . . . the . . . that thing you turn to open a door, but then the water went off, and John jumped back. He walked silently down the hall to pretend he hadn't heard her, didn't know, hadn't almost come in.

He *should* have gone in, he realizes now. Maybe she would still love him if he had gone in. He's sorry he didn't go into the bathroom. If he could do it over, he would have gone in and not let her pretend to be fine. He would've let her be not-fine. They could've been not-fine together.

But too much time passed, blurry time that John doesn't remember. Then Barb was happy because of the baby, the girl baby, and he was the one who was alone. He was alone and no one listened to him, and he wasn't sure what to say, anyway. He wanted four children, but there was only one and she was Barb's, until a long time later, another one came, and this time, it was his baby. This time, he wasn't shut away. He got to be needed again.

Sadie. Sadie!

He smiles because he remembered her name. Sadie. Such a pretty, happy name.

He tries to say it, but no sound comes out. His mouth is moving, but not the part that makes sound.

He wishes he could tell his daughter he remembers her name. He wishes he could say, *Hi, Sadie*, and make her smile and hug him. But he can't, and this makes his eyes water, and so he tilts his head back and escapes to sleep once more.

CHAPTER EIGHTEEN

Juliet

It wasn't anything to be ashamed of. Juliet knew this. That being said, she wouldn't mind a paper bag to put over her head right now. Or no, a silk bag. They could afford it, that was for sure. That way, no one would have to look at each other and pass judgment.

Park Avenue Aesthetics.

Yep.

There were four of them, three women, including Juliet, and one man. One woman had that freakish, ageless look that didn't say youth, but did say that plastic surgery was a legit addiction. Her skin was so tight it seemed like her whole face would crack if she blinked, which she seemed unable to do. Another woman was stunningly beautiful and, honestly, why was she here? Could she be a day over thirty? *Don't buy into the patriarchy, sweetheart! You're perfect!* Then again, what if she'd been *made* perfect here? If so, could Juliet have what she was having? The man was a normal-looking guy who had a pleasant face and fit-enough physique. What did he want to change? Why?

Go home, people, she wanted to say, hypocrite that she was.

Clearly, business was booming, because the office occupied two floors of a Park Avenue building and had a waterfall in the lobby. She'd been offered a bottle of mineral water when she came in, and the chairs were luxuriously comfy. Harp music interwoven with whale song was playing from discreetly placed speakers. There were many brochures on the table, but Juliet couldn't bring herself to look at them.

Oliver would not be happy about this. Hopefully, he would never know. Juliet had taken out a separate credit card to hide the cost. Not that he would deny her anything (and not that she needed his approval to spend her hard-earned money) . . . she just didn't want him to know she was here. That fear—if she pointed out an imperfection, he'd say, "You know what? You're right."

He, of course, was aging perfectly, as had his grandfather, who died at the age of 104 and looked about sixty. Helen, Oliver's mother, could be a model, and she was seventy-five. That peachy British skin.

But Juliet was American, and ageism was a real issue.

Last week, Kathy Walker, who was six years older than Juliet, had come into the office with shocking red hair. Prior to this, Kathy had worn her prematurely white hair in a very elegant French twist, saying she couldn't be bothered to color it. Now, it was cherry red and short—quite a lot like Arwen's cut, gosh golly, big coincidence there.

Kathy had also taken to wearing stilettos with red soles . . . Christian Louboutins, which cost a small fortune. Juliet could afford them, too, but it felt morally wrong, paying two grand for a pair of painful shoes. Kathy had been swinging by Arwen's office more and more, and Juliet's less and less. When Juliet texted her, asking if she wanted to grab a drink, Kathy responded that it was a nice idea and she'd get back to her. That was three weeks ago.

Back when Juliet had been new, she and Kathy were the only women in the New Haven office of DJK, and they'd supported each other, eventually becoming friends. They'd had dinners together, sometimes with their husbands. Juliet and Oliver had gone to Kathy's son's wedding last year. Before Arwen got hired, Kathy and she speculated about when a new partner would be named, since they were both on track to be tapped.

The past few months, Kathy had cooled considerably.

It didn't matter, Juliet told herself. She'd keep her head down and do her job. Her work had always spoken for itself. Sadie was the fun one, the kind of person who made a new friend every fifteen minutes, or had people telling her their life stories after ten seconds in her presence. Juliet was the worker. Organized, determined, a big-picture thinker with a list of details. Clear eyes, full heart, can't lose, as *Friday Night Lights* told her. That slogan had always spoken to her. Her heart had always been full, because she truly felt blessed in life, with a mother who encouraged and guided her, a stellar education, a wonderful husband, healthy children, a job she loved.

Clear eyes meant seeing what needed to be done. Oliver often marveled at her organizational skills. She had a monthly meal plan she put together so grocery shopping and dinner prep would go smoothly. Chore charts for the girls. She maintained the family calendar, juggled her and Oliver's work schedules so at least one parent would be present at every school or sport event. She researched their vacation destinations, booked flights, found hotels or rentals. Scheduled the dentist, the doctor, took the girls shopping for clothes (by the way, Brianna probably needed a bra, and she'd try to make that a bonding experience, the way her mom had done for her).

It was the *can't lose* part of the phrase that was coming into question. When Dave had appointed Arwen as the lead of the Hermanos building, Juliet had lost project management to a woman far less experienced than she was. She may have lost Kathy as well.

"Juliet Smith?" A strikingly beautiful woman with dark, dark skin and a shaved head stood in the doorway. "Ms. Smith?"

That was her. She'd given a fake name. "Hi," she said, standing up.

"Right this way," said the woman, smiling gently. "You're new to us?"

"I am."

"Welcome." She was shown into an exam room, and the woman smiled and left.

God. Juliet was sweating now. Why was she here? She'd never thought of herself as beautiful, but she liked her face. She looked a lot like her father, she knew, and had what Oliver's mother called a sporty face. Strong bone structure, symmetrical enough, not particularly girly-pretty, in that she didn't have full lips or doe-like eyes.

That was fine. She was attractive. With some makeup, she could look quite nice. She had good skin, in that it was clear and even-toned, more or less. She'd always thought she was aging well. Sure, she had crow's-feet, which she rather liked. And yes, her throat was starting to get crepey. And her hands looked like a crone's if she didn't drink enough water. And there was a wrinkle on her cheek when she smiled that hadn't been there last year.

But look at Helen Mirren. Meryl Streep. Don't even get started on Angela Bassett. They were older than she was and had never been more beautiful.

And yet, here Juliet was, at a posh New York plastic surgeon's office because she was terrified. She was forty-three, and Arwen was thirty-one, and maybe—gah—looking a little younger would remind the partners and perhaps the world that she was still a young(ish) woman, but really, why would you *want* a young architect? Wouldn't you want someone with experience and maturity? They made buildings! Experience was a good thing if you didn't want things crashing down on your head!

And yet she'd been passed over for the Forty Under Forty. *Vanity Fair* was doing a profile on Arwen. *Vanity* fucking *Fair.* "Women Who Are Changing the World." After being lead designer on three entire projects.

Three.

So yeah. That's why Juliet was here. It went against everything she believed in, and here she was. Not a proud moment, but she wasn't racing for the door, either.

The door opened. "Hello! I'm Dr. Brian. How are you? Juliet . . . Smith! What a pretty name."

He was about sixty and wore a white doctor's coat over jeans and a button-down shirt. And he was no supermodel himself. Should she trust a plastic surgeon with a nose that size? Why hadn't he gotten anything tweaked? Look at those wrinkles! *And* he was balding. "Hi," she said.

"What are you thinking of today, Juliet?"

Juliet took a deep breath, noticing that her hands were shaking. "I'd like to look . . . a little younger. Not different, just . . . rejuvenated." She closed her eyes at the overused word.

"Face? Body? Labia and vagina?"

"Jesus, no." She paused. "What's that? The vagina thing?"

He smiled pleasantly. "We can plump up your labia, maybe trim them, since they can get stretched out—"

Her knees locked together. "Trim my labia? Are you kidding?"

"No, not at all. We can get a very nice effect. We can also tighten your vagina. It says on your form you've had two children?"

"Mm-hm."

"Which can stretch you out, obviously. A few well-placed stitches, and—"

"Okay, no. I'm not comfortable talking about this." Did *men* do this? Was there any male at DJK who was being told his sac should be a little tighter and higher?

"I just want something quick and easy and very subtle," Juliet said. "I don't want to look frozen. I don't want to look weird or different or carved up . . . I just want to look like me, five or ten years ago. No scalpels." Her hands were tingling. A panic attack was lurking.

"Got it. Let's have a look." Another pleasant smile. "Listen, Juliet, it's normal to be nervous. I promise not to slice and dice when you're not looking." He laughed, and she felt a little better. He tilted her head, pushed her hair back, lifted her eyebrow, tapped on the underside of her chin. "What brings you in at this point in your life? Big birthday coming up, or anything like that?"

What the hell. "There's a woman at work who's younger than I am by about ten years. She's getting a lot of plum assignments and kind of leaping up the food chain, and I can't help but think it's because she's so attractive. At least in part. The new kid on the block, you know?"

"What kind of work do you do?"

"I'm an . . . uh . . . uh, a magazine writer?" *I'm a world-class architect. You've probably seen my work. You may have been in one of my buildings.*

"Neat! What magazine?"

"It's . . . an online thing."

"Okay," he said. "Here's what I'd recommend. You're already a beautiful woman, and we can make you even more beautiful. You have some puffiness above your eyelids, which is very normal for a woman your age, and your jawline is starting to soften, which gives the appearance of jowls and definitely makes you look older. We'd cut some tiny holes, insert a laser—"

"A laser?"

"That's right! The heat will cause contracting and stimulate collagen growth. Or, for something more dramatic, a neck lift would give you great results, along with a lower face lift."

"No. No cutting."

"Fine, fine. You could go for an eye lift, since your lids are looking a tiny bit heavy, but you said something quick. Some lip plumping would definitely add to a more youthful appearance. Subtle. You, but five years ago." He smiled, trying to reassure her, which was nice of him, since she felt like puking on his shoes. "We can do some Botox injections to lift the brow. Some filler between your eyes to get rid of that." He touched between her eyebrows where, yes, she did have a crease. "There are also some more superficial things I'd recommend.

Lash extensions, teeth whitening. A sassy haircut, even. You know we have an aesthetician wing here."

Juliet touched her hair. It was all one length, cut (rather well, she thought) straight across with a razor every two months or so. Not one bit of body to it, so it was reliably straight day in and day out. She could wear it in a ponytail or a bun, or just down, which was what she did most days.

Oliver loved her hair. Plus, Arwen had a sassy haircut, and Kathy had just gotten one as well, and Juliet didn't want to look like a follower.

"Um . . . okay, but not a haircut."

"Trust me?"

"I just met you."

He smiled. "Well, I'm a board-certified plastic surgeon. Dartmouth, Johns Hopkins, NYU residency. I've been practicing for twenty-two years."

Just not on yourself, apparently. She clenched her fists. "Okay. Let's do this. I'll be able to go home looking normal, right?"

"Of course."

"Not a lot of Botox. I don't want to look like those freaky Real Housewives."

"Two of them are my patients," he said. "But I hear you. Just a sprinkling. You'll look like you came back from a wonderfully restful vacation."

A wonderfully restful vacation where she fell asleep in the sun for eight hours, apparently.

"Am I bweeding?" she said, looking closer.

Her lips were swollen, which would subside, Dr. Brian said. He'd better not be lying. And for God's sake, she could hardly see through the forest on her upper lids.

"There are a few little dots, yes, but that's normal." He blotted her forehead, and the gauze showed blood.

"I—I can't go home wike this." Her glowing white teeth flashed against her red, red skin and swollen lips.

"It will just take a day or two."

"You said an hour!" She was blinking, the lash extensions so long they hit her cheeks (and possibly her eyebrows, but she couldn't feel those). She looked like Bambi trying to flirt. An evil, demonic Bambi. She tried to draw her eyebrows together, but they were no longer functioning eyebrows. She could lift them maybe a millimeter.

The redness. Jesus. Her face was the color of boiled lobster.

And those eyelashes. That was a mistake. "I thought it would wook more natural."

Dr. Brian smiled. "You look *beautiful*. The redness and swelling will go down, and the lashes will come off in a couple of weeks, so you may want to schedule a fill appointment now."

She cringed. "It wooks wike I have a small animal sitting on my eyewids."

A jolly chuckle. "No! You look amazing. Just make sure to brush them out when they get wet, or they clump together."

Great. Add that to her list of things to do every morning. "Can you twim them, at weast?" She sounded like the priest in *The Princess Bride*.

"Why don't you just sit with them a little while and get used to them. I'm telling you, you look wonderful. I can tell. This is my job. When that redness fades, you'll be very happy, I'm confident. You wanted to look younger, and you will."

She studied her reflection in the mirror. Maybe he was right. The redness was distracting, and the eyelashes were . . . long. And fanned out, like a peacock tail. Her lips were sore from the injections, and her gums throbbed from that thing they'd stuck in her mouth while whitening her teeth.

She wouldn't want her girls to do this. Ever.

I'm sorry I put you through this, Face, she thought.

"Here's the numbing cream," Dr. Brian said. "In case the pain gets worse."

. . .

The pain got worse. Juliet called her office from I-95, said she had a migraine and went home. Thank God she'd taken the first available appointment of the day; the girls weren't home yet, and she could have some time to ice her face. If they saw her like this, Brianna would give her that disgusted look she'd mastered this past year, and Sloane might cry.

Juliet's face was still bright red. Some blood had crusted around her nose in tiny droplets. Not a great look. Frozen eyebrows. Her lips were throbbing and not noticeably fuller. Those ridiculous lashes. No one on earth would think they were natural.

There was only one person to call. She got into the house, tossed her bag on the table and took out her phone. "Mom? I'm having kind of a . . . cwisis here. Can you come over?"

"What's wrong, sweetheart? Are the girls okay?"

"It's nothing, except I need a wittle help. You'll see when you get here."

"Sure thing, hon. Give me fifteen minutes. I have to cancel a conference call."

Juliet's guilt was drowned out by gratitude. "Thanks, Mom."

When her mom got there, her eyebrows shot up (lucky thing). "Oh, sweetheart. What did you do? One of those facial peels?"

"Something with needles."

"I don't think those false eyelashes are doing you any favors, hon."

"They're extensions. Can you twim them for me?"

Mom put down her coat and purse. "You betcha. Let's get some ice on that face. It looks hot and painful."

"It is." She felt like crying. "I went to a pwastic surgeon. It's so humiwiating. I just thought I needed a wittle . . . fweshening."

"Why, honey? You're beautiful just the way God made you." Her mom smiled and kissed her forehead. "Let's get you into bed. Go on now. Change into your jammies and I'll get some stuff together down here."

Juliet went upstairs and did as she was told. She had friends whose mothers were, to put it bluntly, ass pains. Kathy's mother called her every day to complain that Kathy never called her. Jen's mother had a gambling problem and constantly begged for money so she could buy scratch offs. Iris's mother was cold and disapproving.

And Barb Frost was perfect. Oh, maybe not perfect, but damn near close. Who else would understand this ridiculous problem and help her fix it without judgment?

Mom came in with an ice pack wrapped in a dishcloth, and a cup of tea. She went into the bathroom and ran the water, then came out with a facecloth.

"Let's get that blood off your face, okay?"

The cloth was warm, and Mom dabbed carefully. It felt so nice, being taken care of after putting herself through the torture of this morning, that a few tears did slip out.

"Everything okay with you and Oliver?" Mom asked.

"Yes. He's wonderful. But I don't want him to know I did this."

"What exactly was it that you did, honey?"

"Micwoneedwing, eyewash extensions, wip injections, Botox and teeth whitening. I wook wike an idiot, and I feel worse."

"Why did you do all that, hm?"

If Juliet told her the truth, Mom would worry. She had enough on her plate these days. Plus, Barb hated when she couldn't help, and there was no helping here. She'd be distressed to hear that Juliet was aging out, that there was that tremor in the Force that had become a constant rumble, that someone else was now the favorite child. She'd given everything to Juliet, and it would distress her no end to hear her daughter was struggling.

And so she said, "Kathy wecommended it, and she wooked gweat, so I gave it a shot."

"Well, Kathy *needs* it, hon. You can tell she was a sun worshipper. Skin like leather. You don't need anything. Okay. Let's take a look at these silly lashes." She smiled. "You girls. So beautiful, and always trying new things when you don't need to. Hold still and I'll trim these a little."

"Thanks, Mama."

Yes. Forty-three years old and still calling her mother mama. Sometimes, Juliet thought her mom was the only person with whom she could be one hundred percent herself.

It was such a relief.

An hour later, the redness had faded. Her lips were less numb (though hardly at all fuller). Her lashes looked thick but not fake. "Looks like you had a little allergic reaction," Mom said, and there it was, the perfect lie, the thing she could tell her husband and children.

"I love you, Mom." Looked like she had her *l*'s back.

"I love you, too, sweetheart. So much. Oh! I'm having a little dinner party this weekend. You and Oliver are invited, of course. I'm inviting the event planner who's helping with the town's anniversary, she's just been wonderful. And she's single, and Sadie's bringing her single teacher friend from New York. And you know, Sadie has no friends here, so I figured I'd get a little business done and help Sadie, too. Caro and Ted are coming, and I thought maybe it would do your father some good, having folks around. Can you make it? Friday night around seven."

"I'll call Riley and see if she can babysit," Juliet said. "Thanks, Mom. Let me know what I can bring."

"I have to get back to work now," she said. "You just take a nap, all right? The girls will be home in an hour, so you just rest, honey. Everyone needs a break once in a while."

Mom kissed her on the forehead, smoothed back her hair, and before she'd even left, Juliet was asleep.

CHAPTER NINETEEN

Barb

Two days after Juliet needed me (the thought still gave me a warm feeling), Caro and I walked into a little café in Middle Haddam, which was far enough from Stoningham that we weren't likely to run into anyone we knew.

We were meeting WORK.

"Cute place," Caro said. "And clearly she's not here yet. Let me get us something. You want a tea, I already know. Any cake or cookies?"

"I'm good, Caro. Thanks." I wasn't good. I was nervous. And still angry. And sad. And humiliated. And gosh-darn tired, too. I got up every night at three a.m. to give John his medication, and I wasn't a young woman anymore. It often took me an hour or more to fall back asleep.

John had been home now for weeks. LeVon had become a fixture in our house, and that was a real blessing, I'll tell you.

Sometimes, it felt like he was the son I'd never had. That first pregnancy of mine . . . I'd always thought the baby was a boy, and . . . well, sometimes I liked to picture what life would be like if that baby had lived. He'd be about LeVon's age—late forties. Maybe John and I wouldn't have grown apart if I hadn't struggled with infertility. Maybe Juliet would have relaxed a little more with a big brother to tease her, and Sadie would look up to him and be a little more responsible with him as a role model.

Most days, LeVon stayed a little late, joining me in a cup of tea before he left. It felt so comforting. Like he was protecting me, in some inexplicable way. He said he'd be with us until John's recovery was mostly done, and gosh, that was a relief. I'd adopt him if I could, but he had a wife and three kids, and his parents lived next door to him, so I guess that was out.

"Okay," Caro said, sitting down. "Any idea what she looks like?"

"Your guess is as good as mine."

"So they didn't text pictures."

"No. Thank God they didn't do that, you know? I'd hate to have to see a dick pic."

"The first selectman of Stoningham just said 'dick pic'!" Caro said.

It wasn't funny. It was awful. But it felt so good to laugh.

We settled down. I sipped my tea. Caro had already put in the sugar. She was drinking some monstrous thing with whipped cream. She also had a slab of coconut cake. "Go on, take a bite," she said, sliding into the booth next to me. "You know you're going to."

I did. Oh, it was good. I needed to bake a cake. Maybe LeVon could bring half of it home to his family. Maybe John would like it, since his swallowing had improved and he could eat almost anything now.

"Is John getting any better, do they think?" Caro asked. "Mentally?"

"In little ways. He seems more alert from time to time. His walking is better, but he still needs help getting in and out of bed. He makes some sounds, but talking isn't going so well. LeVon gave him a pen and paper, but he didn't seem to know what to do with it."

"Jesus, Barb. I don't know how you do it."

"In sickness and in health."

"Yeah, and forsaking all others. Let's not forget why we're here, after all."

The door opened, and a young couple came in with their baby. "How's your grandbaby doing, by the way?" I asked, and Carol pulled out her phone to show me the latest pictures of Garrett, her second grandson. "Beautiful. Looks like you, Caro."

She flashed me that gorgeous smile that lit up her whole face. "I thought so, too," she said.

Then the door opened, and a woman came in, late fifties, maybe.

"Hey," Caro said. "We know her. It's . . . uh . . . oh, shit, I can't remember."

"It's Karen, the teacher from ballroom dancing, remember?" I had great facial recall, which helped in my job. Also, we took those lessons for a few months, in those days when I'd still been trying to work on my marriage, making sure John had enough fun, trying to feel something other than irritation toward him.

"Right!" Caro said. "Hi, Karen! How are you?"

Karen looked over, then flinched.

The penny dropped, as the saying goes.

Seems we had just met WORK.

"Come on over!" Caro called. "Remember us? We took dance classes from you. We were all terrible."

Karen came over, her arms crossed tightly in front of her.

Caro went on blithely. "This is Barb Frost, and I'm Caro, and . . . oh. Oh, shit. It's you, isn't it?"

Yep. Her eyes darted between us.

"Here to meet my husband?" I asked, oddly numb.

"Um . . . uh . . ." She closed her eyes. "I think I might faint."

"Great. A drama queen," Caro said. "Well, faint away. We'll throw a bucket of water on you. You're not leaving till you've answered some questions."

"It's just that I only had a kale smoothie for breakfast, and—"

"We don't care," I said. "Sit down, you . . . adulteress."

"Oh, Barb," Caro said. "Call her what she is. Sit down, slut."

"Where's John?" she asked, holding her giant fabric bag in front of her.

"We'll get to that," I said.

Karen. Karen something boring. Sanders or Saunders.

She sat across from Caro and me, and I took a long look at her. Her face was flushing a dull red, and she looked at the table. Dyed black hair, a dull, drab color that came from a drugstore, not a salon. *I* was a natural blond, and over the years my hair had gradually become streaked with silver. Never colored it a day in my life. *She* was dressed like a twenty-year-old bohemian—long full skirt, a low-cut leotard showing off her speckled, bony chest. Hard features, small eyes, but cunning, like a . . . like a rhino. A beaky nose, thin lips.

Well, he wasn't with her because of her looks.

"So I guess you know," she said, swallowing.

"I sure do, Karen. Or should I call you angel kitten?"

"Barb's been texting you for almost two months. You didn't even know it wasn't your tiger," Caro said.

"How dare you?" she said, and Caro and I both laughed.

"Barb," Caro said, "the slut is mad because you pretended to be John."

"Caro," I said, "I'm mad because the slut was sleeping with my husband."

"It wasn't like that!" Karen said.

"Oh, please," Caro said.

She twisted one of her silver bracelets. "I . . . we love each other. And you didn't understand him," she said. "He said your marriage had been over for years."

"Jeesh," I said. "The oldest line in the book, kitten. Did you fall for that? He gave me a beautiful ruby pendant for Christmas." Juliet had picked it out, of course, but technically, it was from him. "Did he mention how much fun we had with our *children* and *grandchildren*?"

She glanced away. "Does he know you're meeting me?"

"I'll ask the questions, kitten," I said. "Let me guess. He and I had grown apart. He wasn't happy anymore. You made him feel young. He didn't know what love was until he found you, and if only he'd met you first, gosh golly, life would've been super great. He'd leave me, but the children. Or the . . . what, Caro?"

"Or the fact that a divorce would cost him every dime he ever made," she supplied.

"That's true, now, isn't it? Hm."

Karen's little eyes darted between us, and she fiddled with her ugly bag. "He *was* going to leave you. He probably still is."

Caro laughed.

"Is that what you want? Would you marry him, kitten?" I asked.

"Please stop calling me that," she said. "And yes. I love him."

"Oh. How touching," Caro said. "She loves him, Barb."

"My heart." This was oddly fun. "Well, you can have him, Karen. In sickness and in health." I took a bite of Caro's cake. "Tell me, what makes a woman go after a married man? Don't you have any morals?"

"I am a good Christian woman," she said, huffing.

Caro and I looked at each other and laughed. "Isn't there a tiny commandment about adultery?" Caro asked.

"You know, Caro, I think there is. I'm sure of it."

"This is different," Karen said.

"How so, dear?" I asked.

She glanced around. That hair was not only unnatural in color, it didn't move a bit when she turned her head. Helmet hair, my girls would call it. "Look. I'm sorry he doesn't love you anymore. But we didn't plan this. It just happened."

"So . . . you fell into a deep sleep and when you woke up, you were screwing another woman's husband?" Caro asked.

"No! We . . . we ran into each other at a treadmill class last spring."

I rolled my eyes. Just when you thought it couldn't get worse. "You had to take a class to learn how to walk on a treadmill?"

"It's more complicated than that."

"And then what happened, angel kitten?"

"We remembered each other. We got a carrot juice at the juice bar. We just . . . clicked. We ended up talking for hours. It was amazing."

"No, it wasn't," I said. "It was inappropriate and dishonest. He's married. Which you well knew. What God has put together, let no one put asunder, good Christian woman."

"I'm telling you, it wasn't like we planned to have an affair. It was just juice at first. But I started to look forward to it. He's so . . . wonderful. A brilliant man." Caro snorted. "The chemistry was undeniable. And *you* didn't even notice." She straightened her shoulders a bit, and her sternum bones showed even more.

She did have a point. I hadn't noticed. Last spring, Sloane had appendicitis, and I stayed with Juliet for four nights and played board games with Brianna and cooked for the family. I'd also been doing the job Stoningham's residents had elected me to do.

"How long did it take for these juice dates to lead to adultery?" I asked.

"About a week." She smirked, obviously proud of herself.

The words hit me in the heart like a hammer shattering glass.

A week. That's how much time and consideration he gave our marriage. Our vows. Our *five* decades together.

One goddamn week.

"The attraction was just so strong," she said, raising her penciled eyebrows at me. "I'm not that type of girl—"

"You haven't been a girl in sixty years," Caro said.

"—and I've *never* done anything like that before. But I believe God put us in each other's path, and life is too short. The past isn't a compass for the future. You have to give yourself permission to chart a new course."

"Been reading Snapple caps?" Caro asked.

"I won't apologize for loving someone with all my heart." Her little rhino eyes teared up. "I take it you gave him an ultimatum. What are you holding over his head, Barb? Is this why he hasn't been in touch?

He said you were controlling and had anger issues, but this is beyond the pale."

"Oh, hush," I said. "I'm not holding anything over his head. He had a stroke." She sucked in a breath, her sharp nostrils flaring. "I found out about *you* when I was at the hospital. While my husband was having brain surgery to save his life, I got to read his idiotic, juvenile sexting with you."

"He had an operation? How is he now?"

For some reason, it was hard to say the words. "You tell her, Caro."

"Well, funny you should ask, kitten," Caro said. "He has the IQ of a celery stalk."

Karen jerked back. "What do you mean?"

"He's nonverbal and needs a full-time caregiver," I said. "Good thing you love him so very, very much. This must be why God put him in your path."

"Barb," Caro said, putting her hand on my shoulder, "I'm so glad you won't be shackled to him anymore, now that Sex Kitten will take over. You know, since their love is more special and so different from any love the world has ever seen."

"The house is in my name," I said. "And I have power of attorney over our finances. But I'm sure you're not materialistic. Good thing, too, since you won't be getting a fucking cent."

Her eyelids fluttered.

"I love that you said fucking," Caro said.

"It felt good."

Karen started to stand, then sat back down. "So he won't get better?"

"You'd have to ask God about that, Karen, since you and He are on such close terms. John can't talk, and he can't write, but he did learn to toilet himself, so he only wets the bed once in a while."

"What would Jesus do?" Caro asked. "I bet Jesus would comfort the sick, don't you, kitten? Small price to pay for ruining a marriage."

"I . . . I have to go," Karen said.

"Yes. You do." My voice was hard.

She got up and wobbled over to the door, and then she was gone.

"Well, we've seen the last of her," Caro said. "Good riddance to bad rubbish."

"Yep. That's true."

Caro looked at me with her kind, dark eyes and gave a sad smile, and that was it. The tears came hard and fast, and I cried in gulping sobs that made the other folks in the café look at me, but I couldn't seem to stop.

Caro put her arm around me, and we sat there for a long, long time, and a thought came to me. I didn't have a great husband, and maybe I never had.

But I sure had a wonderful friend.

CHAPTER TWENTY

Sadie

I got a dog. I *needed* a dog, for several reasons: company, of course; and snuggles; protection from murderers, since I didn't live close enough to anyone and my screams would go unnoticed during said murder; and to run for help if my house fell in on top of me, as it seemed intent on doing.

Stoningham's animal shelter had only three doggies—a wee little purse dog, who, though tempting, would not protect me (not very well, anyway) should a serial killer come knocking. Then there was a wheezing, balding sheepdog who was blind and deaf but also spoken for (God bless *that* person). And finally, Pepper.

Pepper was a mutt of House Mutt, proud descendant of mutts. Shepherd-bloodhound-rottweiler-something-something else, we'd never know. She was reddish-brown with some black markings, about thirty pounds and growing, and when I came to her little kennel, she wagged her tail so hard she fell down. Her ears were silky soft, and the top of her snout was velvety and plush. If she wasn't going to defend me, at least I'd have a sweet, wagging pup as the last thing I saw as I slipped this mortal coil.

Her talents seemed to be licking people and pouncing on leaves. And cuddling. She was great at cuddling. Also, barking at such threats as wind, rain, the coffeepot and my cowboy boots.

I'd had her a week and now couldn't imagine life without her. I talked to her a lot—"Do you think this bucket is big enough to catch the leaks?" I'd ask, or "Should I have fish for dinner, or popcorn?"

The truth was, I was lonelier than I'd anticipated. The temporary loss of my dad made me realize how much and how often we talked and texted. Sometimes, it was just silly things—a photo of that grimy Elmo in Times Square, or a pigeon sitting on the shoulder of a sleeping man in Central Park. Sometimes it was an article . . . I'd send him links to writing workshops, hoping he'd still give it a shot, or events that he might want to come down for. He'd send me cartoons or make Dad jokes, teasing me for not drinking more, saying I was sullying his legacy.

Sometimes he'd just call me to say he loved me and was thinking of me and wondering what I was looking at.

Juliet was a good-enough sister, though we didn't have much in common. I loved her daughters and always had fun with them, but less was more in that respect. You couldn't be the cool auntie if you were around all the time. My mother was very . . . competent. But I had never met my Minnesotan relatives; Mom didn't get on with anyone except Aunt Nancy, and Dad was an only child. So as family went, Dad was kind of it for me. Dad, and Alexander, and I missed them both so much. Missed my life in New York fiercely.

But Alexander was coming to visit this weekend, thank God, and Carter had broken his vow never to leave the five boroughs and was coming up tonight for Mom's dinner party, though he'd booked an Airbnb after I FaceTimed him from my house.

It was so quiet here. Quieter in this little house than my parents', where there was always some kind of noise—cars, neighbors, the distant thump of music from the restaurants on Water Street, just two blocks away. Stoningham always had some event on the weekends—the library fund-raiser, a Presidents' Day trivia contest at the library, storytelling night and open mic night at the local bar. To its credit, Stoningham tried very hard not to be a summertime-only seaside town.

I hadn't realized how much my mother did. When she had run for first selectman, I thought it was cute, and pictured her sitting on a panel, fielding questions from disgruntled residents. Now I knew she worked with the state government, figured out how any federal and state budget cuts would affect Stoningham, built partnerships with the business community, tried to woo the kind of industry to town that would be green, clean and employ locals . . . and yes, handled complaints from disgruntled residents.

I felt a little bad that Dad and I had made some jokes about her being the queen of Stoningham.

And now she was having a dinner party, to which I was invited. The first time I'd be my mother's guest at something other than a family event. It felt kind of strange. Alexander was due in this afternoon . . . March was a busy time for him—all those rich folks getting itchy for summers on the Vineyard or Penobscot Bay or in San Diego. Many yachts to sell. We'd only seen each other three times since I moved back here—two quick runs back to the city for me, and once, dinner in New Haven. But he was coming tonight, staying all weekend, and I couldn't wait.

To show how strange life had become, I found myself looking forward to going to Mom's. It was the highlight of my social life since coming home.

Stoningham hadn't exactly welcomed me back with open arms. I was a local who'd let it be known I couldn't *wait* to leave my posh and pretty hometown behind, eager to be a New Yorker. Some of my classmates had never left, and I understood. It was a beautiful area. Others left to go to URI or UConn, came back and settled in, happy as clams. Mickey, Noah's baby mama, had done that—she was the music teacher at the elementary school and taught piano and violin on the side. Some kids, like Juliet, left and came back wreathed in glory, the local success stories, living in the best neighborhoods.

And then there were the blue-collar folks of any place like this . . . those who worked for the submarine plant in Groton or for the wealthier residents through skilled or unskilled labor. The townies who had struggled to make their peace with a fishing village turned summer retreat for the wealthy. Noah was one of those; his dad remembered when most of Stoningham was dairy farms with a few gracious houses on the water.

And then there was me. I'd run into a few old classmates since coming home, and they seemed confused to see me. Wasn't I in New York? Art, right? Still painting? Anything good? Oh. Private collections? (It sounded better than couch paintings.) What was I doing back? Was I staying? No kids? Oh. Still not married? This last one was always said with a little meanness, as if getting married would have proven my worth in a way that the other parts of my life could not.

I was a stranger in my hometown, in some respects. I knew the names of the people I'd grown up with—Mrs. Churchill from the library and her four grown sons, or Caroline DeAngelo, who taught me to double Dutch in sixth grade. There were the kids I used to babysit, now grown, and their parents, who still recognized me. There were the middle-aged women who used to babysit *me*.

So I knew people, but I didn't have any friends here. Jules let me come over and hang with the girls, and Oliver smiled and smiled. My New York pals felt far away, and the truth was, I didn't have a lot to say to them on the phone. *My dad is still recovering. I'm painting a little. I, uh . . . got a dog. No, I can't have guests just yet, it's kind of tiny here, and the roof leaks . . .*

There were nights when I was alone in my little house, wishing someone would text me or drop by, feeling a little afraid to reach out in case I'd be rejected. (You'd think a woman in her thirties wouldn't have those feelings. You'd be wrong.) I worked on the house every morning, learning what wood rot was, finding mouse droppings in my insulation, realizing that one outlet downstairs was probably not enough. In the evenings, I painted for my interior decorators—they'd send me a swatch of fabric or take pictures of a throw pillow and instruct me on what the homeowner wanted—those "little dot paintings" (Seurat, I assumed) or "swirly" (Van Gogh) or "messy" (Pollock) or "those weird stick figures where the person only has one eye" (Picasso). My favorite was "little bitty brushstrokes so up close you can't tell what it is but from far away, you can, like those Magic Eye puzzles" (Monet. So sorry, Claude).

The only time I felt like my old self was when I was with my dad. He'd made some real progress from those terrifying first days in January. He wasn't talking or otherwise communicating yet . . . I'd been trying some sign language with him, since I knew a little from St. Catherine's, where it was taught one day a week. LeVon was trying that, too, but we'd yet to have an Anne Sullivan/Helen Keller breakthrough. Not yet. He was right on the cusp, it seemed. I could sense it.

He smelled different, my father. It was one of those things you didn't know would affect you until you were crying in the bathroom.

Mom and Juliet were there, and I was sure they missed him, too, but they hid it well. I had the feeling Mom wished he had just died.

But he *was* getting better. "It's tempting to read into every little thing," LeVon had warned me. "If he's having a breakthrough, we'll know, but it'll be harder if you attribute every reflex to meaningful interaction." He put a big hand on my shoulder. "But I agree with you. He's making progress."

We all fricking loved LeVon.

Meanwhile, something was happening to me.

It was the view. My house might be a decrepit pile of mold and decaying wood, but damn, that view. Because my house was on a little hill, I could watch both the sunrise and the sunset. Every morning, I woke up to the sun streaming in my room at the literal crack of dawn. I'd take Pepper out and let her romp and chase the dead leaves, and we'd watch the sun come out from behind the clouds, beams of light stretching out their arms. I'd sit on the porch with my coffee, listening to the birds. Each week they got more vocal—the chickadees, red-winged blackbirds, blue jays, ducks and geese. A blue heron hung out at the bend of the river, just past the bridge.

At night, if I was home from my parents' house in time, I'd watch the sun set over the water, and it was even more startling in its beauty than the sunrise. Sometimes, the sun would glitter over the ocean, not a cloud in the sky, and after it sank below the horizon, a band of yellow and gold would linger for an hour as the stars came out. Other times, the clouds would catch and throw the light in all the shades of color I knew and then some—dianthus pink, iridescent pale gold, French blue, Montserrat orange. This past week had been milder, and Pepper and I stayed out till the last bird sang, and the smell of earth was strong as the sky deepened bit by bit.

I'd sit there and watch and listen, and all the yoga classes in all the world didn't make me feel this way. Still. Awed. I hadn't come back to Stoningham for Noah—I couldn't, not the way he'd demanded it of me, not under the weight of his expectations. But even though it was temporary, I was glad I was here now. The town was less insipid than I'd painted it as a teenager; the people were more layered than I'd imagined them to be. Maybe it had been a necessary exercise to prepare for the New York phase of my life. Maybe I'd had to minimize what home meant to me so I could leave it behind.

I loved my New York life. But I loved this, too. I was . . . happy.

Happy. Even though I was here for a terrible reason, the happiness, the peace, snuck in. Right now, there was nowhere else I should be, could be or wanted to be.

The dinner party did not get off to a great start.

For one, Alexander was running late. "Babe. I'm so sorry, but this traffic is horrible."

"Well, what time did you leave?" I asked.

"At four."

"That's way too late! I told you to get out of the city by two thirty!" I groaned. "Honey. We haven't seen each other in weeks. I wanted to get you in bed before this party. Now you'll have to come straight to my mother's."

"I know. I'm so sorry. I had all this paperwork to file, and time just got away from me. I'll be there as soon as I can. I've missed you so much."

I sighed. "It's okay. Just . . . drive carefully. I love you."

"Love you, too." He clicked off.

I got ready, which meant showering downstairs (I'd installed a makeshift showerhead) and being licked by Pepper as I got out (she loved the taste of my soap). I got dressed in a skirt and shirt, then ditched it for a flowered dress and little sweater. Couldn't find my blue pumps so I wore the cowboy boots that made Pepper bark, and so I left the house with a dog who simultaneously loved me and feared my footwear. Getting her into the car took some effort, torn as she was. Right as I pulled up to Mom's, I realized I'd offered to bring wine, so I had to run to the package store and buy some that would pass the snob test. Jules and Oliver had a wine cellar *and* a wine fridge.

Finally, I got to the house. Pepper liked my dad, and he seemed to be interested in her. She bolted for the dining room the minute we got in. From the sound of it, people were already here.

"There you are," Mom said. "I said six o'clock. It's almost seven. Your friend Carter made it on time from New York. You had two miles, Sadie."

"I know, and Alexander will be late, too, I'm afraid. Here." I handed her the wine. "Hi, Mom. You look pretty."

She sighed and took the two wine bottles into the kitchen. I checked on my dad before going into the family room, where everyone else seemed to be. Sure enough, Pepper was already curled up on his bed.

"You're Pepper's favorite, Daddy," I said.

He didn't look at me. He was just looking ahead, but his hand was on Pepper's bony little head.

"You like her, Dad? Do you like the dog?"

He looked at me then, and my heart leaped. "You do, right? You like Pepper?"

She licked his hand, and he smiled.

Oh, my God, he smiled! "Good job, Daddy," I whispered around the immediate lump in my throat.

"Hey. I didn't know you were here." It was Jules. "Where's your boy toy? Also, did you know your friend Carter is gay?"

"Why, yes, I did, since I've known him for years and years. Jules, Dad just smiled at me! Because of Pepper!"

"Right. You got a dog."

"Juliet. Our father just *smiled*."

"Good. Great job, Dad." She took a sip of her wine. "You coming to join the rest of us? Also, you should've told Mom your friend is gay. She's trying to fix him up with one of her guests. A woman."

"Oh, shit."

"Also, Sadie, remember what the doctor said. Smiling could just be a reflex, you know?"

"No, Jules, it wasn't. I asked him if he liked Pepper, and she licked his hand, and he smiled. That's significant."

"Sure."

"What is *with* you? Did he beat you or lock you in the cellar before I was born? Why aren't you more excited?"

"He's asleep now. You gonna join us or what?"

I closed my eyes briefly, then looked at my father. He *was* asleep, Pepper's head on his leg. I covered them both with a soft throw and followed my sister into the back. "You look good, by the way," I told her.

"Are you making fun of me?" She jerked to a stop in the hallway and turned to glare at me.

"No! Why? Should I have said you look like shit? You just look . . . pretty. I'm sorry. Was that a wrong thing to say? No. It's not. I revoke my apology."

"Can you do me one favor? Be nice to Mom."

"I . . . okay. Check."

Carter saw me first and gave me a big bear hug. "I've missed you so desperately! How are you, precious?" He lowered his voice to a whisper. "Why does your mother think I'm straight? Will she stone me if I tell her I like boys?"

"She's very accepting, if obtuse. I'm so sorry. I missed you, too!" I kissed him on the cheek. "We're still on for tomorrow morning, right?"

"What's tomorrow morning?"

"I show you my house, you wave your magical *Queer Eye* wand and boom! It's beautiful, and we go out for brunch with Alexander."

"Oh, honey, I'm sorry. I'm going to the casino tomorrow with Josh. He loves the craps table."

"You brought Josh?"

"He's coming tomorrow." Carter paused for effect. "It's official. He's my boyfriend, and we're getting matching tattoos. Now come. Mingle, and break the news to your mother that I won't be dating that nice girl in the corner."

The family room was two steps down, and there were more people here than I'd expected. Oliver (smiling, ever smiling, which shouldn't irritate me as much as it did), Caro and her boo, Ted or Theo or Tim, I could never remember, and . . .

Oh, crap. Noah. And (not crap) Mickey and their baby. Little Marcus was being cooed over by my mother at the moment.

That could've been her grandchild. The thought came unbidden. But yeah. Once, I thought I'd be the mother of Noah's children, long before I'd asked myself if I wanted to be a mother at all.

Shit. Where was Alexander?

I turned, then froze. Sweet baby Jesus. Though I hadn't ever seen her in person, I knew her right away. Gillian Epstein. Noah's ex-fiancée.

What the *what*?

She looked up at me, and she obviously recognized me, too, because she flinched the teeniest bit. "Hi," she said after a beat. "I'm Gillian Epstein." Ah. A hard *G*, not the *J* sound. I hadn't expected that.

"I'm Sadie. Barb's daughter."

"Believe me, I know who you are." She forced a smile. "I was engaged to Noah a few years back."

"Right. I knew that. From Facebook, that is. You know. We have mutual friends, I mean, of course we do, we grew up together, Noah and I that is, not you and me"—*stop yourself, Sadie*—"and I guess one of my friends commented on your picture, and you'd tagged Noah, so I . . . well. I knew he was engaged."

She looked to the left, hoping for someone to save her, no doubt. I, too, cast about for a savior. Where had Carter gone? And why, *why* did Alexander have to be late today?

Gillian—I kind of hated the hard *G*—was even prettier in person. Olive skin, green eyes, really good lashes (natural, damn her). Perfect body, nice clothes. She even smelled nice, like oranges.

"So you and Noah stayed friends, I guess?" I said.

"No. It's kind of hard to stay friends with the person who broke your heart and embarrassed you by calling off your wedding."

Youch. "Yeah, that would be . . . tricky." I felt sweat prickling in my armpits. "You're very honest."

"Are *you* and Noah still friends?" she asked.

"Oh, uh . . . yes? Sort of? Not really, no. I mean, it's different, since he and I have known each other since kindergarten. Maybe before that. And we were never, um, engaged."

She cocked a well-groomed eyebrow, as if doubting me.

"Gillian, uh . . . you mind if I ask why you're here?"

"Your mother invited me. I'm an event planner, and I'm handling the town's three hundred and fiftieth anniversary weekend. I wasn't aware Noah and his . . . partner . . . would be here."

"Mickey." I lowered my voice. "She's gay. They're just coparents. It's not romantic."

"I *know* that."

"Cool. Great. Information is good to have. That's great." I needed a drink. Gillian probably needed more to drink. Or a Xanax.

Ah. My mother was handing the baby off to Mickey. "Mom! Let me help you with dinner!" I said. "Excuse me, Gillian. So nice to meet you."

I dragged my mom into the kitchen. "What are you doing?" I hissed.

"As usual, Sadie, I have no idea what you're talking about."

"Gillian Epstein and Noah used to be engaged."

"Oh. Oh, dear. I didn't think of that." She blinked at me. She looked tired, I suddenly noticed. Of course she did, living with Dad, doing her part in his care.

"Also . . . I used to date Noah, remember? It's awkward to have to schmooze with his ex. And it might be awkward for him, too, don't you think? And, not to put too fine a point on it, awkward for me to be with both of them."

"I just told you, Sadie, I forgot! I invited her because she'd mentioned how hard it was to meet a nice man, and I thought maybe your friend and she would hit it off."

"My friend is gay. And thirty years older than Gillian."

"Do you have to jump down my throat with a houseful of guests here? Hm? Do you? Noah's been very kind to your father. And you, missy. Didn't he fix your furnace?"

"Yes. But—"

"Gillian is handling the town's anniversary, and who knows? Maybe Noah will realize he made a big mistake."

I blinked. "I don't think you should try to get them back together."

"You have a boyfriend, Sadie. It's not really your business, is it?"

Ouch. "I don't. I mean . . . I just think it's weird to try to fix up your daughter's ex-boyfriend with his ex-fiancée."

Caro popped her head in. "Need help, Barb? Hi, Sadie, sweetheart."

"Hi, Caro. You look beautiful, as always."

"I know, and thank you, angel. Barb, what can I do?"

"We'll be eating in a few minutes, so if you could start herding everyone in here, that'd be great."

Caro flashed her dimples at me and popped back out.

"So. You won't try to push Gillian and Noah together," I said, just to be clear.

"Whatever happens with them happens, Sadie. She does a lot of events in town and she knows everyone. Maybe she can help you find a job while you're here, who knows? You could run errands for her."

Nice. "I have a job," I said.

"Is that right."

"I paint."

"Of course. Now, would you mind getting your father so we can eat?" She went back into the family room, all smiles for everyone but me.

It would be nice to like my mother as much as other people did. Then again, they didn't get the side of her I did—the slightly irritated, impatient, better-things-to-do mother who already had a perfect daughter and couldn't be bothered with me. She had a knack for peeing on everything I liked or did in ways both subtle and obvious and then wondered why I didn't seek her out the way Juliet did. It was exhausting.

I took a deep breath and went back to the dining room. I bet my dad missed being in a proper bedroom. Pepper was still curled at his side, looking like a giant cinnamon bun, snoring gently. My father's eyes were open. "Hey, Dad," I said. "Mom's driving me crazy, but what else is new, right?"

He glanced at me, looking blank, and my eyes filled. "It's me, Dad. Sadie. You know who I am, right?"

I thought his expression softened a little. "Of course you do. I'm your daughter, and I love you." Pepper's tail wagged, beating on the bed. "And my little doggy loves you, too. Right, Pepper?"

"Do you need help?"

Noah. I wiped my eyes before turning. "Sure. Thanks." He came closer, and his hair was extra curly. Must've just washed it. Not that I was thinking about Noah in the shower or anything. I cleared my throat. "Hey, I'm sorry my mom invited your . . . um, Gillian."

"Why?"

"Because it might be awkward for you."

"It's not. She's a good person." There was already an edge in his voice.

"I'm sure she is."

"Is it awkward for you?"

"Of course not! Why would it be? I'm great! How's the baby, by the way? And Mickey's still nursing? Is it going well?"

He gave me a pained look. "Why don't you ask her?"

"I will do so." Blathering like an idiot yet again, and over my father's balding head. "Come on, Dad. Time for dinner." Noah took one of his arms, and I took the other.

"Whose dog is this?" Noah asked.

"Mine. Pepper, meet Noah. Noah, this is my puppy, Pepper."

She licked his face, and he laughed.

Oh, that laugh. That sooty, low scraping laugh. A hundred memories of Noah laughing flashed through my head—hearing it in high school, turning to see him smiling at me, the two of us walking to get coffee, his big, strong hand holding mine, or best of all, in bed, his skin warm against mine, that soft, tangled black hair framing his face.

Yep.

Pepper was going to town on him, lucky thing, and he picked her up and set her on the floor. "Okay, Mr. Frost, one, two, three. There you go."

Together, we helped Dad get his walker and come into the kitchen.

It was really, really unfortunate that my boyfriend was stuck in traffic. I could use an ally to fight these memories before I fell in love with Noah Pelletier all over again.

CHAPTER TWENTY-ONE

Juliet

Juliet Frost had seduction on her mind, which was hard enough since she was in her mother's house with her brain-damaged father, her yappy sister and about six other people.

But sex with Oliver was on her list of things to do tonight, and she owed him some sparkly time. She sipped the wine she'd brought and smiled hard.

Knowing that her father had had an affair had shaken her to the roots. That her father—her *father*, that steadiest of men, married for *fifty* years—could have an affair made her feel that every second Oliver was not in view, he, too, could be screwing some other woman, or thinking about it, or flirting or looking or . . . or smelling some other woman.

Perhaps she should lay off the wine.

Which wouldn't calm her fears. Oliver had never once indicated anything but happiness in their marriage, but it happened. Half of marriages ended in divorce! Half! Why were she and Ollie any better than anyone else? She'd spent half her workday Googling "why do men have affairs?" It happens even in the best marriages, the literature said darkly.

So it *could* happen to them. Had she and Oliver fought? Of course. About stupid things, like . . . well, like the time she had to leave vacation early because of a work crisis a few years ago. The time he broke her favorite mug, because even though she told him it was fragile and special to her, he handled dishes as if he didn't have opposable thumbs. The way he let Brianna get away with things when Juliet tried to lay down the law. But they'd never spoken about unhappiness or a lack of love. Never. They'd never raised their voices to each other. Never.

Mom and Dad had never fought, either.

So reminding Oliver that she was a desirable woman who loved sex and was spontaneous and adventuresome, especially after she hadn't been able to kiss him for the past three days, thanks to those stupid injections . . . that was on her list. As was coming to this party, because Mom was utterly heroic, doing all this, trying to get people around Dad. (God. If she only knew.)

Juliet had dressed up for this evening, which Mom always appreciated, and wore a stretchy white dress that required a serious bra, which currently seemed to be intent on embedding itself in her rib cage. Three-inch red suede heels she hadn't worn in years. A thong for the planned seduction. A thong that may or may not have worked itself into her lower intestine.

Sparkly. Sparkly. She had to be sparkly. She'd talked to everyone here tonight—the event planner Mom thought so highly of, Noah, Mickey Watkins, Ted, Caro, Sadie's friend from the city, who was very nice. She'd held little Marcus. Endured Sadie's predictions of a full recovery for their father. If only *Sadie* knew. God. That would kill her, knowing their dad had had an affair. The two of them had always been so close. Dad had never paid too much interest in Juliet. Not that she resented it. Much. Anymore.

She finished her glass of wine and got another before everyone sat down. Sadie had been in charge of the wine tonight, and Juliet had brought a couple of additional bottles, correctly anticipating that her sister wouldn't bring enough. Not that she was cheap; she just wouldn't think too hard about how many people were coming.

"How's the house, Sadie?" she asked brightly as everyone sat down to dinner. "Fallen in the Sound yet?"

"Not yet," Sadie said. "A few shingles blew off the roof last night, but I plan on getting up there and fixing all that."

"Please don't," Noah said. "Hire someone."

"I think I'm very handy, actually," she said. "But thanks for your concern."

"You're handy?" Carter asked. Yes, Carter, that was his name. The friendly friend from the city. "Remember when you broke the sink in the teachers' bathroom because you forgot which way the knobs turned?"

"I have no recollection of that event, no," Sadie said, grinning. Always getting away with being a ditz and thinking it was charm. Maybe it was. Maybe Juliet should try it.

"Does anyone mind if I breastfeed?" asked Mickey, and, not waiting, pulled up her shirt and attached the baby. "No one is scared of boobs, right? Although I have to say, they do look a little scary these days. No one told me I'd become Joan from *Mad Men* after popping out this little bruiser. I was a 34-B before Noah knocked me up." She glanced at Gillian, who looked green. "Sorry. Shit, Gillian, I'm really sorry. You too, Sadie."

Right. Right. The event planner had been engaged to Noah. The baby was making smacking sounds.

Sadie's teacher friend smiled. "I love watching a woman breastfeed," he said. "So natural."

"Thanks, dude," Mickey said. "You're okay."

Dad, too, was staring at Mickey's breast. It was hard to miss, but was he looking at it lustfully? And if so, doubly gross, because (a) it belonged to a woman not his wife and (b) it was feeding a baby, so lusting was just icky.

She *really* had to tell her mother about that other woman. Or she really shouldn't *ever* tell her mother. God! How could her father be such an asshole? She hated him . . . except seeing him wobbly and silent and staring at a strange woman's boob made her both want to curl into a ball and sob or kick him and also have him just die already and let her mother be free.

"Barb, this asparagus is wonderful," said the event planner. Gillian.

"It is," Oliver agreed. "You're a smashing cook, Mum."

The nicest man in the world was her husband. Time for a little seduction. She slid off her shoe (blessed relief) and reached her foot out to slide up his pant leg. Nothing . . . nothing . . . Could a foot grope? If so, her foot was groping into emptiness. There.

She hooked her toe in his pants and slid it up.

Mickey jumped. Oliver didn't. Shit. Wrong leg. Mickey gave her a reproachful look over her baby's head.

"Sorry," Juliet murmured. "I thought you were my husband."

"That's what they all say."

Okay, so no foot sex or whatever that move was called. More wine was a good idea.

Caro and Ted seemed to be fighting in whispers. Gillian looked wretched. "My mom says you're amazing at what you do, Gillian," Juliet said. "How did you get started?"

"Oh, funny story," Gillian said. "So, it was my mom and dad's thirty-fifth anniversary, and I thought, why not throw them a big party? And I got the bug! I just love organizing."

Juliet waited for the funny part, but apparently Gillian was done.

"That *is* funny. Ha. Ha ha." Yes. She was a little drunk. Dad was looking at Gillian now. Maybe he was interested in her in his foggy, befuddled state. Like the woman he'd been kissing, Gillian had dark hair.

How many women wished their fathers were dead after seeing them cheating on their moms? CNN should do a poll.

A knock came on the kitchen door.

"Who could that be?" Barb asked, getting up to answer it.

"Elijah the prophet?" Oliver suggested. It was his go-to joke when someone interrupted dinner, and it always made her laugh. No one else got it, apparently, and her laugh sounded too loud in the vacuum.

"Can I help you?" Barb said. "Oh! Hello there!"

It was Janet, the woman from Gaylord whose brother had been down the hall from Dad. She'd been really nice, Juliet remembered, if fashion challenged. Her hair was in two long, gray braids, and she wore overalls over a flannel shirt. "Oh, shit," she said. "You're having a party. I'm so sorry. I was in the neighborhood. Thought I'd drop in."

"No, no, come in. Please. Girls, do you remember Janet? How's your brother, Janet? Have a seat. Would you like some wine?"

"No, thanks. I don't drink. Hey, Juliet. Sadie. Everyone else." Her eyes stopped on Dad's face. "Hey, John. How's it going, buddy?"

Dad's mouth hung open for a second, then he burst into a big smile. "You!" he said. "You."

There was a moment of silence.

"That's *right*, Dad," said Sadie, her voice breathless. "You know her!"

"You sure do," Janet said, going closer. "How's my old pal?"

Dad grabbed her hand and kissed it. Jesus. How nice for Mom. Had he slept with Janet while at Gaylord? Probably not, but still. Cheating asshole.

"You," he repeated.

His first word since the stroke, and it wasn't even directed at a family member, the bastard. Why put family first when he'd had his tongue down some other woman's throat? When he didn't even have the decency to divorce Mom before cheating on her? That slut should be the one stuck with him now.

Forty-three years old, and feeling like Brianna, sullen and judgmental and wishing she could kick a sick old man. Not a proud moment. She poured herself more wine and drank it, grateful that tomorrow was the weekend.

. . .

An hour later, Sadie was still happily snuffling her tears of joy. Mom had called LeVon, who said this was a very good sign, and Caro had gotten Janet a plate and heated it up in the microwave. Janet was talking about her brother's progress at Rose Hill, a care facility north of Stoningham. Noah was holding his sleeping baby, Mickey was in the bathroom, Gillian was subtly texting someone for help, no doubt, and Juliet was drunk.

That was when the vacuous waste of space known as her sister's boyfriend walked in.

"Our yacht salesman is here! The man of the people has arrived!" Juliet announced.

"Hon," Oliver said in a low voice, "I think you should tone it down a little."

"Why? He's three hours late."

Sadie got up and hugged him, but not before shooting a look at Noah. "Honey! You made it. Guess what? My father spoke tonight! He recognized Janet!"

"And who's Janet?" he said. "Mrs. Frost, I'm so sorry I'm late."

"Don't worry about it, dear," she said. "Do you know everyone? This is Janet, our friend from Gaylord, and Noah and Mickey and their little boy, and this is Gillian, a friend of mine."

"Hello. Nice to meet you," Alexander said, smiling blandly.

"We've met, actually," Gillian said. "I organized the yacht christening in Clinton last fall. The Parkers?"

"Oh, right!" he said, clearly not recognizing her. "Small world."

Mickey came in, still buckling her pants. "How long did it take for your period to get back to normal after you had babies, Juliet?" she asked.

"Nope. Not gonna talk periods at a dinner party," she answered.

"Thank you!" said Alexander, and Juliet rolled her eyes.

Bad idea. The room was starting to spin a little. "Let's go home and get naked," she whispered to Oliver. He gave her a look that did not say *great idea*.

Perhaps she had been a little loud.

Gillian stood up. "I should go. This has been . . . yes! Thank you, Barb. I'll be in touch. So good to see everyone."

Poor thing. "Sorry!" Juliet called. "We're usually better company than this."

"I'm taking you home," Oliver murmured.

"I should stay and clean up."

"No, you should come home and sleep it off. Come on. Mum, thank you. We have to get going." They muttered a minute, talking about her, no doubt.

As soon as they were in the car, Oliver said, "What on earth is going on with you?" His voice was sharp.

"Um . . . nothing?"

"You were *really* off tonight."

"Why?"

"You're pissed, for one."

"You know what, Oliver? It's kind of hard to see my father like this. Then he recognizes that woman? Not me, not Sadie, and God forbid, not Mom. Some woman he barely knows."

"So that makes it all right for you to get drunk at your mum's party? Does that make it easier on anyone?"

"Yes, Oliver. It makes it easier on me." She looked at him. "Don't be mad. I'm just a little"—*past my prime at work and hiding a horrible secret about my father and considering a job as a smoke jumper and not sure our older child loves me anymore and a little terrified that you'll leave me someday*—"stressed. Take me home and ravish me."

"I don't think so," Oliver said. "I don't ravish drunk women."

"Even your wife, who just asked you to?"

"When you've sobered up, I'd really like us to have a meaningful conversation."

Shit. Panic threaded through her foggy brain. "About what?"

"Darling. You're drunk. You had at least three glasses of wine."

"In England, that would be called a good start."

"You haven't been yourself lately, and it's not just your dad, though of course that's hard. But something's off, and it has been for months."

"Pull over."

"What?"

"I'm gonna puke."

And so her evening ended, barfing in front of the McMasterons' house, her husband sighing and holding back her hair.

So much for seduction.

CHAPTER TWENTY-TWO

Barb

LeVon was leaving us.

I knew the day would come, but I cried just the same. He was going to Rose Hill Rehabilitation and Care Center a half an hour north, the place Genevieve London had endowed before her death. LeVon would be director of patient services, and of course I couldn't begrudge him the change. He said it was his dream job.

"We'll stay friends," he said over tea, kindly covering my hand with his. "And I can recommend some great caregivers and therapists."

I nodded. "You're irreplaceable, LeVon." I had to wipe my eyes on a napkin.

"I think you're pretty amazing yourself, Barb. A lot of people fall apart when something like this happens."

"They must not be from Minnesota." He laughed, those kind eyes and ready smile. I squeezed his hand. "If I'd ever had a son, I hope he would've been like you, LeVon."

It was his turn to get teary. "That means a lot to me. I'll be here till the end of the month, so don't you worry. I'm not abandoning this ship."

"Will he get better, LeVon? I know you're not supposed to guess, but what do you think?"

He took a deep breath and let it out slowly. "Technically, you're right. I can't guess, and patients surprise us all the time. But I don't think he'll ever recover completely, no. Most of the patients I've seen with hemorrhagic stroke and traumatic brain injuries . . . at his age, no, I don't think he'll ever go back to being the guy you used to know."

I nodded, my heart sinking even though I'd kinda known that already. "Well. Thank you."

Sadie wasn't coming today; she had to do something with that little pile of sticks she called a house, so I'd left work early. I had to e-mail Gillian about the town's birthday (and apologize for that wretched dinner party) and call Juliet (who had been a bit tipsy, which wasn't like her). I had a speech to write for the Small Town Coalition and a few e-mails to return. A phone call to Lucille Dworkin, who had been pestering Lindsey to see if we would arrest her neighbor for using his leaf blower before eight a.m. on a Saturday.

I looked in on John, who was asleep in his chair, and took the soft cashmere throw I'd splurged on last year, tucking it around him in case he was cold. Regulating his body temperature was one of his medical issues these days. His hair was sticking up on one side, and I smoothed it down. He didn't stir. I hadn't shaved him today, because it made him agitated, and he had a fuzz of white stubble on his face.

He looked so old.

A knock came on the door, and it was a relief to answer it.

Janet Hubb, who had crashed our dinner party and inspired John to say his first intelligible, post-stroke word, stood there, smiling.

"Hey, Barb," she said. "On my way to see my brother, thought I'd pop by."

"Hello, Janet. Come on in."

I wasn't sure why I liked Janet, but I did. She was the type of woman who didn't care about postmenopausal facial hair—I had to force my eyes not to study her lip—and she only seemed to wear overalls and those awful gardening clogs. I liked her hair, her granny glasses, her bulky, hand-knit sweaters (although perhaps I'd knit her something with a little less hay in it, fewer dropped stitches).

"How you doing today, friend?" she asked, taking a seat at the kitchen table. "How's our John?"

Our John. "He's resting."

"Yeah. So it's none of my business, but I picked up some weird vibes last weekend, and I just wanted to check on you."

"Ah. Yes."

"How are you feeling? I mean, you've been through the wringer. Your kids, too. The drunk one? I thought she might stab me with her fork."

"Oh, Juliet is lovely. She would never stab anyone with a fork. Or any instrument." I sat down, too. "Tell me, Janet. You obviously like John for some reason."

"Yeah. He's cool."

"Why would you say that?"

"I don't know. He listens really well."

"He has no choice, does he?"

She smiled. "Good point. I feel like he hears me, though."

"I feel like he hears you, too. He always brightened up when you came into his room at Gaylord, and the fact that he spoke when he saw you . . . that was a real breakthrough."

"Has he started talking more?"

"No." Just those three *you*s when he saw Janet. Apparently, the women who inspired John were not in his family. I wondered what he'd do or say if Karen visited, but she wouldn't, would she? Theirs was a love that was more than a love only when she thought he was wealthy. She wasn't the type who would wipe drool from a man's face.

As Janet had last weekend, after the hand kissing.

"This is a really pretty house, by the way," Janet said.

"John cheated on me," I said. "I only found out after his stroke."

"Well . . . fuck."

"Yes. My daughters don't know."

"So you're all alone with this?"

"My best friend knows. Would you like some coffee? I baked cookies with my granddaughters yesterday, too."

"I love cookies. Sure, I'll take a coffee. Thanks, Barb."

For the next hour, we talked. Janet told me about her brother and his progress. They only had each other, she said; their parents died when they were teenagers, and Janet had become Frank's legal guardian at the age of eighteen to his twelve. They'd had no other relatives for most of their lives, and they were so close they lived on the same street before his accident.

I thought about my six siblings. Nancy had sent a card when I told her about John via e-mail, but otherwise, I hadn't heard from anyone.

"Have you thought about putting John in Rose Hill?" Janet asked. "It's fab. They have a saltwater pool, and the food is great."

For a second, I imagined the freedom of having John in a facility. Those weeks when he was at Gaylord and I was alone in the house, and how . . . peaceful they had been. I was so tired these days.

Then I pictured myself in his situation, away from home, surrounded by strangers.

"I don't know that he meets the criteria," I said. Rose Hill was for the profoundly disabled, so far as I knew, and John could walk and do some of the tasks of daily living. "My girls and I can take care of him, anyway."

"You're good people, Barb."

"Thank you. You too."

"Okay if I visit with the old man?"

"Absolutely. He's in the living room, sleeping in the recliner."

She popped the last cookie in her mouth, waggled her impressive eyebrows and left the room.

It was strange, how many people had come to visit John. Caro's Ted came fairly often, even though the men had never been particularly close outside of our couple nights. Noah brought his baby over at least once a week, and seeing John hold sweet little Marcus made me happy and brokenhearted and angry. If Sadie ever had a baby, would John know it was hers? Would it break Sadie's heart, knowing her father could never be the type of grandfather who'd give piggyback rides and read stories? Not that he'd done that with Sloane or Brianna, mind you. Always with one foot out of the room, John.

Juliet and Oliver came, too, often bringing the girls. And Sadie was here every day. She was so devoted. Had it been me in that recliner, I wondered if she would've moved back.

Well. Apparently John had a way with people. Just not with me. Our window had closed long before his stroke, and maybe long before I decided to divorce him.

It takes two to make a good marriage, and only one to ruin it. But in the past several weeks, I'd been spending a lot of time awake at night, thinking about my role as a wife. I had stopped making John a priority a long time ago. When Juliet came into this world, she had outshone everything, and I resented his half attention to her, the way he didn't seem to adore her as much as I did. He became superfluous to our life. If I hadn't had Sadie, I wondered if we might have divorced years ago.

I had tried, yes. Those dance classes (ugh), the forced conversations, the date nights, all that. But maybe it had been too little, too late. Maybe John had been waiting for *me* all those years when I gave him my half attention, my irritation, the unpleasant but honest feeling that he was in the way. I wanted to love him, and I'd thought I might again . . . but the truth was, I'd cast him in the role of inept and irritating husband long ago.

Not that it excused his affair, not at all. I'd been ready to divorce him; he'd gone the cheap and easy way of cheating.

Sometimes, though, I'd remember the way his eyes lit up when I came into the room in our little red house in Cranston. I'd had that, and yet somewhere during the in-between spaces of our lives, I let it slip away. Infertility had eaten away at me, and I'd tried to drown my sorrow by becoming part of Stoningham, and then, when motherhood did come, we stopped being a real couple. Maybe we would've faded away no matter what, but I didn't try real hard, either.

So maybe I owed John more than I wanted to admit. To love, honor and cherish . . . maybe I'd broken my vows, too.

CHAPTER TWENTY-THREE

Sadie

It was so, so good to spend the weekend with Alexander. He reminded me of who I was outside of my family, something more than the "other" daughter, the one who wasn't as smart, accomplished or wealthy, or married and a mom.

With Alexander, I was fun, smart, hot, interesting—a person he wanted to be with. Same as my dad (minus the hot part, obviously). We drove up to the casino for dinner with Carter and Josh. Carter, ever on my side, made a few little hints about marriage—"Can't wait to be your man of honor"—okay, pretty big hints. Alexander put his arm around me and kissed my temple. He picked up the tab with great flourish, and we all left fatter and happy and full of laughter and friendship. I felt loved again. I really did.

I felt better than I had since Dad's stroke. The way he'd recognized Janet was astonishing, and I'd been over every day, trying to get him to say another word (my name, can you blame me?). The speech therapist and I talked for two hours, and I went to the house when she was there.

He might've said *dog* when Pepper jumped on his lap. *Duh* . . . It was close to *dog*, right? He was getting there.

But today, I told Mom I had to spend some time on my house and had already painted the upstairs bedroom pale gray. If Dad improved enough, I could go back to the city in the fall, so this little hovel had to be on the market for summer. Hours on the Internet had taught me everything I needed to know. Ikea was my friend, and yes, I could wield the sledgehammer taken from my parents' shed.

My plan was to knock down the wall separating the kitchen and living room, put in white cabinets and a couple of rough wooden shelves (so on trend), and make or buy a butcher block island for the middle. Small, yes, but also smart. Buff out those old floors, stain them dark walnut, spring for a new couch, and hang a Sadie Frost original abstract on the wall. Throw pillows. Rocking chair from my old room. A coffee table made from some cool wood. Bamboo and rice-paper blinds so the serial killers couldn't see in. Sand the rust out of the bathtub, bleach the shit out of the tile floor, buy some bright blue towels, and voilà. A summertime jewel.

You'd think with an architect sister, I might get some help. You'd be wrong. Juliet was weird lately. Jumpy. I invited her over one night, hoping for some advice and (cough) sisterly bonding, but she said she had to spend time working on Sloane's reading skills. Fair enough.

Time to take down that wall. "Okay, Pepper Puppy, stand back," I said, and she cocked her head at me, pricking her silky ears. "Maybe you should go outside," I said, remembering that people usually wore respirators for this kind of thing. I let her out; she never ran away, good doggy that she was. Then I tied a dishcloth over my face, cranked up Prince for company—"I Would Die 4 U"—and got a-swingin'.

Boom! Ohh. Therapy *and* home improvement rolled into one. Boom! Swinging a sledgehammer was fun!

And honestly, it didn't take that long, probably because the house was older than dirt, the Sheetrock crumbly with years of humidity and mold. Even the two-by-fours came down easily enough, crooked old nails and bits of other types of wood testifying that the house had been built by someone without a license.

Twenty minutes later, I stood in a much bigger area, a pile of rubble at my feet. "Take that, Jules," I said, and texted her a picture of my destroyed wall.

DIY, baby!

Then I turned off the music, went outside to get the dust out of my lungs. My dishcloth was covered in nastiness, which I hopefully hadn't inhaled.

Pepper lay on the lawn, gnawing on a stick, which I pried out of her mouth and threw.

"Fetch!" I said, and she raced after it, picked it up and lay down again. "Bring it here, Pepper! Here! Come! Come on!"

Nothing. Well, we all had our talents. I sat on the front steps of the porch and felt the stillness settle over me, seep into my bones.

The air was heavy with the smell of brackish water. The tide was coming in, the river rushing along the reed-filled banks, and the sunset was setting up to be glorious.

If I were to paint the scene, I'd use my palest blue for the sky, and slate gray for the clouds, edging them with tangerine and apricot, and a hint of gold. Every minute, the color changed, deepening, sliding from one shade to the next. The tidal river picked up some reflected color—red, salmon, pink—and the gold of the grasses seemed to glow. The red-winged blackbirds chuckled, and somewhere far away a wood thrush sang, rich and full.

This porch was perfect for sunset viewing. A little wicker couch, or two Adirondack chairs and a little table to hold your wineglass.

An osprey flew over me, its white belly and striped tail feathers picking up the gold of the setting sun. That would be in my painting, too. I glanced over my shoulder and saw someone driving over the bridge now, a pickup truck, its headlights sweeping the increasing dusk.

Yes. This would be my painting. This moment, right here, right now. *Homecoming*, I'd call it.

Not that I did that kind of thing anymore.

But suddenly, I wanted to.

I hadn't painted a skyscape in years and years. Not since I left for school and found out the art world didn't want pretty pictures of pretty places.

Fuck the art world. I headed inside for my camera to capture the colors, the moment, the scope and feeling.

Just as I went into the house, a pickup truck came into my driveway at top speed. I paused.

It was Noah, practically leaping out of his truck. "Sadie! Get out of the house!" Pepper ran to him, wagging her tail so hard it looked like it was going in circles as she yipped with joy.

"Hi!" I said. "What are you doing here?"

He ran up onto the porch, grabbed my arm and dragged me back into the yard. "Your sister texted me. You just knocked down a load-bearing wall."

"Is that bad?" I asked.

"Honey, get away from the house, okay?" He held my arms as if he wanted to plant me in place. "Let me see if I can get something up before the second floor falls in."

Honey. He called me honey.

Le sigh.

Then I blinked. "What? Shit! Let me help you. What's a load-bearing wall?"

"The kind that holds up the second floor." He cut me a look. "You need to stop being handy." He opened the door. "Jesus. You're lucky you're not buried right now. Come on. I have support beams in my truck. And a stepladder. Quick."

I helped him haul the materials in.

Support beams, I quickly learned, were the kind that hold up second stories after people who watched too much HGTV did idiotic things. Noah quickly made two inverted Vs of fresh two-by-fours to hold up the second floor, securing them so they were jammed tight between floor and ceiling.

When he stood on the ladder to nail them in, his T-shirt pulled out of his jeans, exposing a strip of his lean belly, a trail of hair running from his navel into his waistband. I swallowed.

He knew what he was doing, this guy. Nail gun, drill, a few swear words, big, thick, strong arms, that beautiful head of hair . . . everything you'd want in a carpenter.

"You can't sleep here tonight," he said. "I'll come back tomorrow and put in a permanent beam, but this should hold it for now. Can you stop watching HGTV?"

"That's exactly what Jules said."

"She might know something, don't you think?"

"Yeah. Okay. I'm . . . I . . . thank you, Noah. You saved me. And Pepper." At the sound of her name, my dog collapsed on his work boots, rolling over to expose her belly should he be so moved as to rub it.

He obeyed her silent command. "Just leave the carpentry to the carpenters."

"Yes, Mr. Pelletier."

He almost smiled at that. "You know," he said, jerking his chin at the front of my house, "I'd get rid of this picture window here and put in three floor-to-ceiling windows. The view is the only thing this house has going for it. Might as well make the most of it."

"Do you know any carpenters who might be available?"

"Finlay Construction. They're the best."

"I was broadly hinting that you might do this for me, Noah. I'll pay you, of course."

"I don't really do construction. I'm a finish carpenter. I work for Finlay on a lot of jobs. Furniture, doorframes, trim work."

"But you *could* do it. You are capable of doing it."

He looked at me assessingly. "I'm expensive."

"I just won Powerball. I can afford you."

"Good, because I'll charge you an irritation fee." He folded up the stepladder and grabbed his nail gun or screw gun or whatever the yellow thingy was called. "Don't go upstairs for anything. Your mom or Juliet will have a toothbrush and clothes you can borrow."

True enough. "Want a beer?" I asked. "We can drink it on the porch. Or in the back of your pickup." Well, didn't that sound like a proposition. "Or on the porch. If it's safe."

He hesitated before answering. "Sure."

As Noah put his stuff back in the truck, I got two IPAs from my fridge, uncapped them (gently, in case the noise caused my bedroom to fall on me), and went out to the porch. Noah came and sat next to me, keeping a couple of feet between us. From somewhere behind us, the peepers were singing. It was full dark now, but the moon was rising.

"Full moon," I said.

Pepper lay down between us, and Noah petted her idly.

"Almost full. Tomorrow. The pink moon." He took a swig of beer.

"How do you know it'll be pink?"

"That's what the full moon in April is called."

"They have names?" I asked. What a cute idea.

"Yep."

"What's March's full moon called?"

"The worm moon."

"Really? Poor March. What about May?"

"Flower moon." He glanced at me.

"Are you making this up?"

He grinned. "Nope. Just a *Farmers' Almanac* geek."

I took a sip of beer, too. The peepers were so shrill and sweet. I'd forgotten that sound. "How are you, Noah? Are you happy?"

"Sure."

"Did fatherhood do that for you?"

"Mm-hm."

"It's nice, seeing you with a baby. You look like a natural."

He didn't answer for a minute. "I always thought we'd have kids together."

There it was.

"Me too," I whispered, then cleared my throat. "Yeah. Me too. Life is funny that way."

"Are *you* happy, Sadie?"

Earlier that evening, I had been. But right now, sitting next to my first love, the song of the little frogs in the background, the gurgle of the tidal river and the almost-full moon rising, all I felt was the sorrow of what could have been. The fullness and heft of it.

My eyes were wet, and I was grateful for the relative darkness. I took a drink of my beer, and Noah let my lack of an answer go. Pepper spied a leaf and bolted off the porch to pounce on it, then rolled in the grass.

"Cute dog," he said.

"She is."

We watched her antics another minute.

"Hey, Noah? You know how you told me we weren't going to be friends?"

He nodded, not looking at me.

"I was wondering if you might reconsider."

He closed his eyes a second, then put his arm around me, pulling me a little closer. "Sure."

He was warm and solid, and his good Noah smell and the tickle of his hair made me want to go back to that pub across from Grand Central Station and figure out a way that I could have said yes. I would've told those two stubborn, stupid kids to wrap themselves around each other, to look into each other's eyes, to kiss with all the love and passion in their souls, and instead of talking about all the reasons why it wouldn't work, just say yes, goddamnit. Yes, yes, we'll find a way, because a love like this doesn't come around twice.

"I should go," Noah said, putting down his half-empty beer bottle and standing up. "I'll come by tomorrow if the wind hasn't knocked this place down."

"I wish people would stop saying that." I couldn't look at him, so I let Pepper lick my hands instead. "You're the best, Noah. Thank you."

He started to say something, then stopped. "Good night, Sadie."

I watched him drive off, the earlier image of homecoming in reverse. His headlights cut through the night, then disappeared, and the sky seemed cold and lonely.

I opted to sleep over at Juliet's and spent the rest of the evening playing Apples to Apples with Sloane, then lying on Brianna's bed as she stroked Pepper's ears. My niece told me about her friends and why they weren't really her friends, and how she wanted them back but didn't actually like them anymore and wished she could go to boarding school. "This town is so stupid," she said.

"It is, and it isn't," I said. "It's a good place to grow up."

"You couldn't wait to get out of here."

"And here I am, back again."

"Only because of Grampy." She rolled onto her belly and propped herself up with her elbows, my sister's little miniature. "Is he going to die, Sadie?"

"Nope," I said. "I mean, what happened was scary, and it *was* life-threatening, but he's out of the woods now." I tapped her little nose. "You don't have to worry about that."

"Then why does Mommy cry in her closet?"

Juliet? Cry? "Uh . . . well, it's stressful, you know?" Shit. "I mean, Grampy's getting better, but he's not his old self, and I'm sure she misses that. I do. Do you?"

She shrugged. "I guess so. I like Nana better, to be honest. She's the fun one."

"What does she do that's fun?" As ever, that image stung—my mother, a completely different person when I wasn't around. I listened as Brianna detailed things like planting seeds to grow flowers for the garden, baking, taking her clothes shopping, going to the movies just the two of them, getting matching pedicures.

Sounded damn nice. I hadn't known my grandmothers.

"Bedtime!" Juliet called, lurching to a stop as she saw me on her daughter's bed. "Sadie, the guest room's all made up." Pepper leaped off the bed, ready for the next adventure.

"Thanks," I said. "Good night, Princess Brianna. I love you!"

"Love you too, Sadie," she said with a smile. "Good night, Pepper."

A little while later, Jules stopped in my room. I had already thanked her profusely for sending Noah over, admitted my inadequacies as a home renovator and sworn to listen better and be nicer to Mom.

"Got everything you need?" she asked.

"Yes. Thank you again." Humility was the price I had to pay. "Hey, Jules. Brianna said . . ."

"What? Is she cutting herself?"

"No! Jesus. Is she?"

"I just asked you!"

"Well, not that I know of or saw. She was wearing shorty pajamas, and her skin is perfect." My sister's shoulders relaxed a few inches. "No, but she said she heard you crying? In your closet."

Jules grimaced. "Oh."

"You're okay, right?"

"Yeah. A work thing. Plus Dad and Mom."

"Do you want to talk about it?"

She sighed. Glanced down the hallway and came in, shutting the door behind her. "There's this woman at work. She's great. Very talented. I hired her, and I have nothing but good things to say about her, but . . ." She stopped. "Don't tell Oliver. Or Mom. Do not tell Mom."

"Okay." Wow. I didn't know that Jules and I had ever had a secret, especially one we kept from our mother. "So what about her?"

"She's been . . . anointed. I don't know how or why, but suddenly, I seem to be yesterday's news."

I started to answer, then stopped. This was the closest Perfection from Conception had ever come to asking for advice or sharing anything except perfect nuggets from her perfect life. My answer had to be good.

"I can't imagine that someone with your talent and work ethic, with all the beautiful buildings you've designed, could ever be yesterday's news." I paused, curling my toes, and pulled out one of my best lines for my little students when they confided in me. "But that must be very hard."

Jules looked at me a second, and I wondered if maybe I blew it. Then she gave me a fast, hard hug, and left. "Sleep well," she said.

Then she was back. "And thanks for being so great with Brianna. She worships you."

She was gone again.

Well, well, well. "Pepper," I said to my dog, who was already asleep in the middle of my bed, "I think I've just had a bonding moment with my sister."

I got into bed, content with the world. Noah . . . well, we were friends again, at least. Dad was getting better. Juliet had said something nice to me. I loved my nieces.

And I had a very good dog.

If Sister Mary could've heard my thoughts, she would've said, "Count your blessings before the shit hits the fan."

A wise woman, that.

By the time I got back to my house the next day, Noah had been there and left, and there was a new and very sturdy-looking beam where the wall had once been. *Safe to go upstairs* said the note taped to it. *I'll be back later. Clean up the rubble in the meantime.*

So bossy. But it gave me a warm feeling, knowing Noah had been here. I'd have to sell a few more couch paintings to afford paying him. Maybe more than a few. Maybe I'd have to take out a bank loan.

Whatever it cost, I didn't care.

Alexander texted me, asking if I could come to the city tonight for dinner and stay over. I was just about to turn him down, since I had homeownery things to do, when a car pulled into my little driveway. An Audi.

It was Gillian Epstein of Epstein Events.

Pepper, faithless cur that she was, bounded over to her. I wish I could report that Gillian was the type to shriek and be afraid and fuss over any fur on her clothes, but instead she bent down and rubbed Pepper's neck and spoke to her, my dog's tail beating the air so fast it was a blur.

Then she straightened up. "Got a minute?"

"You betcha!" I said. Sometimes my mother's Minnesotan accent just popped out of me.

Gillian was dressed in a red pencil skirt, a pretty white peasant blouse and a brown suede jacket I wanted to marry. I was dressed in yesterday's jeans and a shirt I swiped from Oliver. She had that walk that some women have . . . the swaying, the grace, the somewhat arrogant stride that said, "Yes, I'm really this pretty."

"My house is under construction, so it's probably best if we sit out here. Um, hang on, I'll grab a chair."

I only had one, so I graciously gave it to her, then leaned tentatively against my decrepit railing, hoping it would hold me. It did. "Uh . . . that dinner party the other night . . . I hope it wasn't too horrible."

"Oh, it was," she said. "Your mother is wonderful, though. Such an impressive woman. I don't think she remembered Noah and I were . . . together once. It's fine."

"Mickey's pretty great, though, don't you think?" I asked. "I love her. Breast is best for baby, right? Funny that both you and I probably once thought we . . . Mickey, though, huh? She's so open and fun and . . ." My hands flailed for something. "Yeah. Just great. Sense of humor. She's very honest." *Stop talking. Stop talking.*

Gillian stared at me. She took a breath, then exhaled through her nostrils in a very evil-Disney-villain kind of way. "I don't know if I should tell you this, but my therapist recommended it."

Fuck. I had been discussed in therapy. That was never a good sign. "Okay. Fire away."

"I obviously have . . . *feelings* . . . regarding you, since Noah . . . well. That's neither here nor there."

Since Noah *what*? "Mm-hm." Traitorous Pepper put her head on Gillian's lap and gazed at her adoringly.

"So. I'm going to tell you this only because I feel it's the right thing to do. Not because I'm trying to make trouble or because I'm jealous of you. I have a very strong working relationship with your mother and the entire board of selectmen, and I don't want that to jeopardize—"

"Just spit it out, Gillian. It's fine. Go ahead."

Another breath. "You're dating Alexander Mitchum, correct?"

"Yep."

"Your mother told me you'd been seeing each other a couple of years."

"Correct."

"I mentioned at the dinner party that he and I had met last spring at a yacht christening."

I suddenly had a bad feeling about this. "Uh-huh."

She looked at me, her red-painted lips tight. "He made a pretty hard pass at me."

"Oh." My eyelids seemed to be blinking too fast. "Uh . . . are you sure?"

"Yes."

"Last . . . last spring."

"Yes. May seventeenth. I checked my planner."

"And by 'hard pass,' what are we talking about? Because he's nice to everyone, and you know, schmoozing is part of his—"

"He pressed me against a wall, kissed my neck and asked me if I wanted to spend the night at the Madison Beach Hotel with him."

Oh, the fuckery.

"That is a pass. Okay. Yep. You're right." I felt a little dizzy.

"And when I said no, he told me I didn't know what I was missing.

He gave me his room key and told me I should change my mind so he could rock my world."

"Dick move." I swallowed.

"I thought so."

My legs felt weak, so I sat down, my knees wobbling like a newborn foal's. My breathing sounded funny. Too loud.

Rock your world. He'd said that to me on more than one occasion. *Want to come back to my place so I can rock your world?* I thought he meant it to be funny, and I always laughed.

And last May—I remembered it was May because of the lilacs—he'd called me and told me to take the train up to Madison. Spur of the moment, he said, because it had been late in the day on Saturday. We'd have fun. And I did, and we did, and I'd been his second choice. At *least* his second choice, because who knows if he'd made that offer to someone else at the yacht christening party?

"Look," Gillian said, and her voice was gentler now. "I'm sorry to tell you this. I know it must seem like I'm trying to get revenge because of Noah, but I'm not. I just thought I'd want to know if my boyfriend made a pass at someone else."

"No, I appreciate it," I whispered.

"Do you want a glass of water?"

"No, thanks." Pepper left Gillian and came over to me and tried to sit on my lap.

"Do you want to call someone, maybe? Your sister? Mom?"

I blinked. Put my chin on Pepper's head, getting my ear licked as thanks. "I'm okay, Gillian. I . . . I appreciate you telling me this."

She stood up, smoothed her skirt and walked past me on the steps. "I love your jacket," I whispered.

She put her hand on my shoulder. "In another world, we'd probably be friends."

Would we? "Drive safely. Bye."

She strode to her car, hips swaying the perfect amount, got in and gave me a little finger wave.

Just then, my phone beeped. I took it out. Another text from my loving boyfriend.

Please come, babe. I miss you!

Did he now?

On my way, I typed.

CHAPTER TWENTY-FOUR

John

There was another woman. In the not-so long-ago, he had been with another woman.

John remembers her hard face, which he had thought was not pretty when they met. (A party? There was dancing.) But the face became prettier as she said things he liked, things Barb didn't say anymore. He knows now he should have been smarter. That these were the things all bored old men want to hear. He thought he deserved those things. He was a man, and men should be told those things.

Handsome. Smart. Funny. Strong. Those were some of the feelings or words she had said.

He said things to that woman, and most of them were lies. He lied about Barb. He lied about his unhappiness being her fault when she had always worked so hard. He remembers how hard Barb tried to fit in, to be not so different, because she thought being from Minnesota made her less . . . something . . . than other women. He told that other woman about that, and they *laughed.* The hard-faced woman laughed at his *wife*, and John had been *glad* and it makes no sense now.

Now he remembers the meals Barb made, the cookbooks she bought, the vegetables she grew. How pretty their house was, how nice it always smelled. He remembers how loving she was with Juliet, how delighted Juliet made her.

Juliet. John knows he could have been a better father to her. He should have tried more. She is an important person in the world somehow. People know her. She is impressive.

That other woman, whose name he doesn't remember, doesn't want to remember, was like . . . like . . . like that plant that grows up a tree and chokes it. That invader. Invasive species, that's it. Kudzu. The word flies into his brain. She was kudzu, taking over, blotting out the view, tangling, and he let her.

Words are flying back into his head. Unfaithful. Cheater. Liar.

Cliché.

When his friend came, the new friend with the hair like pieces of rope, he was so happy. *She* didn't know him when he was wrong, when he was a liar and stupid. She only knows him the way he is now, and there is no disappointment or hope in her eyes, no expectation that he will be anything other than what he is. She talks to him and talks to him, and laughs. She is not pretty, not like his girls or Barb or even the other woman, but Janet—yes, her name is Janet—makes him feel at peace.

A fear seeps through him, its tentacles cold and coiling. That he has done something terrible by being sick, and his family needs him to be the father again, the husband, and that he will never be able to do this. That he has to fix something or his wife and daughters will never get . . . never be . . . never know . . .

The thought is gone.

Shame. Another word he knows now. He is ashamed of himself, for lying to Barb, about Barb. For telling the invasive species his wife was cold and self-absorbed. That she didn't care about him anymore, didn't want to talk to him, when he knows that he should've turned that knob and opened the door to the bathroom that day in the long-ago, held her close and cried with her. He knows in doing so, he could have changed the course of their lives.

That is the thought that won't go away. He hears her crying in the bathroom as he sleeps, and when he wakes up, he is so sad.

There is something about a flower he has to tell Barb. Something important. Something that will fix things, but the flower floats away. It has to come back. He has to make it come back. He has to tell her about the flower, but LeVon makes him exercise and the bossy woman asks him to make sounds, and now he is trying, trying hard, because he has something important to say.

CHAPTER TWENTY-FIVE

Sadie

I chose the restaurant in which I planned to dump Alexander, and I made sure it was as expensive as I could find, which was really saying something in New York City.

He was there already, handsome, charming . . . shithead.

"You look beautiful, as always," he said, leaning in for a kiss. I gave him my cheek. The maître d' showed us to our table, which was in a corner, because Alexander always asked for a great table. The restaurant was everything I hoped it would be—sleekly decorated, Michelin starred, quiet, with well-dressed people murmuring and drinking.

I didn't plan on murmuring, but first, I did want to order pretty much everything on the menu. Alexander, my soon-to-be ex-boyfriend, wasn't getting out of here without bleeding money.

The waiter came over. "Hello!" I said, as was my way. "How are you tonight?"

"I'm quite well, *signorina*. My name is Luciano, and it is my pleasure to serve you tonight."

"What a beautiful name," I said. "Please tell your mom she chose well! Luciano, I'll have the Fiorentino, please." I pointed to the drink that cost, yes, forty-nine dollars. Only in New York, folks.

"I thought you didn't like brandy," Alexander said.

"I've grown and changed." I smiled brightly. "What are you having, hon?" The endearment felt like poison on my lips.

"I'll have the Dante," he said.

"Very good, *signore*," Luciano said.

"Oh, and we'll have a bottle of Cristal with dinner, okay?" I said, smiling my sparkliest smile.

"Excellent! Which year?"

"Surprise us. It's a special night." I'd studied the champagne list after picking this place. The cheapest bottle of Cristal cost six hundred dollars, and the most expensive was well over a thousand.

"Babe," Alexander said, "uh, that's kind of expensive."

"Oh! We can call him back, then, babe." I raised my hand, knowing he would stop me. It would look like he couldn't afford it, and he would hate that, especially here.

As predicted . . . "No, no, it's fine. A special night, like you said. How are you, babe? How was your week?"

"So good, Alexander. So good."

He smiled, not picking up on the venom in my voice. "Well, it's great to see you. I hope you can stay a few nights. I'll be in town for four days. We could have a lot of fun. The Guggenheim has a new show, and—"

I stopped listening.

He had made a pass at another woman. He wanted to sleep with her in the hotel where we'd had sex. That image of him kissing her on the neck . . . it was kind of a specialty of his.

I wished Gillian had kicked him in the nutsack.

When the waiter came back, I was ready. "I'm starving!" I announced cheerfully to both men. "It's been a tough couple of weeks, Luciano, and I haven't been in the city in ages, and I think I want a bite of everything! How about the sea urchin with pickled fennel, the Chinese caviar, maybe . . . hmm . . . the red prawn antipasto, and the garden salad, and oh! That lobster risotto sounds great! And for my main course, the sirloin, please. With the roasted potatoes, please. And heck, throw in those wild mushrooms, too."

Luciano was in love with me now. "Excellent choices, *signorina*. For the *signore*?"

Alexander looked incredulous. "Are you sure you can eat all that, babe?"

"I'm super hungry, babe." Sparkle sparkle. "Plus, you know how these Michelin-star places are. Every plate is basically two bites of food."

Luciano chuckled warmly. "*Signorina*, you are correct. Just enough to whet the appetite for the next course, *si*?"

"*Si*," I said, beaming.

"*Signore*? For you?"

"I'll have the sea bass," he said.

"Oh, come on!" I said. "You can't let me sit here and eat all those courses and just have one! This is an Italian restaurant! To eat is to love, right, Luciano?"

"*Si, signorina*. The beautiful lady is correct, of course."

I winked at him. Alexander had flaws, but being a shitty tipper was not among them, and Luciano would leave here with hundreds of dollars from our meal alone.

Alexander ordered a pasta course and the grilled octopus. I would also be ordering dessert. Possibly a dessert martini. Carter had already been notified about my romantic drama as I drove to the New Haven train station, and had ordered me to sleep over tonight, bless him.

I drank the cocktail, wincing a little at the taste but appreciating the warmth.

How could Alexander *do* this to me? Why? Wasn't I the easiest, most laid-back girlfriend in the world? Had I ever complained about his travel schedule? Ever insisted he come to a school event or birthday party? Before my father's stroke, he'd only visited Stoningham once. I was always cheerful and upbeat around him because I *was* those things, goddamnit.

Luciano brought our courses. I ate, laughed, murmured in the appropriate places. The food was amazing. At least there was that. Also, the champagne, my God. So good. I might even order a second bottle.

As I watched Alexander, I saw it. The performance. The need for validation. He was working hard to make sure we were The Couple To Be at this swanky, sophisticated restaurant. When I fake laughed, he'd glance around to make sure people saw that he had the power to bring humor. He smiled a lot, and where my dorky brother-in-law also smiled a lot, Oliver was . . . sincere. He loved my sister and his daughters. He adored my parents. He even loved me, not that I'd given him much reason to.

We ordered dessert (though I was going to go into a coma soon if I ate much more).

"Babe," Alexander said now, "I know this has been a rough couple of months for you."

"You, sir, are absolutely right." I was tipsy and enjoying it. It was fueling my rage.

"So I wanted to give this to you, and hope it will make things a little happier."

He reached into his breast pocket and pulled out a little velvet box.

Shit. If there was an engagement ring in there, I knew it would be big, and I'd want it, and I wouldn't be able to have it, and everyone in here would feel bad for the poor guy who proposed and got shot down. Cringing internally, I waited for him to get down on one knee.

Thank God, no. He just passed it across the many plates and smiled.

"Aw. So sweet of you!" I opened it and, shit, it was a beautiful necklace. A chunky bezel-set diamond surrounded by pink gold with a matching chain. "I love it." I did, damn it. I'd keep it, too. I could sell it and pay for something in my house. "Thank you. How much did it cost?"

"Oh, babe. Whatever it cost, you're worth ten times that much."

"So . . . what are we talking? A thousand dollars?"

He grinned. "More. Significantly more. Here, let me put it on you."

Ass. I allowed it. He sat back down, smug and pleased (glancing around to see if everyone had noticed).

"It's beautiful," said the woman from the next table.

"Thank you," Alexander and I said in unison.

"Hey, Alexander, I have a quick question for you, babe."

"Sure, babe."

"When you came to my mom's dinner party, did you remember Gillian?"

"Uh . . . the one with the baby?"

"No. That's Mickey. The very pretty woman?"

"Other than you, babe?"

"The one you made a pass at last May. At the yacht christening party she mentioned."

He blinked. "I think she . . . no. I've never met her."

"She said you pressed her against a wall, kissed her neck, gave her your room key to the Madison Beach Hotel. Where we then spent the night after she turned you down."

His neck was getting red. "She must have me confused with someone else."

"You said you'd 'rock her world.'"

He didn't answer.

Luciano came with our desserts. "The bomboloni for *signorina*, the cheesecake for *signore*."

"Thank you so much," I said sweetly. He left. "Anything to say, Alexander? You made a pass at a woman and then called me as your B-list fuck. Why would you *do* that? You were going to cheat on me!" My voice may have risen a teeny bit.

"Look," he said, glancing around, his hands up in the universal male sign for *don't make this a big deal, you hysterical female.* "We never said we were exclusive."

"What? We *were* exclusive! We've been dating for two years! We spend holidays together!"

"Calm down," he said.

"How dare you tell me to calm down!" But yes, people were staring.

"I never said we were exclusive," he repeated through gritted teeth.

"What does that mean? You get to sleep with other women?"

"Yes."

The bald-faced admission was like a bucket of ice water. "Do I need to get tested?" I hissed. Thank God we'd always used condoms *and* the Pill. But I did. I'd need to get tested. Good God!

"Look." He glanced around. "It's not like I'm promiscuous, okay? I'm not on Tinder. But yes, I have two other relationships."

"What?" There was the screeching again. Luciano was huddled with the maître d' in the front, casting us concerned looks, so I lowered my voice. "Explain yourself."

He looked at the restaurant ceiling, clearly aggrieved. "There's Toni in San Diego and Paige in North Carolina. I've been seeing Toni for four years, Paige for three."

"And me for two."

"Yes."

"So *I'm* the other woman?"

"No, no. Well . . . yes, I guess so. I don't see it that way."

"How do *they* see it?"

"They don't know about you. Why would I tell them, right? When I'm in San Diego, I see Toni. When I'm down south, I see Paige. But mostly, there's you, babe."

"Do not call me babe. Ever again."

"Listen, Sadie. You're my favorite," he said, leaning forward with a smile.

"I *proposed* to you," I hissed.

"And when I get married, you'll probably be my first choice. You know. When I'm ready."

Jesus. I stood up and threw my napkin on the table. "I'll send you the bill for my STD panel," I said loudly. "Make sure you leave Luciano a thirty percent tip. And I'm keeping this necklace." I looked down at the table. "And these little donuts."

Luciano patted my hand and waited for the cab with me, as I was busy crying (and eating the bomboloni), the shock of what I'd learned settling in.

Shit. It was so obvious now. The three days in San Diego turning into five. The many times North Carolina had thunderstorms that shut down the airport (not that I bothered to check the Weather Channel, because I was trusting and an idiot). The "turned-off" phone. All those yacht emergencies. How tired he could be after coming home from schmoozing and screwing his other girlfriends. The holiday weekends when he was traveling, or visiting his "mother." The truth was, he was probably taking Paige or Toni on lovely weekend getaways, same as he'd done for me.

I'd have to find them through his Facebook page or Instagram and tell them.

Shit. Shit, shit, shit.

I went to Carter's apartment and spilled. He made the appropriate noises, cursed occasionally, ate my remaining donuts and made me drink water.

"I know it's too soon to say this, honey, but you're better off without him," he said as I hiccuped and clutched his aging, obese cat to my chest. "Now go to bed. Uncle Carter's giving you some Motrin and water, and don't even think about puking in the guest room. Janice just redid it. I'll make you a nice big breakfast in the morning, okay?"

"How's Josh?" I asked, remembering that my friend was happy, and we talked about how Sister Mary had invited the guys over for dinner and told them to get married and not live together first.

Good. There was love in the world, even if I was a jerk.

I got in my pajamas, washed my face and brushed my teeth, avoiding my reflection in the mirror, and got into the wonderfully soft bed.

As I lay there, slightly drunk, tears leaking into the pillow, feeling as dumb as I'd ever felt, I had two overwhelming thoughts.

The first was that I missed my dad so, so much. That he would've known more than anyone how to make me feel better about this—less ridiculous, less like the younger, stupid Frost daughter.

The second was that Noah wouldn't have cheated on me with a gun to the back of his head.

CHAPTER TWENTY-SIX

Juliet

On Wednesday, Kathy stopped by Juliet's office, her gossip face on—eyes sliding from the left to the right, eyebrow raised (lucky . . . Juliet's were still frozen). She came in and closed the door. "Guess who was just named project manager on the school Beyoncé is building in Houston?"

"What Beyoncé school?" This was the first Juliet had heard of it.

Kathy sat down, looking too pleased with herself. "Yeah. Her."

"Arwen?"

"Who else?"

Anyone else, that's who. Matt, who was nine years senior to Arwen. Elena, who was six. Brett and Christopher, four.

"Are you going to talk to Dave?" Kathy asked, running a hand through her bright red hair.

"Are you?"

"No. Of course not. It's not like I could be PM, though I'm definitely hoping to be on the interior team. Maybe meet Queen Bey."

Juliet was very sure Kathy was too old and white to be using that nickname. She glanced out the window, her stomach clenching with nerves. "Did you know we were pitching Beyoncé?"

"Arwen mentioned it. It's really Beyoncé's foundation. Her PR team asked us to keep it a secret till ground is broken."

Beyoncé. Jesus. And Kathy knew, but hadn't said a word till now.

"Well. I have work to do, Kathy."

"I'm sure you do."

What did that mean? She and Kathy used to be friends, but Kathy had always been the office gossip. Juliet felt she'd been immune to that.

Now it was hard to trust her, with that Arwen haircut and the way Kathy brayed laughter from Arwen's office at least twice a day. Kathy was here to gather intel, that's what she was doing. To plant seeds and make trouble.

It worked.

A few hours later, so it wouldn't be so obvious, she went down the hall to Dave's office with the excuse of showing him the plans on a house for a former senator. She liked doing residences once in a while—she'd done her own house, obviously, and occasionally offered to do one at work, though it was small potatoes for her. She'd volunteered to do this one because it was fun and had a limitless budget, which was always pleasant.

"Is he available?" she asked the side-eying Laurie (who may have been casting a spell on her).

Laurie shrugged and jerked her chin, indicating that it was okay for Juliet to go in. Her boss had his feet up on the desk and was gazing out the window. Hard to believe he'd been a force in architecture once, since he mostly napped and went out for lunch these days.

"Hey, Dave, I've got the elevations on that house in Maryland. Want to have a look?"

"Sure." She sat down and watched as he gave them a glance. "Nice job, Juliet."

"Thanks. It's a beautiful site."

"That it is."

"So, Dave . . . I heard a rumor. You made Arwen the PM on a school for Beyoncé's foundation?"

He avoided looking at her, studying the house plans as if he'd just realized they'd come down from Mount Sinai in the hands of Moses. "Mm," he offered.

Be careful, a voice in her head warned her. But screw that. She'd earned her place here. "Since when does such a green architect get that kind of high-profile job? I thought the firm had a system. A ladder." One that she'd climbed, step-by-step, never skipping a single rung.

Dave sighed. Still didn't look up. "Arwen is very talented."

"I'm aware of that, Dave. But she's only thirty-one. She still needs supervision."

"Or does she? She's quite ambitious. People respond to her."

"There are a lot of ambitious people here who outrank her. Matt. Elena. Brett." She paused. "Me. I'm a little shocked that I wasn't informed we were pitching this job, frankly. I'm the senior project manager at this firm."

"Look, Juliet," he said, finally looking at her. Her chin, to be exact. "You've done some remarkable work for us."

"I *am* doing remarkable work for you, Dave." Her voice was firm but she made sure not to be too angry, because God forbid her boss had to deal with an angry female. "I realize Arwen is the shiny new thing, but my record speaks for itself, doesn't it?"

"I'm a fan of yours, Juliet. Don't get hostile."

Oh, the *fuckery*. "I'm not being hostile. I'm pointing out facts."

"Maybe if you smiled more, people would—"

"Dave. Do not finish that sentence."

"I'm just saying, Arwen is a really positive person. *She* smiles all the time."

"Are you giving her a promotion because she *smiles*?" she asked.

"There's that hostility." He smiled ruefully.

"It's disbelief, not hostility."

"Juliet, you're very serious."

"About my work, absolutely. You could say that's a positive attribute in an architect."

He put his hands behind his head. "Listen. You're right. Arwen is new and exciting, and the world seems to love her."

Time to be dead honest. "But her work isn't particularly special, and you must know that."

"Be careful, Juliet. You're sounding very jealous and competitive."

Hostile, *serious*, *jealous and competitive*. All code for bitch, or worse. If she were a man, it would be *fiery*, *dedicated*, *strategic* and *ambitious*.

But here she was, in a male-owned, male-run firm. So she lowered her voice to a tone Dave could tolerate. "I've always put the firm's best interests first and foremost, Dave. I'm your senior architect. I've never let you down, have I?"

He tilted his head. "Nothing is coming to mind, no."

"Because it's never happened."

"What's your point, Juliet?" He glanced at his phone.

You could lose me. I might quit. I could sue you for ageism and discrimination.

Except Kathy was older and wasn't saying boo. And it would be hard to prove discrimination on the basis of gender, given that Arwen was a woman, too. A gay woman, for that matter, something Juliet had only found out a few weeks ago when she and Saanvi had had drinks at the same bar where Arwen had been with a woman, and they'd kissed once or twice. Arwen hadn't seen Juliet, and Juliet hadn't gone over, not wanting to intrude.

Now Juliet glanced out the window, then back at her boss. "Just be thoughtful, Dave. A green architect on a high-profile client's project could be risky."

"Fortune favors the bold," he said. "And you know how we like to think outside the box at DJK. Thanks for bringing me your concerns. I think we've cleared the air. And I'll see you at your party this weekend, right?"

Dismissed. "Yes. Thanks for hearing me out." She left his office, past the silent Laurie, the plans for the senator's house clenched in her hands.

Today was one of the days she left early and worked from home. She grabbed her stuff, fake smiled at her colleagues and got out of there as soon as possible. In her car, she sat for a minute, gripping the steering wheel, stymied, frustrated and . . . scared.

She could leave the firm and start her own. The thought had crossed her mind from time to time, but DJK had always been the best of both worlds—creativity within an established, respected firm. Starting her own would be twice the workload, and the girls still needed her. She could put out some feelers at other firms, but the truth was, if she left now . . . well. It would look exactly like what it was. She was leaving because another architect was taking over.

Was it possible she had peaked? Were her best days behind her? She was forty-three, and she hadn't recycled an idea yet. Maybe this was just a normal phase of a career, being established and therefore slightly less exciting.

But the thought of aging out struck a nerve. Arwen was so beautiful . . . That had to be a factor, even if it wasn't ever going to be acknowledged. Juliet looked in the rearview mirror. She was still attractive. Of course she was! She had decades of youth in front of her! She was in her prime. Look at Meryl Streep! Look at . . . um . . . Sofía Vergara! And JLo! She'd just spent three grand on looking even younger, goddamnit.

She was too serious, was she? She should smile more? How dare her boss imply that she was . . . was stale and boring! She was absolutely not those things. Oliver still adored her. Even if they'd settled into a routine, it was a good routine.

Sort of like Mom and Dad.

Shit.

She flew up 95 to Stoningham. Oliver was working from home today with a slight cold and being an utter infant about it. He was about to have his mind blown. Time to be shiny, spontaneous and bold.

Oliver was in the laundry room, putting sheets in the dryer because Juliet still hadn't hired a new cleaning lady, goddamnit.

"All right, love?" he said as she came in.

"I want you," she said.

He side-eyed her. "Darling, I have a man-cold. I'm hovering at the precipice of death." He coughed to prove it, a meaty, phlegmy sound.

"I don't care. I'm so . . ." Shit. She should've paid more attention to the three pornos she'd seen in her entire lifetime. "I'm so . . . wet." Ick. It sounded like she'd peed her pants.

"I wouldn't wish this cold on my worst enemy, my darling girl."

"I won't kiss you on the mouth, then."

She dropped to her knees and started to untie his sweatpants.

"It's a lovely thought, darling," Oliver said, putting his hand on her head. His voice was thick with the cold. "Perhaps a rain check."

"No. I need you now. Here. Like this."

"Darling. I feel wretched."

He'd change his mind. She pulled down his pants. "It's so, um, big." Gah. It wasn't, not at the moment. She screwed her eyes shut and gathered her courage.

He stopped her, thank God, and pulled his pants back up. "Juliet, what are you *doing*?"

"Trying to give you a BJ." Men were supposed to love this shit.

"The girls will be home in five minutes."

Right. "Then I'll be quick."

"I swear that I'm thrilled about this theoretically, but seriously, darling, can we reschedule?"

"No."

"Juliet." He pulled her to her feet. "What's got into you?"

"I'm trying to be fun and spontaneous and . . . not so serious."

"Darling, we're married with two children. Spontaneous happens only when we put it on the calendar."

Well. She just couldn't fucking win, could she? Everything Oliver said was true, and he looked like vomit warmed over, but it didn't do much for her battered ego.

At that moment, the door banged open. "Daddy! Mommy!" yelled Sloane. "Guess what? Brianna got her period!"

"I rest my case," Oliver murmured.

"Shut up, Sloane! I hate you!" Brianna said.

Juliet opened the laundry room door as Brianna flew by, her eyes red.

"She's a woman now," Sloane said solemnly. "She could have a baby."

"Sloanie-Pop, this is a personal matter," Oliver said. "Let's get you a snack while Mummy talks to your sister, right?"

Sure. Give the hard child to me, Juliet thought. But yes. This was a mother's job.

She went to Brianna's room and knocked once. There was no answer, so she went in. Brianna was lying on the bed, sobbing.

Juliet didn't know what to say, so she just put her hand on her daughter's hair. "Hello, baby," she said.

"It was horrible! It was in math class, and I felt this stickiness, and then George Tanner said, 'Don't mess with Brianna, she's on her period,' and everyone laughed. The blood was on my jeans, Mom! You knew I had cramps last night! Why didn't you tell me to wear a pad?"

Yes. Why hadn't Juliet been more psychic? The fact that Brianna had been claiming to have cramps every time she wanted to get out of a chore for two solid years was probably not what she wanted to hear.

"I'm sorry, honey. If it's any consolation, I've gotten blood on my pants, too. So has Sadie, and just about every female I know." Except Arwen. It probably hadn't happened to her.

Brianna gave her a sullen look. "I thought it would be different," she said, tears still dripping down her face. "I thought it would be cool and I'd feel sophisticated and in some kind of older girls club, but it's just gross and my stomach hurts and my legs do, too."

"I'll get you some Motrin," Juliet said. "And a hot-water bottle. It'll feel good against your tummy."

She went into her own bathroom and got the necessary items. A pad, just in case, and a tampon, too. She'd bought Brianna her own supplies last year, as well as a book about periods, but nothing ever did prepare you, did it?

She went back into Brianna's room and gave her the Motrin and a glass of water. Put the hot-water bottle against her daughter's abdomen and nodded at the tampons and pads. "In case you need it."

"I have my own," Brianna muttered. She rolled away from Juliet. "You can go now, Mom. Thanks."

Once again, dismissed. What would Barb, the perfect mother, do? "You'll always be my little girl. No matter how old you get."

"Thanks. Could you go? I just want to sleep."

"Right. Sleep tight."

By the time Juliet had made dinner and cleaned up, even though it was Oliver's turn (but he was suffering greatly), and checked on Brianna and helped Sloane with her reading and took a shower and got into bed, Oliver was asleep. He rolled over and put his arm around her, then started gently snoring in her ear.

So much for being the spontaneous, sexy, positive lover.

CHAPTER TWENTY-SEVEN

Barb

LeVon had gone to his new job, and John had recovered enough that he could handle the stairs. We moved him back into his bedroom, and the dining room furniture was returned. A home health aide named Kit came to keep him company and make his meals, but she was sullen and didn't talk much, and was no replacement for LeVon. Sadie also came over every day, always optimistic, always talking up John's mental progress (which I sure couldn't see, though having him go up the stairs was great, don't get me wrong). The speech therapist continued to come three times a week, and while John did seem to be trying to say words from time to time, the only clear thing he'd said was *you* the first day Janet came over.

Janet still visited once or twice a week, and I was grateful, if a bit mystified at her motives. If I was home when she visited, we'd have coffee and talk; if I was at work, she'd leave me a nice little note and, once, a pot of pansies. She worked at a nursery. I took to making sure there was some baked good in the house, cake or cookies, and always texted her to help herself.

Juliet was working like crazy these days. Caro, too. Sadie would move back to the city eventually; those paintings she did were fine as a side job, but I knew she wasn't exactly fulfilled (as I had predicted all those years ago, but who listened?). She seemed to like teaching in New York, and sooner or later, she'd get restless and leave again.

So this was what the rest of my life would be like. Alone, but a caregiver. Married, but to a man I'd wanted to leave, a man who'd found someone else and had been stepping out on me for God knew how long.

On a soft, gentle evening in April, I herded John onto the slate patio. Sloane and Brianna and I had planted pansies in the window boxes out here, and the birds were singing, and it was real nice. I settled John in a chaise longue, covered him with a blanket and got myself a glass of wine, then came back out and sat down next to him. Gosh, I was tired. I had a dozen things to do, but technically, I didn't have to work sixteen-hour days.

Everything could wait. My back twinged as I leaned back, and I wished I had a pillow, or someone who would bring a pillow to me. It was fine. The twinge stopped after a minute, and John was silent and still.

I loved this patio. We used to eat out here when the weather was nice, the whole family. I'd combed the countryside for antiques to decorate the space—a granite horse head sculpture sitting on the gatepost to the backyard, an old millstone, the iron planters.

The wine tasted so good—a fat, buttery chardonnay that John had hated, being the kind of wine snob who only drank reds, or port as an after-dinner drink. He'd made fun of me in that wine-tasting class. *Barb's the type who thinks there's nothing wrong with ice cubes in her pinot grigio.* The teacher had winced before recovering.

"Guess I got the last laugh," I said now, even though he couldn't know what I was talking about. "No more alcohol for you, John. I bet you miss it."

He was listening. Sometimes he just stared off into the middle distance, but tonight, he seemed a little more present.

"Juliet's party is this Saturday," I said. "I'm sorry I'm not bringing you. It's just that I need a little break. A few hours with people who like me, don't you know?" Another sip of the glorious chardonnay. "I've been wondering when you stopped, by the way. We were happy once. We were solid for a long time, I thought. Not exactly setting the bedroom on fire, but I liked our life. Thought you liked us, too. We had the girls and then the grandbabies. That was enough for me."

Except it hadn't been. Not really, if I was going to be honest.

"I'll tell you something, John. I was planning on divorcing you. I was going to tell you on our anniversary, for effect. 'Hey, we've been married for fifty years and I'd like a divorce. Happy anniversary.' I didn't know you were cheating. I was just done with you. It was how little you thought of me, John. I wonder how often I crossed your mind, even living in the same house."

"Dig," he said, startling me. I looked at him, and he scowled.

"That's good, John. Keep trying. You're doing real good." Or was he just making noise, poor thing?

"Horse."

"That's right. The horse head. You never liked it." These word bursts were a good sign. *Dig* could be because of the gardening, but maybe that was a stretch.

His mouth worked.

"Got anything else to say there, John?" I asked.

He scowled again and pulled the blanket up to his chin, sulking much like Brianna did these days. Well, maybe he liked me talking to him as if he could understand. Maybe he could, who knew?

"I met a friend of yours." I poured a second glass of wine, glad I'd brought the bottle with me. "Karen. Your girlfriend. WORK, as she was listed in your phone. Gotta say, I was surprised when I saw her. Then again, I don't really know your type, except that I'm not it. She didn't seem like the brightest bulb in the box, but I suppose IQ isn't high up there on the list of things an old man looks for in a mistress."

He was still scowling.

"Caro and I met her for coffee. I told her about your stroke and whatnot."

His face changed, the scowl sliding down into old-man sadness.

I reached over and patted his hand. "I'd like to tell you she sent a card or stopped by or texted you, but she hasn't. I'm sorry about that."

Listen to me, apologizing that Karen didn't give a good gosh darn about him. Must've been the wine.

"Hello? Anyone home?"

"We're on the patio, Caro!" I said, letting go of John's hand. "Grab a wineglass. The bottle's out here." I heard the cupboard open, and a second later, there she was, looking so stylish and pretty.

"You two look cozy," she said, pouring herself some wine and taking a seat across from us.

"I've just been telling John about our meeting with Karen."

"Oh, that slut." She looked at John. "You do not deserve Barb, John. You hear me? You don't deserve to clean her toilet."

"Hush now," I said. "He's my husband. Not a great one, mind you, John, but my husband just the same."

"You're too good, Barb."

"You betcha," I said, and we laughed, Caro and I, and maybe, just maybe, John smiled a little bit, too. I closed my eyes, listening to the birds.

If this was my life now, I guess I'd have to take it. Aside from a cheating husband, I'd been real blessed. My girls, my friend, my home, this town . . .

"Go to bed, Barb," Caro said. "You must be exhausted."

"I'm pretty tired, I'll give you that."

"I'll get this old bastard settled, and I'll hardly kick him at all. How's that, John?"

"Oh, Caro. You're all talk. Don't listen to her, John. She'll take real good care of you."

And I did go to bed, not even brushing my teeth first. My clothes felt as heavy as lead.

Would John live a long time? Would I be able to keep this up?

Thank God for Caro. I lay down, comforted by the sound of my best friend's voice as she talked to my husband. I was asleep almost before my head hit the pillow.

CHAPTER TWENTY-EIGHT

Sadie

For the first time in years and years, Noah and I were in a car together.

It brought back a lot. Sure, we were driving down I-95 to Brooklyn, but memories of steamy windows, hands under shirts, lush kissing, panting breath, the way he knew exactly how I—

"You okay?" he asked.

"Yes! Why? Jeesh."

"You just squeaked."

"Did I? I don't think so. Must've been the truck."

This was going to be a long ride.

Why were we going to New York together, you ask?

I was delivering a painting to Janice, the interior decorator. This one was a "huge painting with those big flowers that look like vaginas. It's a lesbian couple, so don't hold back."

When I called her to ask about the delivery, Janice had been more frantic than her usual self. "Can you come down and hang it yourself?

This whole job is going to shit. It's a brownstone, and it needs custom work, and the guy who was supposed to make the window seat on the staircase landing just bailed, and I'm telling you, no one is available unless you book a year in advance these days, and they discontinued the wallpaper the owners loved and I'm pulling my hair out."

"Sure, I'll come," I said. Janice had probably forgotten that I was here in Connecticut with my dad, but I could use a day in the city. I hadn't spent any time there except to dump Alexander a few weeks ago, and I'd been in a state, obviously. It would be good for the soul, as it always was. There was nothing like a spring day in Brooklyn.

An idea popped into my head. "Hey, Janice, I might know someone who can make a window seat."

"Really? Oh, Sadie. That would be *miraculous*."

"I'll call you back." I hung up, then looked at my dog. "Don't judge," I said. "It's only business." She wagged kindly, her eyes suggesting I wasn't fooling anyone.

Noah had put in the beam so my house was no longer in danger of falling in on itself. He'd also put in the picture windows, and it was amazing how it changed the look of the house, both from the outside and the inside. Sure, it was still a bit crooked, but Noah said if I put on a new roof, it could be fixed. The thing about house renovation, I was learning, was that the more you did, the more you wanted to do. The huge vagina flower painting (sorry, Georgia O'Keeffe) would put some money in the bank.

A big butcher block island with stools would let you eat while staring out at the salt marsh. Maybe Noah could put in a spiral staircase, like Juliet's. Maybe he could make the entire northern wall a bookcase.

Maybe I just wanted to spend more time with Noah.

I was still recovering from Alexander's cheating and lying, granted. I had loved him, or the him I thought he was. Then there were the feelings of stupidity and humiliation, of being less than, because he needed *three* girlfriends, not just me. I'd thought I found a man who loved me without that sense of . . . expectation Noah always had. Like, until I lived life the way Noah wanted me to—that was, move to Stonington and start popping out babies—I was a disappointment.

Alexander had taken me exactly as I was. He'd been generous, fun, not unintelligent, easygoing. All he needed was two other women to make his life complete.

Oh, the fuckery of it all.

At any rate, I'd called Noah, told him two wealthy brownstone owners needed a window seat pronto, did he want a quick job in the city? Much to my surprise, he said yes.

When I arrived at his house this morning, he'd been passing off Marcus to Mickey in the front yard, daffodils blooming, sun shining on his hair.

"Girlfriend!" sang Mickey. "How you doing? Damn, you're so stinkin' cute. I could be gay for you."

"You *are* gay, you tease. Hi, Marcus." The baby smiled at me, and my ovaries spontaneously frothed over with eggs.

"Want to hold him?"

"We need to get on the road," Noah said at the same moment I said, "God, yes."

Mickey smiled and passed me her son. The warm, wriggly weight of him, his sturdy little legs kicking, and yes, people, the smell of his head . . . God. "Hello, gorgeous," I said. His lashes were so long and silky, and his cheeks were fat and pink and delicious.

"Dwah!" he said, taking a fistful of my hair and tugging. "Baba!"

"He's a genius!" I said to the parents.

Noah was smiling. Just a little, and probably at his son.

"Please, please, let's get together," Mickey said. "I want to see your goofy little house and drink wine."

"Done," said I.

"You're nursing," Noah said.

"Oh, am I, Noah? I forgot that my breasts are as big as watermelons and my nipples look like saucers and milk spurts out of me every time this baby smiles." She rolled her eyes. "Mansplainer. Shame on you! I'll pump that night and chuck it. Jeez. The nursing police here, Sadie."

"He's horrible. I'm sorry for all you endure." She grinned. I liked her so much.

"We do need to go, Sadie," Noah said.

I kissed the baby's head—oh! The soft spot! So dear!—and handed him back to Mickey. "I'll call you."

"You better. Bye, Noah! Marcus, wave bye to Daddy!" She held up his fat fist and jiggled it.

Noah leaned in and kissed his child. "I love you," he said, and my ovaries frothed again. "See you tomorrow, sweetheart."

Which brought us to my current horndog state, sitting in Noah's truck, his tools and some walnut planks in the back, the smell of wood and coffee the best foreplay I could think of. "I brought pastries from Sweetie Pies," I said. "Want something?"

"Sure."

I handed him a chocolate croissant and watched as he ate it, his jaw moving hypnotically. Would it be inappropriate to brush the crumbs out of his lap?

"Who's watching your dog today?" he asked.

"What? Nothing! Oh. My nieces." I took a calming breath and chose a cheese and raspberry Danish to get my mind off Noah's lap.

"How are they?"

"They're good. Brianna got her period and is officially a horrible adolescent, and Sloane is a little behind in school, but they're awesome."

He smiled, and I had to look out the window to avoid wrapping myself around him like an octopus.

When we got to the brownstone, all was chaos, as it tended to be with Janice. Movers were bringing in furniture, painters were finishing up, and she pounced on me, despite the fact that I was carrying the huge wonkin' vagina flower painting wrapped in brown paper.

"Let me see it! Let's get it inside. Up those stairs, second door on the right."

Noah followed with his toolbox.

"You must be Noah, thank you for coming, you're an angel, you really are, I hope you're good enough to do this right because I don't really have a choice right now. Unwrap the painting, Sadie, let's have a look!"

I glanced at Noah with a smile. Hopefully Janice hadn't offended him with her run-on sentences and half praise. He smiled back.

Unwrapping the painting carefully, I leaned it against the bed. "What do you think?"

"Oh, Sadie! It's beautiful! You signed it, right?"

"Mm-hm."

"*Look* how it matches the comforter!"

I suppressed a sigh. This was my bread and butter, after all.

The painting was a close-up of lilies, that most vaginal of all flowers, and sweet peas (labia), and I was rather proud of it. The lesbian couple could go to town under that painting. Unlike the "swirly" or "scribbly" paintings I often did, this one had taken more work and time. Sure, it was an O'Keeffe knockoff, but it was beautiful, and not just an imitation. Oil this time, with more texture and detail than the great Georgia. Her style with a tiny bit of my own.

"It's really pretty, Sadie," Noah said, staring at the painting, his head tilted the slightest bit. "Very . . . detailed." Then his dark eyes cut to me with a slight smile, and I felt my skin prickle with a blush. There was a bed right behind me. Just sayin'.

"Okay, hang it up, and Noah? It's Noah, right? Let's get you started on the window seat. You got the pictures I sent you, right? Can you match that? Did you bring wood?"

Yes, Noah, did you bring wood? God. I was ridiculous.

I hung the painting, chatted with the movers, wandered through the brownstone. What a lucky couple! I'd always been a Manhattanite, Brooklyn being too hip for me, but damn. The building was a block off Prospect Park on a street with fully leafed-out maples. All the windows were open, and the sun shone through the stained glass window on the landing, making it appear that Noah worked in a church.

He did look like an angel. Or maybe Joseph, Jesus's dad. The carpenter dad, not the God dad. Or with that black, unruly hair, scruffy beard and olive skin, maybe Jesus himself.

"Stop looking at me," he said without looking at me.

"Need a helper?" I asked.

"Sure. Sit there and don't touch or do anything." He cut me a look, and I felt it in my stomach. He had a black elastic on his wrist and, in a practiced movement I remembered well, pulled his hair back into a short ponytail to keep it out of his eyes as he worked. A few curls escaped.

Heathcliff hair. Jon Snow hair. Darcy hair. *Damn you, Noah*, I thought. *You've only gotten better.* Watching him work, his movements sure and confident, it hit me again that my wild boy was a man. A father, and who could be a better father than Noah?

"How's your dad?" he asked, picking up on paternal vibes.

"He's doing well," I said. "He's trying to talk, and write. I mean, he held a pen the other day, but he didn't write anything. Still, he held it the right way. Mom said he said 'horse' the other day. And maybe 'dog.' He definitely responds to Pepper."

"Good. He likes Marcus, too."

"Everyone loves that baby."

No response. He ran his hand over the walnut panel, which he'd already varnished. Lucky panel. "Pass me the hollow ground planer blade."

"I heard the words, but they mean nothing to me."

A flash of a smile. "Maybe you can walk around the block a couple times, hm?"

"Are you saying I'm in the way?"

"Yes. You're in the way, Sadie." His eyes met mine. "Take a walk, Special."

Time stopped. That name. It sliced into my heart like a burning arrow.

"How's it going here?" Janice said, racing up the stairs, her arms full of pillows. "Will you be finished by three, do you think? They're having a housewarming party! Tonight! It's just crazy! I have to stage the whole house, get fresh flowers and make all the beds and hang the towels and put this damn cow statue somewhere, what was I thinking when I ordered it, oh, and guess who doesn't like fake orchids? My lesbians, that's who!"

Good for the lesbians. "Can I help?" I asked. "I'm just in Noah's way, and I'm great at making beds and such."

"You're an angel, Sadie! An angel! Noah, three o'clock?"

"No problem," he said, looking back down at his work.

By three o'clock, the house was more or less in order, Noah was finished, Janice was thrilled with the window seat and now on her phone, yelling at someone. She handed us two envelopes, mouthed, *Angels!* and waved goodbye.

We walked out of the brownstone, despite the fact that I'd sort of been hoping to meet the owners and be invited to the party and end up snogging Noah on a pile of coats somewhere.

Noah opened his envelope. "Holy shit," he said. "This is twenty percent more than my estimate."

"She pays a rush fee. She's a little crazy, but she's kind of wonderful, too."

"I should work here more often."

Words I would've killed to hear once upon a time. I let it go, but the casual way he said it scraped my heart. "Well, now that she's seen your work, she may well call you again."

"Thanks for the referral, Sadie."

"Of course."

"You gonna see your boyfriend tonight?" he asked as we walked toward the truck.

"Oh. No. We broke up. He had a girl in every port, as the old saying goes. Or two ports, anyway."

Noah stopped in his tracks. "Shit."

"Yeah."

"You heartbroken?"

For someone with the kind of verbal diarrhea I had, it was oddly hard to talk about this. Because it was him. Noah, the real breaker of hearts. "A little bit. I feel pretty dumb."

"Because you didn't know?"

"Yeah." Naive, dopey, innocent Sadie.

"Because you trusted him to be honest."

"Yep."

"That's not dumb, Sadie. That's just . . . you. You believe in people."

The wind rustled the maple leaves, which were so green and fresh they glowed. "Thanks, Noah."

"You want me to beat him up for you?"

I laughed. "Nah. He's a soft yacht salesman. You're a badass carpenter. It would hardly be fair."

The corner of his mouth tugged up. "Well, then. You wanna eat? I'm starving."

"You mean here? In this horrible city you hate?"

"I don't hate Brooklyn. Brooklyn's nice."

"Jump on the bandwagon, why don't you? Sure, let's go eat some street meat. It smells incredible."

And so we got a couple gyros on Seventh Avenue and took them up to Prospect Park to eat while we sat on a bench overlooking the grassy field. When we were done, I said, "Come on, wild boy. Let me show you the botanical gardens. You think you like Brooklyn now, just wait. It's the perfect day for it."

And it was. Late April, the cherry trees so fat and fluffy with pink blossoms, a few drifting down into Noah's hair, which I left for effect. What the lad didn't know wouldn't hurt him. Thousands upon thousands of flowers were in bloom, and Canada geese strutted about, their little goslings following in quick, darting movements. The constant noise of traffic and music that defined the city was silent here, and the smell of grass and flowers combined in the perfect perfume. Ahead of us was a guide dog, a Golden retriever, and I thought of Pepper. Would she like the city? Probably not at all, given what she was used to, romping on the shores of the tidal river, going for swims in the Sound, rolling in dead seagull whenever possible. Maybe she'd transition to pigeons. The thought made me wince. The pavement in New York could get so hot that . . .

Okay, no. I wasn't going to worry about that right now. My father was getting better, and I'd be in Stoningham till the end of summer, and it wasn't even May. People had dogs in New York. Pepper would be fine.

And I was with Noah, whose hair had escaped the elastic. Women looked at him, and so did a few men—he was cooler than cool because he wasn't trying at all. Levi's and work boots that actually saw work, a worn flannel shirt over a dark green T-shirt devoid of ironic sayings or rock band names. He was authentic, and that was something rare in this part of Brooklyn, especially among men our age.

"This is so beautiful," Noah said as we walked under an archway of entwined cherry blossoms. "I can see why you love this part of the city. There's a lot more to it than cement and noise."

My heart hurt. "True," I whispered.

"I'm glad we're friends again."

"Me too, Noah. I missed you." There it was, my heart on a plate, waiting for him.

He nodded. "Same."

A man of few words. We looked at each other a long minute. "Okay," he said briskly. "What's in that glass place there?"

"A whole lotta fun, that's what," I said, a little relieved. "Off we go!"

The conservatory *was* fun, a creative array of biospheres to explore. I tucked the hurt away, not saying anything about how things could've been if only he'd been a little more open-minded back then, and just . . . relaxed.

But Noah knew me. He could practically read my mind, and I could read his. We weren't going to have a summer romance. At the end of the day, I'd be coming back here, and he had a child and a full life in Stoningham, and if we broke each other's hearts again, it would be unbearable.

For just this day, we'd be friends again, like we'd been before we ever started dating, when just being together and talking was as uncomplicated and easy and as natural as breathing. For this day, I'd pretend not to be in love with him, because there was simply nowhere to go with that without leading to hurt. I'd cut off my hand before I hurt Noah Sebastian Pelletier again.

We ended up eating dinner at a little Italian restaurant and drove home late. I fell asleep at some point and woke up as we pulled off the highway to Stoningham.

"Sorry," I said.

"No need to be sorry."

"This was a great day."

"It was."

I guess the chatty part of it had ended, though. Noah didn't say anything else as we drove through town, past the now-closed shops and restaurants. I thought about asking him to drop me off at my parents' so I could check on my dad, but it was almost eleven.

Pepper had been returned, and as soon as we pulled into my driveway, I heard her happy barking. Noah got out, too, and a warm tingle began low in my stomach, spreading to my arms and legs.

If he kissed me, if he wanted to stay, I'd be helpless to say no, given the lust factor, the love, the everything he was.

He walked me up to the porch. "How's the roof?" he asked.

"Still leaking in a hard rain."

"I'll try to come over one day this week. There's a storm due about Wednesday."

"That's okay. I'll get to it."

"Why does the image of you on a ladder make me think of ambulances? Save your mother the worry. Let me do it."

Pepper was going crazy inside, so I opened the door and let her out. She waggled at me, licking my hands, and I bent down to pet her. She repeated the action on Noah with a little leg hump attempt. Like owner, like dog. "Off you go, girl," he said, sending her down the steps with a gentle shove.

"Want . . . coffee? Or water? I have water."

"I'm good." The wind blew then, and he pushed my hair back, his fingers sliding against my scalp. I closed my eyes for just a second. Then I was in his arms, and he was hugging me . . . not kissing, but a full-on, all-enveloping hug that made me feel so good, so safe and so . . . loved. I could feel his heart slamming against my chest. He smelled like home. Felt so perfect. I hugged him back for all I was worth, feeling his solid muscle, his collarbone against my cheek.

"I better go," he whispered.

"Okay." Neither of us let go. For a second, he hugged me that much closer, and every inch of me wanted him.

Then he stepped back, took a shaky breath and said, "Okay. Bye."

And that was that. A second later, he started up his truck and backed out, and I stood there, watching him leave.

Story of my life.

CHAPTER TWENTY-NINE

Juliet

Juliet hated throwing parties. This was unfortunate, given that she was doing just that.

Even having her small book club over caused her a great deal of agita—what drinks should she serve? If she made cocktails, would everyone be okay to drive? Was wine boring? Should she have baked something? Why had she chosen a nonfiction book? Was popcorn an acceptable snack?

This party was ten times the size of her book club. Had she had a couple of horse tranquilizers, she would happily take them. At least she had help for this one, but the stress level was even higher, given the work week she'd had.

But it was May first, and this was their tradition, hers and Oliver's. When they first moved to Stoningham, bought the old house that had once stood here, torn it down and created this gorgeous structure of wood and glass, they'd had a housewarming party on the first of May. It became a tradition. Cocktails served by a bartender, caterers with trays of food, fairy lights strung in the trees, the house filled with bouquets of lilacs, and the rooftop deck shaded by the retractable awning. Square cement planters burst with ornamental grasses, and every table had a centerpiece—pots of live moss and ferns, very Brooklyn, very cool. The food was all farm-to-table, and four high school girls were earning twenty-five dollars an hour to serve and clear.

Juliet knew her house was extraordinary—a slender, four-story structure of dark wood and glass. It was an upside-down house—The ground floor had a beautiful entryway, a mudroom, a family room, a game or craft room, depending on the girls' interests, and Oliver's study. The second floor held the bedrooms—four of them, three full baths, as well as a cozy reading room with couches where she and Oliver read to the girls at night, or where they now read to themselves. The third floor held the huge kitchen, dining room and Juliet's spacious office, complete with antique drafting table and a huge desk for her computer monitors.

And the fourth story was what Brianna, then age four, had dubbed the sky room. One giant room on the entire floor. The view was so vast that on a clear day, you could see the very tip of Long Island. It was a gorgeous place to watch storms, the lightning crackling from sky to ocean, or the snow blowing against the windows, making you feel as safe and charmed as the heroine in a fairy tale. The pièce de résistance was a rooftop deck with cable railings and a retractable awning, couches and lounge chairs, a small bar and outdoor kitchen, and planters bursting with whatever annuals struck Juliet's fancy that year.

It was clearly an architect's house, meant both to impress visitors and shelter and nurture the family. This party was intended to remind people that the Frost-Smitherington family was here, that they cared about the neighborhood and community. That she was a Frost of the Stoningham Frosts. Barb's daughter.

It should've been nice. It usually was, hostess nerves aside.

But this year, Juliet wasn't feeling it. She stood in the sky room, feeling awkward and alone and hoping it didn't show. Oliver was laughing with some of his work friends—one woman was standing awfully close and tossing her hair. Should she go over and make a claim, slide her arm around his waist and say, "Back off, bitch?" Was that how her father's affair had started, with someone from work? Who *was* that practically drooling on Oliver? Had Juliet ever met her? Oh, now she was laying her hand on Oliver's arm, and was he doing a damn thing about it? No.

"Juliet, what a lovely party, as always!" Saanvi Talwar, their neighbor and Juliet's almost friend, smiled as she hugged her. "Now that Genevieve is gone, you're taking over as Stoningham's most beloved hostess."

Shit, I hope not. "So glad to see you, Saanvi. How are things at the hospital?"

"Oh, God, the insurance companies are killing medicine as we know it, but we soldier on!"

"Well, I'm sure you're doing great work. Did you try the dumplings? Make sure you do. I think you'll love them."

"Let's get together sometime, just us two," Saanvi said. "We should make a monthly wine date."

"I would love that." She would. But when? Was Saanvi just being her kind self? Would it be rude to whip out her phone and force her to commit?

"Oh, there's Ellen. I haven't see her in ages! Thank you again for having us, Juliet. This house is such a showplace." Saanvi smiled and walked away, effortless in her social grace. Juliet had to fake it.

She should've become a doctor, like Saanvi and her husband. Doctors didn't get upstaged by younglings, did they? They just got better and more esteemed.

Speaking of upstart younglings, here came Arwen. She drifted gracefully over to Juliet, almost floating as heads turned. "Thank you for inviting me, Juliet. What a lovely home you have!" The European air-kiss on each cheek.

"So glad you could make it. Hello, hello!" God.

Arwen wore a long white dress and simple sandals, looking like a

Greek goddess with a badass haircut. Sandals, a toe ring, and a brown leather bracelet set with a single turquoise stone. One gold ring on her index finger, just above the second knuckle. She held a glass of rosé that seemed to complement her skin tone and outfit, her graceful fingers cupping the stemless glass.

Juliet felt immediately outclassed and overdressed. The formfitting black cocktail dress was meant to show that yes, she ran six miles on the treadmill every single day. No stockings, black kitten heels that had cost a fortune but suddenly felt a bit old-school.

"Oliver!" she called. "You remember Arwen!" She waved at her husband, who finally left the hair-tossing hand-layer and ambled over, drink in hand.

"Hello, Arwen. So nice to see you again. Did you bring a friend?"

"I did. Cecille, come meet our wonderful hosts." Arwen waved to a very tall woman with a beautiful Afro. "Cecille, this is my colleague, Juliet Frost, and her husband, Oliver."

Colleague? She was Arwen's boss.

"So nice to meet you," Cecille said. "What a gorgeous view. Did you guys build this house, Mrs. Frost?"

Mrs. Frost. Gah. "Call me Juliet. And yes, we did." She described the tear-down in quick terms, glancing at Arwen's face as she did so. Unimpressed. Bored, even.

"My wife is a genius," Oliver said, putting his arm around Juliet. "Every detail was her idea." He kissed her temple. "I'm so lucky to be married to an architect. I'd be living in a shoebox if not for her. No taste whatsoever. This is all her."

Juliet smiled gratefully.

"Oh, are you an architect, too?" Cecille asked. "I thought you were . . . in administration?"

Juliet made sure not to look at Arwen and arranged her face in what she hoped was a pleasant expression. "I'm an architect, first and foremost, but I also manage projects." Arwen hadn't mentioned what she did? Who she was? She didn't say, *My boss is having a party and we have to go*? "I'm Arwen's boss," she continued. "I oversee all her work, and the work of four other architects at DJK." She smiled (hopefully) and tipped her head against Oliver's shoulder. "Please enjoy yourselves, ladies. There's a deck on the roof. That spiral staircase in the corner will take you right up, and the view is gorgeous."

They went off, hand in hand. Juliet thought she heard the words *so nineties*, but she couldn't be sure.

"They're rather nice," Oliver said.

Her head snapped around to look at him. "Nice?"

"Aren't they?"

Of course she couldn't tell him. Not here, not now. Maybe not ever. "I need a drink."

"Sure thing. What would you like? And just a word of caution, love . . ." He lowered his voice. "Try not to overdo it tonight."

"Jesus, Oliver."

"Just putting it out there. I'll get it for you. Chardonnay?"

"I'll get it myself." She loved chardonnay. She loved cosmos, too, but they were so cliché now, so middle-aged. She even liked appletinis, goddamnit. She went out onto the deck, where one of the two bars was set up. "I'll have a glass of rosé," she told the bartender, hating herself. But she didn't dare look any more outdated than she already felt.

"Sweetheart!" Her mother extricated herself from a knot of people and came over, patting her cheek. "What a triumph this is! You've outdone yourself, and I know I say that every year, but that's because every year, it's true."

Finally, a true ally. "Hi, Mommy. Hi, Caro. Did you bring Ted?"

"Ted and I are on the rocks," Caro said, grinning. "You can see I'm really broken up about it."

"Oh! Um . . . well, I'm glad you could make it."

"Wouldn't miss it!"

Riley London, Genevieve's great-granddaughter and Juliet's favorite babysitter for the girls, ran past, chasing Sloane and a little girl with wild hair. The Finlay kid, maybe? "Hi, Ms. Frost!" Riley said over her shoulder. She was with Rav Talwar, Saanvi's son. Juliet had hired her to keep an eye on some of the younger kids, a move appreciated by the guests who had youngsters. Brianna could've done it, too, but she wasn't that kind of twelve-year-old, and besides, twelve was a little young . . . or was Juliet just making excuses for her? Should she have forced Brianna into service? What if she became one of those horrible, entitled kids, or was she already? Had Juliet failed her? Should she make Brianna volunteer at more than the town arts festival? Maybe bring her to a nursing home and—

"Everything all right, darling?" Mom asked.

"Just fine. Great! How are you? Remember, you're a guest here. Don't let everyone talk your ear off. I want you to relax. Did you have something to drink? The food is great, too. Go! Enjoy."

"Mrs. Frost, could I have a second of your time?" asked a woman whose name Juliet could never remember. "It's an issue involving some water runoff in my yard, and we left a voice mail with your office last night, but we haven't heard from you."

"Probably because it's Saturday, and even the first selectman gets a day off," Juliet said, smiling to soften the words. "My mom is officially off duty."

"No, it's fine. What's going on?" Mom said, ever gracious, and Juliet wondered if anyone had any idea how much work she did.

Juliet texted Brianna—ridiculous, yes, but she had sixty people here, and didn't have the time to go up and down four flights, looking for her eldest, who was doubtlessly hiding.

Nana and Auntie Caro could use some company and a bodyguard. Would you mind hanging out with them?

Sure, came the answer.

Good. That was nice. Maybe Brianna wasn't beyond salvaging. Now Juliet would know where her daughter was and that Mom was with one of her favorite people.

A burst of laughter came from a group in the corner—Emma London, who was Riley the babysitter's mom, Jamilah Finlay, whom

Juliet knew from the Stoningham Women's Association, and Beth, who worked as the manager at Harvest, where she and Oliver ate from time to time. This reminded her that they hadn't gone on a date in ages. The women were all younger than she was—more like Arwen's age. Evelyn from her book club was here, as well as Lucia and Emiko, all women Juliet knew and liked. The folks from Oliver's work.

A lot of people she knew, but not a lot who were close friends. This was the toll of having a career that took her all over the world, of trying to be there for the girls at least ninety percent of the time, of having a marriage that wasn't lying neglected in some ditch of her life.

She didn't have friends. Not really. Not like the closeness Mom and Caro had.

Juliet suddenly felt like crying.

"Hey." It was Sadie. "How's it going?"

"Shitty. I hate parties."

"You hide it very well, then. The house looks gorgeous, and everyone seems to be having a great time."

"How are you?" Juliet asked. "Is Alexander here?"

"Ah, no. We broke up."

Juliet blinked. "Oh! Are you . . . are you okay?"

"You were right. He's an asshole. Feel good about yourself? Oh, hey, person with the tray, stop right there." Sadie grabbed three shrimp wrapped in bacon and popped one in her mouth, then looked back at Juliet. "You look stressed."

"Thanks. What do I say to that?"

"I don't know! I'm your sister. I'm supposed to worry about you. Everything okay?"

"Yes. Are you, though? You and Doofus were serious, weren't you?"

"I thought so. His two other girlfriends might disagree."

Juliet's jaw dropped. "Oh, that entitled little penis scum. Shit. Did you—" She lowered her voice. "Did you get checked by a doctor?"

"Yeah. I'm fine, thank God. I also found his other girlfriends on

Facebook and told them. They seemed really nice. One was really broken up."

"Let me know if you want a building to fall on him."

Sadie grinned. "You're okay, Jules, you know that?" She looked around, eating the other shrimp. "Anyone I know here other than Mom and Caro?"

"Probably not. Come on, let me introduce you to some folks." She led her sister to the younger women of Stoningham and introduced them. Sadie mentioned to Emma London that she'd almost taken an internship with her grandmother's company one summer, and before Juliet knew it, Sadie was one of the gang, laughing, asking personal questions without restraint, getting answers. No doubt she'd be having them over for margaritas before the week was done, because that's how things always worked for Sadie.

Juliet went up the (not-anywhere-near-the-nineties) staircase to the rooftop, a feature so impressive that even the late great tastemaker Genevieve London had admired it. She took a deep breath and tried to shed the anxiety building in her.

But no.

"Juliet," came a voice, and it was Dave Kingston. And shit, Edward Decker was there, too. Both partners from DJK. Edward rarely spoke, and while he nodded during her yearly review and approved her raises, Juliet never knew exactly where she stood with him.

"So glad you could make it," she lied, air-kissing them as Arwen had air-kissed her. "Are you having a nice time?"

"Very nice," Dave said. "Listen, Juliet." Her heart curled in on itself. "We're a team at DJK, as I'm sure you know."

"Of course!"

"So this . . . chain of command thing. It's not necessary, is it?"

"I'm not sure what you're talking about."

"Arwen mentioned you 'put her in her place,'" Edward said, using air quotes and looking ridiculous doing it.

Shit. If Edward spoke, it was dire. "I did what, exactly?"

"Said you made it clear you outranked her in front of her . . . partner."

"Uh . . . no. Her friend asked if I was an architect, and I . . . I just explained that I was both a project manager and—"

"It doesn't matter," Dave said. "Titles are so misleading, anyway, don't you think? We like to color outside the lines at DJK, and we're a meritocracy. The optics aren't great if you're . . . well. You know."

"No, Dave, I don't," she said, starch in her voice. "Arwen *does* work for me. I have eleven years more experience than she does, and it would be irresponsible for us not to provide her with oversight and mentorship."

"Still, there's no need to throw her under the bus," Dave said.

"How did I—"

Edward interrupted. "The attention she's brought to the firm is in everyone's best interest, Juliet. Let's make sure she stays happy, shall we?"

The prickling panic had started in her feet. "Of course. Understood."

"Good."

Juliet glanced over at Arwen, who was pointing out something on the Sound to Cecille. *She told on you*, Juliet's brain informed her. *You spoke up for yourself, and she tattled, and the bosses are on her side.*

"Excuse me," she said. "I need to check on something. Please enjoy the party." She forced her cheek muscles to retract in what might pass for a smile. The panic was in her knees now, and breathing had become a problem.

Down the staircase into the sky room, down the next staircase, *hello, hello, are you enjoying yourself, good, wonderful, make sure you try the cream puffs, they're so delicious, you're welcome, nice to see you.* Down the next staircase, take a left, here come the tears, but it was okay, here was her bedroom, close the door, check to make sure no one was in here, and they better not be, this was her *bedroom*, into the closet, close the door, safe, safe, safe.

She was crying. *Faint*, she ordered herself. Faint. *Go to the hospital, even, and make everyone feel fucking horrible for taking Arwen's side.* Maybe Juliet had some tragic wasting disease that would excuse her from everything except sitting in the sky room and coloring with Sloane, and Brianna would love her again, and the disease would last until the girls were grown and then she could just slip away, looking at the clouds over the ocean, and wouldn't that be fan-fucking-tastic.

Or maybe she'd just quit her job, pack her suitcase and head for Montana. Dedicate her life to saving others as a smoke jumper. The girls would miss her, but they could visit. If she died, at least it would be for a good cause. Oliver would be fine without her. He'd remarry in a matter of weeks. The thought made her sob.

Maybe she needed a therapist. That would be an hour a week she just didn't have. Other than Mom, there was no one she could talk to, and Mom had enough on her plate. Sure, people accepted her invitation to the party and made small talk and hugged her, but when was the last time someone asked her how she was and really listened?

She hated entertaining. Hated it. Hated trying to be friends with people who didn't reciprocate (okay, yes, Saanvi had invited her over once, but Juliet had to go to Dubai for two nights, and other than the very occasional glass of wine in New Haven, which was always Juliet's initiation, Saanvi never asked again, except for maybe suggesting something vague earlier). Juliet shouldn't have thrown this party. She should've spent the night sitting in the hot tub and watching a movie. Which she never did anymore, but still.

Breathe in, breathe out. Breathe in love, exhale insecurity, as her meditation app told her to do. Another thing she'd let slide.

What was *happening*? She'd followed all the rules, but here she was, in her closet, and there was nowhere else she'd rather be.

But the partners were here, and Arwen was here, and Kathy, too, somewhere, and she had to put on a strong, confident front and show them that she was one hundred percent together. She was going to have to push for partner at DJK. Until the past six months, that had been almost a given. No other architect there had as many successful projects under their belts. No one had brought in as many clients. Partnership would guarantee her income for life. No one would be able to touch her. Even if Arwen eventually got on the partnership track, that would be fine. That would be fantastic, because two women partners would mean equal representation.

If she didn't make partner, though . . .

Not a tolerable thought.

She stood up, went into the bathroom, cleaned up her makeup, put on some bright red lipstick, and changed into a flowing black jumpsuit and the fat diamond earrings Oliver had given her for their tenth anniversary.

"You are a successful, confident woman," she said, ignoring the tremor in her hands. "This is your party. Your beautiful home. Your wonderful husband. Your healthy children. You made this all happen. You belong here."

She went back to the party and pretended not to mind that Arwen was making Dave and Edward laugh uproariously, pretended not to see the woman who'd been close-talking with Oliver was at his side again, pretended not to care that Sadie was having a great time with people Juliet had met first but didn't really know. She endured. For the next four hours, she sucked it up, buttercup. That's what her life was about these days. Making it through the day until it was acceptable to go to bed.

When the party was finally, finally over and the high school girls had done their best to clean up, and Sloane and Brianna were sound asleep, Oliver poured her a glass of chardonnay (thank God, because the rosé had been utterly insipid). They sat down in the sky room, since the mosquitoes were out in force on the deck.

"Great party, hon," she lied.

"I didn't think so." His voice was uncharacteristically tight.

"What? Why?"

"Where the hell did you go? You were missing for at least a half hour! Kathy was looking for you, and I had no idea where you were. Saanvi and Vikram had to leave without saying goodbye, and I had no cash to pay Riley, and the entire time, I couldn't find you. What is going on, Juliet?"

If she were a porcupine, all her quills would be up and ready.

"I had to change," she said.

"Why?"

"I . . . spilled something on my dress."

"And it took you all that time? You're lying. Why are you *lying* to me?"

She pressed her lips together.

Oliver crossed his arms. "For months, you've been at bits and pieces, Juliet. Before your father's stroke, before Sadie came back. You're hardly here anymore even when you're sitting right in front of us. You're constantly distracted, and believe me, I've noticed. So have the girls."

Whatever had been holding her together snapped, and it felt huge and delicious and black. She jolted to her feet, sloshing her wine.

"How dare you, Oliver? How fucking *dare* you? You're damn right I'm distracted. I'm fucking terrified. I've given everything to everyone, and my everything is a lot, not to blow my own horn. But somehow, that's never enough."

He started to speak, but she cut him off. "Do you know how hard I try, Oliver? Do you? You think it's easy to have my job and work full-time and still be here for the girls and still bake those fucking gluten-free vegan cupcakes and take Brianna to lacrosse and Sloane to violin and work on Sloane's reading and make sure we have downtime and organize the meal calendar and serve on committees and have sex with you at least twice a week? I have to be at a hundred percent all the time on every front, and it's fucking hard!"

His mouth hung open. "Darling," he began.

"And you, Oliver, *you* get to be the nice parent, the perfect husband with all the women just waiting for a crack in our marriage so they can slide in, and you think I didn't notice that slut hanging all over you tonight? Who is she?"

"What? Who? No one was—"

"Oh, sure. You're so fucking clueless. Next thing you know, you'll be cheating. Just like my father." Tears were streaming down her face, and the breath was ripping in and out of her.

"Cheating? Me?"

"I'm tired, Oliver! I can't do this anymore! I can't be perfect and work and shower and pretend to like salmon so the girls will eat it. I hate salmon! I got a warning tonight to pretend I'm not Arwen's boss because it offends her, and she gives good press! My father's a lump, my sister lives in her own little world, and I'm watching my mother fade away. What am I going to do if she dies? I have no friends! Brianna hates me, Sloane's behind in school, and I'm outranked at work by someone eleven years younger than me! I feel like I'm screaming and no one can hear!"

"Darling," he said, going to her, but she didn't want him to touch her, because she felt so brittle, she was afraid she'd shatter.

She stood up, avoiding his open arms. "I'm going to my mother's for a few days. I just . . . Tell the girls she needs extra help with my father."

"Please don't," he said. "Let's talk, sweetheart. You've just said so much, I can barely process it."

"No. I never want to talk again. I hate everything I just said."

"Juliet. Sweetheart."

"I'll see you in a few days."

With that, she went back to her closet, her safe space, threw some clothes into her carry-on and left.

CHAPTER THIRTY

Sadie

Pepper and I went over to my parents' house the day after Juliet's party and found my sister crying at the kitchen table, Mom patting her hand.

"What happened?" I said. "Where's Dad?" Panic speared my heart.

"He's fine. He's watching *SpongeBob*," Mom said.

"What's wrong, Jules?"

"Nothing," she wept. Pepper tried to crawl on her lap, whining. "I'm fine."

"Okay, liar. First, I'm going to change the channel. *SpongeBob*? Is there something wrong with National Geographic? Then I'm coming back in here for the truth."

"You can't handle the truth," Mom said.

"Mom! Did you make a joke? A Tom Cruise joke? What is this weird parallel universe I'm living in? Be right back."

My father was smiling at the TV. "Hi, Dad," I said.

He looked up at me. "Say."

My heart leaped. "Yes! Sadie! That's right! Great job, Dad!" He smiled at me and looked back at the TV. I kissed his head. "Got anything else for me? Can you say 'hi'?"

Nothing. Well. That was okay. He'd almost said my name. "I'll be back in a bit," I told him. "Juliet's having a crisis, and since this has never happened before, I want a front-row seat."

He didn't respond or look at me. I left *SpongeBob* on and returned to the kitchen. "I think Dad just said my name."

"Good for you," Mom said.

My sister looked like hell, despite the fact that Pepper was now licking away her tears. "What's wrong, sis?" I asked.

"My life is falling apart."

"Oh, that." My mom cut me a look. "Sorry. Is it really, Jules? You have the world's best husband, two healthy girls, that incredible job, a house, health care, money . . ."

She started crying again, and I felt evil. But come on. First-world problems, people!

"She's overwhelmed," Mom said. "She's allowed to be overwhelmed, Sadie. Your sister has done more with her life than anyone I know."

"Point taken. You have, Jules. You're amazing and impressive and sometimes even likable."

"Sadie!" Mom snapped, but my sister snorted a little, then blew her nose.

"Here's an idea," I said. "Mom, no offense, but you look wrung out. As much as we all enjoy my role as flaky little sister, why don't you let me take over for a couple days? You two go to . . . I don't know. Go to the city. Go to Boston. I'll stay with Dad, and if your girls need anything, I can handle it if Oliver's at work."

"Sadie. The town's anniversary is less than a month away," Mom started. "I have a thousand things to do."

"I think you're allowed to have a day or two off, even if you run the universe, Mother. Especially after the winter you've had."

"She's right," Juliet said, her voice thick, tears still dripping. "You need some time to recharge."

"You're going, too, Juliet. The two of you are best friends, and don't bother denying it. I'm Dad's favorite, at least. Oh! I know. That shithead Alexander took me to this great place last year. If he was good at anything, it was self-indulgence." I pulled out my phone and typed a few words. "The Mandarin Oriental in Boston. Amazing spa." Expensive spa. "I'll treat. I just sold a big painting."

"I'll pay," Jules said.

"Let me be the rich one this time," I said, tapping away. "Okay? Okay. That's settled. Ta-da! I just booked you a room for two nights with a couple hours at the spa. You go, girls. Throw some stuff into a bag, order room service, shop, eat, go on a duck boat. Enjoy. Relax. It's an order."

They looked at each other. "I will if you will," Jules said, and Mom smiled and went upstairs to pack

A half hour later, they were gone, and I had to admit, it was kind of nice, being all bossy and in charge, like my mother.

I went into the living room. "Crisis averted, or at least delayed," I told my father. "So now it's just you and me, Dad." My doggy was creeping into the chair next to him, trying to be tiny. "And Pepper, of course."

"Dog."

"Yes! High five, Dad!" I held up my hand, but he didn't respond. "You're really getting better. I'm so proud of you. Can you say that again? Dog? Dog?"

He didn't. The words were infrequent, but they were words. That brain elasticity was coming back.

For the rest of the day, we hung out. Took a slow walk around the town green, saying hi to some people we knew, stopping in the library to breathe in the good smell. I took out a book about real-life dog rescues and brought it home, made lunch and read to him. We went out onto the patio, and I deadheaded the flowers Mom had planted and made myself useful while narrating everything I was doing. Mom didn't seem to talk much to him, and Juliet didn't either. I made up for that.

Dad didn't try any more words, and his expression didn't change much. Those little flashes were few and far between, but at least they were progress.

Jules texted me a picture of her and Mom in big white robes, both of them looking a lot happier, and I texted back hearts and make sure you get the aromatherapy facial. Yes, it would be expensive, and no, I didn't care. It felt nice to be the generous one. I didn't even mind that the two of them were bonding (yet again) without me.

When Dad started to yawn, I brought him back inside, where he settled back into his recliner and promptly fell asleep, Pepper curled at his side, pressing herself against him. It was three thirty.

I wandered through the house. I didn't have a lot of downtime when I was here, since I tried to keep moving forward with the work LeVon did, making sure we took walks now that the weather was nice, did art therapy, worked on motor skills and all that. It felt like a long time since I'd really seen the house.

Mom had done a lot of work here. Every picture, every piece of furniture and art was thoughtful and well chosen. She even had a small acrylic I'd done in college (hanging in the downstairs bathroom, since it matched the wallpaper). Pictures of the family were framed and placed at even intervals up the stairs.

It was a lovely house. Sunny and classic, homey and elegant. Not my style, but really pretty. I should tell my mother that. She'd like hearing it.

My room had been remade into the guest room before I'd even graduated from college, and that was fine, too. Still, it was a little strange . . . nothing of me remained anymore. The horse figurines I collected in middle school had been given away, the bulletin board that had been plastered with pictures of my high school friends (and Noah) gone. The room was painted pale yellow now; when it was mine, two walls had been black, two purple. Couldn't fault Mom there.

I lay back on the bed. Ah, there was something familiar. The ceiling. That fuzzy-looking paint they used to use. I'd always liked that—it looked like a snowfield, and when I was little, I'd imagine tiny people crossing it, upside-down nomads huddling down for the night, coming to sleep under my pillow if it got too cold.

One time when I was about nine, I'd been really, really sick with strep throat, the bane of my elementary school years. This time was extra fierce, though. My throat had hurt so much I had to drool into a towel, completely unable to talk, let alone swallow medicine. I was limp with dehydration, and the doctor told me to push fluids when I couldn't even swallow spit, or I'd have to get IV hydration.

Mom made me a vanilla milkshake and told me to drink it down. "It'll numb your throat, and you have to drink something, or you'll end up in the hospital." I glared at her, sulky and sick, wishing she was more sympathetic, more worried and less . . . resigned. Maybe I *should* go to the hospital. Then everyone would feel sorry for me.

"Drink, Sadie." Her voice had been firm, and she was right; the milkshake was so cold, it took the hurt away. When I had finished, she told me there were two raw eggs in there as well as my antibiotics and Motrin, masked by the taste of the extra vanilla extract she'd added. Then she tucked me in and pulled the shades, and I remembered falling asleep to the sounds of the other kids walking home from school and my mother in the kitchen.

I knew I'd never have the same relationship Juliet had with our mom. Truth was, I didn't really deserve it. I had been Daddy's girl from the start. But she'd always taken care of me just the same. She always knew what to do, even if she . . . no. She always knew what to do. Full stop. It was time for Barb Frost to get some respect from her younger child.

I called the Mandarin Oriental and ordered flowers and a bottle of champagne sent to their room. Yes, yes, it cost the earth. So what? I didn't have children. I could afford it. "And for the card," I asked the hotel clerk, "would you write, 'To the best mother and sister in the world. Relax and enjoy. You deserve it. Love, Sadie.' Thank you so much!"

The warm fuzzies I got were only slightly more fun than picturing their shock that I was so damn wonderful.

That night, after I'd made mac and cheese for Dad (it was easy for him to spear with his fork), Dad watched a documentary on the wolves of Yellowstone that made Pepper tremble with the call of the wild (or terror, but I was going with the former). I set up my easel in the little glass bump-out that abutted the living room, having made a run home for some things while Kit, the rather bitchy home health aide, was here earlier. She was efficient, but she wasn't very nice. I'd have to help Mom find someone better.

But for now, all was well. Call me sentimental, but I was drawing a picture of my dad in charcoal. I wanted to capture him in one of his alert moments, with Pepper against him. His shirt was buttoned wrong, but in my picture, I'd fixed that, as well as the tuft of hair that just wouldn't sit flat on the left side of his head, where he'd had his surgery.

Sometimes, a picture took on a life of its own, almost against the artist's will. This was such a time. I mean, sure, I knew how to draw a human. I was nothing if not technically proficient, as a wretched professor had once told me. But the Dad in my drawing looked too sad, and lonely, and nothing I did was fixing that. Every line I added just seemed to emphasize the feeling of being lost.

Sometimes, the picture told the artist the truth.

A knock came on the door, and I answered it, expecting Caro.

It was Noah. And Mickey, holding the baby. "Hey!" I said.

"Yay!" said Mickey. "We came to see your dad, but we get you, too! Bonus points!"

"Come on in," I said. Stepping aside, I glanced at Noah, feeling shy and blushy. His eyes. That hug. Curly hair. Et cetera.

"Hi, Mr. Frost," Mickey said. "Oh, hi, doggy! Look, Marcus! A doggy! Woof woof!"

"Dog," my father said.

"He's talking so much," I told them, giving Dad's shoulder a squeeze.

Mickey deposited the baby on my father's lap, and Dad held him. He smiled, even. There. Not lost or sad or lonely. My drawing was wrong.

"I hope it's okay that we're here," Noah said.

"Yes, of course. It's really nice of you." My cheeks were hot.

"Your mom is the bomb," Mickey said. "She really helped me last year when I was pregnant. My own mom died a few years ago."

"Shit, Mickey. I didn't know that. I'm so sorry."

"No worries. But it was hard. Pancreatic fucking cancer. She and Barb were friends, and we got close. Plus, Noah here has always had a soft spot for your family."

"Is this true?" I asked.

He shrugged amiably. "Sure."

Marcus was babbling cheerfully and fascinated with my dad's ear. I would need to trim some ear hair soon. Such was the life of a loving daughter. Maybe he'd like to go to the real barber in town, like he used to, every four weeks.

"You guys want something to drink?" I asked.

"I'll have a beer," Mickey said. "Half a beer. It's good for nursing mothers. Don't stink-eye me, Noah Pelletier. Split a brewski with me."

"Okay." He smiled at her, and my heart pulled a little.

They were a couple. A family. Not a romantic couple, but families came in all shapes and sizes, didn't they? The ease between them, the affection, the way they were both so natural with their son . . . it was really lovely.

I was jealous. The certainty between Mickey and Noah was not something I'd ever had. Not with Noah, because we'd been too young, of course, and later because we'd wanted different things. And not with anyone else. The past few weeks since dumping Alexander, I'd come to realize that I'd filled in a lot of his blanks with answers I'd wanted, always making the best assumptions about him, never once wondering if he was lying to me.

Stupid.

I got the beer, and one for myself, poured them in glasses, because we were civilized and all that, and went back into the living room, doling out the sad little half beers to Noah and Mickey and feeling very grown-up with my full glass. Mickey took the baby, who was starting to fuss, and clucked at him, making him utterly delighted.

"Do you want kids, Sadie?" Mickey asked.

"I see we're going straight for the deeply personal questions," Noah said, rolling his eyes.

"You don't have to answer," Mickey said. "Sorry. Too personal? Is he right?"

"No! No. Um . . . you know, maybe?" I answered, trying not to look at the man who'd once told me he wanted me to bear five children. "I love kids. I'm a teacher. An auntie. I just never was . . . I don't know. In the position of really having one."

"Squatting, you mean? Or feet in stirrups?" Mickey grinned.

"Please tell me your birthing story," I said, smiling back (and relieved not to have to dissect my thoughts on being a mother). "You know you want to."

"I do!" she said. "Because I was fucking heroic, right, Noah?"

"You were. Are. Every day."

"Spoken like a well-trained man." She hiked up her shirt, whipped out a boob and started feeding Marcus. "Okay. So there I was, driving down the fucking highway."

"Marcus's first word is going to be 'fuck,'" Noah said.

"And suddenly I'm sitting in a puddle, and I think, shit, did I just pee myself? But no! My water broke!"

Like every woman on the face of the earth, Mickey thought her labor was the most special thing that ever happened. And, like every woman, she was right. She walked me through the details of contractions and transition, the pain, the pushing, her fear of pooping herself. I glanced at my dad, but he seemed content, his hand on Pepper's head.

"And then they put the mirror up so I can see his little furry head coming out, and I'm thinking, 'Is that even me? It looks like the surface of fucking Mars or something!' You ever see your parts stretched out like that, Sadie?"

"Sadly, no, but I can't wait after hearing this."

"So anyway, I'm half-horrified, half-fascinated, half in love with myself because my fucking body is producing a *human child*, and Noah is crying—"

"Were you?" I asked.

"Manly tears. Yes." He smiled, that fast, flashing smile that was like a bucket of lust splashed over me.

"And then the baby's head pops out, and there's this gross little spurt of blood because of the *tearing*—"

"Oh, sweet Jesus," I said, my stomach rolling.

"—but it's a baby, right? A baby!"

"As opposed to the hippo we'd been praying for," Noah said.

"And then one more push, and there he was, all gross and slimy and fucking beautiful." Her eyes were full of tears. "Best day of my life."

"Mine, too," Noah said, and he got up, kissed her head and sat down next to her, an arm around her shoulders.

"Well," I said, "that was disgusting, but I'm glad you went through it, because I'm rather fond of this little guy."

"Here's my advice. Don't have kids if you're not dying to. They're adorable, tiny terrorists, that's what they are, holding you hostage till the day you die." She slid her little finger into the baby's mouth, and he popped off, treating me to a graphic view of Mickey's nipple. Then she passed the baby to Noah, who put him on his shoulder and patted his back.

Noah Sebastian Pelletier was so . . . perfect. My face felt soft and gooey with adoration, same as when I saw pictures of Chris Hemsworth holding his children.

"What's the prognosis on your dad?" Noah asked. "Any updates?"

"What? Oh. No updates, but he's getting a lot better. Right, Dad? He said my name today. He's a lot more attentive, too. Doing great."

"No," said my father, and we all froze.

"What's that, Daddy?" I said.

"No."

"Are you . . . Do you need something? Are you okay?" Keep it simple, LeVon had said over and over. "Dad. Are you in pain?"

"No."

"Do you need something?"

"No." His eyes, once the same seaglass blue as mine with a burst of gold around the iris, seemed faded and tired, but his gaze was steady on me.

My heart was pounding. He was trying to tell me something. Not just a word, but something important.

"Do you want us to leave, Mr. Frost?" Noah asked.

"No."

"Um . . . are you worried about something, Dad?"

His face muscles worked as he tried to get the word out. "Bahr."

"Barb? You worried about Mom?"

He didn't say no. My shoulders relaxed. "Mom and Jules are in Boston. They're having a little girl time. Here." I pulled my phone from my pocket and showed him the picture. "See? They're at a spa. Don't they look happy? But I'm here. I'll take care of you."

He sat for a minute, looking peeved. Then he got up out of his chair, struggling a bit, and Noah passed the baby to Mickey and was by his side in a flash. "Where are we headed, Mr. Frost?"

Dad walked to the stairs, listing a little.

"I guess he wants to go to bed," I said. "I'll take care of this. You guys stay put and relax. I'll be right down."

Dad was halfway up the stairs, and I ran to catch up. He went to his old room, the one he'd shared with Mom. I steered him to Juliet's old room, where he'd slept for years because his snoring kept mom awake. The bed there had rails for him to grab, and to keep him from falling out.

"You're doing great, Daddy," I said. "I'm so proud of you. I know you're trying really hard, and you're getting there." There was a sick feeling in my stomach, though, and I didn't know why.

I helped him get into his pajamas and put toothpaste on his brush. He knew how to brush his teeth. When he first had the stroke, he couldn't even breathe on his own. Of course he was getting better.

He got into bed, and I secured the railing, then bent over and kissed his forehead. "I'm here for you, Dad. I know you're in there, and I want you to know that however long it takes, I'll be here. I love you."

He closed his eyes.

Maybe he was just tired. That was probably it. Mom got him ready for bed most nights. He'd probably been trying to say he was done with visiting and wanted Mom to help him. That made the most sense.

I washed my hands in the bathroom across the hall and looked at myself for a minute. I hadn't had a haircut in a while, and the longer it got, the worse it looked. I thought of the salon I went to in the Bronx, wondered if Robert, my stylist, missed me or wondered why I hadn't been in. It seemed like a long time ago, that New York life.

When I got downstairs, Mickey and the baby were gone, and Noah was standing at my easel.

"Shit," I said. "I'm sorry they left."

"Marcus has a window of time where he needs to get to sleep or he'll be up all night," Noah said. "Is your dad okay?"

"Worn out. I mean, he spoke more today than he has since the stroke, at least on my watch. So it was a great day. I think he was just tired."

He looked at me a minute. "You're a good daughter, Sadie."

"He was a great dad. *Is* a great dad."

"And Juliet and your mom? How come they got to go to Boston and you didn't?"

I sat down on the couch and smiled. "I sent them away like a benevolent overlord. Jules is stressed about something at work, and Mom is exhausted."

"You must be, too."

"Nah. I'm fine."

"Mickey really likes you."

"She's great, Noah. You couldn't have found a better baby mama." Whoops. He let it slide. "I mean, she's really fun. And open. Just . . . seems like a great person."

"She is."

He nodded at my drawing. "This is really . . . touching."

"Oh, that. I was just . . . goofing around."

"It's beautiful."

"Thanks. Um, do you want another beer? A whole beer, just for you?"

"I'm good. Thank you."

So. We were going to sit and look at each other and exchange pleasantries? Nah. That would be boring. "Noah, can I ask you a personal question?"

"No."

"Why didn't you—oh. Sorry."

He laughed, that low, dirty sound. "Go ahead, Sadie. You know you can't stop yourself."

I pulled a face. He was right. "Why didn't you wait to find someone to marry if you wanted kids?"

"I told you. I tried that. Twice."

"By which you mean me and Gillian?"

"Yes, Sadie. You and Gillian."

"I'm not wild about the hard 'G' on that. I like the other way better. Jillian. Much nicer."

"I'll be sure to tell her."

"So why have a baby with Mickey? You're not that old."

He looked at his glass. "I'll take that beer after all." He got up and helped himself, then came back and sat down in the easy chair. "I wanted to be a dad. Always have. Gillian and I didn't work out, and I wasn't . . . I didn't find anyone else. One day Mickey and I ran into each other at Frankie's, and we had a drink, and we started talking. She got pregnant two months later."

"And how was that? Sex with a lesbian?"

"You're incredibly rude and nosy."

"And yet you feel compelled to answer." I grinned at him, knowing he'd spill.

"Let's just say we were both thinking of someone else."

"Heidi Klum? For both of you?"

Another laugh. "Something like that."

"How many times did you—"

"Once, okay?"

"Wow. She's fertile. Lucky."

He smiled at his beer, shaking his head.

"And what about Gillian?" I said. "Why not her? I saw your . . . ah, shit, I might as well come clean. I stalked her Facebook page and saw your pictures. You looked really happy, Noah."

"Yeah. We were happy for a while." I waited. He didn't say any more.

"Did she cheat on you?" I asked, wanting to kick her if the answer was yes. How could you cheat on Noah? Noah! Was it because he was a blue-collar guy and she was—

"No, no. Nothing like that. She . . . she's got a lot of really great qualities."

"You're making her sound like a monster."

His mouth pulled up. "She's not. She was a little crazy with the wedding planning, but it goes with the territory, right? That was fine. Things were . . . nice. We'd even put an offer on a house."

"Wow." I already knew this, thanks to her Facebook posts, but hearing it from Noah, the news had more of a resonance. That would have been huge for him, buying a house with someone.

"Yeah. So we . . . disagreed on decorating." He looked at his beer.

"Ah, yes, I can see how that would split you right down the middle. 'Blue? I hate blue! It's over!'" He smiled a little. "So what really happened, Noah?"

He was staring into that beer real hard. "She wanted me to get rid of something that meant a lot to me."

"Was it your hair? She was Delilah to your Sampson?"

"No, not my hair, idiot."

"Your first tooth? The family Bible? What?"

He didn't answer for a beat or two. Kept staring into that beer. "A painting some girl gave me a long time ago."

He looked up then, and I felt the full force of his dark eyes like a rogue wave, knocking my heart over with its power.

"You broke up over a painting?"

"More or less."

"My painting? The clouds? You kept that?"

"Of course I kept it."

I couldn't believe it. If it had been me, I would've burned anything related to me after I'd turned down his marriage proposal. Proposals, plural. "That goofy sunrise painting?"

"Don't sound so surprised. And don't call my painting goofy." His voice was low, and there was a . . . a light in his eyes, and that half grin of his was . . . affecting me. Do not underestimate the power of a crooked smile, ladies and gentlemen.

He and Gillian broke up because he wouldn't get rid of my painting.

Man, oh man alive.

"You . . . you . . . you wanna make out?" I croaked.

Such eloquence. It did the trick, though. Noah stood up, which was good, because my knees were already useless and weak and tingling. He came across the room and slowly, so slowly, knelt in front of me, held my face in his big, warm, manly hands and kissed me.

It had been so long.

Our kissing was slow and hot, and yet I was desperate for him. I'd missed him so much, my wild boy. One of my hands clenched in his hair, and the other was against his neck, feeling the fast, hard thud of his pulse. He tasted so good, felt so good, so right, it was like coming home. I couldn't think of anything except him, his mouth, his hands. Us. The two of us.

When he stopped kissing me, he wiped under my eyes with his thumbs, because I guess I was crying a little. "Oh, Special," he said, "you'll be the end of me."

Then we were kissing again. I slid to the floor, my bones useless, and we tangled into each other as if no time had ever passed and also like we'd never so much as touched. Every brush of his fingers, every time he kissed my lips, my neck, my hand, jolts of liquid electricity surged and hummed in my veins. I wrapped my arms around his neck and held him so tight, and it still wasn't close enough.

When his hand worked its way under my shirt, I managed to remember—with great difficulty—that my father was upstairs and prone to wandering the house at night. "My dad," I whispered.

"Got it. Just like old times," Noah murmured against my mouth, and I felt him smiling.

Old and new. He felt different now, bigger, stronger, heavier, but he was Noah, *my* Noah, and let's be honest. He'd had my heart since before I knew what love was.

CHAPTER THIRTY-ONE

Barb

You could've knocked me over with a feather when Sadie took charge like that. I'll admit I had no idea she could afford to pay for a weekend at this real nice hotel, no sir.

Gosh, I couldn't remember when I'd felt so relaxed. I'd have to tell Caro all about this, and we could come here the two of us sometime. But for now, it was so special, being here with my sweet little girl. Of course, she was forty-three. I knew that. When she turned up at my door Saturday night, crying, it had felt like she was little again. I made her a hot toddy, listened as she talked tangles about work and Oliver and Brianna, then tucked her into bed. Being Juliet's mother was the one place where I always knew what I was doing.

Being sent to this fancy-pants hotel with Sadie all cheerful and efficient . . . that was just extra.

Juliet and I had been scrubbed and massaged and had breathed in all sorts of lovely aromatherapy mists and whatnot. The sauna, the Jacuzzi, the steam room, a bowl of fruit, and glasses of delicious cucumber water. I felt warm and smooth and smelled like oranges.

Then we got back to the room, and there were flowers and champagne from Sadie!

It was a real nice surprise, don't you know. Real nice.

"Sadie is my absolute favorite sister," Juliet said, then giggled. My favorite sound in the world was my girls laughing, and boy, Juliet needed it.

"She's my favorite second child," I said, and we laughed together. "I hope she won't have to sell her apartment to afford this."

"Oh, I'll pay her back."

"No, you won't, Juliet Elizabeth. You let your sister do this nice thing for you. Don't take that away from her."

"You're right, Mom. As usual."

We were both wearing fluffy white robes and comfy slippers, sitting under the covers in the enormous king-size bed. That champagne went down nicely.

"So what's going on, honey?" I asked, turning to look at her. "You weren't making a whole lot of sense last night."

"I don't know, Mom. That's the problem. I have no idea. It's like all the rules have changed, and no one told me. I was playing one game, and I was winning, and now I'm not."

"Do you mean work?"

"Yes. There's this associate named Arwen—you met her at the party, and that time you came to the office last fall?" I nodded. "She's . . . there's absolutely nothing wrong with her. She's a good architect. She's good with people. She's ambitious and smart. But you'd think she was the first woman architect ever. *Vanity Fair* is doing a profile on her. She's up for the Moira Gemmill Prize, Mom!"

I gathered that was something real prestigious, and made a sympathetic noise.

"And I just don't see it," Juliet went on. "She's good. She's not great, but the partners *love* her, and clients are asking for her by name, and that leaves me pedaling in the air." She sighed and finished her champagne.

"That sounds awfully hard," I said.

"I'm a little bit afraid that my career is coming to an end. Maybe a lot afraid."

"Oh, honey. Don't be silly." She cut me a look. "'In the past decade, Juliet Frost has designed some of the most impressive buildings in North America.' You know who said that? The *New York Times*, that's who."

"Oh, yeah. They did, didn't they?"

"Four years ago."

"See, that's the thing. Four years ago. Today, I'm old news. It's not Arwen so much, Mom. It's that feeling that I did everything right, and I got screwed anyway."

I was quiet for a moment, then took her hand. "I know that feeling, hon. I'm sorry. All you can do is the right thing. You're talented and hardworking and ethical. No one can take that away from you."

Her eyes filled. "Thanks, Mama. I was afraid you'd be disappointed in me."

"That will never happen, Juliet. You're my pride and joy, and you know it."

She hugged me a long, long time, and I petted her silky hair while she cried. Oh, it felt so wonderful to be needed by my little girl, even if she was a mother herself. There was nothing like it, this moment, the two of us.

I said a silent thanks to Sadie, then added a quick apology.

Juliet took a deep, shuddering breath, the sign that she was done crying. She got up, blew her nose, and then poured us more champagne. "Did I mention I love Sadie? To Sadie."

"To Sadie," I echoed. "I should check in."

"No, Mom, not yet. You said you knew that feeling of doing everything right and getting the short end of the stick. Is that . . . is that at work?"

I took a deep breath. "No. Not there. I love my job. I guess I meant, well . . . being married. I love your dad, of course"—that wasn't exactly the truth—"but we drifted apart. You know that."

"Yeah. I do." Her voice was odd, and I glanced at her, but she was staring straight ahead.

"We just didn't have a lot to say to each other, even before his stroke. I felt like I tried, but I could never seem to do the right things. I didn't know what they were."

Juliet burst into fresh tears. "Mom," she sobbed, "I'm so sorry to have to tell you this, but you can't blame yourself. Dad . . . Dad was having an affair."

"Oh, yeah, I know, honey."

That stopped her. "What?"

"I do know that."

"When?"

"I found out when he was in the hospital."

"Holy shit, Mom."

"Watch your mouth, honey. But yes. Holy shit." I snort-laughed, and she did, too. "How did *you* know, sweetheart?"

"I saw him with another woman in New Haven this past fall. They were making out on the sidewalk outside the restaurant where I was having lunch. It was disgusting."

"You've known longer than I have, then. Oh, honey. I'm so sorry."

She started to cry again. "I should've told you, but it was just a couple weeks before Thanksgiving, and then Christmas, and then your fiftieth . . . I'm so sorry, Mom. I wanted to, and I dreaded it, too."

"No, no, honey. Your father is the one who did something wrong. Not you. You were between a rock and a hard place, that's all. Don't cry, sweetheart."

My words made her cry even harder. "You know what I wish? I wish Dad had died. That makes me a horrible daughter, but then you'd be free, Mom. I know he's been a pretty good dad and all that, but he ignored you for so long." She grabbed a tissue and blew her nose. "You deserve someone better."

"That might be the nicest thing anyone's ever said to me," I said. "You know, I always felt like people looked at us and thought the opposite. Like *he* could've done better. I'm just a girl from Nowhere, Minnesota, who took some legal secretary courses. He married down. He's a Frost from Stoningham."

Juliet huffed, then blew her nose again. "No, Mom. *You* built this family. You made our home. We're the Frosts of Stoningham because of *you*. It's not his last name; it's everything you've done for the past forty-plus years. You think people don't know that? Of course they do."

I guessed it was my turn to get all teary-eyed. "Thank you, honey." I toyed with the ends of my bathrobe sash. "Are you worried about anything in your marriage, honey?"

She closed her eyes. "No. Yes. I mean, part of me thinks if Dad could cheat on you, then Oliver could cheat on me." Her lips trembled a little, just as they had when she was little. "Ollie's so wonderful, Mommy. He's kind of perfect, and I have this stupid fear that he's going to wake up and think, 'Oh, my God, I could do so much better than her.'"

"There is no one better than you, Juliet," I said firmly. "Trust me. That man adores you. He lights up when you come into a room, and I can tell you, your dad sure never did that with me. Well. Not after the first couple of years, anyway. Oliver's different."

She swallowed. "You think so?"

"No. I know it. Plus, I'd stab him in the soft parts if he so much as looked at another woman. But he won't. You two are the real deal."

She put her head back on my shoulder. "You're the best mother ever."

"Mm. Tell that to Sadie."

"I do. And she doesn't have to be me, Mom. All the love you gave her isn't wasted. It just doesn't show up the same way."

"You're a wise woman, honeybun." I stroked her silky hair and kissed her head. "Don't tell her about your dad, okay? It would break her heart."

"I won't," said Juliet. "She's been great this whole time. And look at her, sending us off, taking charge. She sent us flowers, even!"

"And we smell so good, too. I might never shower again."

We started laughing, and then we couldn't stop, that wonderful, unstoppable laughter that made me run for the gorgeous bathroom, which made us both laugh harder.

Maybe it was the champagne. But I didn't think so. I think it was relief, and a little exhaustion, and most of all, love.

CHAPTER THIRTY-TWO

Juliet

Sadie knew a thing or two. The two nights in Boston had been heaven.

Juliet hadn't cried so much . . . well, ever. But they were the good kind of tears, the kind that washed away the dirt from your soul. Mom was magical. She could make every situation better just by her pragmatism, her dry sense of humor, her conviction. If the woman Juliet most admired in the world thought Juliet was the bomb, who was Juliet to disagree?

Even so, she felt nervous when she got home. Oliver could well be furious with her. When she texted to say she was going away for a couple of nights with her mom, his response had been, "Have fun."

That was it.

He was home when she got back . . . His car was in the garage, at least. Sloane swarmed her at the door, full of questions, wondering what presents she was about to receive. Juliet gathered her up and smooched her cheeks before doling out the gifts—a fake Boston Police Department badge, since Sloane wanted to be a cop, and a T-shirt that said *Chowdahead*. For Brianna, she'd bought a replica of the statue that showed Mrs. Mallard leading her ducklings through Boston Common.

"I loved this book when I was little," Brianna said.

"I know."

Brianna looked at her. "I'm not little anymore. Here, Sloane. You can have it."

"Yay!" Sloane said.

"I got you a T-shirt, too," Juliet said, holding it up. *Wicked Smaaht.*

"Thanks anyway."

Okeydokey, then. "Where's Daddy?"

"Daddy!" Sloane bellowed. "Mommy's back! She brought presents!"

He came up the stairs. "Hello, darling."

"Hi."

"Did you have a good time?"

"Yes. Definitely."

"Brilliant." His voice was tight. "Girls, would you mind going to your rooms?"

"Are you fighting?" Brianna asked.

"Not at all," Oliver said. But his eyes were not happy. "Darling, shall we go up to the deck?"

"Sure!" Too enthusiastic. Shit.

It was a gorgeous day, full-on May glory, the lilacs blooming below, their scent heavy in the air, the wind gentle off the water. She still felt like throwing up.

"Right. Well. You said some things the other night," Oliver began.

"Listen, I—"

"No, no. My turn. It's only fair, isn't it?"

She nodded. Sat down on the sofa and tried not to cry.

Oliver took out a piece of paper.

"Do you want to sit down?" she asked.

"No. Please. Just let me read this." He cleared his throat. "Dear Juliet, you told me you were tired of trying to be perfect and that you were afraid I would cheat on you if you were anything less than one hundred percent. Please allow me to share the following with you." He glanced at her, frowning, and her toes curled in her shoes.

"The first time I saw you at Yale, you were standing in the rain at the corner of York and Elm, and I stopped in my tracks because I knew the world had just changed. Then, rather unfortunately, a cabbie blew past you, soaking you, and I felt it would be ungentlemanly to approach you."

Oh, God. She remembered that. She'd been drenched to the skin with filthy gray water, and the driver hadn't so much as tapped his brakes.

"The second time I saw you, you were buying tampons at the CVS just off the green, and again, the time didn't seem right to engage in witty conversation with you, because, knowing me, I'd have said something less than clever, such as 'Oh! I see you're menstruating! How wonderful!' and you rightly would've dismissed me as a wanker."

She felt a smile start in her heart.

"The third time I saw you, you were going into a party in Saybrook, and I begged my former flat mate to get me in so I could be in the same room as you, and when I saw you, my heart was pounding so hard, I thought I might vomit, and I was terrified you'd turn away and talk to your extremely good-looking and fit boyfriend, who would no doubt go on to become president of the United States or cure cancer. But you didn't turn away, and you didn't have a boyfriend, and you graciously said yes when I asked you out after forty-five agonizing minutes of mindless chatter, the subject of which I still have no recollection."

His eyes were tearing up. "You are the most beautiful woman I've ever seen, never more so than after you had our daughters, or when you're folding laundry, or in the car, or at your desk. You never have to eat salmon again. I will henceforth take on all the baking of the fucking gluten-free vegan cupcakes, and I can assure you that our firstborn doesn't hate you at all, she is merely blinded by the horrors of adolescence and will once again become your darling girl."

He folded the paper and put it in his back pocket. "I love you. It's pathetic, really. I worship you. You at twenty percent is more than every other woman in the world at one hundred, and you at one hundred is nothing short of a magnificent tornado, but if you need help, darling, please, ask for it. That's my job. To take care of you."

She was crying again, but the tears felt wonderful this time. "Why haven't you told me this before? I always . . . I never . . . I never knew you watched me buy tampons."

"Darling, I'm British. Free expression of emotion is forbidden by the Crown." He looked down. "I just assumed you knew."

"I love you."

"Thank God, because I'm nothing without you, Juliet Frost."

They were in each other's arms then, holding on tight, kissing with relief and love and blessed familiarity. His darling bald spot and strong arms, the smell of his soap, how they were the perfect height for each other.

"They're kissing," came Sloane's voice.

"Gross," said Brianna, and Juliet smiled against her husband's mouth.

What a joy, what a blessing to know that after all this time, love could grow and flourish like the lilacs below, growing stronger and intertwining, becoming more beautiful with each passing year.

The next day, almost purring from the lack of sleep and an abundance of sex, Juliet went into DJK and buckled down to work. A phone conference with a client, design tweaks on the senator's house, a long meeting with Brett on an airport addition. Nothing bothered her. Work was finally as it used to be.

To her surprise, Arwen stopped in her office around five. "Would you like to have a drink after work?" she said.

"Oh! Sure. Where did you have in mind?"

"Barcelona at six?"

"Sounds good."

And so, at six on the dot, she opened the heavy wooden door of the restaurant and went in. Arwen was already there at a high top. "Just a Perrier for me," Juliet said to the server.

"Same," Arwen said. "And privacy, please." She smiled at the server to soften the words. "How was your time off, Juliet?"

One day off. One day. "Lovely," Juliet said. "My mom and I went to Boston."

"Fun."

"Are you close with your mother?"

"Sure. Of course." She offered no further details, and Juliet realized she really didn't know Arwen at all.

The server brought their water and slipped away. "What's up?" Juliet asked.

"I'll get right to it. I'm leaving DJK and starting my own firm."

"My goodness." That was fast. Not entirely unexpected, and not terribly unwelcome news. "Are you sure you're ready?"

"Positive. It'll be called Arwen Alexander Architecture."

"Triple A."

"Exactly. I've already had a logo designed."

Juliet opted not to point out the car association. "Why are you telling me this?"

"I want you to be part of it."

Okay, now that was surprising. "That's very flattering. Thank you."

"You know I've gotten a lot of attention recently, and it'd be foolish not to seize on it and make a move now."

Smart woman. "There will be the usual noncompete issues, of course."

"Of course. I'm not worried. Are you interested?"

"What's the offer? I assume I'd be a partner."

Arwen sipped her water, maintaining steady eye contact, then set her glass down. "Actually, no. I'd like you to come on as senior associate."

The *nerve*. Eleven years her junior, and she wanted Juliet to be subordinate. "Who are the partners, then?"

"Just myself and Kathy."

Kathy? That was . . . wow. Kathy. "Well, good luck." DJK would go back to the way it was. No more It Girl, no more fawning over the shiny new thing. Good.

"Juliet," Arwen said, "please think about it. You're very reliable, you multitask well, and you're . . . well, steady."

"Gosh golly. Thank you so much, Arwen."

Arwen twisted her straw into a knot. "DJK just offered me a partnership. So you might be thinking it'll be nice not to have me around, but you'll still know that I leapfrogged over you. If—*if* they offer you a partnership—and I think it's odd they haven't yet—you'll have to live with the fact that you're their second choice. After you put in more than fifteen years with them, they offered it to me."

Well, shit. She was right. Juliet straightened her cocktail napkin. "Can I share something with you, Arwen?"

"Of course."

"I was you. Ten years ago, I was pretty much exactly where you are."

"Were you, though?"

"No, you're right. You've gotten much more attention than I ever did. But I got my fair share. I also listened to architects who were better than I was. I put in the work and the time, and I became a better architect, because I knew I had to, and I wanted to."

"So is this the 'I paved the way for you' speech?"

"No. It's me telling you you're not as good as you think you are. But you *could* be great. Someday. And you *won't* be great if you believe all the buzz around you. If your name had been Lorna Kapinski and you weren't quite so photogenic, I doubt you'd be getting all this attention. I, on the other hand, picked you for your potential as an architect. Nothing more, nothing less."

"I'm taking this as a no," Arwen said. "Thank you for your time, Juliet."

"Thank you for your offer."

With that, Juliet slid off the stool, pushed her hair behind her ears, and grabbed her bag. "Good luck, Arwen."

Arwen wasn't at work the next day, and her office was empty. Kathy, too, was gone, not so much as an e-mail of goodbye after all this time. That hurt, since Juliet thought they'd been friends. But Barb Frost hadn't raised any fools. Juliet had always been wary of Kathy.

Meanwhile, the rumor mill was churning out stories, and Edward and Dave were in a huddle in Edward's office. Juliet closed her door and did her work.

It was no surprise when Dave and Edward called her into the conference room at five.

"Juliet!" Dave said as if he hadn't seen her seventeen times today. "You look amazing! That week off did you some good, did it?"

"One day, Dave. One day off. And yes, it did."

Edward was staring at his iPad. "Let's get to it, shall we? We'd like to make you a partner, Juliet. Your excellent contributions here have not gone unnoticed or unappreciated."

"So true! We're a meritocracy, and you have merit, all right," Dave chuckled.

She listened as the men wooed her with phrases like *percentage of profits*, *principal ownership*, *staff management*, *increased vacation time*. When they were done, she folded her hands neatly in front of her.

"Arwen turned you down, I take it?"

The men exchanged glances. "Uh . . . well, she's decided to pursue other opportunities," Dave said.

"I know. She asked me to join her firm." They flinched in unison.

"Well, we know you're a team player, Juliet," Dave said. "Loyal. We gave you your start, after all."

"When I got my license, I had offers from nine firms, Dave," she said.

"But you came here, and I think we've treated you very well."

She could do it. Sure, they offered Arwen the spot first, but business was business, and Juliet wouldn't take it personally.

It was the recent memory of the two of them lecturing her in her own home just a few days ago that did them in.

"No thanks," she said. "I hereby tender my resignation. All the best to you, gentlemen."

She called Oliver from the car, and he congratulated her and said they'd talk more when she got home, but he was very proud.

Her righteous badassery lasted the entire drive home and up to dinner (which was not salmon, but a delicious roast chicken. Juliet's favorite. Oliver had served it with a flourish and a kiss).

"I quit my job today," she announced as the girls bickered. That did silence them.

"Hear, hear, darling," Oliver said, toasting her.

"Seriously?" Brianna said. "You *quit*? That's just great. Are we still going to Hawaii this summer? Has it occurred to you that you make more than Dad and maybe quitting isn't a great idea?"

The little . . . brat. "You know what, Brianna? Maybe we'll go to Hawaii, and maybe not. Maybe, if you don't lose the attitude, we three will go and you can stay with Nana and help with Grampy, because you're not . . . how should I put this? You're not bringing much to the table these days. I mean, we love you, but you're a real pain in the ass lately, and I'm not sure you deserve a vacation at all."

Brianna's mouth dropped open.

"Sorry, sweetheart," Oliver said, putting his hand over Juliet's. "But Mum's got a point."

"Am *I* a pain in the ass?" Sloane asked.

"Not yet, honey, and hopefully not ever," Juliet said. "Brianna, you need to try harder. Okay? Great. Also, I'll be taking your phone for the rest of the school year. I don't think it's good for you, being attached to it as much as you are."

If looks could kill . . . There was no love in that glare, that was for sure.

Shit. The panic attack was coming. She'd quit her *job*. She'd turned down frickin' *partner* and was currently unemployed for the first time in her *life* and her daughter hated her and they might *not* go to Hawaii, and she had really, really been looking forward to it, and— "Excuse me."

Down the stairs, down the hall, into the closet. *Breathebreathebreathe*, nope not working. She lay down, legs weak, and wished she'd thought to bring a paper bag. Her vision grayed, but this time she didn't want to faint. She just wanted . . . she just wanted nothing.

The truth was, she had everything.

She'd find a job. She could start her own firm. She'd be fine. Oliver made a decent enough living. They could switch their health care to his work, even if it was a worse plan, and . . .

"Mommy?" Brianna sounded like a little girl again, scared from a bad dream. Shit. Had she done that?

"Yes, honey?" Juliet said, sitting up.

"Are you really that mad at me?"

"No! No. Just tired of the . . . bitchiness."

"You still like me, though, right?"

"Of course!" A lie, but really. Parenthood was ninety percent forgiveness, ten percent lies and a hundred percent love.

"Why are you in the closet?"

"Oh, I guess I'm . . . hiding from life. Sometimes I feel scared about things."

"Like what?"

"Like, am I a good mother? Have I been helpful and kind today? Will everyone I love be okay? Can I be doing more?"

"That's a lot." Brianna sat down next to her and picked up one of Juliet's shoes, fiddling with the strap.

"It is."

"Is being a grown-up hard?"

"Sometimes."

Brianna started to cry, her sweet little face crumpling. "I don't want to grow up, Mom. I hate all this, the periods and zits and boobs and boys and the drama. I want to be eight again. Eight was really fun." Her voice squeaked on the last word, and Juliet gathered her up against her, every molecule in her body wanting to wrap around her child and protect her from every hurt, every bad feeling.

"I understand, honey. I do. I remember how hard it is." She kissed Brianna's hair. "But you know what? You're going to like your body pretty soon. It's so weird, but you will. This is the hardest time. You'll get through it. Daddy and I are with you every step of the way."

"Is there *anything* good about being a grown-up?"

Juliet laughed. "Sure. You can pick someone really great, like your dad, to be your best friend, and you get to live with each other. You can find a job that you love doing."

"I don't know what I want to do. I hate when grown-ups ask me that."

"You're not supposed to know. Tell them that. Say, 'Hey, I'm twelve. Give me some room here.'"

Brianna laughed a little.

"You know what the best part of being a grown-up is?" Juliet asked.

"No."

"You get to be a mommy if you want."

"I thought I was a pain in the ass," Brianna muttered.

"You are. But you're *my* pain in the ass. I wouldn't trade you for anything."

Brianna didn't answer, didn't hug her any tighter, didn't say, *I love you so much*, or *You always make me feel better*, as Juliet would have said to her own mom.

Brianna didn't have to. Juliet already knew.

A few hours later, when the girls were in bed, and Oliver was "thoroughly shagged" and sound asleep, Juliet went to her computer and typed an e-mail.

To: arwenalexander@gmail.com
Subject: job offer
The firm's name will be Frost/Alexander. I'll get 33% ownership, the tie-breaking vote if one is needed, head of design. Take it or leave it.
Juliet

A few minutes later, the one-word answer came.

Done.

CHAPTER THIRTY-THREE

John

Dog. *Daw*. Baby. *Bay . . . bee*. Barb. *Baahr*. Juliet. *Zhool*. Sadie. *Say*. Tired. *Tahr*.

No. *No*. He has this one down.

These are the words he can say now, though the effort makes him feel foolish and old. Most times, words come out of his mouth wrong, sounding huge and shapeless, or like other words. He can look at a tree and think *tree*, but the word that comes out is *roo,* which means *root*. Sometimes he's understood, most times he's not. His mouth muscles are tired, and the bossy lady doesn't care.

Sadie does, though. She can understand his connections. Not always, but sometimes.

He wants to say, *I'm sorry, Barb*. Because she knows about the hard-faced woman who has never been to see him. He knows this. Barb told him, and Barb doesn't lie. He wants to talk about the flower, but he can't, and he doesn't remember why it's so important, but it is, and he tries to pull it close.

Ted still comes to visit, and John is glad. Noah comes, too, sometimes to fix something for Barb, and sometimes to let him see the baby, who is solid and warm and harder to hold now because he is growing. His daughters come. Juliet doesn't look at him much, which is better than Sadie with the hope in her eyes. John doesn't know which is harder to see, the mad or the hope.

Janet comes, too. She knows about the flower. Sometimes she brings him flowers that she grows. She works in a place that grows plants or babies, but the word is long and hard for his mind to remember. She talks and talks, gentle words falling around him like warm rain.

He loves her. Not the way he loved Barb, or the hard-faced woman, but in a new way. She is the only one who wants nothing from him. She has no hope or sadness or disappointment or . . . what is the word? Tired. She has no tired on her face.

He is not getting better. John understands this. The words he says are so hard and the trying is so heavy that he won't be able to do more. He wants to stop trying. The way he talked long ago, the way other people have the words tumble out of their mouths is not for him anymore. The doctor says words, and Sadie with hope in her eyes . . . no. He can feel it. He knows. He isn't trapped inside his body. This *is* himself. He will be this way always. His now-self, not his old self.

With Janet, his now-self is fine.

What he has to do is make his wife understand. He has to be the husband again, just for a little while. The father.

Images flutter from the long-ago. John would come home from the place where he did the work. The office. He would drive the car into the driveway and go into the house. Sadie was little in the long-ago, and Juliet was bigger, and Sadie would run to him, and he would pick her up and smile, and Juliet would wait in the kitchen doorway, and he would remember to give her a hug, too.

Then he would kiss Barb on the cheek, not really listening as she talked, but smelling the good smells of the kitchen, feeling like a husband, a father. A man.

He needs to get to that place again, to be that man. It is like crawling through a snowstorm, up a mountain in a snowstorm on the darkest night. But he will get there. He will find the flower. He will be husband and father again for a moment, and then he can go back to being the now-self, who listens to the birds and the little baby and the warm rain voice, the now-self who likes to have the dog close to him, who can go to sleep whenever he wants.

CHAPTER THIRTY-FOUR

Sadie

The storm was full of bluster and drenching rain, a nice old-fashioned nor'easter, raging all day long. My little house sang and shook in the wind, creaking and groaning, sounds I decided to like, rather than worry that the roof was going to blow off. The rain slapped against the windows in sheets, and I couldn't have been cozier. I'd ventured into my attic the day before and nailed up some tarp until I could really fix the roof, and so far, I only needed one bucket for the leaks. The sound of the dripping was strangely companionable. Pepper was asleep on the couch, curled into her little cinnamon bun position, snoring gently.

Me, I was painting. Painting something because I wanted to, not because it matched a comforter or a couch.

Without a lot of forethought, I'd gotten out my paints, set up my easel, taken a canvas, prepped it and, before I could talk myself out of it, squeezed out the delicious, shiny blobs of oil paint onto my palette—cadmium red, cerulean blue, burnt umber, titanium white, Naples yellow, magenta, black—and put paint on canvas as fast as I could.

The sky.

I was painting the sky, lost in the smell of the oil paint, the bite of turpentine, the swirl of colors, the gentle, wet whisper of the brush against the canvas. The sun, the clouds, the sea.

A sunset, the most painted scene in the world, and I didn't care. I was lost in colors—and the infinite possibilities of mixing shades that created turquoise, lavender, purple, rose. Pushing the paint, dragging it, twisting it, dabbing, brushing, watching in an almost out-of-body experience as the sky began to form.

This wasn't a couch painting. This was an impulse. Instinct. For weeks, I'd been wanting to paint the sky, and I'd found all sorts of reasons not to start.

Today was different. Now that I'd started, I couldn't stop. Lightening the red here, bringing up the blue, adding more black and purple to the water and the clouds. Time was marked by the dripping in the bucket and the shifting gray afternoon light, and that was all.

I had nowhere to go. A branch had fallen just behind the car this morning (thank God it hadn't fallen *on* the car, since it was Juliet's). It was big enough that I couldn't drag it out of the way; I'd need a chainsaw to cut it and move it. I'd called Mom and Juliet and let them know I was stuck for the day, and an hour later, the storm knocked out the power. I had a battery lantern on in the kitchen, and the gray, watery light poured through the new windows Noah had put in.

So I was stuck, and I could do nothing outside, and I had to release some of the energy and electricity that had been building since my marathon make-out session with Noah.

Somewhere around one a.m. that night, he'd said, "I better go," and we disentangled from each other. I was barely able to stand, so turned on I felt like I could float, but also like my legs wouldn't hold me. Noah was in no better shape.

"Time for a swim in the Sound," he said. "Hope the water's cold enough."

"I wish I could come with you," I said, and we were kissing again. It took him fifteen minutes to get from the living room to the door, because we just couldn't stop kissing, touching, winding ourselves around each other, our hands stopping to admire, caress, feel.

Finally, he caught both my hands in his and kissed them. Then he just looked at me, his hair tangled and wild, his eyes so dark and happy, and he smiled, and finally left the house, leaving me to collapse on the couch in a pile of raging pheromones.

Joy. That's what it was. It was joy. Whatever our future was, it was best to stay right here, right now, and let the joy fill me and lift me, because Noah and I were something. I didn't know what, but we were something to each other, and something important.

For now, that was enough. I didn't let myself think past that.

And it clearly had an effect on my mood. My house was immaculate, Pepper and I had gone for a five-mile run last night, knowing the storm would keep us inside. I sanded the butcher-block island I'd bought on Etsy, oiled it and then made spaghetti sauce from scratch.

Today, when the branch fell and the power went out, I busted out the paints.

It was time. All that joy, that floating, buoyant emotion, needed to come out on a canvas.

God, I'd missed this. It felt so good to see the painting bloom as my brush danced and bustled. All these weeks I'd been in this house staring west in the evenings, watching the sunset, the moon rise, the rain blow the reeds of the salt marsh. For the first time in years, painting once again felt like my destiny. For the first time since I could remember, I felt like myself again.

The painting was nearly finished—half of art was knowing when to stop—when Pepper jumped up and started to tremble and whine, pressing her nose against the front window. She did this when a fox or coyote was in the area, or a deer, or a mouse, or a worm. Often, I couldn't see what she saw, but I always took a look, because who wanted to miss out on seeing a little red fox, right?

I set my palette down, rested the brush on the easel lip and went to see.

Nothing. "Is one of your friends out there?" I asked. She started moaning, trembling violently now. I took my phone in case it was something cute and I could snap a picture for Carter, who loved hearing about wildlife, New Yorker that he was.

"Okay. Let's get your leash on, Pepper Puppy," I said, and she wagged gratefully, still pressing her nose against the glass. I got my slicker and her shoulder harness, since she was a puller.

The wind battered us the second we stepped out the door, but Pepper leaped and tugged me down toward the river. The tide was going out, so the river was getting more and more shallow, and the rain-soaked, salty mud made walking hard.

"Easy, girl, easy!" I said. The rain had already soaked my face and the front of my jeans, but my good old L.L.Bean boots kept my feet dry. A gust of wind made me stagger back a couple of steps, my foot nearly coming out of the boot, but Pepper was on fire to get to the water.

"Pepper!" I yelled. "Stay with me!"

Then I saw what she'd seen.

It was a beached dolphin. And it was alive! Holy crap. The storm must've pushed it up here, and it didn't have enough water to swim. Oh, it was tragic, flapping and struggling there. Pepper was crooning at it, her tail wagging madly, and the dolphin blew hard out of its blowhole in a whooshing sound.

Thank God I had my phone. I dragged Pepper a few yards away and tied her leash to a scrubby bush. She wanted to play with the dolphin, dropping her shoulders down, barking and wagging.

"It doesn't know what you are, Pepper," I said. "Settle down. But yes! This is very exciting!"

I pulled out my phone. One bar. I dialed 911, but the call dropped before it connected. I tried again. Same result. My one bar went away, and the dreaded words *No Service* appeared.

I texted Noah, Mickey, Mom and Juliet—in a nutshell, every capable person I knew. Dolphin stuck in tidal river by my house, please call someone, I have no service.

My phone told me the message was not delivered. "Shit!" I said.

I went closer to the dolphin—it may have been dying. Sometimes they stranded themselves, right? She (I thought it was a girl for some reason) struggled a little more and made a squeaking sound, and the noise hit me right in the heart.

"Okay. Hang on, honey. Help is on the way. I'll be right back."

I went back to the bush, untied my dog, had to practically drag her back to the house and shoved her inside. "Sorry, baby, you're not going to be much help here." I checked my phone—still no service, which had happened a few times since I moved here. That was okay. I'd get in my car and drive to Mom's or Noah's—

Right. My car was blocked by the tree branch.

I took a deep breath and thought. Google would be real handy right about now, but I had no power, and therefore no Wi-Fi.

Looked like I was about to become a dolphin rescuer. I grabbed a bucket, so I could pour water on her (because maybe she needed that?), and a shovel. I could dig the muck and maybe make a trench for her, and then as the tide came back in, maybe she could swim? Or I could carry her to deeper water, maybe? Oh, yes, a tarp. I could get her on it and drag her to deeper water.

"You were right, Mom," I said aloud. "I should've gone to college for something more practical. Marine biology, in this case."

Well, there was a little dolphin out there and she'd squeaked at me, and I wasn't going to leave her alone to die. I grabbed my New York Yankees cap to keep the rain off my face and set off with my makeshift dolphin rescue kit.

She was still there. Maybe not flipping her tail as much. I knelt down next to her. "Hi, honey. I'm going to try to help you." I stuck out my hand, in case she wanted to sniff it, like a dog, and she lifted her head up a little bit, and I swore to God she looked at me and knew I was one of the good guys. You could touch dolphins and not hurt them, right? Of course. They let you swim with them at those resort places in

Florida. I touched her just south of her blowhole, and she was cold and firm and smooth. "I'll do my best, honey. Stay with me."

She flapped again, utterly helpless on the sand. I ran down the river to where the water was deeper and got a bucketful to pour over her. She did seem to like that, flipping and wriggling with more energy. Then I started digging the trench, which filled up with water immediately. Maybe if I could position her toward the river, she could sort of flop her way down . . .

"I'm going to touch you now, honey," I said. "Okay? I'm going to try to turn you."

She was, as best I knew, a bottlenose dolphin, and a little one. Maybe half-grown? I loved nature documentaries, but I was just guessing here. I knew dolphins were smart, maybe smarter than humans. And they traveled in groups—pods?—so maybe her family was waiting for her in the deeper water. Stoningham was the only town in Connecticut that had a little bit of oceanfront; most of the town hugged the very end of Long Island Sound. But out here, where I was, it was possible (if you were a dolphin, for example) to swim straight from the Atlantic, past Fishers Island to the east, and right here to the tidal river.

Taking a deep breath, I put my hands on either side of her and moved her so she faced the trench. She flapped her tail up and down, seeming to know that she had to do her part. A foot. Two feet. I dug some more, moved her a few inches in the inch or two of water, dug some more. I tried to pick her up, then abandoned the plan, afraid I would drop her. She was awkward and heavy, maybe seventy-five or a hundred pounds.

The tidal river was just too shallow, and getting more so every minute. Honey—I'd named her now—seemed to be getting tired. Her breathing wasn't as loud or frequent, and her efforts weren't as strong. The tide was going out too fast for my plan.

"Okay," I said after maybe an hour had passed. I was panting myself, my jeans wet and sandy, making my skin feel raw. I got another bucket of water and dumped it over Honey, then considered the tarp. If I could roll her onto it without hurting her, I could drag her closer to the Sound. It was better than nothing. I didn't know if the rain was hurting her skin, or if it was good for her, or if she was hungry and I should've brought that envelope of tuna in my cupboard to feed her.

I spread out the tarp next to her and knelt, putting my hands on her. If I rolled her, would it hurt her fin? I tucked it against her and looked in her eye. "I hope this won't hurt you, Honey," I said. "I just want to get you back to your family, okay? Okay. So on three, we'll roll. One, two . . . three."

She was heavy, but she rolled over pretty easily onto her back, and I managed to tuck her other fin so it wouldn't get hurt, and rolled her the rest of the way. She lay on her stomach, but now on the tarp. "You okay, Honey?"

She didn't answer, just blew hard. No more squeaks.

I went to the front of the tarp and started dragging it. God! She was heavy! I had to walk backward, and after a few steps, I tripped and landed flat on my ass in the wet sand. Got up and started trying again. She wasn't even trying to flap her tail fin anymore. "Please don't die, Honey," I said. "I'm giving it my best here."

I had never been this soaked. Even my raincoat was soaked through, and I was sweaty and clammy and shaking with exhaustion, but we'd come this far, Honey and I. I wasn't going to leave her now.

"Sadie! Hey!" Noah, his hair whipping across his face, was standing on the hill my house perched on.

"Oh, thank God," I said.

He ran toward me. "What are you doing?"

"Just saving a dolphin. You know."

"Did you call anyone?"

"I tried. No cell service out here, and my car's blocked in."

"Yeah, I saw. No service in town, either. I tried calling you to see if you were okay, then came out to check." He bent down to look at my new friend. "Have you named her?"

He knew me well. He really did.

"Honey."

"Yes, dear?"

"No, that's *her* name." I smiled at him. Noah, flirting with me over a baby dolphin. God! The feels! "Think we can pull her to the water? She's getting tired, and the tide is going out."

"Let's go."

It was a good quarter mile to the Sound. I talked almost nonstop to my little dolphin friend, telling her to be brave, be strong, relax and enjoy the ride. It was tough going, and Noah and I both fell once or twice more (fine, I fell twice, and he stumbled). By the time we reached the ocean, I could barely stand, I was so tired.

"Okay, Honey, let's go," Noah said.

We pulled her into the water, and my faithful L.L.Bean boots filled up immediately, the fleece lining acting like a sponge. The water was bitingly cold and stung my raw skin.

Honey didn't seem to rouse much. Flapped a little, but didn't make it off the tarp.

"Let's take her in a little deeper," I said. I put my hand on Honey's back. "Come on, sweetie. You can do it." We were knee-deep now, then thigh deep. She flapped once, and the tarp slid out from under her.

She sank.

"No! Come on, Honey! Up you go!" I reached in and pulled her up so she could breathe. "Here, baby. Just sit a minute. Get your bearings."

"She might be sick, Sadie," Noah said.

"She's not." Stupid of me to say, but I didn't want her to be. My throat tightened with tears. All this to watch my little friend drown? No.

I took her out a few more feet, now waist deep in the ocean, the waves slapping me, sliding over Honey's blowhole, soaking my sweater. "Maybe you can run back to your truck and drive into town and get some help," I said, my teeth starting to chatter.

"I'm not leaving you in the ocean by yourself. With a dolphin. It's not even fifty degrees today, Special."

"Well . . . maybe if we swim her out a little more, she'll catch on."

Noah looked dubious.

"Please?" I added. "You're a father. She's a baby. Doesn't this inspire your paternal instincts?"

He shook his head, smiling a little. "Sure. Okay." We took her out a little more, and her tail moved. I was up to my shoulders now. She wasn't sinking, but we were holding her up, and let me tell you, a baby dolphin is not a tiny thing.

"Any other ideas?" Noah asked. A wave slapped me in the face, and I choked. "Pretty soon we'll be dead, so think of something."

I couldn't help a sputtering laugh.

And then, like magic, like proof of God, a full-grown dolphin leaped out of the water *right* in front of us, and I screamed a little as it splashed down. Honey began squeaking and wriggling, and then, just like that, she gave a flip of her powerful tail and swam toward her mother (I thought it was her mother, anyway). She was a dark shape in the water, and then she was gone.

"Yes! Way to go, Honey!" Noah said.

But I felt suddenly . . . bereft. That was it? After two hours together?

It wasn't. In a glorious whoosh of water that pulled around my legs, Honey and her mama circled us, once, then twice, and for one beautiful second, we could hear their clicking and squeaking.

Then they were ten feet away, surfacing for air side by side, then twenty, and then they disappeared, indiscernible from the choppy waves in the darkening sea.

"They thanked you," Noah said, wonder in his voice. "Now that doesn't happen every day."

I was crying with the beauty of it. Wrapped my arms around Noah and sobbed, then kissed him full on the mouth, tasting the salt of my tears and the ocean.

"Okay, dolphin girl," he said, pushing my wet hair off my face. "Let's get you home."

. . .

Because God obviously approved of my efforts, the power came on five minutes after we got back to the house. Pepper greeted us ecstatically, and I bent down to kiss her. "We did it! She's back with her mommy! All because you saw her, Pepper!" I swear she knew what I meant, because she did a victory lap around the downstairs, found her squeaky possum toy and started the musical portion of our evening.

"Go take a hot shower before you get hypothermia," Noah said, scrubbing a hand through his wet hair. "Your lips are blue."

"*You* go take a hot shower before *you* get hypothermia," I said. "You were just a Good Samaritan, whereas Pepper and I have trained for this all our lives."

He rolled his eyes (fondly, I thought). "Don't be dumb, Sadie. You were out there a lot longer than I was."

"Warmed by my love of marine mammals, though."

"Get in the shower."

"I have to see if my phone will dry out."

"Forget your phone."

"I have to post something on social media so the world knows of my greatness."

"Damn you, Sadie," he growled, and then—finally—he was on me, mouth on mine, arms around me, tongue against mine. He lifted me up on the butcher block, muttering, "I could've made something a lot better than this piece of crap," before yanking open my jacket, pushing it down my arms so I was pinned. He kissed me like he was drowning, dying, and I was the only one who could save him.

And you know, saving *was* kind of my thing that day, so I wrapped my legs around him and kissed him back, freeing one arm so I could grip his wet hair.

"I have eight minutes of hot water in that tank," I said, gasping a little. "Let's make them count."

He still knew how to undress a woman with great efficiency. He could still carry me. He still had that look of intense concentration when he worked, and he still smiled during a kiss, hot water running over us, soap sliding between us. He still knew every place I loved to be touched, where I was ticklish, how to make my knees buckle.

But he was new as well. He turned off the water when it started to cool, stepped out and wrapped me in a towel. Dried himself off fast, his six-pack rippling, his shoulders smooth and hypnotic with muscle. Then he kissed me and kissed me, sliding his hands under my ass, picked me up and carried me upstairs.

"I'm on the Pill and passed my STD panel with flying colors," I said as he dumped me on the bed.

"I see your dirty talk hasn't improved," he said.

"I just want you to know, I'd never take any chances with you, Noah." I was abruptly serious. "Even if we . . . I mean, if we're about to do this, I just wanted you to . . . feel safe."

He lay down on top of me, his skin so smooth and warm, still damp, his wet curls hanging around his face. "Special," he whispered, "the last thing I feel with you is safe."

I didn't know why the words were so romantic, why they wrapped around my heart and pulled.

But they did, and when we were finally making love, finally, finally together again, I knew I was home.

CHAPTER THIRTY-FIVE

Barb

The morning after the big storm, I had to take John back to Gaylord for an assessment with his team. He'd had another MRI, and they were going to go over the results with us and talk about future therapy and all that.

Driving the hour plus to Wallingford was almost peaceful. John didn't talk, though he'd been making more noise lately, trying to say words. And I tried to understand them, but it was tough. Sadie thought it meant a full recovery was just around the corner, but I wasn't so sure. He seemed to check out a lot, and those words . . . I knew he wanted to tell me *something*, but his speech was so unclear, and the effort exhausted him.

Poor John. I wondered if he'd have been so bad off if he hadn't been riding his bike that day. If someone had been there and saw him fall, gotten to him sooner. If he hadn't banged his head in addition to having the stroke. In other words, if he hadn't been having an affair and training for a triathlon in January, maybe the stroke wouldn't have been so bad.

But the anger and humiliation I felt had seeped away. It's real hard to be upset with a man who can't cut his own food.

I'd been awfully busy yesterday, fielding calls from people reporting power outages and downed trees, and sent the fire department out to help the Patrick family get their generator started, since Violet had a condition where she couldn't regulate her body temperature, and if their house got cold, she'd get so cold she'd have to check into the hospital. The Fieldings lost their cat, so once the fire department was done at the Patricks', they headed over there, and I went, too, since Juliet came over and said she'd watch her dad. I loved cats. Always wanted to get one, but John was severely allergic. We did find the sweet little thing, crouched under the car, scared of the wind.

Aside from storm issues, there was the impending town-wide celebration for the 350th anniversary of our founding. The garden club needed more volunteers, the auction that would raise money for college scholarships needed more donations, and half the people who'd answered the e-mail about hosting open houses hadn't filled in their forms.

I guess you could say I had a lot on my mind, plus John's future. Gosh, it made me tired.

"All right, John, we're here," I said, getting out of the car. I had to unbuckle him, because he couldn't seem to grasp that one. I wished LeVon was still with Gaylord. He'd come by last week to check in and, after John had fallen asleep, stayed for a cup of tea with me. It had been so nice, talking to him again.

It was slow going to the conference room, since John seemed to wander to the left, and I had to half tow him down the long hallway. The whole team was there—Betsy, the speech therapist; Evan, the head of physical and occupational therapy; Dr. McIntyre, the head of outpatient rehabilitation; two physiatrists. They all had iPads and folders, and I suddenly had a bad feeling in my stomach.

"Lovely to see you again," Dr. McIntyre said. She'd been wonderful this whole time, sometimes even calling me on the weekend to check in. We all sat around the table, and my heart started jumping like a scared rabbit.

"So," Dr. McIntyre said. "I'm afraid the news isn't great, which doesn't mean it's horrible. John seems to have had at least two smaller strokes since the big one. That explains why his left side seems weaker than before, and why he's struggling with mobility more than he was a month ago."

I put my hand over John's, not sure what he understood. He seemed calm and unchanged. Sleepy, even. "Oh," I said, my voice small.

"He *has* made a little progress with speech," Betsy said. "But that seems to have plateaued. He can say a few words, but he's not putting them together in a meaningful way."

"Yes, I . . . I thought so, too." Oh, gosh. This was going to hit Sadie real hard. It was hitting me, hard, too. "Um . . . the strokes. Does that mean he'll have more?"

Dr. McIntyre looked kind. "We're adjusting his medications, but it's definitely possible."

John was asleep now, his chin on his chest. Good. I didn't want him to have to hear this. Know this. Oh, he looked so old, so sad!

"He's probably safer using the walker all the time," Evan said. "A wheelchair for when he's tired. You may want to look into hiring a full-time caregiver. We can give you referrals, of course."

"Gotcha. I . . . So he's not . . . going to improve." No one said anything. "Do you have any guesses on how long he'll . . . be with us?"

"It's always so hard to predict," the doctor said.

So they weren't going to say the words outright. "Can I have a sec?" I asked.

"Of course," Dr. McIntyre said. "Use the room next door."

I practically ran to it, closed the door and started to shake.

So this was it, then. My husband, the once intelligent, wry attorney, was gone. He'd never talk to his grandchildren again. Sadie and Juliet wouldn't get him back. We'd never have another night where talking was even a possibility, and suddenly, those silent nights of him watching television and me answering e-mails felt awfully precious.

I shouldn't have let them operate on him that day in January. I should've let him go, but gosh, I don't even remember that being presented as an option.

This was his life now. He'd just slip away, inch by inch, confused and scared and exhausted until he died. And not to put too fine a point on it, I'd be his caregiver for the rest of his life, or the rest of mine. Almost without knowing it, I pulled out my phone.

"Caro?" I said.

"What's wrong, honey?" The concern in her voice brought me to tears.

"He's not going to get better. He's had a couple of little strokes, and . . . and he's not getting better." I started to cry.

"Oh, shit, Barb. I'm so sorry. Are you at Gaylord now?"

"Yes. I didn't want the girls to come, because I suspected there would be bad news. I just didn't know it would be so . . . definite."

"Barb, why didn't you call me? I would've come! We're best friends, for God's sake!"

"I should have."

"Okay, here's what we'll do. You come home, I'll bring dinner tonight, and wine and lots of it, and we can talk to the girls and go from there. Don't worry, hon. We've got this."

We. A person forgot what a beautiful word that was when it had been *you* for so long.

CHAPTER THIRTY-SIX

Sadie

Noah left before dawn, kissing me gently on the lips, whispering that he wanted to see Marcus before he went to work. I spent a blissful half hour dozing, Pepper by my side, before getting up to take her for a walk. There was no evidence of our dolphin rescue; the tide had erased any tracks, and the birds were nearly deafening. I felt as happy as I'd ever felt in my life.

Grateful . . . a word made sappy by a million tacky wooden signs, yet a feeling that was so powerful. I felt as if sunbeams were shining from my skin. My dad was getting better. Noah loved me. We'd saved a baby dolphin! I had a dog! I'd painted a sunset yesterday, and the coffee was on.

I took in a few deep breaths of the salt-kissed air, the sun warm on my face. Noticed that Noah had moved the branch that had fallen behind the car. Of course he had.

God, I *loved* him. Alexander was barely a memory, though the other two women were my Facebook friends now, and we'd all shared our Alexander Breakup stories. I'd always known he was a pale shadow compared with Noah. I just hadn't wanted to dwell on it, feeling that *good enough* was about all I could expect.

Noah was amazing. He was so kind and decent and trustworthy and good in bed that he was a unicorn among men. I said a prayer of thanks that we were getting this second chance. If yesterday had shown me anything other than the fact that I loved baby dolphins, it was that I loved Noah more.

The coffee was extra delicious this morning. I took my mug and laptop onto the porch, sat on the step and let Pepper frolic on the lawn. Checked my e-mails.

Then I jolted upright so fast, my coffee sloshed.

To: SadieFrost1335@gmail.com
From: hasan@HasanSadikSoho.com
Re: your painting at Harriet White/Darcy Cummings house

Dear Ms. Frost,

I was recently at a housewarming party hosted by Harriet and Darcy in Brooklyn. They showed me your incredible painting, knowing I have a special interest in emerging artists. I was able to obtain your e-mail from their interior decorator.

I would be very interested in talking with you about showing in my SoHo gallery this coming fall and perhaps, if you'd be so kind, having the chance to see your portfolio. Is there any possibility you are available to meet? I am desperately hoping you don't have exclusive contracts elsewhere.

The very best to you,
Hasan
Hasan Sadik SoHo
29 Walker Street, New York, NY 10013

I reread the e-mail four times.

I'd *been* to that gallery. It was one of *those* galleries. The "I can make your career in one show" galleries. Aneni had had a show there, during which time a curator for the Guggenheim had bought one of her paintings. The Guggenheim!

In fact, Hasan Sadik SoHo was the gallery where I'd tried to explain to Noah why my skyscape paintings were touristy drivel and not true art.

And now the owner—Hasan Sadik himself—was desperately hoping I was free to show at his place. Just like that, a chance came out of the clear blue sky.

This could make my career. Every dream I'd ever had about art reared up and hugged me tight.

All I had to do was bang out some more Georgia O'Keeffe–type work, using the same kinds of touches I'd used on the vagina painting to make it clear that it wasn't just a knockoff and . . . and . . .

Shit. I'd be established. I'd be *that* New York artist, discovered after teaching Catholic school for years and years and making paintings that matched upholstery. It *was* a great story!

I needed to get to work. Mom had Dad at Gaylord today, so my schedule was clear.

I took a few deep breaths and, hands shaking, wrote back to Hasan Sadik, saying I'd love to meet with him and was a great admirer of his gallery. Kept it short and sweet, and nearly fainted when he wrote back *immediately*, offering to send a car to pick me up, and perhaps we could also have lunch? And did I have an agent he should be including in these e-mails?

I'll be in touch in the next day or two, I wrote, too overwhelmed at the moment, and afraid I'd say something stupid. Thank you so much for your interest.

Thank God I'd taken down my website years ago so he couldn't see all my previous attempts to be artistic and unique (or read my idiotic bio where I mentioned Robert Frost). I pulled up some images of Georgia O'Keeffe's work and printed out a couple for inspiration. Somewhere in one of my unpacked boxes was a juicy coffee table book on her flower paintings. Which box was it, dang it?

Listen. All work was derivative. It wasn't like I was doing anything that hadn't been done a million times before. I found the book, flipped through it and settled on a white rose, the oriental poppies and an iris.

A chance like this did not come around very often. I'd be an idiot to turn it aside. "Mommy's going to be a famous artist," I told Pepper, who nuzzled my hand encouragingly. "Let's get to work, shall we?" I set aside my sunset painting from yesterday, got a couple of canvases out of the closet, and started working, ignoring the little voice in the back of my head that was telling me to slow down.

I painted all day. Noah texted, asking me if I wanted to come to his house that evening, and I told him yes, I had some really exciting news and couldn't wait to see him, but had to have dinner at my mom's first to talk about Dad's progress.

I've been thinking about you all day, he wrote, and my heart melted.

Same here, I texted. Debated saying, *I love you*, even though he knew already, and kept on painting, with a little more depth, deeper color.

Noah was good for my art. He always had been. I hoped I was good for him. I made him laugh. I knew him in a way that started in the very center of my heart. I had always believed in him, his goodness, his kindness, his talent at what he did. Also, I gave him the chance to save me from a collapsing house *and* the opportunity to save a dolphin.

I loved him. I loved him. I loved him so much. Small wonder that I was singing as I painted.

"So, girls," Mom said. "Sit down."

Jules and I had been cleaning up after dinner. We'd eaten Caro's delicious chicken and salsa verde casserole, and Dad had been settled in front of the TV with Pepper.

We sat, exchanging glances. Juliet looked spiffy as always in her chic, tailored clothes. I had paint on the back of my hand and wore stained leggings and a T-shirt with Bill Murray's face on it. The fact that Oliver and the girls weren't here struck me as ominous all of a sudden. So did the fact that Caro had stayed.

Shit.

"The news isn't good," Mom said. "I'm sorry."

"What news? Dad's news?" I asked. "How could it not be good? He's been doing great!"

"Could you let her talk?" Juliet snapped.

"Yes! Fine! I'm just . . . Go ahead, Mom."

She glanced at Caro, who gave her a little smile. "Well, girls, your dad's not progressing, I'm sorry to say," Mom said. "He's had two more smaller strokes, and he's likely to have more."

I jerked back. "Okay, first of all, when were these other strokes?" I asked. "I think we'd notice. And secondly, he's *talking* now! How can they say he's not progressing?"

Caro covered my hand. "This is hard news, I know, honey."

"No, it's not! It's just wrong news."

"Calm down, Sadie," Juliet muttered, and I wanted to bite her.

"He can say a few words, but there's more weakness on his left side," Mom went on. Juliet scootched her chair closer and put her arm around her. "So he'll keep needing care. That's the long and short of it. Our insurance will cover an aide for when I'm at work, and we'll figure the rest out as we go along."

"I think we should look into a nursing home," Juliet said.

"No! Absolutely not!" I said.

"Mom does eighty-five percent of the work, Sadie. She's seventy years old."

"I'm not exactly dead yet," Mom said.

"You're getting worn out, Mom."

"I just sent you two to a spa for a rest!" I said, knowing it was ridiculous.

"Two nights isn't going to be enough, unless it's two nights a week, Sadie," Jules said. She looked at our mother. "I'm worried about you. Insurance would cover—"

"Would cover a shithole, Juliet!"

"Keep your voice down," she said. "Oliver and I can help."

"Juliet, you're starting your own firm, honey. You keep your money.

Sadie's right. This is my responsibility, and with a little help from the visiting nurses and such, your father and I will be okay."

I glared at my sister. She'd put Dad in a kennel if I let her.

"What?" she snapped. "I don't see *you* making plans to stay here permanently. You want Dad cared for, maybe you have to do more than come over and paint and let your dog watch TV with him."

"That's not fair. I've done everything I can for him. God forbid you interrupt your perfect life—"

"That's enough, girls," Caro and Mom said in unison, then smiled at each other. I pressed my lips together and tried not to cry.

"The truth is, you're both right," Mom said. "I can't see putting him into a nursing home when all he needs is . . . well, a keeper. And yes, I'm tired. It hasn't been easy."

"In sickness and in health," I said.

"Exactly," Mom said.

"Fuck you, Sadie," Juliet said.

"Wow! Angry much, Jules? You *know* he'd take care of her if the situation were reversed."

"You're an idiot. And you don't know the half of it."

"Well, this has been wonderful," Mom said. "Now, both of you get home. You're upsetting me."

"I'm sorry, Mom," Jules said. "But if she knew . . ."

"If I knew what?"

"How hard it is for our mother," Jules ground out. "Getting him in and out of bed, showered, shaved, dressed, making sure there's enough food in the house, paying the bills, working more than a full-time job, checking in on him on her lunch hour or on the app—"

"Mom," I interrupted. "I know how devoted you are. And I admire you for it. I really do."

"Well, thanks, now, hon. It's still time for you both to get on home. Sadie, your dog is curled up with your dad, why don't you just leave her here tonight? Juliet, honey, I'll see you for lunch tomorrow. Caro, want to stay for a glass of wine?"

My sister and I were dismissed. We went outside, giving each other plenty of space.

"How's my car, by the way?" she asked.

"Oh, Jesus. It's fine. Thank you for being so benevolent and generous, thou perfect human."

"Good. You can keep it as long as you're here. And if you wanted to move back forever and be Dad's caregiver twenty-four seven, I'd give it to you."

"Okay, I'm leaving now."

"As you do."

I sucked in a sharp breath. "Juliet, what do you expect me to say? I have a job and an apartment in the city. I have a second career as a painter, as much as you like to laugh at it. I know you're used to being the important one in the family, but that doesn't mean I can magically become a nurse and leave the life I built in the city. Dad and Mom are married. This is part of the territory. Would you want Oliver to stick you in a nursing home?"

"Yes! If it made his life better, you're damn right I would."

"And would you stick *him* in one?"

Ha. I had her there. She looked away, conceding defeat, and I got into the car and backed out of the driveway, heading for Noah's.

Those doctors were wrong. Dad was clearly getting better. They didn't spend as much time with him as I did. I mean, seriously. When was the last time they'd even seen him?

I was crying, and crying while driving was not safe. I pulled over and let myself bawl a little. Two more strokes? When? Yes, he'd been a little . . . wandery lately, listing off to the left, but . . . but . . . the idea that I'd never have the old Dad back was intolerable.

Deep breaths. Deep breaths. My father *was* getting better, and . . . and I didn't know what else, but that had to be true. It had to be.

I hadn't been to Noah's house since I came back. I knew the address well, though; it was his parents' old house—Mom had told me years ago that the elder Pelletiers had moved to Ottawa, where Noah's grandmother lived.

The Pelletier home was in one of Stoningham's quiet little areas, the houses shaded by big maples whose branches wove together above the street as if the trees were holding hands. The sidewalk was pleasantly uneven from their roots.

I ran a hand through my hair and looked at my face in the rearview mirror. Red eyes, blotchy face. Another deep breath. Seeing Noah would make me feel better. He'd put things in perspective.

As you might expect, since both he and his father were carpenters, Noah's house was lovely. It was white, with a wide front porch, two stories. It had changed quite a bit since I was here: bigger windows, a new front door, the garage resembling a barn now. There was a baby swing hanging from a branch in the crab apple tree in the front yard.

It was a house for a family, that was for sure. Not like my crooked little place.

I knocked on the door, wishing I'd thought to bring something.

Mickey answered. "Hey! Heard you two got it on last night."

I couldn't help a smile. "Wow. He spilled, did he?"

"Well, we agreed that if one of us was in a relationship, the other should know. Well done. He looks very happy. Come on in. He's giving Marcus a bath."

The house was beautiful—different from when I was here last, when Noah and I were still hanging on to the threads of our relationship. Back in the day, Mrs. Pelletier would pop out of her study—she'd been a science editor for a news organization—and tell me to help myself to whatever was in the fridge. The floor plan was now open and bright, wide oak planks having replaced the beige carpeting. Ridiculously tidy, with sturdy furniture, and all the beautiful touches you'd expect from a carpenter. Cabinets with glass panes, a beautiful mantelpiece, built-in bookcases.

I followed Mickey toward the kitchen, then jolted to a stop.

There, on the stair landing, was the painting I'd made for him when I was sixteen years old. The one he'd refused to give up for Gillian.

Just a blue sky with soft, golden clouds.

No. There was nothing "just" about it. I hadn't seen that painting in years, and it hit me. The sky was cerulean, the clouds lit with gold and edged with Noah-red. The sun had been just about to rise that day, and I'd painted the sky from memory, not a photo. I could almost see the clouds drifting past on the soft breeze and hear the birds, feel the damp air of the early morning and smell the muffins baking at Sweetie Pies. I'd ridden my bike out to watch, to the bridge near where I now lived, in fact, and with all that young love in my heart, made this painting for Noah.

It was so beautiful.

"In here," Mickey called.

I snapped myself out of my reverie and went into the kitchen, which was cobalt blue and white. "Did the photographers just leave?" I asked. "Seriously. What man has a white kitchen?"

"I know. I can't wait till Marcus starts walking and his grubby little hands turn everything gray. I'll feel less inferior then. I'm not quite the housekeeper Noah is. When are you going to come over to my place, by the way? Tonight would work, since it's Noah's night with the little prince. Hang on, you probably want to nail the carpenter, right? See what I did there?" She laughed. "Don't scar my kid. Then again, Marcus *does* sleep through everything. Even that storm yesterday. So if you two *were* going to fool around—"

"Yeah, okay, let's change the subject. Speaking of the storm, did Noah tell you about the dolphin?"

"Is that a euphemism for penis or something? Want a beer or some wine or whatever he has?"

"Yes to wine, and no, a real dolphin." I sat at the kitchen table and told her the story.

"My God! You rock, kid," she said. "You both do. A fricking dolphin!"

"Thanks. In this case, I'd have to agree with you." I took a sip of wine. "Where do you live, Mickey?"

"Right next door."

"Oh, my gosh, how perfect."

"Yeah. No point in making life harder on the kid, right? So if you two are gonna get married, we should probably have a serious talk, don't you think?"

"Marriage is not currently being discussed."

"But you're gonna get there eventually, right?"

"Uh . . . how long do baths usually take?"

"As long as the baby wants," Noah said, and there he was, his son in his arms. He smiled at me; my face grew hot. Other parts, too.

"Hi, Marcus," I mumbled.

"Abwee!" he answered.

"Want to hold him?" Noah said. "He smells good. Now. That was definitely not true half an hour ago."

"Poop explosion!" Mickey said cheerfully.

I took the little guy. Oh, wow. He did smell good. He was a sturdy baby, and his black hair stood straight up. Dark eyes, like his father.

"How old is he now?" I asked.

"Six months," the proud parents answered in unison. Like Mom and Caro.

Had my parents ever been like that, so in sync that they finished each other's sentences? I couldn't remember.

Marcus yanked my hair. "You're pretty cute, kid," I said, untangling the strand from his chubby little fist. "Pretty cute indeed."

"Well, I'm feeling very third wheel here," Mickey said. "Should I go?"

"No! No, stay," I said. "Um, I got an exciting e-mail today. I think I might be having a gallery show in New York. Noah, remember that painting I did for the brownstone people? One of their friends owns a gallery, and he wants to feature me."

"Holy shit! That's great!" Mickey said.

"Yeah. It's funny, it's actually a gallery you've seen, Noah. Way back when."

"Really."

It wasn't a happy and excited word, not the way he used it. "Yep. So I'll be wicked busy for the next week or so. Painting. More of the same stuff, you know? Those flowers?" For some reason, I was glad to be holding the baby.

Noah took him from me, reading my mind as he usually did. "Mickey, would you mind taking Marcus next door? I'll come back for him in a little bit."

"Sure! Glad to. I need to nurse anyway." She shot me a look. "Maybe see you later? But not if you two are fighting, because I'm on his side. It's a coparenting loyalty thing."

"We're not fighting!" Shit. We were about to fight, weren't we?

Mickey left, Marcus babbling away.

"So," Noah said, sitting down across the table from me. "A gallery show. Wow."

"Yeah. Hasan Sadik. Very, very prestigious."

"For that flowery porn painting."

"Well, yeah. I mean, that's one way of putting it, sure. I think the interior designer called it a huge vagina painting. So I have to make more of the same. That's what I was doing most of today."

"How are you gonna work that?"

"Uh . . . what do you mean?"

"Are you moving back to the city?"

"Um . . . I don't know. I mean, eventually. I have a job there. Teaching. So yeah. I guess so. But the problem is, my father isn't—"

He threw up his hands. "Are you kidding me?"

"No. Why?"

"Jesus, Sadie! We slept together!"

"I know! I was there! And I'm really happy about that."

"Are you? Because I'm feeling used all of a sudden."

I tried a smile. "I think it was a mutual using, pal."

"I *love* you, Sadie."

"I love y—"

"I never stopped. So we spend more than a decade apart, and then you come home and we get back together, and now you're leaving again? For that same New York bullshit?"

"Okay, for one, it's not—"

"Your sister is right. You're unreliable."

"—bullshit. Noah. It's what I've worked for all my life. And when did Juliet say I was unreliable?"

"Once your father's situation is settled, you're done, aren't you? You'll go back to the city and maybe come out here to visit a couple times a year."

"And for two, my father's situation is a long way from settled." My eyes filled again at the thought of Dad, but I refused to cry right now.

Noah clenched his jaw and looked out the window. "I have a son now. A family. You can't pop in and out of our life whenever you feel like it. You have to make a plan, Sadie, and it's clear I'm not in it, and Jesus Christ, I can't believe I fell for this again."

"I think you missed the part where I said I loved you."

"And what exactly does that mean?"

"It means exactly what I said! I love you, Noah!"

"Are you gonna stay here? Are you going to marry me?"

"This is hauntingly familiar, you giving me ultimatums and telling me how life should be."

"Are you going to stay?"

"I don't *know*!" I shouted. "Should I? What's even here for me anymore? Maybe you, if I meet all your criteria? The father who loved me is gone, and according to my mother, he's not getting better. *You* have a family without me and you're just fine with that, you've made that clear. My sister and mother are in a club I was never asked to join. I was recently told by my boyfriend that out of all his girlfriends, he was almost sure I was his favorite. I teach school and earn just above the poverty rate and I'm making these fucking couch paintings and somewhere along the line, I seem to have lost my soul, and then I *finally* get a huge, life-changing chance to show at a dream gallery, and yesterday we sleep together and you tell me you love me, but today you don't want me. What the hell am I *supposed* to do?"

I sat back, panting, then drained my wine.

"You're still with your boyfriend?"

"No! I'm leaving. I'm furious and upset, Noah. Maybe I'll see you soon, and maybe you'll be sticking pins in a voodoo doll of me. I have no idea and I don't care right now. I'm going home to paint."

"Sadie." He stood up. "One thing. Your flower painting, the one you did for the brownstone ladies. That's not you. That's you pretending to be someone else. *That's* a couch painting."

"Fuck off, Noah." I slammed the door on my way out. You know. Just in case he missed thc point.

CHAPTER THIRTY-SEVEN

Sadie

It was here. The biggest moment of my professional life.

Hasan Sadik had greeted me, kissing me on both cheeks, told his silent and beautiful assistant to get me an espresso (I hated espresso). He had me place my paintings on the waiting easels and now was looking at them, walking slowly past each one, pausing, tilting his head, waiting for them to "talk to me and tell me their story."

This required silence. The assistant was barefoot, lest her footfalls interrupt Hasan's conversation with my work. I sat, pressing my knees together, pretending to sip the bitter coffee, and tried to exude confidence.

Juliet had loaned me an outfit and jewelry (she had her flaws as a sister, but staying mad wasn't one of them). I was dressed better than I'd ever been—black tuxedo pants, red patent leather pumps with a chunky heel, a sleeveless ivory top with a slightly draped neckline, and a gray "jardigan" (new term for me, but Brianna had told me it was very on trend). Dangly gold earrings, one plain gold ring on my right forefinger.

It was how I thought a successful artist should look. Cool, simple, wealthy (thanks, Jules) and sophisticated.

Hasan, tastemaker of the New York art world, broker of some of the most lucrative deals for artists today, wore Levi's, a white T-shirt and Converse sneakers and somehow outclassed me by a thousand points. I owned the same outfit many times over. Should've worn it so we could bond over our matching look.

In the week since he'd e-mailed, I'd worked twenty hours a day, making seven more flower paintings. Iris, rose, peony, carnation, tulip, poppy and maple leaves (to show my range). At six this morning, I'd finished drying the last one with my blow-dryer, put them in my portfolio, left Brianna a note about Pepper's new propensity to eat worms, and drove down here two hours early, killing the remainder of time by sitting in my car, sweating with nerves and pressing tissues into my armpits.

I'd never been at this kind of meeting. Never been that chic woman who had something New York wanted to see. This was it. I was, as they say, having a moment.

If only my father could see me now. The thought made my throat tighten with emotion.

He wasn't getting better. I pressed my lips together, hard. I'd think about that later. He'd *want* me present, to soak it all in. I wanted that, too, but somehow, I felt hollow. Maybe because he wasn't quite here to share it. Juliet had wished me the best and hugged me, and Mom said she thought the paintings were "real pretty," but the hollow, fake feeling remained.

After all, I wasn't even wearing my own clothes.

I should've come in wearing one of my teacher dresses, which were invariably flowered or striped, because my students were little kids, after all, and loved bright colors.

I missed them. I missed St. Catherine's and Sister Mary and Carter and the gang, but it seemed more and more that my New York life was a light post on the highway that I could only see in the rearview mirror. A life left behind.

I missed Noah.

Last night, he'd knocked on my door at ten o'clock, stood there awkwardly as Pepper pounced on his shoes.

"Listen," he said the second I opened the door. "I'm really sorry for what I said. I know how much this means to you, and I'm pulling for you. Okay?"

"Thank you," I whispered.

He nodded. "Knock 'em dead tomorrow."

"Did Mickey send you?"

He laughed at that, but his eyes were sad. "No," he said. "All my idea."

"Thank you, Noah," I said. "It means a lot."

He nodded once, then left before either of us made things more complicated.

So here I was, lunch planned with Hasan afterward.

He made another turn, another stroll, little humming noises coming from his throat. I kept my mouth shut to maintain an air of mystery and also not babble like an idiot, which was, of course, my way.

I glanced out the window, and there I was, looking in. Not me, not really, but some kid—God, so young, probably not even twenty. He wore black jeans and a black T-shirt and had dyed, messy black hair, a bull nose ring and pierced eyebrow. Yep. Me, fifteen years ago. I smiled a little. He gave me a nod, then kept going.

I remembered that feeling. That outside-looking-in feeling. The someday-that-will-be-me feeling. I had it right now, even though I was literally on the inside.

The paintings . . . well, they were frickin' beautiful, no doubt. How could they not be? They were flowers. The colors were rich and deep, the technique well executed. All week long, I'd painted with every damn emotion in the world—fear about my father, anger and love for Noah, ambition, hope, peace, contentment, joy, terror, uncertainty.

But looking at them here, where they might well sell for tens of thousands of bucks apiece, I had to admit it. Noah was right.

They were couch paintings, and they weren't me. They were the me of college, trying to be something I was not. I'd been telling myself I stumbled onto something with the vagina flower painting, but I hadn't. I'd done an O'Keeffe and added a few squiggles, and it was a cheap trick. These seven at least, had been done with some passion and energy. But they still weren't me.

That stupid sunset was. The one I'd practically flung off the easel to make these porn flowers.

"It's . . . interesting," Hasan finally said, looking at me. "When I saw the painting at the party, I was struck by its intensity and authenticity. These . . . I just don't think they have the same impact, and I'm trying to figure out why."

Well, shit. "Hm."

"There's something missing in these, whereas the lilies and sweet pea painting had such a stark disparity, such a contrast between the lush sensuality and the void of emotional despair. It was a battle between chastity and vulgarity." He shook his head. "I'm just not feeling that same emotional upheaval here."

Oh, the fuckery. "Interesting." It seemed like a safe word. Chastity and vulgarity? The void of emotional despair? Words that had never once entered my brain as I made the brownstone painting. These seven? The entire tornado of human emotions.

"Tell me about the lily painting, Sadie," Hasan said. "What was in your heart when you painted it? How can we capture that mood again? Because that painting was special, and I think, if you can tap into that darkness, that fury and sexuality once again, we would be onto something here. Perhaps you know I consider myself not just a collector, but a mentor as well. Someone who nurtures the expression of passion and emotion."

Jesus. Had this kind of talk always sounded so ridiculous?

"What was in your heart, Sadie Frost?" he asked again, putting his hand against his chin.

I nodded. "My heart. Yes. Well, Hasan, to be honest, money was in my heart, because I was getting six grand for that painting. Also, copying was in my heart, because anyone could see it was a Georgia O'Keeffe knockoff. I just played with some texture in the oils to make it a little different. Aside from that, I didn't have much in my heart at all."

"Oh. That's . . . that's disappointing."

"Hasan. I'm a hack. I painted those lilies to match the owners' comforter. These . . ." I gestured to the paintings in front of us. "These are me trying to please you. Maybe I should've used some fabric swatches as inspiration."

He frowned. "You clearly have talent. Did you bring anything else?"

I hesitated. Why not? My dad would want me to. *I* wanted me to. At least I could show this guy something that was authentically mine. "Yes, as a matter of fact, I did."

In the last pocket in my portfolio was the sunset picture, the one I'd painted the day of the storm. To me, it was the best thing I'd painted. Ever.

Except for Noah's clouds.

I pulled it out and watched him take it in. And I took it in as well. I could almost feel the calm of that day, hear the birds, the distant shush of the ocean, feel the damp salt air of springtime.

"Eh," he said. "Any art student could do that. That's not the kind of thing my clients are looking for."

"I didn't think so. Thank you for the opportunity." I started gathering up my sexy-beast flowers.

"I'm sorry, Sadie," he said. "I've wasted your day."

"It's okay. Really. These aren't me, these flowers. That sunset is, and I understand SoHo is not the place for sunset pictures."

"Would you still like to have lunch? Perhaps I could give you some guidance about where the market is these days."

"I think I'll get back to Connecticut. But thank you." I shook his hand, and left.

It was official. I was never going to be that artist.

But I'd had the chance. The big break. I'd been considered by a major gallery owner who had loved something I did. That was more than most artists got, regardless of their talent and training and outlook.

So I'd done it. I'd made it through the doors, and that—much to my surprise—was enough. There was a spring in my step as I lugged the paintings down the street. I wasn't going to make it, but I hadn't sold my soul, either.

I'd give the flower paintings as presents, maybe even keep one or two. Maybe send one to the lesbians, since they were so nice to play a part in getting me today's chance.

But right now, I wanted to go home. I wanted to go home and play with my dog and sit on my battered front porch and watch another sunset.

CHAPTER THIRTY-EIGHT

John

He knows what is happening. Barb is going to take care of him forever now.

He is sliding away, not toward, and he still has not said the right words. The flower word that will save his wife. The other words he wants to say. He needs his girls to be here, and Barb, and when that happens, he has to be ready. He has to be *here*.

But the world is grainy and blank, and the feelings come without words. He keeps trying, but he is slipping down the mountain he was trying so hard to climb. The snow is too heavy, and he is so tired. Days pass, and he is unaware. Sometimes everyone is here, sometimes he seems alone, sometimes he is asleep and sometimes in the snow. He has to say the words. He has to tell his Barb about the long-ago.

And then one day, he wakes up on the patio, in the chair that lets his legs stick out straight. It is warm and his daughters and wife and his friend with the warm rain voice are all here.

This is his chance, he knows. It will not come again. He knows that, too.

He grabs the arm of the person closest to him. Juliet, his oldest, his perfect girl, and she jumps. "You!" he says. He forces his mouth and his brain to work together. "Poor," comes out, the word tortured and heavy.

The women look at each other, confused.

"Pour?" Sadie asks "You want a drink?"

"No!" He looks at Juliet again. "Prow. Prow."

There is a silence, and the word slips away, Juliet's word, and John's eyes are wet because she didn't understand, and now the word is gone.

"Proud," Barb says. "He's proud of you."

She *knows*. She knows! John nods and takes Juliet's hand and kisses it.

"Oh, Dad," she says, and her eyes are raining, which is not the right word, but he has made her happy and sad. It was her word, and he gave it to her, at last.

Sadie kneels in front of him and says words, but they're blurring and tumbling in his head.

"Joy," he says, touching her face.

"Joy," she repeats, nodding. "Yes. Joy."

His heart is so full, and his eyes are raining, too.

Just a little more now. The snow has held off, but the clouds are heavy with it. "Bar," he says, and his wife comes closer. Sits on the chair next to him. She waits for her word, too.

Bathroom. The closed door. Crying. Sorry. I should have gone in and I didn't.

But the words are too many and too hard.

"Rose," he says. "Rose." The flower word! He said it at last.

"That's real nice, John," she says, patting his hand, but she doesn't know that this is the word that will set her free.

"No! Rose . . . Heel."

Everyone freezes. The snow is coming, and is this why no one is moving? Just a little longer, that's all he needs.

"Rose Hill?" says his friend, and he nods again, his head wobbling on his neck. He is an old man now. He closes his eyes just for a second.

"What do you mean, Dad?" Juliet asks. "You want to live at Rose Hill?"

He nods again.

"And not live here anymore." She is clarifying, his older girl, and he knows that is her way.

He nods. Oh, he is tired now, but he forces his eyes to open.

Sadie's face is crumpled and sad. Juliet is crying, yes, that is the word. Janet is smiling her nice smile, her rope-hair so tidy and twisty.

But there is one more word Barb needs to hear. One more word for John to tell her before the snow comes, because he knows the snow won't stop this time.

"Barb," he says, looking at her. He takes her hand, bringing it against his face. "Barb."

Sorry. Forgive. Love.

"Divorce," he says, and it is the right word.

They talk then, and he can hear their voices but not understand their words.

It doesn't matter. He knows he made it. He said the words they needed, and they understand.

The snow comes, but it is warm and light, and he falls into it, knowing he has once again been a father . . . knowing that, for the first time in a long time, and for the last time ever, he was a good husband.

CHAPTER THIRTY-NINE

Barb

John was going to Rose Hill. There was room for him, and the facility took every kind of insurance and made up the rest of the cost, thanks to its endowment.

He wanted a *divorce*. Now, after all these years, when he needed me more than ever, he was divorcing me. I wasn't sure I could go through with it, but . . . well, my eyes teared up every time I thought of it.

That thing men say when they're cheating . . . that their wives don't understand them. The real problem is, we do. And I did. John had said *divorce* to give me the last thing I wanted from him. When he'd taken my hand and said the words, something happened. He knew we'd failed at marriage, and he was letting me go.

Closure. They say you can never really have it, but here it was.

I wasn't sure if I was going to file the papers, but my attorney had said we should discuss it. Financial reasons, that kind of thing.

Even if we did get divorced, I'd still look after him, of course. I wasn't the kind of person who'd turn her back on a sick man after fifty years, no matter what he'd done.

We visited Rose Hill, and John hadn't wanted to leave. It was a beautiful facility, and when I saw LeVon, I started to cry.

"I'm so glad he's coming here," LeVon said, hugging me. "I'll get to see you all the time." Gosh, what a comfort that was!

Janet was there, too, since she visited her brother four or five times a week. John's face lit up when he saw her, and I had to shake my head. Leave it to that old dog to find another woman, even in his current state.

But I was grateful. I didn't have someone else, of course, and I didn't even know if I would ever want that. But for the first time in decades, I felt like my husband had really seen me and understood me.

LeVon had suggested easing John into life at Rose Hill, so one night, just before Memorial Day weekend and the big town anniversary, I drove John up there and got him settled, then left. It was harder than I expected, coming back to my quiet, lovely house.

I went out on the patio and thought maybe I'd call the girls, but then decided against it. Juliet had her own family, and I'd just seen her two nights ago at her place. Besides, this is what the future would look like. Quiet and peaceful, maybe a little bit lonely. But beautiful, too, out here on the patio, a glass of wine in my hand.

"You home?" came Caro's voice.

"On the patio," I called.

"I brought wine."

"I already have some, but grab yourself a glass, hon."

She came out a minute later and sat next to me. "How are you? Did it go all right at Rose Hill?"

"Oh, sure. He seems to like it there a lot."

"But how are you, Barb?"

I smiled, feeling tears prick my eyes just a little bit. "Doing good. How about you? I feel like we haven't talked about you in ages."

She sighed and settled back. "Ted and I are done for good now."

"Is that right? What happened?"

She shrugged. "Is it callous of me to say I don't know and don't care enough to analyze it? We didn't have anything to say to each other these past few years, and I thought, why am I bothering? It's not like we're married."

"Is he sad?"

"No. He's dating a forty-eight-year-old."

"Oh, that's just gross, now."

"Tell me about it." She sighed. "I might get a condo, Barb. The house seems so big these days."

"Move in with me."

She smiled. "That'd be so much fun, wouldn't it?"

I sat up straighter. "Caro. Move in with me."

She shifted to face me. "Don't you want to be alone?" she asked. "After all this time? Date somebody, maybe? Join Tinder? Get laid?"

I laughed. "Does that sound like me?" I thought a minute. "I've been thinking a lot about marriage these days, Caro. What it means, what love is, commitment, all that."

"Sure you have. It's been a rough few months."

"The thing is . . . well, I'm not a lesbian, you know? I don't think so, anyway. No, I'm not. You're beautiful, of course, don't take it personally."

She threw back her head and laughed.

My throat grew tight. I always loved her laugh, her smile, those dimples and the way her eyes crinkled, making her look forty years younger. "Caro, I think you're the love of my life. No one's been there for me like you have. You're the best friend I ever had, the person I can really talk to. You can make me laugh at everything, even my husband cheating on me." I reached over and took her hand. "I can't think of anything nicer than us sharing a house."

"I *have* always loved your house more than mine," she said. "You know what? I'll think about it. We could do it on a trial basis, maybe. Let me run it past my boys and see what they think."

"That sounds great."

We kept holding hands, listening to the birds as they sang their evening songs, sipping our wine.

"The love of your life, huh?" she said.

"Well, it's sure not John."

She laughed. "Then I guess you're the love of mine, too."

"Girl power, as the kids say," I said.

"Friends till the end."

"I do love you."

She squeezed my hand. "I love you, too." She clinked her glass against mine. "Here's to housemates. Who cares what the boys think? I'm bringing my purple chair, though."

"You better. I love that chair."

We chatted until it grew dark and the mosquitoes found us, and then moved inside.

Life partner. Longtime companion. Cherished friend.

Such beautiful words.

Love didn't have to be romantic to encircle you in its arms. It didn't have to make your heart race or your toes curl. Love could be just this, the sound of laughter on a warm night, the absolute comfort of being exactly who you were with the person who knew you inside and out.

CHAPTER FORTY

Juliet

She'd thought she would hate being the one in charge of the details, the legalities, the administration. She was wrong. It was completely different when it was a thing of your own.

Frost/Alexander opened three weeks after Juliet quit, the week before Memorial Day. Arwen and Juliet might never be friends, but they were a good team—Arwen giving the firm some buzz, Juliet backing that up with her reputation. They hired three other architects on a trial basis and already had six clients. Smaller projects than airport wings and Dubai skyscrapers, but they were just getting started.

The offices were in Mystic, so Juliet could be closer to home. DJK Architects had been housed in a sleek and stark building; Frost/Alexander occupied a four-story Victorian with stained glass and beautiful bookcases. She hired Noah to put in new windows and fix the front porch, but they were already working there. Arwen was moving from her loft in New Haven, and Juliet had recommended a real estate agent. Kathy was spending two weeks in Napa before starting.

"Kathy is a little miffed that you're senior partner," Arwen had told her over dinner. "But so be it. We needed your experience. And I have to be honest. You have balls, telling me your name goes first." She raised an eyebrow. "I respect that."

"Good," Juliet said. "I respect you, too, Arwen, striking out on your own so young. You're a very impressive person."

"Let's order a bottle of champagne," Arwen said. "To celebrate ourselves and each other."

"Maybe we should wait for when Kathy can join us."

"We can order it then, too," Arwen said. She waved the waiter over. "Bring us a bottle of your best champagne," she said.

"Mind the budget," Juliet murmured.

"Bring us a bottle of your cheapest champagne," Arwen amended, and they laughed. And cheap champagne . . . hey. It's not awful.

A few days later, Kathy showed up at Juliet's house around dinnertime. "I need to talk to you," she said tightly.

"Sure. Come on in and say hi to Oliver and the girls." She led Kathy up to the kitchen.

"Hi, Kathy," Sloane said, the friendlier child. So much like Sadie.

"Hi, Kathy," Brianna echoed, barely looking up from her math homework. *Just like I used to be*, she thought, smiling.

"Kathy!" Oliver said. "How lovely to see you! Shall I fix you a drink, then?"

Dear Oliver. So oblivious sometimes. Kathy's face was already blotchy with anger, and she ignored him. Instead, she jammed her hands on her hips and glared at Juliet. *Here we go*, Juliet thought. *Women tearing other women down.* She tilted her head, waiting.

"How *dare* you move in on my company?" Kathy said, ignoring the fact that the girls were at the table and now gawping at her. "This was mine! *I* was supposed to be Arwen's partner! What did you tell her? How did you weasel your way in?"

"She asked me," Juliet said, her voice calm.

"To *work* for us. Not to be one of us! Senior partner? That's ridiculous! I didn't agree to that!"

Juliet raised her eyebrow (she could again, thank God, since the Botox had worn off). "That will be a problem, then, since Arwen and I can outvote you."

"You *bitch*. You've always had to be the star," Kathy said. "You think your shit doesn't stink, and you—"

"Shut up!" Brianna barked. "How dare you talk to my mother like that! She's one of the best architects in the country, for one, and for two, this is our house. You should leave now."

"Yeah," Sloane added. "Get out. You're mean. And quite rude."

Oh, that *feeling*. That feeling! Pride and warmth and love and surprise. Her girls, defending her from a bully. "Thank you, my darlings."

"My daughters have a completely valid point, Kathy," Oliver said. "I'll walk you out."

"I'll do it, honey," she said, but Kathy was already striding out on her own, hissing like an old radiator. Juliet caught up to her on the driveway as Kathy yanked open the door of her little MINI Cooper.

"Kathy, wait. Why are you upset? We've worked so well together all these years."

Kathy stopped and turned, jamming her fists on her hips. "Jesus, Juliet. I wanted to get away from *you*. You think you've struggled with Arwen being the golden girl for the past two years? Oh, you're too superior to admit it, but I knew. Well, try that fifteen years."

Juliet blinked. "We do entirely different things, Kathy."

"Really? I had no idea. Please, lecture me."

"I honestly don't understand the problem."

"Well, it's not my job to educate you. Just think about this. I've worked with Arwen since she got here. I coached her and whispered in her ear about how good she was and got her half of those interviews so that she'd do exactly what she did. Leave and take me with her. But instead, you just step in at the last second and somehow get your name on the door. It was supposed to be Alexander Walker."

"Not according to Arwen." She looked at Kathy, who suddenly seemed a little pathetic with her cherry-red hair and painful high heels. "I think you underestimated her. Maybe she worked you a little bit, too."

"You both went behind my back."

"No, Kathy. If you can't hold your own, don't blame someone else. I gave Arwen my terms, and she accepted them. Clearly, she was in the position to make those decisions. Now. If your tantrum is over, I'd like you to stay with us. If it's not, we'll have to part ways." And get a new partner, probably. Brett, maybe. Or Elena.

"I've already talked to Dave about coming back."

"Then I wish you the best." All those lunches together, all those conversations, watching each other's kids grow up . . . it had meant something to Juliet. Quite a lot. But not to Kathy, apparently, because she just snorted and got into her car. Juliet watched as she sped down the street.

"I never really liked her," Oliver said as she came back into the kitchen. He sensed her lingering sadness and put his arm around her.

"I never liked her, neither," said Sloane.

"Me neither," echoed Brianna. "She was always jealous of you, Mom."

Out of the mouths of tweens came wisdom . . . sometimes, at least. Juliet smiled at her oldest, and, a little miraculously, Brianna smiled back.

"I think we should go out for ice cream tonight," Juliet said, earning a cheer from both her girls.

Life was good. She and Oliver were better than ever, and that was saying something. The girls were wonderful, even if Brianna was still sulky and hormonal, and Sloane would probably go through that, too. Mom was going to have an easier life when Dad went to Rose Hill, and Dad . . . well, she hadn't forgiven her father. Maybe she never would. Maybe some things shouldn't be forgiven.

But being angry was too great a burden to carry, and Juliet felt it slip away, there in the warm sunshine of the May evening. She owned her own business. She and Arwen would find a new partner. She loved her husband and daughters, mother and sister. There would be grief and loss and conflict ahead, and she'd get through it all.

She was her mother's girl, after all.

CHAPTER FORTY-ONE

Sadie

Joy. That was the word my father had given me, pulled with such effort from the depths of his heart and mind. I knew it was his way of telling me I'd brought him joy, and yet, I'd been thinking it might have been more, too.

Maybe . . . maybe it was advice.

Ever since I left Stoningham at eighteen, I'd been looking for that moment when everything in my life came together the way I dreamed it would. It never had, though, had it? I liked teaching quite a bit, loved my little students, St. Catherine's, loved New York with all its treasures, felt a bit of pride that my couch paintings paid the bills. I'd created a good-enough life in New York. A solid life, a happy life.

But joy was a different animal, wasn't it?

Joy was a quiet night watching the sunset, stroking Pepper's silky ears, laughing at her antics. Joy was painting those damn skies. Talking with my nieces. Taking care of my dad. Sending my mom and sister to Boston. Joy was that moment when the dolphin and her mama had swum around my legs before speeding out to sea. Joy was walking through the streets of New York looking up, always up, at the beautiful architecture, the sky, breathing in the smell of the city, listening to the constant song of traffic and languages and feeling that surge of life, all that life, swirling around me.

Joy was being with Noah, from the first time I'd seen him with that beautiful baby strapped to his chest, to irritating him as he fixed my furnace, to walking through a shower of cherry blossoms with him, to finally kissing him again.

But as much as I loved Noah Pelletier, the fact remained that I didn't want the life he did. I didn't really know what life I *did* want, even now. A little of everything, whereas Noah wanted a lot of one thing. He wanted home, a partner who was always there, more kids, and who could blame him? Those were nice, good things to want.

I was pretty sure I didn't want those things. Oh, I loved my nieces, loved little Marcus even, loved hearing Mickey talk about the horrors and wonders of motherhood. But in my heart of hearts, I wasn't sure it was for me. My mother had once called me a butterfly, flitting to whatever bright thing caught my attention, and she wasn't wrong.

I just wasn't sure how to make a life around being a butterfly. I mean, those things didn't live real long, did they?

A few days after my meeting in New York, I went to the hardware store for some more plastic to patch up another hole in my roof. I turned down the aisle and there was Noah, studying a drill bit. He did a quick double take when he saw me.

"Hey," he said.

"Hi." My insides flooded with heat, my heart pulsing with that beautiful scarlet red only he could incite.

"How was New York?"

"Oh . . . it was . . . it didn't work out. My stuff wasn't what he was looking for."

"Then he's an idiot."

I snorted a little. "An idiot with a lot of influence."

He just looked at me a minute. "I'm sorry, Sadie."

"No, it's fine. It's nothing I haven't heard a hundred times before. Two hundred. Five, maybe. Anyway. How are you?"

"Good."

That seemed to be all. "Well," I said. "Nice to see you. Love you." *Shit.* "I do. I mean, you know that. Anyway. Have a good day."

I left before I made things worse, and went to see my dad.

He hadn't spoken again since that day. It was awfully hard, finally admitting he was the man in front of me, in a place I couldn't reach or see. Maybe he'd have another breakthrough, but I had a feeling he was done.

Rose Hill had space for him in their new wing. It was only a half hour away. Still, the tears slid down my face. I'd visit a lot.

"I'm thinking about staying in Stoningham, Dad," I said. His expression didn't change. "Maybe I can get a teaching job up here. Keep doing my couch paintings, pop down to the city once in a while, keep the apartment on Airbnb. I don't know. Maybe not Stoningham, since it would be hard to see Noah, you know? Maybe Mystic or Old Lyme."

I sighed. Even talking to myself, I couldn't make up my mind.

Hasan had told me what I'd always known. Those skyscapes weren't all that special. Not to the New York art world. Any first-year art student could do them. They weren't even that hard, technically speaking.

"I'm not that good as an artist, Dad," I told him, and tears filled my eyes. He didn't answer, but I wedged myself in the chair against him and put my head on his shoulder. His arm came around me, just like old times, but for once—for the first time since his stroke—I didn't look for more. Sometimes an arm around you is all you need.

"Thanks, Daddy," I whispered, and there it was again. Joy, soft and quiet this time. My father loved me. It was May. I had a good dog and options in front of me. Joy would be the key to my life. Be in the places that made my heart sing, do the things that made me feel whole and fulfilled, spend time with the people who did the same. No more phoning it in, no more *good enough for now.* I would find a way to make a life based on joy, because really. What if you fell off your bicycle one day and injured your brain?

"Thanks for the pep talk, Dad," I said, and maybe it was my imagination, but I thought he held me a little closer.

On Memorial Day weekend, Stoningham celebrated its 350th birthday. I had to hand it to Gillian, my mother and the scores of volunteers. It was beautiful.

We started the day with a parade. I brought Pepper, since she loved people, and she wagged joyfully at every person she saw. At the last minute, I'd found myself one of the volunteers—the person in charge of the nursery school float had had a meltdown over the responsibility of it all, and my mom recommended me to step in. It was right up my alley, after all. Kids. Art. Last-minute accomplishments.

There's something so tender about a small-town parade. The handful of Stoningham veterans, some of them so old, so noble, riding in a convertible, waving with a gnarled hand as the townspeople cheered and teared up. The National Guard volunteers, somber in their uniforms. My mom, looking beautiful in a blue pantsuit with a red scarf, and the other two selectmen. The town clergy—Rabbi Fierstein, whose daughter had been my bus buddy in grammar school; Reverend Bateman, who used to read *The Giving Tree* on Easter Sunday; the handsome Catholic priest.

Then came the kids. The 4-H club, the sailing club, the school music bands (including Brianna on trumpet). The Brownies, Sloane looking so stinking cute in her uniform, saying, "Hi, Auntie!" like she hadn't just seen me that morning.

Then came my float, bright as a garden, decorated in hundreds and hundreds of crepe paper flowers (not the vaginal kind), all the little kids wearing (or taking off) the beaks and wings I'd made out of papier-mâché. Damn cute. *Fly, Little Birds, Fly!* I'd written across the banner, making the letters out of their handprints. As I said, it was my groove.

I saw Noah, Mickey and Marcus across the street. Mickey waved, nudged Noah, and he waved, too.

We hadn't spoken since the hardware store run-in. I understood. His son needed stability. Noah needed stability, and I wasn't exactly that. Love was not all you needed. You needed to match, to fit, to want the same things. I had never wanted five kids. I wasn't sure I wanted any. I'd never really known what I wanted, except to be a painter.

But my heart hurt just the same, looking at him. I loved him, and I didn't make him happy, and that was an awful ache I didn't know how to fix. I petted Pepper to remind myself I wasn't alone in the world.

After the parade, the shops and businesses of Water Street hosted a sidewalk stroll, serving snacks and drinks, putting bowls of water out for doggies. Sheerwater, that splendid house the town now owned, was open all day, the garden club giving tours and hosting a high tea. There was a small regatta (we were Connecticut, after all). In the evening, there'd be the auction to raise money for scholarships.

I hung out with my nieces, letting Oliver and Jules go to the high tea so my brother-in-law could get his Brit fix. When the girls got hot and tired, we went to my parents' house for a little rest, and I parked them in my old room and put cool cloths on their heads, like my mom used to do for me when I was little.

"Rest, little ones," I said, and they both smiled, even though they were pretty big. Dad was asleep downstairs, back from his overnight at Rose Hill, Pepper curled up next to him, good pup that she was.

My father had never been a great husband. It didn't take a rocket scientist to know that. These past few weeks, I'd seen some looks exchanged between Mom and Jules, and overheard a few whispers.

It was dawning on me that my father may have had an affair. Honestly, I didn't want to know. It was a moot point now. He was still our dad. He'd released my mom from her duties, something she would never have done for herself.

I looked at him now, the old man who needed his eyebrows trimmed. "You're a good guy, Daddy," I said. Maybe not the perfect man I'd once thought, but good enough. I could still love him, and he deserved that love.

Then I got the scissors and took care of those eyebrows.

That evening, Brianna, Sloane and I walked to the green for the auction, which was the crowning event of the weekend. Gillian was there, zipping around like a gerbil on speed, flitting to my mom every thirty seconds. I chatted with some of the women I'd met at Juliet's party—Emma London, Beth, Jamilah Finlay with the cute little boys. There were Jules and Oliver, holding hands. They had such a good thing going, those two. I was glad for my sister. Ollie got on my nerves from time to time, but honestly, if his greatest flaw was smiling too much, then he was pretty damn great. The girls cantered over to them.

"Hang out with us," Jules said.

"Nah. I'm feeling melancholy and want to brood," I said.

"You're so weird," Brianna said.

"Takes one to know one," I said, and she grinned. "See you guys later."

I found a spot under a tree where I could watch the auction. Some of the big-ticket items were grotesque, thanks to Stoningham's summer people trying to outdo each other. It was a good cause—college scholarships for low-income families—so God bless, but even so. *A week at our ten-bedroom house in Jackson Hole, butler included! Starting bid $2,500. Dinner with Lin-Manuel Miranda after a* Hamilton *show! Starting bid $5,000.* (I would totally bid on that one, had I any money to spare, but I really wanted a new roof.) *Design for an addition on your house, courtesy of Frost/Alexander Architecture, starting bid $7,500.*

I hadn't been asked to donate anything. The truth was, it would be embarrassing to offer up a painting that my sister would pity-buy.

"Hey, Sadie! Do you teach painting?" came a voice. It was Emma London.

"I do," I said. "You interested?"

"Oh, God, no. I mean, I've been kicked out of those paint and drink nights, you know? Stick figures is the best I can do." She smiled.

"I was thinking of lessons for a little friend of mine. She's four and a little wild."

"Sure. I could do that. I used to teach elementary school art."

"Cool! Thanks, Sadie. Hey, there's my guy. The father of your potential student, Miller Finlay. Do you know him?"

Of course I did. Miller owned Finlay Construction, and Noah had done an internship with him in high school. We did the two degrees of separation Stoningham thrived on, and then they wandered off. Nice couple.

Bidding was pretty hot and heavy. Dinner with Lin-Manuel went for sixteen grand. Jeez.

Then I saw Noah. He was carrying a painting.

My painting.

The clouds I'd given him for Valentine's Day so long ago.

He set it on an easel and stepped back, and my chest felt sliced open.

The auctioneer looked at his notes. "Next up, folks, something that's not listed in your program. A Sadie Frost original oil painting. Very pretty. Sadie's the daughter of our first selectman, I believe. She works as a . . . a teacher, is that right? An art teacher! Great. Let's start the bidding at . . . a hundred dollars? A hundred dollars, can I have a hundred dollars, thank you, sir. A hundred and fifty, fifty, can I see a hundred and fifty, thank you, ma'am, two hundred, two hundred."

Noah was selling my painting. No. He was giving it away. He was tossing it. He was . . . shit, he was ditching it, because what was that phrase? It didn't spark joy.

He'd kept it all these years. He'd broken up with his fiancée over it, and now he was essentially throwing it in the junk pile, for a couple of hundred dollars, no less.

I got up to leave, tears blurring my vision. Jesus. Why not just burn down my house or stab me in the throat? At least that would've been a little less public.

"Three hundred, three hundred, thank you, can I have four? Four, please?"

"Where are you going?" Mom asked, suddenly at my side.

"I'm . . . gonna see Dad."

"That's your painting, honey!"

"I know."

"You have to stay. Don't be silly, flouncing off." She took my hand, anchoring me to the spot.

"Four fifty, four hundred and fifty, thank you, ma'am."

Noah was still standing at the front, just off to the side of my painting, staring right at me.

Something was happening. I wasn't a hundred percent sure what, but that red flare was burning in my heart, and his dark eyes didn't leave me.

"One thousand, please, one thousand," the auctioneer said. "Thank you, sir, very nice, can I have fifteen hundred?"

"I wish I could bid on it, sweetheart. It's so pretty," Mom said.

"That's okay, Mom," I said. But it was a nice thought. Maybe the first time she'd sincerely praised my work without telling me how impractical it was.

"Two thousand, two thousand to the gentleman in the blue shirt. Do I hear three, three thousand, three, thank you, going to four now . . ."

People—strangers, even—were bidding on my painting. Bidding quite a lot. I didn't know whether to laugh or cry. That was Noah's painting. Noah's.

"This is so cool!" Juliet had come over to Mom and me. "Can you believe it, Sadie?"

"Ten thousand dollars, thank you, sir, can I have eleven, eleven thousand for a Sadie Frost original oil, thank you, ma'am, do I hear twelve?"

Holy crap. That was double my most expensive couch painting.

Something was happening, all right.

Noah left the stage and came walking through the crowd, his eyes never leaving my face.

"Fifteen thousand, fifteen, thank you, sir, can I get seventeen, seventeen thousand . . ."

He was here, right in front of me. "You're giving away my painting," I whispered.

He nodded. "I wanted you to see how beautiful it is. That guy in New York doesn't know anything."

"But it's yours." My lips trembled a little.

"So you'll make me another." He slipped behind me and whispered in my ear. "Look at this, Sadie. Look at that painting and how many people want it. It's beautiful. It makes people happy. *You* do that, Special."

"It's for a good cause," I murmured, hypnotized by the auction.

"Eh," Juliet said. "Dinner with Lin-Manuel went for less than that."

"Gosh, this is exciting," Mom said. "Oh, the Stanleys just bid twenty grand, Sadie! Honey! I'm so proud of you!"

I started to cry.

"Maybe we should subtly drift away, Mom," Juliet said.

"Why? Do you . . . Oh, okay. Not too far, though. You okay, hon?" she asked me.

I nodded, wiping my eyes.

"Going once for twenty-two thousand . . . going twice . . . last chance to bid on this magnificent Sadie Frost original . . . sold to the man in the blue shirt!"

The crowd burst into applause.

Noah turned me around and kept his hands on my shoulders. His big, warm, manly hands. "Sadie, I've looked at that painting every day since you gave it to me. It's part of me."

"Then why'd you put it up for sale?"

"Because I wanted to show what you do. How beautiful your paintings are. I'm not the only one who sees it."

"But you won't have it anymore." A little sob popped out, and I covered my mouth.

"That's okay. That was the old us. That painting has tortured me for years now, reminding me that I've only ever loved you."

"Well, you're quite a masochist then, hanging it in your house. You could've just burned it."

"Absolutely not. Being mad at you was better than not having you at all. It was a way to see you every day. But, Special, I can't do that anymore. I can't keep you, and I can't let go of you again. I love you. I love that you're a painter. What you do is important and beautiful and . . . and magic. You just saw that. If you need to be in New York, I understand. We can make it work. I want to make it work. I've been in love with you since I was fifteen. I'm not gonna wreck that again."

I seemed to be crying. Nope. Definitely crying. My mother and sister watched, smiling.

"I don't want five children," I said. "I don't know if I want any."

"I already have the world's greatest kid, and he has the world's greatest mother."

"I live in a crooked house that hasn't passed inspection."

"I can fix that. Or you can marry me and live in my house."

"I have a place in New York." I dashed a hand across my eyes.

"You can spend as much time there as you want. I'll even come visit when you want."

"Did you . . . did you just propose?"

"Yes. For the third time, I might add."

He was smiling.

"Are you sure, Noah?" I whispered.

He dropped down on one knee, and the folks around us cooed. A few people whipped out their phones. "Home is where you are, Sadie. I shouldn't have tried to make everything fit how I wanted it. Marry me. Be my son's stepmother. Be my wife. Go to New York if you need to, but come home to me, Sadie Frost. I love you with everything I have."

I looked down into his dark, dark eyes. They were full of love and happiness and . . . certainty.

"Third time's the charm, then," I said. "Yes, Noah Pelletier, I will marry you."

I kissed him then, threading my fingers through his curly hair, feeling so much love, so much joy. My father's word to me was the key to everything.

Home had never been a place. Noah, my wild boy, *was* my home, my heart, my joy. Part of me had always known it, and now I would stake my claim and build from here.

EPILOGUE

Barb

Two years after he moved into Rose Hill, John died. In bed. With Janet.

They hadn't had a sexual relationship, she told me. They just liked sleeping together. I believed her. It was nice to think that he died next to a woman he loved, who loved him as he was, and had never known him any other way.

So I was a widow now. I never had divorced him. Just couldn't bring myself to sign the final papers. I had Caro, who'd moved in almost as soon as I asked her to. I hadn't known life could be so happy and fun, so free. I didn't need a divorce, wasn't interested in dating. I'd won another term as first selectman, and so I had at least two years more of working, and that was wonderful.

Juliet and Oliver were better than ever, and Brianna and Sloane were the lights of my life. I still saw them a few times a week, but . . . well, things had changed a little bit. Juliet was still my darling girl, but she had come into her own. She was more relaxed now, and I had to admit, she didn't need me as much as she used to. That was just fine.

That was wonderful, in fact. The girls were putting them through their paces, and she was handling it like a real champ. Her firm was going gangbusters, and gosh, I was proud.

Noah and Sadie had gotten married about a month after the art auction. Just a little backyard affair here, at my house, with Caro officiating, since she was a justice of the peace. Brianna and Sloane were her bridesmaids, and Noah's parents came down from Ottawa. Nice people. Even Sadie's little dog got to come, and ate some cake before it was time, but we just cut it from the other side.

Now, too, I had little Marcus, who called me Nana and often came running into the town hall to give me a hug when Noah was there, filing paperwork with the building department. Mickey was a hoot and a holler, and she was a regular at our family gatherings. She loved to tease Caro and me about being lesbian wannabes, and we'd laugh so much at her comments.

Sadie had made good on her promise to flip that little house of hers. Granted, her sister was an architect and her husband was a carpenter, but she did most of the work herself, and it was quite the little charmer when it was finished. Her friend Carter and his husband bought it and called it their country house and often had lovely parties there. Caro and I were always invited.

Sadie had started an art gallery here in Stoningham. The Frost Gallery. It had her own pieces and some sculptures and photos by other artists, too. The summer folks gobbled it up. Another way our name was growing. Frost/Alexander, now the Frost Gallery. Sadie lived with Noah most of the time, though she'd flit off to the city for a few days here, a week there. She was a little bird, my daughter, always flying somewhere, but always coming back. Sometimes Noah would go to New York with her, and Caro and I would petition to take Marcus for a night or two, letting him stay in the bathtub till his fingers were pruney, then cuddling him and reading to him, kissing his dark curls.

The garden club had proposed an area at Sheerwater to be named after me. The garden would have all the types of flowers that bloomed when the weather was still cold—the Frost Garden. It was quite an honor, and I was so proud of my girls, and myself, and our name—we Frost women were an impressive lot.

When John died, I was sadder than I expected to be. I knew it was coming; those little strokes had chipped away at him, but now that he was really gone, I kept remembering snippets of our marriage that I'd forgotten.

There was one morning during the infertility years after I'd had an awful night. Cried in the little bathroom in the Cranston house and ran the tap so John wouldn't hear me, since there was nothing he could do. I'd been embarrassed about being so sad over something I couldn't control. Sad again, sad every month, and I knew it had to wear at him, the feeling of helplessness, so I kept it to myself as best I could.

But the next morning, he'd made me French toast with powdered sugar, my favorite. We'd had it on our honeymoon—the first time in my life I'd had French toast, and I was so delighted with the powdered sugar and the sliced-up strawberries, John had laughed at my happiness.

And then there it was, on a regular morning when we both had to go to work. French toast and warm maple syrup, powdered sugar and sliced strawberries.

I hadn't thought of that since it happened, but now, those kinds of memories were slipping in.

Love isn't always the thing that fills up the room, or your heart. Sometimes, it's what sneaks into the in-between spaces. I never thought the love of my life would be my best friend. I never expected to get to the point where I found Sadie's butterfly life to be so enjoyable to watch. I never knew I'd get to have a grandson who wasn't technically mine, or that my family would grow to include the lesbian baby mama of my son-in-law, or the woman who was in bed with my husband when he died.

But here we all are.

I wouldn't have it any other way.

Always the Last to Know

Kristan Higgins

Questions for Discussion

1. Relationships take a lot of compromise, and we can see Noah demonstrating this when he tries to live in New York for Sadie. Sadie also compromises, telling him to go back home when it's clear he's unhappy in the city she loves. For the sake of their relationship, do you think Sadie should have compromised the lifestyle she always wanted, or do you agree that they were too young at that point to make such large sacrifices?

2. What is the right time to adjust your dreams for someone else? The author makes no secret that Sadie and Noah love each other, but neither feels at home in the other's world. Do you think one of them should have bent a little more, or do you think they made the right choices? (Also, how unromantic were Noah's marriage proposals?)

3. Were you surprised with Barb's decision in the end, despite everything that happened and went wrong in her and John's marriage? Why do you think she chose what she did? What do you think about her view on marriage as opposed to what John's actions told us about his?

4. Juliet has a memorable visit to a plastic surgeon. We've all felt the pressure to look or act a certain way because of our age or what society deems appropriate or good. Can you think of a particular circumstance in which this happened? How did you handle it?

5. Have you ever felt the way Juliet did: that the window was closing on your chances, or that you'd aged out of an opportunity? What did you think of Arwen? Is she arrogant or just confident? Juliet is careful never to stoop to gossiping or complaining about Arwen, yet her confusion is obvious. Have you been in a similar situation?

6. How could both John and Barb have done things differently to understand each other and keep their marriage happy? They're not happy for a long time, but do you think they're just accustomed to the status quo? Do you know any long-married couples who seem to be getting things right? What are some keys to a long, happy relationship, or is that a myth?

7. One of the many types of relationships we see in this novel is the co-parenting relationship between Noah and Mickey. Though they aren't romantically involved, their relationship is one of the most functional partnerships in the book. How do you think they make it work? Do you think this kind of relationship could work for you?

8. The theme of not being good enough is prevalent in this book, including feelings of not being a good mom, partner or artist. Can you relate to any of the insecurities that the characters feel? Do you tackle these insecurities head-on or ignore them and

hope better days are ahead? Everyone feels insecure or inadequate at some point in their lives. What are some positive ways to deal with that?

9. Caro and Barb have such a close, loving and unconditional friendship that truly makes them soul mates. How does it differ from Barb's relationship with John? What do you think are the key factors that brought Caro and Barb together and make their relationship work? How are the women different, and how are they the same? Who is your oldest or closest friend? What makes your friendship special?

10. Do you think reading John's perspective throughout the book made you a little more forgiving toward him? How might you have felt had the author decided to include only the Frost women's points of view?

11. In what ways do Juliet and her daughters' relationships reflect her own mother's relationships with Juliet and Sadie? What do you think of Juliet and Barb as mothers? If you're a mother yourself, have you struggled with one child more than another?

12. The Frost women are quite different from one another. To whom do you relate the most? Can you see yourself in all of them?